PRAISE FOR KIM KELLY

'With her keen ear for a poetic and authentic Australian vernacular, Kelly is a masterful creator of character and voice ... Reminiscent of Mark Twain's dry humour, this rollicking ride through the 1860s' goldfields of NSW – part romance, part colonial picaresque – reveals a landscape of hatred and brutality but also unexpected acts of kindness.' – Julian Leatherdale, bestselling author of *Palace of Tears*

'Kim Kelly seems to understand the sounds and scents of the country' – *West Australian*

'storytelling is clearly encoded in her DNA' – *Writerful Books*

'It is uplifting to know that there are people who can write like this, with clarity, a bit of devilment and a hint of a smile ... Why can't more people write like this?' – *Canberra Times*

'marvellous depth and authenticity based on some impressive research, and her characters, plot and fluid prose draw the reader into this world' – *Daily Telegraph*

'colourful, evocative and energetic' – *Sydney Morning Herald*

'storytelling that breaks the rules so beautifully' – Jenn J McLeod, author of *A Place to Remember*

'Kim Kelly's writing is magnificent' – *With Love for Books*

ALSO BY KIM KELLY

Black Diamonds
This Red Earth
The Blue Mile
Paper Daisies
Wild Chicory
Jewel Sea

KIM KELLY

LADY BIRD
&
THE FOX

First published 2018 by Jazz Monkey Publications

Copyright © Kim Kelly 2018

The moral right of the author has been asserted.

A CIP record for this book is available at the National Library of Australia.

Design: Alissa Dinallo
Cover image: Shutterstock montage
Author photograph: Dean Brownlee
Printing: IngramSpark

Publishing services provided by Critical Mass
www.critmassconsulting.com

For Deano, who brought me west

Lady bird, lady bird, fly away home,
Your house is on fire, your children are gone,
All except one, and that's little Ann,
For she hid under the frying pan

AUTHOR UNKNOWN, eighteenth century

*

'For I know the plans I have for you,' said the Lord.
'Plans to prosper you and not to harm you.
Plans to give you hope and a future.'

JEREMIAH 29:11

*

No conviction, no reward.

DISTRICT SUPERINTENDENT C. U. SLATER,
Mildew Flat, Western Goldfields,
New South Wales,
May 2, 1868

GO WEST

ANNIE

'Annie! Annie! Are you there? Is that you, Annie?'

Yes, I am here. And this is what you would call a disaster. I see what it is, on the front step of our home, not yet in the door to get the fire on. It shivers up through the soles of my boots, freezing my knees with seeing it, even while my mind is busy spinning, thinking that I've never before this moment known just what a disaster is. It's one of those words, isn't it? You say it all the time not knowing what it truly means. Disaster. And so here it is. And I know, even as I am standing on this step, this moment is just the small beginning of it.

'Annie!'

Dad's been felled by a tree. He's calling out to me from the shadows inside, from the parlour room. I can see his new boots up on the sofa: wrong and mad.

'Branch got him – huge, it were – straight across his middle,' Gudge is still going on, explaining beside me on the step. I look at Gudge – Abel Gudge, chief of our most recent lot of feckless farmhands, half a brain shared between him and that shabby mob he wandered down from the hills with. He nods at me: 'Were at the river, Miss Annie, as I tell you, on the rocks below them experimentals. Don't know how long he were there. Were some hard work dragging him up through the beetroots all the way here, I tell you.'

I don't tell him he wouldn't know hard work if it smacked him a swift one between the eyes. I can only feel Dad's pain falling over me like a dark, dark dream.

'Dad?' Somehow I am in the door and beside him now, my knees dropped to the floor.

I see my dad on the sofa here before me, laid out and moaning through every line in his old face. 'Oh Jesus. Oh Jesus,' he's praying to the rafters, and his hand is crushing mine.

This is a disaster. A disaster. Oh, Heavenly Father, please help my dad. But even as I pray with him I know this is no good. My poor father is broken. As I'm looking at him here, at his pale face and the sweat streaming into his beard from his suffering, I see a great big branch off one of the trees down at the riverbank lashing out at him, grabbing him up and shaking him. Breaking him. Why? He would only have been going down there to bring up the fish trap, as we do of a Wednesday afternoon. It should have been me down there. And it would have been me most likely if I hadn't gone into Richmond with Sis, to the shops. For what? Nothing. McGowans were having a clearing-out sale on old gloves and bonnet trimmings and all sorts of remnant bits, so we went in for a bargain, but there was nothing there for us; nothing I would let Sis have, anyhow. I should have been down at the river, pulling up a basket full of mullet and sweet silver eels. The river is jumping with mullet. The tree would not have fallen upon me. I would have heard the split and crack of the branch; I would have dived into the water and swum away.

And Dad would never have been harmed. He'd be inspecting his rows of beetroot for leaf worm.

'Oh no, poor Dad,' is about all I can say of the whole great terror of it.

He doesn't care what I might say. He's talking to Jesus, lips trembling at some conversation between them.

'Dad? Dad?' I'm asking and asking him.

'I should run up to get the doc, you reckon?' says Gudge, wringing his hat beside me.

I think he should better get Reverend Thorne, but I don't say that. I don't want to think that. I feel the join of the boards sharp under my bony knees as I hold Dad's hand, touch his brow with the other. His skin is cold. He sweats so much but he is cold. Sweating and trembling like that plough horse we had that snapped a fetlock in the deep mud. Poor old horse. Dad had to —

'Dad, everything will be all right,' I lie to him with every hope I have, squeezing it into his hand even as I feel his grasp weakening in return, and I tell Gudge over my shoulder: 'Get me a glass of rum.'

'Rum, Miss Annie?' Gudge is that much of a cabbage he has to ask, and I can't help taking a second to blink at him even in this devastating circumstance: what is it about this colony that attracts so many boatloads of cabbages and sends them all tramping through here?

'For Dad,' I tell him through my teeth; Dad, who'd give a cabbage a job when no-one else would. 'Get him some rum for the pain – on the sideboard behind you.'

I turn back to Dad. My dad. He likes a rum of a Saturday evening; finds it reviving. He plays fiddle at the Coach and Horses when they have a shindy on and he's especially revived. Revive now! I reach behind his head to ready him to take his rum, and as I do I find his neck is soaked with sweat – streaming. All the water in him is pouring into my hand, taking with it all the colour in him, too; his face is so leached, he's pale as the threads of white in his red beard. He stares and stares into the rafters, scaring me. 'Dad – can you hear me?'

'Annie?' Of a sudden he does and he finds me; eyes wild and urgent, trying to grasp my hand again, but giving up. My hand thumps down to his chest. 'Annie?' He draws me closer still with his fearful eyes.

'What is it, Dad? Tell me.' Whatever I might do to help him, please, I will do it.

He says: 'You see that Sis stays clear of that Mickey Dinnigan, won't you, girl?'

'What?' These could be his last words on earth and he's asking me this? I can no more keep Sis from Mickey Dinnigan than I can keep Dad from his suffering. Just as I can no more tell Dad that Mickey is most likely who Sis is loitering with right this minute – back in Richmond, I left her, on the road outside the Brown Jug, with sixpence for the lemonade and soda water she demanded in place of the whorish lace gloves with the tear at the wrist I wouldn't let her have at McGowans. I was so cross from bickering about it

I threw the money at her feet and called her a nasty little tart as I hoofed off without her.

In place of telling Dad how sorry I am for all that now, I bend further to him and kiss his forehead, as if I might press into him the will to fight.

But he only closes his eyes. He sinks back against me, into my arms. He is not a big man, but he is so heavy in my arms, the little of him I can hold.

'Dad!' I yell at him, for the want of yelling life back into him.

He's only fainted from the pain of the injury, I tell myself over the walloping of my pulse. That's what's happened. I see my whole life laid out in this second, looking after an invalid father. That's my lot in life, right here in my arms. My fate spun out in the time it takes a spindle to turn once around. And I will be a grateful daughter every second of every day, please, I pray. I will care for my father as no daughter ever has; I never expected any more or less than to help my dad, anyhow. This is life; our life. I will get the beetroots up over May; I will get another man or two on it to help. Mr Webb will be understanding: Dad's managed these fields for him for twenty years, since the year before I was born, and I keep the books as well as any man might: two for the price of one, Mr Webb calls us with a smile, always pleased with Dad and me. We will get by.

But this isn't my lot in life. Because Dad has not fainted.

He is gone from us.

He is dead.

He doesn't take another breath. I lay him back on the sofa and stare at his stillness. I place his hands on his heart and I neaten his hair, as if I might make him ready for church.

I don't believe it.

Dad?

'Here you go.' Gudge is at my shoulder with the glass of rum I asked for a lifetime ago.

'Get away with you.' I push him back as I stand. The rum flings up in the air, time gone so slow and so fast I see it fly out of the cup in a wave. Drops falling, gold and shining. Drops of sunlight hanging before my eyes. The last of the sunlight coming in through the still-open doorway and up the hall.

I walk right out of it and down the back as the sun falls dead behind the mountains across the river. The air is cold. The light is cold. End of April cold. Clouds rising up above the range.

Dad?

Dad can't die. Not this way, not so unfair as this. He's not old enough to die – he's only forty-nine. Plenty die younger – but no, not *mine*. He's done everything right his whole life, except the one thing that brought him here. He stole a bag of oranges as a boy, fourteen years' worth of transportation to New South Wales for it – or free passage out of the Liverpool dockyards and the terrible hunger and hopelessness there, is how he saw it. Best thing that ever happened, he always said. Said? No. No! Why is he punished now when he has paid for his crime? He found his redemption in the Lord and his strength in clean air and fresh fruit and vegetables. He is the manager of Cygnet Farm here at Castlereagh; he has been here under Mr Webb since he earned his ticket-of-leave. He is a model man. He is kind and humble and honest and respected by everyone who knows him. A hero of the floods last winter, going out on the boats, setting up tents, and feeding everyone brought up to our higher ground from Penrith where the river cut them off from the town. Sis and me made that much onion soup out of our ruined, soggy crop I can't tolerate the smell of onions anymore. Dad and his mates played and sang all night, so the children wouldn't be frightened by the storm that came again and the mud and the crowd; took the little ones around and around on Mr Nettleby's donkey, from next door. And our Lord takes only the good unto his bosom, always taking the best too soon.

Dad. Such a good man. The very best of fathers. He has brought up Sis and me so well and all on his own after our mother was taken by the bronchitis, bless her sweet memory. I was only seven; Sis not yet four. No greater testament to Dad that we never felt Mother's going as any kind of a terror: she was returned to the Lord, who took up her suffering as His own. And now Dad has been returned to her. Our parents were perfect, both of them; they always will be. Never missed church and Dad made sure I went right through school with barely a day missed there, either – a man needs someone to read the *Empire* to him of an evening, the paper he loves for his hero the Honourable Mr Henry Parkes prints it so that the common man can know the world and better himself. Dad never learned his letters; he was very sure we did. I went right the way to the finish of primary-school lessons, as far as one like me can go – and better at those lessons than any other girls around here. Better than Sis – she stopped going when I did, no-one to pull her along by the plait. *Any man that doesn't want a smart girl can't be too smart himself*, Dad always says to us. Said. No: he will always say this to me. I can read and write as well as any man and I am so good at figures I have always been Dad's eyes on the ledger. Always. We will get by. I will get by.

I am nineteen years old, twenty in September. The cold grabs me around the shoulders like a shroud. I am a woman, sudden and now: no more a girl. No more a child to anyone. I must stand on my own two feet. Where are my feet? I have walked from the house and six acres out through the potatoes, and I am standing in the beans. Dad's prize-winning French fines, just finished picking. This field will need turning over, get the stakes up, ready for the carrots to get in there for next crop. Essie is crying out to be milked right this moment. I'm so cross with Sis. It's her job to tend to Ess. My sister is so lazy and vain. And our father is dead.

I keep walking, out across to the experimental field, where the beetroots are. This would have been Dad's next triumph, for he's got so much sweetness into them: a prize he will not see. So much work and no reward. Not here on earth, anyhow. I see him carrying a basket of the plumpest and reddest of the beetroots to Saint Peter. He will have his supper with the Lord: bright sliced beetroots and a fat roasted catfish. And a rum.

Oh, Dad. I walk the path of the torn and trodden leaves that saw Dad's last way home, dragged up by Gudge, and I follow it to the edge of the field, to the top of the steep bank here and I look down at the wide, cold river. The Nepean River. Our mother used to call it something else now and again; I can't remember what, I was so small then. I look at the horrible trees leaning out above the rocks here. The cane basket of our fish trap lying there, pulled up and empty.

This is a disaster.

A disaster.

And I don't know the first thing about it yet.

JEM

'I do not care if the archangel Gabriel sent you in his stead, there is no place here at this mine for you,' this fellow at the kerosene diggings is informing me, for the second time. A gristly old codger called Grindle. Filthy leather apron straining around a fat belly, filthy fat fingers to match and a pencil behind his ear, he appears to be made out of charcoal and lard. And he's definitely the codger I'm supposed to see – Grindle, that's the name all right. And there is definitely supposed to be a position waiting here for me – one I am compelled to take up or suffer a far harsher penalty as yet undisclosed but perhaps involving a custodial sentence of some kind.

I ask the man Grindle again: 'Are you certain? There's no-one here at all expecting me? Jeremy Fox – or Jem, or perhaps mistaken for a Jim? J.G. Fox – that's me. You're not in need of a, errr, a clerk of some kind, perhaps ...? Or ... ah ... I don't know ... Hm?' Hopefully, nothing involved with the actual mining here: I can see out to the top of the workings through the wide-open carriage doors beyond Grindle's head, down what appears to be the bottomless drop of a cliff face, windlass creaking up and back with buckets of rock and an assortment of charcoaled men. I have no intention of going out there, except that not going might bring me worse. I am a jeweller by trade, when I must, for God's sake. What do they want me to do here – fix their pulley chains and pick-axes? Consider the value of coal chips? Or, perhaps not too improbably, steward the draught horses? Now, that would be kind, on me, if not the team of six at work here, hauling that windlass up and back all day long. 'Erm,' I ask Grindle, as if he might yet have forgotten: 'Not someone for your horses? Perhaps the stable-master might know …?'

'I am the foreman here at Comet's Kerosene.' Grindle squares at me. 'I am the one who knows and says what goes and I say I am not expecting you any more than I am a cartload of mangy rabbit skins.'

'Right. Good. Fair enough.' I scratch my head. Beggar me, I am out of luck here, it would seem. And I don't know what I should do. Go back to Sydney? Perhaps there's been some sort of mistake or muddle-up, a delay in the communique advising my arrival? Perhaps I should wait here a day or two. I look out of the window the other way, back onto the road, such that it is: not a lot out there but forest. And an inn, about a mile or so back up the steep mountain track I got here upon – what was it called, Mount Something Road? Somewhere in this place called Petrolia Vale, where the coachman set me down and grunted towards some unseen depth of perdition by way of further direction.

'Well, I'll be out of your way, then, and thank you.' I nod to Grindle. 'My apologies at having interrupted you,' and I pull out what I might of a smile as I ask him: 'You couldn't tell me, though, could you, is there a possibility of sending a message by telegraph from some … where? Around … here?'

Grindle expels another gust of contempt at me: 'With your newspaper ironed and shoes shined too? You ain't in Sydney anymore. Not out here.' He waves me off behind his turning back by way of dismissal. 'Go up and ask at the Royal.'

'Is that the inn, up along the track –?' I begin to ask and stop as he turns back to me once more with some threat now assembling around his impatience.

'Nah, it's Buckingham bleeding Palace,' he says, all Australian charm. 'What do you bloody reckon?'

I reckon I should get quite quickly out of his sight.

Nothing else for it but to return hat to head and trudge back up the track, back to that inn, and ask there, I suppose. I step out into the early evening and the coals of the enormous blacksmith's forge across the way are glowing like the maw of Cerberus warning against the idea, but apart from that, and a great iron chimney stack a little way further down the slope, whose purpose I don't want to begin to guess at, and, of course, several million weary, ragged gum trees enclosing all for a million miles around, there is nowhere else for me to stop the night, or not that I am aware of, anyway. I throw my carpetbag over my shoulder: I don't think I've so much as a box of matches in there, so hastily was I shoved into the coach – and at about two o'clock this morning, still rather drunk – I didn't think for a moment that Pa would ever do anything like this to me, honestly, seriously, I didn't. This is absurd.

But of course, being of generally optimistic disposition as I am, my next thought is: I wonder if there'll be a game on there at the inn? Doubtless there will be: what else does one do for amusement in such a place as this besides drinking and gaming? The soles of my boots slip on the rubble of the track as its incline quickly steepens, and steepens some more still: at least I'll be able to find my way in the dark safely enough, for I'll be crawling on hands and knees in a moment as this mountain pass is all but perpendicularly sat upon the earth. I don't remember it having been so steep as this on the way down.

I'm probably lost. I slip again, elbowing the gravelly turf. I'm going to ruin my new tweed, which I only picked up from Eli the day before yesterday. Would you like that, Pa? Leave a trail of ruined herringbone twill behind me through the wilderness before I disappear altogether? Did I really need to leave the comfort of home for that? A half-moon is rising over this lonely vale, the twilight is steadily swallowed by thickening cloud, and some bird shrieks over the desolation, as if to confirm that my punishment is barely yet commenced. And to remind me that drinking and gaming are precisely what has brought me here, as if I might forget: last night's doorstep, gale-force windbaggery from the Inspector-General of Police, Douglas Fitzworthy, over the whole thing is yet fresh in my ears.

You are fast becoming a nuisance to society, young Mr Fox, a troublesome customer, a larrikin of the worst order, a ne-er do well, a dandy and a wastrel, but nevertheless it has been decided, with your father – and with the weighty bond of his word and his esteemed repute in the community taken into consideration, as well as the fact that custodial sentence will likely only encourage your base proclivities for roguery further and irredeemably – and, I must add, arranged by me at great personal effort and inconvenience – that you will leave this town of Sydney for the Comet Kerosene Company Shale Mine at Petrolia Vale for a term of humble and honest toil under the supervision of Mr Howard Grindle there. Failure to present yourself at the mine office and failure to commit yourself to the labour you are set will see that the law be brought upon your head with redoubled vigour.

Or words to that effect – the man can't speak in sentences less than one thousand words in length.

And the law is an ass, then, in every sense, isn't it – so is my father. It's only ninety-five pounds on the horseflesh, for God's sake – I've done worse at the club before. I'd have won it back, eventually, as luck in its way turns around, and I'd have paid back what I owe at the Hyde Park Hotel the same way – what is it, fifty? As for the fifteen I owe at the Colonnade – that's less than nothing, surely. A bet on which of two goats in the yard would shit first, and I was stinking groggified – tight as a boiled budgie on that occasion. Who takes that sort of a punt seriously? Why were there two goats in the yard in the first place? Whoever gets charged with absconding from a debt for a bet like that, anyway – when I've done no such thing, even if I have often entertained the idea of winning enough one day to return to London and forget I was ever here. I've not absconded anywhere, of my own free will, and I have every intention of fixing up the debts, eventually. I am honourable, if somewhat profligate.

But as for Cornelia Osborne, Inspector-General Fitzworthy's niece – that charge is simply preposterous. I was never going to touch a hair on her pretty head, not in the slightest. It's not my fault young ladies have a tendency to go clucky after me – not my fault Miss Osborne hangs about the shop like a lost lamb whenever I am there. She's a scandal waiting to unfold, that one. Just happens to drop in with a broken catch chain on her bracelet, or something to be engraved by Pa, as if she has a spy set up at the restaurant on the corner, alerting her to my comings and goings. All I did was go after her runaway parasol one blustery afternoon down at the Governor's

Domain a month or so ago when I was on my way through to Woolloomooloo – retrieval of parasol, brief introduction, in company of her silly, giggling friend, and that is *all* I did. Did not attempt to kiss her hand. Did not even breathe in her direction. Nice girl, really – not *my* girl. I like mine with a bit of spark to them, as if my own repute is not well known enough in that regard.

Above all, it's not my fault my father's desperate need to cling to his social rung is more important to him than anything else, is it? He is tired of the embarrassment of me. *And who wouldn't be?* he laments, shaking his palms at me. But it is his embarrassment, not mine. He's the one who's spent his whole existence tiptoeing around on eggshells, making sure he doesn't cough out of place, making sure of every penny – careful not to contribute a farthing more to the New Synagogue Fund than to the Church of England asylum for the poor. Making sure his only son and heir is seen to be a gentleman, as he could never have been himself in London. Too small a fish, too big a pond, in England; too much a silly old Jew in any place. *Jemmy, Jemmy, please understand – with advantage comes responsibility*, he gnashed away at the door of the carriage as he sent me packing, beard trembling with dismay in every conceivable direction. *Jemmy, this coach alone is costing more than I want to pay for you anymore – you have to go. You have to appreciate things.* I appreciate he's more tightly wound than his polishing wheel, God love him – someone must.

God, but this road beggars belief. Up and up it goes, and it's not even a road. There is no such thing as a decent road twenty miles from Sydney, any and all pretence ceasing at Parramatta – indeed, the coach nearly lost a wheel at Penrith, where dawn broke over a pothole big enough to consume a house. I don't know what sort of a gentleman Pa ever expected me to become in a place such as this, wherever this is, or Sydney Town in its entirety. There is nothing – *nothing* – for a gentleman to do; nothing that one might be gentlemanly at, apart from gaming, drinking, women, or some other sport, and a nice bit of horseflesh, not necessarily in that order – which is the very definition of gentleman in this land. Life, gentlemanly or otherwise, is not repairing the setting claws on the jewels of Hebrew wives in the hope that Pa might marry me off to one of their rare and precious daughters, or ship out some long-lost niece from Warsaw for me, or fetch up a horrifically snobbish and expensive creature from Melbourne, so that we can do our bit for Israel by producing three hundred and forty-seven children. I could not be less interested in any of that, no matter how appealing the idea of unlimited matrimonial shagging might be.

But I'm even less interested in going to prison. Coldly sober and alone, I don't now trust that these charges hanging over me are all bluff. I let the threat of them push me the rest of the way up this mountainside – and quick as I can take it, as the night is falling blacker by the second. Twigs crackle under the movement of invisible beasts at the edges of the track. Something growls through the undergrowth. A branch trails a few ghostly fingernails over the top of my head, and I just find the fuzz of the lamp of the inn a little way off before this whole place does me in with the creeps.

I run the last few paces and bound for the door, the bell clanging as I trip up the step and stumble inside.

'Well, well, what have we here?' The fellow behind the bar grins over his counter; thickset, short as he is broad. The room is small, of bare clay and stone, dim and smoky, and crowded with grim, grey faces so that for a moment I wonder if those miners by some trick of time beat me up here. More creeps, but I grin in return over them.

'Good evening,' I greet the innkeeper. 'I seem to have found myself unexpectedly on your doorstep – looking for a room at the inn. Is this the Royal, by any chance?'

The man narrows his eyes at me as if I am lately escaped from an insane asylum; he shakes his head: 'This here is the Pigeon.'

'Right. Good.' A pub is a pub. Grey faces stare blankly at me over their glasses. God, but a pub is not a pub – there's not even a dart board in here. 'It's a very pleasant establishment you have, too,' I say, preparing to plead my case, as it's doubtful I'll be going further than this place tonight. I ask the innkeeper again: 'So, does your fair Pigeon have a bed available, then?'

'That depends,' says the innkeeper. 'Who are you?'

'Jeremy Fox.' I must relate my story to him and his patrons as barely as possible, omitting mention of Inspector-General Fitzworthy and the so far hushed charges against me, naturally, telling them only:

'My father has lately arranged a position for me with the Comet Kerosene Company, but word of my arrival hadn't got through to them. I suppose there's been a mix-up with the mail, a message not received. Hm?' I'm getting tired of this now, and last night's efforts nobbling over billiards at Young's on William Street on the way home, together with the all-dayer in the coach after being prevented from sleeping at and staying home, have overtaken me. I might simply like to sit down in a moment.

The innkeeper shrugs and nods: 'Yestdee's mail was robbed, so it could well be the case, me lad, and today's has been delayed down the mountain.'

'Ah. Good.' I lean on the counter in my relief. 'That explains it. Good. Good.'

'Not good for them that was robbed and them that's waiting on the mail.' The innkeeper frowns and shakes his head – at my hand on his counter, clearly not a counter for me to be leaning on.

'No. No! Not good at all,' I agree, straightening up, giving his counter the respect it is due, and ask again: 'So, would it be possible for me to stop here until I can discover –?'

'Who are you but?' He narrows his eyes suspiciously.

'Jeremy Fox, as I said,' I reply, just as I find the crucifix mounted on the wall behind the bar – for Christ's sake, what kind of pub is this? I plough on regardless. 'Son of Solomon Fox,' I tell him, 'of S.J. Fox & Son, Silversmiths & Jewellers – Sydney.'

'Never heard of you.' The innkeeper shrugs, making a face like a toad with indigestion.

'Well, no, I don't imagine you would have heard of *me*,' I must admit and be glad he hasn't. 'But it's quite a well-known silversmiths – the new Governor, the Earl of Belmore, and his lady the Countess have lately commissioned my father for their incoming requirements. Otherwise, we make bespoke baubles and bijouterie for the upper crust. Continental craftsmanship, valuations, et cetera – in Sydney, George Street, with the foundry for the flatware over on Goulburn Street, on Brickfield Hill.'

'Is it, then.' Mr Innkeeper is in nowise impressed or intrigued. 'Give our regards to the Guv and his missus when you see 'em, won't you. No-one to vouch for you out here?'

'Er, no.' What? At this point, I might slap a pound note on the counter and be done with the charade, only I don't have any such cash on me. 'But – ah!' It occurs: 'The coachman who brought me here today – he'd have stopped with you, surely, to water his horses and himself?' Pa would have paid him his agreed fee in advance, so the fellow will surely vouch; I peer around through the tallow gloom. 'Is he still here?'

'Who?'

'The coachman, from Sydney. I suppose we came in at about three, perhaps half past?' Couldn't tell you exactly as I've left my watch ... somewhere. 'Tall fellow, wearing a brown coat. Gruff. Not too chatty.'

'Never saw him.'

'Really?' I find that somewhat difficult to believe. It's not as if this is George Street. You could not miss a stray goat much less a coach outside this establishment, even if the driver rolled on past with no tip of the hat good-afternoon.

Despite having stated we came up from Sydney, conversation over the possible identity of this coachman ensues – 'Mighta been Sid Avery from Will's Chimney, gone Berghofer way onto his daughter's,' says one grim, grey face – 'Or Bill Chilvers from back o' Weatherboard,' says another, 'he never stops in for a g'day' – 'Nah, he give up the coaching wi' the lack o'trade – and it consumes the entire room for a good few minutes, during which I gather that these patrons of the Pigeon are all inordinately sober, and all local bullock drivers or timber-cutters or relations thereof, before the innkeeper decides: 'No, your coachman is no-one from round here, it looks like. No-one from the mountains. No-one known to us at One Tree.'

'Ah well, never mind,' I say, for if a man is *no-one* to the dozen or so faces in this spiritless chapel of a pub, he doesn't exist, clearly – and a pity because I might have just realised I left my watch, as well as my gloves, on the seat of that phantom coach. But I must ask: 'One Tree, did you say? Where precisely am I?' Not still in Petrolia Vale? Not still in the realm we know as Planet Earth?

The suspicious squint comes at me from the innkeeper again: 'One Tree Hill, this is, on Mount Victoria.'

One Tree Hill? Lying in the midst of a forest as it is? All right, then, let's not query it aloud; I say, 'Good. Excellent. It's a hill up here all right, just as I am who I say I am. You can trust me.' Best and most winning smile to convince them.

But the innkeeper only frowns more deeply, regretfully: 'That I might, me lad, but I can't be too careful, neither – there's too many fakers and cheats abroad to risk it these days. We're good Christians here all the same, though. You can sleep in the shed – it's a cold night coming tonight.'

For God's sake, a little more mercy than that might be nice. 'But fair go, sir, I —'

'Fair go? I'd say your go couldn't have been much fairer. Come on, follow me.' The innkeeper steps out from behind his counter and beckons me towards a door at the rear. 'I'll show you the way.'

Show me that I have no choice but to follow him, beyond the ice chest, beyond the larder, beyond one of the rustic but comfortable-looking guest beds all toasty at the back of the hearth, beyond the verandah and outside to a nest of hay bales under what is little more than an awning stretched between the inn and a water tank.

'Here you are,' the innkeeper says, tossing me a blanket and presenting me my draughty shed for the night. Positively medieval, and I can't buy my way out of it for once. I scraped my last oddments together and spent them on lunch, a rather disgusting mutton hash pushed across a greasy table at me by a spectacularly sour publicaness, somewhere further down the mountain. Well, at least there goes the temptation to put a bet on anything, I suppose. I don't fancy they'd take my credit here, would they. I don't fancy they approve of betting any more than they do drinking, dancing or darts at the Pigeon. They possibly don't approve of telegraphic messages, either.

Was this part of the punishment plan, Pa? Deliver me into the hands of some arcane cult of Methodist bullockies?

Only my guts grumble in reply, for want of dinner, but I'm too weary now that I've sat down to go back and try to beg for any. Besides, as luck would have it, I'm sure I've got that half a quince pie in my bag, left over from breakfast – too crook and crapped out at five o'clock this morning to eat it all at the time, rehorsing at some other revolting place. I shall enjoy it here, then ... While I consider how I shall exist tomorrow.

But hang on, what's this I find as I rummage in the dark? An apple – one I'd quite forgotten I had. How could I? Comely little dollymop over her fruit basket on my way to billiards last night: *Help yerself, sweet'eart.* I did, and as fortune favours the hopeful, indeed I do find a few other comforts here in my bag as well: a copy of last Saturday's *Bell's Life* track news, my shaving case, dressing-gown, a squashed box of Faney's chocolate pastilles, a fresh pair of socks and – here we go, here we go – two sneaky little farthings. Worthless, but mine.

ANNIE

'There can be no delay about the burial, Annie Bird, no delay at all. With the dysentery and pneumonia a scourge throughout from all this autumn dampness in the air, your father will be buried this morning at ten o'clock. Reverend Thorne is already engaged thusly. The cost of the burial has been subtracted from the final account of Mr Bird's wages for this month.'

I stare at Mrs Webb as she hands me an envelope with *R.M. BIRD – APRIL 1868 & FINAL* written on it, and *FINAL* underlined three times. I don't much like her, but here she is and free of any good influence of her Mr Webb. He is away in Sydney on business, at the meeting of the council of the Board of Agriculture, attending to something about land divisions. I'd forgotten that. He won't be back until Sunday, three days away. My thoughts are a bucket of suds turning grey with the wash of all this. Dysentery? Pneumonia? Dad isn't gone from either of them, never been sick a day in all the time I've known him, for his diet of fresh fish and vegetables, he'd tell you if he could. He tells the whole district every Richmond market day, every Friday. I crunch up the envelope in my hand; I feel coins slipping around inside, heavy with all her subtractions – when there's always five crisp one-pound notes in it. Sixty pounds per annum Dad receives, plus the accommodations here on the farm. Mrs Webb won't be paying me sixty pounds per annum to keep the place turning over; Mr Webb neither. What's wages for a farmer's daughter? What am *I* worth? My heart starts drumming with fear and this word *FINAL*.

Mrs Webb's lips are moving as she goes on, but I'm not hearing anything, except for Sis blowing her nose again behind me here on the front step, and Reverend Thorne clearing his throat behind Mrs Webb. She is a mean old cow.

I think this even before Sis shouts out at her: 'No – you can't do that.'

Do what?

'I can indeed,' Mrs Webb goes on with her meanness and her callousness. 'There is a new manager ready and waiting for Cygnet Farm. The crops must be tended to. Life must go on. You are to be removed from the cottage this afternoon. Do not bring trouble upon yourselves by resisting the inevitable.'

I look behind me, past Sis and through the parlour room door, to Dad, laid out as he still is on the sofa there. We've got him bathed and in his best clothes, though he is grey now as my mind, so gone from this life that even the freckles on the back of his hands have left us. He is at peace; his face set into what looks almost like a smile. I whisper to him through my thoughts: *You would think that Mrs Webb arranged for the tree branch to fall on you, wouldn't you, Dad, she is so well organised.* I still can't believe he is not breathing, as I can't believe Mrs Webb is being such a nasty cow.

I turn back to her but I'm asking the sky: 'Where are we to go?'

She says: 'Wherever you must. There is no room for you here. Mr Murgett, the new manager, comes with wife and daughters of his own.'

'So that's it – we are put off?' I look to Reverend Thorne. His eyes are cast at the ground. The coward. And so he should be ashamed of himself: he christened me and Sis. He also just two months ago arranged a collection of fourteen pounds from the whole district for some widow called Mrs Whitmore from Kurrajong when her husband was struck by lightning in their dairy paddock, so she could pay off his mortgage – and she's not even from our church. Reverend Thorne only clears his throat again. Because there's deserving poor and undeserving poor – here it is. I hope the Devil takes him. No, I don't. That's a terrible thought. The Devil must take Mrs Webb first, as I recall that I know that name Murgett from somewhere – from Windsor? I can't put the sense of it together just at this minute.

She says: 'There is plenty of work about – up at the Emu tweed mill, or at the flour mill in Richmond. There are hands needed at Eliot's poultry farm, too, and many, many places in want of domestic servants in any town you like. You can go anywhere for miles around and ask for work, Annie Bird. *Honest* work.'

Like the work I have been at all these years for my dad has not been honest. I've never imagined working in any other way, or for any other master. Oh, Dad, the grief runs through me, shivering and falling, and in it I see the depth of Mrs Webb's disregard for our predicament. There is no work at any mill or farm, not for a girl. All good-paying work is taken up by men come off the goldfields empty-handed, wanting to earn a passage back home, wherever that might be, and there is not enough work to go around for them – they're lucky to get fifteen pounds for the year labouring if they're in work that long. What will become of Sis and me? Girls such as us, if we put ourselves up for service in some house or other, it'd be unlikely we'd get paid at all.

Sis pushes right up beside me at the doorway now with her own question for Mrs Webb: 'Don't s'pose you'll be kicking off Gudge and all them, will you? Just us.'

'That's Mr Murgett's affair,' the old cow sniffs. 'Not mine. He may employ whomsoever he chooses.'

He may employ a crateful of brainless, sluggardly cabbages, but not us. Mrs Webb is telling us we're not chosen, not wanted anywhere. What kind of charity is this?

I look out to the distance, south to the vineyard that ranges up over the hill towards Penrith, and as I do I raise my hand to the glare of the sunrise. I see my hand against the sun: my skin dark in this light. Not nearly so dark as our mother's was, but skin that's coloured enough. Skin that is the reason why we're getting kicked off without a care.

I look back down at Mrs Webb, her lips and cheeks all sucked in and creased with the bitter corruptions of her character, and the step I'm standing on seems a mile above where she is in this life. I say to her: 'Why don't you tell the truth, Mrs Webb. You're kicking us off because, without our father here, we're just a couple of unwanted blacks.' She's never wanted us here, we know it, two little black marks in her white parish, though she would never say it to our faces while our father's labour and skill poured prizes and money into her husband's bank and into her purse. None of her five daughters allowed to sit by us at church or school; cross the other side of the road to avoid a nod of recognition at the shops, lest they might catch something of our blackness. 'Can't wait five minutes to see the back of us, isn't that right?'

She opens her mouth so wide her chin disappears into her scraggedy neck, but she can't deny what I say.

'Now, now,' Reverend Thorne finally has something to say himself. 'There is no need for incivility.'

'Incivility!' My voice hits the clouds and rings across the whole of the district. 'You are only lucky that I am as civilised as I am.'

'You threaten me!' Mrs Webb screeches back.

And I tell her in a blinding flash of the truest of truths I know: 'I don't need to. For I trust that God will deal with you – He'll send some justice more fitting than I could ever dream of.'

'You curse me!' She takes a step back, knocking Reverend Thorne sideways into a puddle.

And I tell her: 'I would if I could – believe you me – only it's not possible to curse the damned, is it.'

'You ingrate! You – you foul-mouthed savage, you wicked little gin!' She can't believe what she just heard.

I can barely believe I said it.

Sis starts laughing – even in our grief and misfortune here, she can't help it roaring out. 'Sticks and stones, you goggle-eyed bitch – I'll show you *thusly*,' she spits down at Mrs Webb and shuts the door on her.

All the good it will do.

I stare down the hall and there's a rushing in my ears, time swishing and swirling all around.

'What are we gunna do?' Sis is asking me.

And I truly don't know before the words come out of my mouth: 'Get packing.'

I walk down the hall and out to the kitchen. Pack what? My Staffordshire teacups and saucers Dad bought for me in Parramatta last year? The sideboard? The sofa? I don't know where to start.

Where to go. But from the back door, I see Dad's swag-roll sitting in the hayloft across the yard looking back at me, and I'm running out and up the ladder to grab it.

'Annie, what are you doing?' Sis is running along behind me.

I don't know, but as I throw the swag down onto the ground, I find I do know something: 'I'm not giving them a chance to shame us one second more. We're leaving – now.'

'What are you talking about? What about Dad!' Sis is screaming up the ladder at me.

'Dad's not going to be worried, is he,' I tell her as I jump down after the swag. 'All he'll be wanting, if he could, is that we keep together and that we not be shunned as they're putting him in the earth.' I don't want to see them put him in the earth, is more of the truth; I can't. I just can't.

'Where are we gunna go?' Sis whines along behind me as I run back into the house.

'Away from here,' I tell her again, because I don't know where we're going to go. We have nowhere to go. I've hardly been across the river my whole life, hardly been beyond the Richmond and Penrith districts, and I've never been to Sydney – who would dare it? A city of two hundred thousand souls, one of the biggest in the world, four times the size of San Francisco, it's said, and who would go there, either? Dad used to swag his way to Parramatta if he ever had to go there, just him and one of Mr Webb's plough horses, as every bed in that town is full of fleas. I can't ride a horse myself, though, never had to, and Dad would never take us to Parramatta, such a rough and dirty town for all its money – worse than Sydney for thieves, he'd warn us. My heart is walloping harder and harder as I race around, ransacking the house for every last coin I can find. What am I going to do? Steal a horse I can't ride? What then? Where are we going to go?

We have no people here to go to. Dad's are all back in England, in Liverpool, whoever they might be – he never expected to see any of them ever again, never wrote because he couldn't do that any more than they could read. And Mother's family – I hardly know them better. Mother herself seems a whisper lost across an age: a small bundle of pictures in my mind, stories told to me by

Dad, and half-remembered dreams. I scramble around for these, too. Our mother's people were the black swan people, who once lived here along the riverbank. *Tragical business*, Dad would only ever say of what happened to them, and I'd never ask more for all his grief over Mother, but he'd tell us all kinds of other stories to raise our chins, make us proud – of her. He'd tell us over and over that our grandfather was a famous tracker, who'd come from way out west, from the river people there. A big man, was our grandfather, so said Dad, tall and handsome, he wore a possum-skin cloak. His name was Kulyan and he was one of them that guided the survey men through the vast, wide lands beyond the mountains. He got a medal from the government for it – or was it a ribbon? Oh Lord, please give me some firm branch-hold of something, some place where we might go.

Go out and find your grandfather, Annie, some kind of something replies. *Go to your grandfather's country – go west, out to the place called Blackman's Swamp*. A strange voice, if it's a voice at all, more a ripple through the air, as I look up to see nothing but the rise of those mountains framed inside the open back door. I think the voice maybe sounds a bit like Dad, I hope maybe it's his spirit guiding me; or maybe it's the voice of the Lord after all, telling me: *Find your grandfather. Find Kulyan.*

Whoever it is, that was a good and clear instruction, one I'm taking for providence, so I say to Sis: 'We're going out west. We're going to find our grandfather.'

'What? I ain't going out to some Never-Never nowhere place for some black feller I ain't ever seen. I'm not leaving my Mickey.' She doesn't move from the hallway while I keep on with scrabbling about the place for any last lost coins – in the drawers, under the beds – wondering if Sis chooses to talk like such a trollop, or she really is one.

'You are coming with me,' I tell her. 'You're going wherever I go. I gave Dad my promise.' I promise him again with a glance over my shoulder.

So Sis and me get our claws out over it, with Sis calling me a 'stubborn streak of snot stain', and a 'screwed-up squealing black witch', and me telling her, with her fairer skin, 'Reckon you're too white to walk beside me, do you? Without me, you're on a fast road to the sluttery!' and her telling me next with her tears streaming, 'I'm going to Mickey right now,' and me telling her, 'No you are not.' Until she hoofs out in a blubbering huff, back over to Yarramundi, two miles north and across the water. I watch her from the back door, skirts flapping across the fields as she storms off, on her way up to the spit across the river at the lagoon, where Mickey Dinnigan's house is, if you can call it a house, rather than a heap of unsightly rubbish.

Don't worry too much for your sister, the voice tells me next, a breath of wind through beet-leaves. *Mickey's not too bad a lad.* It can't be Dad's guidance I'm hearing, then. Maybe it's God being charitable; or maybe it's just me sighing, giving up on Sis because she makes me mad as a wet cat.

I go back inside, to the parlour room, and I look down at Dad once more on the sofa: one fight between me and Sis he didn't have to hear; one final declaration of her intentions to chuck herself at Mickey our dad didn't have to know about, either. Such a good, God-fearing, God-loving man, our father, but with something of a harsh prejudice against Catholics, believing them all to be a bit lazy and degenerate, especially Irish ones that do nothing but go around shooting the royal family, blowing things up with dynamite and never toasting the Queen, sinning and going to confession afterwards and pretending you never wronged at all – they let themselves off a charge too easy. Or off a job. Mickey's got a job, though, a good one, at the tannery. You can smell him coming, but he's a hard worker by any reckoning, not too bad a lad, I suppose that's true, and Sis'll be sixteen in June. I can't tell her what to do anymore. I'm no King of Israel to bring the hammer of judgement down.

Let her go her own way …

She's gone whether I like it or not.

And I'm going too. Going to find our grandfather. I'm going to find us a new home, and then I'll come back and see about Sis, drag her off if Mickey turns out a bad one after all.

I straighten Dad's tie like he might be coming with me.

Oh, Dad.

And I am frantic mad again with disbelief, hurrying while I'm about it. I roll Dad's swag out up the hall, the blue blankets on the inside of the oilskin canvas smelling strong of him as I start gathering all I think I'll need into them. More pictures tumble into my mind as I rush here and there: a summer long ago, when I was very small, Mother showing me a tree, where bark had once been sheared off for canoes; Sis so tiny on her hip. Where were we? Trees so tall … Somewhere in the Mulgoa Forest, it must have been, or Warragamba, as they're the only places we've ever gone for the holiday we take between Christmas and New Year, not five miles south of Penrith, and not for the last few years. We were fishing, swimming; I jumped off the rocks into Mother's arms, all fun and laughter; sun sparkling on the drops of water trickling over her shoulders like stars, while Dad pegged out our tarp between two of those tall —

Tarp. Dad's tarp. I see I might need that, too, if I'm going anywhere without a roof over my head – and I race outside to find it, right up the back of the loft, covered in chaff dust, and heavy for all that it's only made of bran bags stitched together. As I carry it into the house, I don't know how I'm going to lug all I'll need for camping out – in fact, I don't know what I'm thinking I might be doing here at all. Tramping off up through the wild Blue Mountains, a girl all alone? I look around the room at all I've ever known; anger and doubt smack me down: this is my home. But no, it's not. It's about to belong to the Murgetts, whoever they are – and I suddenly remember who they are at this thought of them: relatives of the Billingtons, that's right, Mrs Billington being close in with Mrs Webb at the church. While I am friendless. Friendless as the moon. And no, I can't do this, I can't tramp off alone. Just as sudden, I can't move.

Yes, you can. Don't be a girl.

Don't be a girl? That's a nonsense. What else can I be? A lady taking the coach up and staying in fine hotels all the way to Bathurst? With the paltry five pounds, seventeen shillings and bawbees I have as a sum total to my name? Not likely. I've never been to Bathurst, but I know it's expensive. I don't even know where I'm going at all. Not truly. Only that Blackman's Swamp is somewhere out there – somewhere west.

And that my heart is broken here.

That brings me back to Dad, to look at him again before I can't see him anymore. I have to go before they put him in the ground. I can't watch that. No doubt none of Dad's friends across this valley will have been given notice to come pay respects today; Mrs Webb's sour face will only be gloating over our ousting all the while, thinking up some worse way to spite me. I have to move these feet and get going.

And just as I think I might fall to my knees once more with not being able to, I see something out of the corner of my eye: one of Dad's long field boots slowly flops down over the other there at the end of the sofa, where they've been since I took them from his poor feet yesterday. He only got them last Thursday, and I'd put them on for a laugh when he brought them home from the cobbler at Windsor, they're so tall, but a necessity against snakes along the rows. Our feet are the same size, just about, though mine are skinnier across the toes. We are the same size pretty much all over but for an inch or two in height: we are skinny but strong. And then I see; I hear what I've been told: don't be a girl – be Dad instead.

I hurry ever faster now, before they come for him. I get Dad's gear on me: his second-best moleskin strides, his new boots, his red Crimean flannel, which he wears every Friday to market, and his good felt hat, which I hide all my hair inside. And I take his tobacco pouch as well: I put all the money I have into it, and I pull the drawstring tight, push it deep into the middle of the swag-roll, snug up against my Holy Bible, with my *Certificate of Completion of Primary Education* from Richmond Free Presbyterian Church School snapped safely shut inside as all the proof of what I'm worth in this world and a whisper of the kindness in it, too, for my old teacher, Miss Madden, who stood up for me being at the school in the first place, before she left the year after me to get married and have children of her own. *Such a bright little thing*, she'd tell Dad in the street, and he was never prouder.

And I kiss my dad on the forehead and I kiss him on the cheek, his skin as cold as mine is warm.

Goodbye, Dad.

In my sore, mad mind I imagine he smiles at me from his dream there on the sofa as I lump the swag on my shoulders and the tarp-roll over it, frying pan and billy can hanging off either side, just as he would have them. But I don't look behind me as I go.

I'm going to find my grandfather, Kulyan. I'm going to find whatever family there is of mine to find. I start walking for the Castlereagh Road, for the new bridge at Penrith – I know that leads to the way most direct across the mountains, for that's the way the railway goes, across Emu and up, with the telegraph line. I will follow the tracks. I'll be a railway tracker, I say to myself against the straps of the swag already cutting into my shoulders.

Up at the hut on the roadside, the farm labourers watch me go, three of them come out to stand at the door. But they don't say a word to me, they don't even nod a good day or mumble a condolence, the dirty, rotten-toothed things – whole river to wash in and none of them do, though they sneak a look at me and Sis whenever they can, like we're the strange ones. Or maybe they don't recognise me at all, my costume is too confusing for cabbages. I could jump at them and say, *Watch out! I am the black ghost of Richie Bird, and I am angry at being dead!* But I hardly look at them as I go, only long enough to see that Gudge is not looking out at me with them. Is he ashamed of what Mrs Webb has done? Or is he in on it? Did he push Dad onto the rocks at her bidding? Not a tree falling on him at all but foul play? I discard that thought as quick as it came: Gudge is too stupid for a life of crime. What would I do if he was in league with Mrs Webb, anyhow? Nothing. I'm no-one to speak against them or anyone, if I ever was. It's a rough, rough world, Dad always said, all you can do is hold your head up as high as it'll go above your boots and keep on the way of light.

Come on, Kath, he says to Mother through all time, past old rough prejudice and pain, and she keeps on with him into town, her hand in his arm, little posy of violets pinned to her bonnet, smiling like a sunny day at him, and I look up, finding the bridge ahead: the huge ugly thing of iron. But the river is huge here itself: still high from all the soaking rain we've got this past year, bless those that suffered in the floods. It is broad and green and beautiful, black swans swimming around by the bank here, five of them, their red beaks flashing through the reeds.

My mother used to talk to this river, in her language, her toes in the mud, bending with her hands swishing through the water, calling me to her: *Come here, daughter, stay beside me.* She told me how the rivers join up like arms across the land: the Nepean, the Warragamba, the Grose and the Hawkesbury. I listen and listen now, but I can't hear her name for this place here. Her special name for this water, all the special words she spoke to it – all small pieces of me I can't catch hold of, tiny pieces of home lost to the breeze.

See you again one day, girl. Goodbye ... I think it must be the river talking to me.

Goodbye, I say into the water and into the trees that climb up to the sky along the mountainside ahead. Goodbye, I say as these boots of my dad's go *rough, rough, rough* on my feet across the bridge. Rough, rough world, it is, today. Rough and slippery as a basket of silver eels.

JEM

I have slept like a bear, one that died and suffered a bout of rigor mortis in the night, and as I rise, I stretch out the kink in my back, reminding myself that I have perhaps too regularly awoken in far worse shape. If the truth be confessed, I have awoken in far worse establishments than this; indeed, in far worse haysheds than this. But I have never been quite so stranded. A thick mist sits over the yard I look out upon, and around it ragged gum trees hang impersonating a quiet expeditionary squadron of Death's army, asking me a question: and what precisely is your point, Mr Fox?

A goat bleats plaintively somewhere.

And the door of the inn opens behind me, with the innkeeper shouting: 'Look out!' as he sloshes his night pot off the back step beside me.

'Good morning, sir,' I greet him; let's not mention the piss you've splashed across the toes of my boots.

He gives me a smug little grin, as if he might have intended it precisely. 'Aw – that's right, you're still 'ere.'

'I am, so it would seem.' And won't it be wonderful not to be. He stands there watching me brush bits of hay from my trousers, and I ask him: 'What time generally do you expect the mail?' because I suppose it might be wisest to wait and see if it brings a missive on my fate, one addressed to Comet's Kerosene, before I go off in search of sending any desperate telegrams to Pa.

But the man says: 'The what?' Scratching his head, still in his undershirt, looking away and into the puddle he's made in the yard as if he might find his missing consonants there, lost somewhere back in Hackney. 'Who?'

'The mail – when?' Go on, tell me that it's been decided no mail will ever be delivered to this place again now that I am so unfortunately trapped here.

But he snorts: 'Oh – ha!' And nods to himself, I suppose upon recalling my need. 'Your guess is as good as mine,' he says, before sputtering out another, 'Ha!' and telling me: 'You picked a good time to be after the mail.'

'Why is that?' I dare to ask: it's been decided that bushrangers will rob the mail coach daily?

'They're doing a trial run bringing it up by the train today,' he says, 'which was supposed to happen yestdee for a first but half the bags got left back at the Cobb & Co depot at Penrith and the other half didn't get past Weatherboard as there was a problem with the engine getting through along the track. It's the grand opening on Satdee, you see.' The man grins wider, somewhat proudly.

So that I must ask: 'Grand opening of ...?'

'The Mount Victoria terminus for the Great Western Railway,' he tells me, with that suspicious grimace that also tells me he's shocked I don't know. 'Day after tomorrow,' he adds, pauses and adds again, slowly, 'sat-a-dee.'

'Oh good. That'll be an exciting day for you, will it?'

'Dunno about exciting. Cartload of nobs from Sydney coming to cut a ribbon. You can say g'day to the Governor when he gets here, ay.' The man scratches his balls and winks at me. 'But it'll be good for One Tree Hill, I'll say. From next week, all the mail will be coming up here to the new terminus.' He rocks back on his heels with his pleasure at this. 'We'll be the hub for the Royal Mail, we will.'

'Whenever it gets here ...' I wonder into the mist.

'Or at any rate the Royal Hotel back up on the Bathurst Road will make a right bonanza out of all this,' he's going on. 'Smack in the centre of the business they'll be, with Cobb & Co using their coach house and amenities for all things going west beyond the line.'

And now I remember that man Grindle told me yesterday evening to ask up at the Royal Hotel about sending a telegraph. Of course I'll be able to send a message from a Cobb & Co coach house – they are agents for the Royal Mail. They will help me – they must – and they can bill Pa for their trouble. I ask the innkeeper, and with some urgency: 'Where is this Royal Hotel exactly? I need to have a telegram sent off, to my father.'

'Just back up Mount York Road here, half a mile, and half as much again along the Bathurst Road highway – you can't miss it, at the town.' He points somewhere into the relentless wall of mist and ragged gum. 'You'd have passed it on the way in from Sydney yestdee – two-storey place with a big, grand verandah all round.'

I don't recall having seen such a pub from the road yesterday, I don't recall having seen a station or a town, but I can't say I was looking at anything much at all after seeing my billionth ragged gum on that journey, more than a little ragged myself.

'All right, me lad, wait a moment and I'll take you up there meself – got to go in for some supplies.' The innkeeper takes pity, doubtful of my ability to follow a road, and I am grateful for the offer. It's not unknown for me to lose my way, sometimes for days at a time. I fix hat to head, pick up my bag, and he's already re-emerging from the back door, crumpled paget coat pulled on over undershirt.

He notes me taking stock of his attire, and takes some stock of mine as we set off: 'Seeing you in the light of day now, you look fresh off the boat. Are ya?'

'Not that fresh.' I could almost laugh in return, but as it is I make a sniff at an armpit, and it's heading towards George Street at high noon. 'Been here a decade, almost,' I tell the man, and reflect inwardly that it often seems the better part of a millennium since that particular morning, dragging my heels onto that clipper at Southampton, ripped away from Piccadilly and the arms of an entirely inappropriate girl called Deb Jacobs – eighteen to my fifteen and her father was in prison for fencing stolen buckles and boots – before being expelled down the arse-pipe of the antipodes via eighty-seven days of dread and despair upon the waves. Me, that is; not Abe Jacobs, who's no doubt back in his Houndsditch pawnshop these days. While I am —

'Right fresh, you look, you do,' the innkeeper continues entertaining himself at my appearance, before switching serious once more. 'But, ay, you don't know anything about the workings of them Morse code telegraphic machines, do you?'

'Ah, no.' Not at all technically minded – to me, telegraphy is all merrily convenient witchcraft and magic. 'Why do you ask?'

I have a suspicion that I won't enjoy the answer even before he replies: 'Well, they're having trouble with that one at the Royal, you see. The transmitterer contraption ain't working as it should be. You can get a message in but can't get one out. No-one round here knows what to do with it, so they're waiting on this tinkerer bloke to come up from the Penrith depot to have a look at it.'

'Oh? When is this tinkerer bloke from Penrith due to arrive here, then?'

'Today, on the train, if it gets up here. If not tomorra. Definitely before Satdee – before the grand opening. They'll want it working properly for that, you'd have to reckon,' he says.

'Of course they would,' I reply, but my mind has dissolved in the acid of vexation after vexation, replaced by visions: of Inspector-General Fitzworthy, twisting his moustaches sadistically; Pa shaking his head with the prodigal tragedy of it all. *Jemmy, Jemmy, Jemmy – please, do the right and responsible thing, that's all I ever ask.* I am trying – for once. And poor Pa, he will be racked with worry as it is – and guilt. I must try to get a message off before any far more adverse one reaches him. Silly old Jew or not, I really don't want him to suffer the ignominy of my arrest, trial and imprisonment, any more than I want to suffer such things myself, even if it is entirely my fault that I forced his hand to bring them down upon me.

The mist is clearing, finally, with the warmth of the rising sun, and as it does the trees lengthen above us, making them appear as a tunnel, and I wonder if my best option now might not be simply to keep on walking back to Sydney. How long would it take? Couple of days? Perhaps three? Could I convince someone to let me borrow a horse?

'I'm Fenderly, by the way, Ed Fenderly,' the innkeeper says beside me. 'You have any trouble getting what you need round here, come back and see me, right?'

'Right – thanks. Very good of you,' I say but, good as this man seems to be, I hope never to see him again.

I glance away up to the right, to what looks like some building activity going on in a clearing of the trees.

'Catholics,' Innkeeper Fenderly hawks onto the road, cursing vermin. 'And they want to build a school, too.'

'Right.'

'There's the Royal, there —' he says, regaining his cheer as inexplicably, pointing up towards a rather unmissable timbered edifice, almost as big as a ship, looming out of the forest and over a fork in the road, as he adds: 'The coach-house master's place is just along the highway behind. Dixon is his name – he's a strange one, but never mind, he'll help you if he can. I'm off to get me a side of bacon.' He points down the fork, then rubs his hands together, keen about his bacon.

Good for him, I smile and wave – and the very thought of bacon makes me want to hurl up the innards. Not that I've ever been too careful with kosher, it's just that I can't stomach the smell of sizzling pig fat, some aversion lodged deep down, or perhaps struck into me by divine hand as one small point of consolation for Pa. I'm sorry, Pa – I'm always at least vaguely sorry to disappoint you as I do. But what did you expect, really? My whole life has been a series of ridiculous contradictions since he enrolled me at St Sav's Grammar, at the age of ten, to make me walk that tightrope between gentleman and Jew, to be inevitably expelled six years later for 'academic indifference, loutish insolence, frequent drunkenness and immodesty' and, in invisible print, 'for having an unrepentant Shylock for a father, never mind your two hundred pounds for the chapel fund, thank you'.

'Don't forget, come back to the Pigeon if you get stuck for any need or any place to go,' Innkeeper Fenderly calls back over his shoulder as he drumbles away, and I wave farewell again. No intention of being anywise further stuck, thank you. I'll be getting myself out of this today, one way or another.

I stride a little quicker up past the fork, beyond which indeed lies a small but busy hillside village of white-washed clay, then past the pub, past the sweet waft of a real pub's ale-ingrained timber, I find a stone cottage just the other side of its yard. A sign fitted to the gate says: *Coach-house Master & Booking Office.* This'll be the place, then. Of course there is a huge, steeply gabled coach house beyond it, with *COBB & CO TELEGRAPH LINE OF ROYAL MAIL COACHES* painted, no, shouted, across the side of the building in red and gold. I must have been knocked out passing through here yesterday.

In the gate and down the cobbled path, I ring the bell at this coach-house master's cottage, upon which the door swings open and a tall, thin man with receding hair and rather savage demeanour barks at me: 'About bloody time.'

And we are each perplexed for a moment at the outburst.

'Oh.' The man appears annoyed. 'You're not Tibbins.'

'No, I'm afraid not. I'm here about a telegr—'

'Oh! Cartwright, is it?' The man throws his hands up in the air with some relief. 'You're early up from Penrith, aren't you? How? What the —? Well, I'm glad of it, however you came.'

'No – not Cartwright.' I must disappoint him again, this Mr Dixon, I presume, mistaking me for the machine-tinkerer, I must also presume. 'I had only hoped to send a telegr—'

'No. No! That you cannot do.' The man clasps his brow and shakes his head, then tells the doorframe with all the quietly seething rage of an outcast civil servant: 'Nothing – *nothing* works around here. Ever – *nothing.* How am I supposed to —' The man grinds his chops in disgust and despair.

I think I should get him a brandy or a cup of tea before steam begins to issue out of his red-rimmed ears, or he drops dead from a seizure. I ask him: 'Can I help at all?'

'Not unless you'd like to step in as my stableman this morning and exercise the mail team, while I go and find the stableman who *should* be at the job and ring his bloody neck,' he replies, addressing the doorframe now with homicidal intent.

And I sense an opportunity. 'I can exercise your horses for you – Mr Dixon, isn't it?' I offer and add: 'I have nothing, absolutely nothing else to do, until I can send my telegram, you see.' I see advantage here for me – three, actually. One, I will be engaged in humble and honest toil, fulfilling what I can of the law's demands while awaiting resolution of Comet Kerosene confusion, and two, hopefully earning at least a little bread, ale and a telegram when I'm done, and three, I wouldn't mind meeting the horseflesh – I'd never be averse to such a thing.

'Are you genuine, sir?' Dixon finally looks at me, and he is quite genuine himself, explaining: 'There is no way of knowing if the mail will even go today, if it'll get up past Weatherboard Creek with the track the way it is, or if sudden fares will turn up to warrant the journey without it, but the horses have got to have their exercise nevertheless. They can't be stable-cold if they *are* to go out. They *must* be ready to go if they're going. What experience do you have with horses? What's your name? Who are you?'

'Fox – Jeremy Fox – of S.J. Fox & Son Silversmiths & Jewellers, Sydney, and there's little experience with horses I haven't had.' Never been without a horsey chum since I was that boy of ten nudzhing for a pony, and getting one, on the promise I'd be good at school. Heh. I wonder how my Raj is faring without me, no doubt resentfully stabled himself; you'll be missing me, won't you, boy? Even if no-one much else is. I don't think the Jockey Club is passing around the hat to bail me out today: I owe too much there, also, and at City Tatt's as well – a pound here and five there, it all adds up, doesn't it. I tell Mr Dixon, for my sins and sanity both: 'It would be my pleasure, I'm sure, to spend this morning with your team.'

He looks me up and down, and up and down again. 'Oh but no, I can't ask a gentleman to —'

'Oh but yes you can – I don't mind at all, Mr Dixon. Please.' Don't make me beg, it'll only embarrass us both. 'I really am at a loose end this morning.'

He hesitates, but pragmatism makes a decision: 'All right, then. Come along with me. I do appreciate the favour, I must say. I am up over my head in sorting last night's mail come in from the west – and my assistant, Simpson, is ill with that river fever, got him in the lungs – picked it up in Penrith of course. Excursioning last Sunday in Penrith! Why would anyone want to do that? Bloody Penrith ...'

He ploughs a line of bitter complaint across the stable yard, and I follow him; I don't know how he can bear listening to himself, never mind how his absent lackeys fare with it. I'm not listening to him.

The stable doors are flung wide and – God Almighty. All four of them – tall and handsome bay Arabs. Bred with that broad draught chest and solid cannons that Cobb & Co coachers invariably have. 'Well, beggar me.'

'Beauties, aren't they?' Dixon suspends his bellyaching long enough to note my admiration of them. 'Especially strong, these boys, and they have to be, to take the steep grade at Mitchell's Pass – easy enough on their way down the mountain, but a herculean effort bringing the Gold Escort back up from there. Sixteen miles and they take it at a gallop just about the whole distance, from Binning's Inn at Bowenfels, down in the Lithgow Valley. Maybe. If the bloody train gets here to send them on their way ...'

And off he goes again, about the *bloody* Great *bloody* Western Railway and *bloody* Public Works Department: 'Left hand can't talk to the right, can it? Certainly not without an operating telegraphic machine ...' On and on, you wouldn't know he had other work to do.

I continue admiring the horseflesh. The stallion nearest, dark coffee coat with a thick black mane and a white diamond on his forehead, sighs and raises his nose to me, taking me in his eye, and as he does, I think of the stocky little trotters that brought me up through most of the changes yesterday: quite a different animal from these massive beasts. Cobb & Co have studs all over the colony, tens of thousands of these magnificent creatures, while all other carriage companies take what they can get at ordinary livery-and-lets. I wonder if the final team that brought me to Petrolia Vale stopped here for watering on their way back last night. They must have done, they were driven so hard uphill on their stretch.

I interrupt this Dixon now to ask him: 'I say, you didn't have a team of four trotters stop in here yesterday, did you? Motley lot, private carriage, coachman from Sydney – about your height, brown coat, gruff fellow?'

Dixon appears to rummage his memory, then shakes his head: 'No, and I daresay I'd know if such did stop in here, or so much as look into the yard. I have been keeping my eyes keen about the place, let me tell you. Amid everything else that's gone wrong in the past forty-eight hours, Tuesday's mail was bailed up at Blackheath, not five miles from here. Terrible business. They even stole the jewellery off the two lady passengers on board – including their wedding rings. The bastards – what I'd do to them if I got my hands on them ...'

I'm sure I don't want to know: his ears are going alarmingly red again.

He goes on about the pistol-brandishing blackguards hiding out in the mountains and terrorising the goldfields, and then somehow moves swiftly back to complaining about the Public Works Department spending £4,000 on the railway station building when it would be better spent on tracks that can carry a train.

'Dreadful business,' I murmur, still yet distracted by thoughts of horses – those little trotters yesterday. How any man could fail to stop to rest and water his animals adequately, and after such a haul, I don't know – and the law against that is lax, isn't it, pay your two-pound fine and on your way. That sort of bastardry I'll never understand. The stallion nearest me raises his nose once more and snorts, giving me a nod: *Too right.* My word indeed, but he is a specimen. Not unlike my Raj in his bearing, though Raj is pure-bred Arab and caramel, this one is giving me the hurry-up; he wants to be out and at it, making me want that as well – making me wish there was some decent, respectable way I might work with horses, an occupation to keep me out of trouble for good. I'd be a jockey if I could, if I wasn't so heavy or so averse to whips and spurs, and wouldn't Pa love that. I've only ever raced for larks, and trouble, as my last fine for doing so attests – pulled up at the Prince Albert monument, where they are trying to grow the grass, if not for *reckless ruffians* and *notorious pests* like me. Which reminds me that I haven't paid that fine, either. I meant to, though. I damn well meant to. Together with whatever it is I owe on cards and quoits at the Hand and Heart, by the racetrack over at Randwick, never mind what I've lost there on the jockeyed lot. I have no idea how much in fact I owe in all.

Pa's pleading comes back to me along the stallion's gaze: *Jemmy, Jemmy, please – you must pay your way in this world. Everyone must.* He pays and pays his way, counting out his large donations to the Benevolent Asylum for Old Women, to the Orphan School, to the Wesley City Mission for wayward drunks, while I throw his money away across the other side of Hyde Park, at the racetrack there and the pubs that water it ... God, but I am sorry, Pa. I really am, this time. I will atone. In fact, I will straighten myself out entirely and come to synagogue with you on my return. You win. I will be a different man come this Yom Kippur; make up for last year's effort. When is it this year? September something. I have five months to reform.

The stallion at my shoulder snorts.

'Fox, did you say your name was? Silversmith? Sydney?' I am asked – by this fellow Dixon, and he's taken a stubby little notebook from his pocket, to jot down my particulars.

'That is me,' I assure him. 'S.J. Fox & Son – I'm the son and the jeweller, mostly, when I'm there – George Street, between King and Hunter, and the foundry on Goulburn. My father is the silversmith, quite renowned for it, exhibition awards, salvers, trowels, candelabrum for the new Gov—'

'Oh yes – yes, I do believe I know the name. Fancy work, isn't it, top notch? Yes, well, very pleased to make your acquaintance, and to have your assistance.' He holds out his hand.

And I take it.

He says now, with all his anxiety returned in his grip: 'Treat these stallions as your own, Mr Fox – please. Cobb & Co will have me for dog meat if anything should happen to any one of their horses, but especially, *especially* these. You'll take every care, won't you? Don't leave the yard.'

I shake on that, and I couldn't be more confident: 'Don't you worry about a thing.'

ANNIE

As the morning wears on, I come to reckon this is not the best path I've ever taken. I've never taken a path on my own before to truly know, but this one is a hard road – the Bathurst Road, winding upwards and upwards, and sharp underfoot with stones. Where am I? I don't know. I am in the forest of the Blue Mountains and the forest is dull and grey and endless as the road, and there's not a railway track or telegraph pole in sight here to assure me where I've gone. The sun is high and boiling my head under Dad's good felt hat, and I am full of regret – grief and anger, and sore, sore regret. And I'm feeling it most in my feet: Dad's boots are just that bit too broad, rubbing my small toes and my heels; and the swag is a mountain on my back.

Dad would be in the ground now, and I have left my sister with our bickering unfinished on this terrible day. I have left the Staffordshire teacups Dad gave to me, left them on the kitchen dresser. *My beautiful teacups* – only the four of them and all assorted, but all precious, and I've left them to be stolen from me along with everything else. Why? At the beckoning of some imaginary voice telling me I had to take this road? At the beckoning of panic and madness, that's what's happened here.

But then the anger sends a fire down into my feet again at having no other place to go. Mrs Webb and all her ilk be damned. I'm going to find my grandfather, Kulyan, find him and all the family he must have, family all across the bush out west. I am going to find some place I belong, as every creature on this earth has a God-given right to. Belong. Somewhere ...

My sadness throbs up from the blisters at my heels. I listen to the beat of the frying pan and the billy whacking the swag either side, and I call on the strength of my dad to continue. The strength of our parents both, the strength of their faith, of Moses leading the Israelites from Egypt, out through the desert, under a sun much fiercer than this one is on me today.

But as I keep on, the heaving and straining in my body and my breath takes on some strange other sound – a sound like a steam-roller, like that one which was brought to repair the road ahead of the Penrith bridge after the floods. *Pushhh, pushhh, pushhh.* Sis and me went to watch it, huffing and punching and rolling, up and down, up and down. We'd never seen anything like it. Monstrous thing. I am a monstrous thing. Huffing and stomping up this mountain.

Only the sound is not coming from me. It's coming from the bush behind me, coming up from the east.

I stop still, except for my knees trembling from effort and from fear at what might be coming for me now.

A great jet of smoke, thick and billowing, shooting up through the trees, and hissing everywhere with steam – and I see tracks again, curving around out of the tall timber towards me, at last. It's only the train, black and stinking and monstrous in its usual way. Of course it's the train; you'd think I'd never seen one before, though they come and go from Richmond and Windsor twice every day, screeching in and out of the station, morning and evening.

I stand where I am and watch this one pass. Carriages crowded with ladies' bonnets all gay with bright ribbons and high-class roses spilling out from under their brims; a man waves down from a window with a cheerful smile, and it's gone. Huffing and stamping away, and blessedly showing me that I am heading in the right direction and on the right road, whatever I might be doing here upon it.

But I don't move on after the train. My knees are still trembling – from weariness, caught right up and gone past me now I've stopped. I let the swag slump from my shoulders, and the tarp after it, and I slump down on top of them both. I will just sit and fret a while, I reckon, until I don't.

Until about two heartbeats later when I hear the steady stamp of hooves and a crunch of cartwheels coming up along the road – I'd better shift or I'll be colloped. Somehow with my skinny, leaden arms, I push the swag and the tarp away off to the side of the road and slump straight back down on them as this team of heavy horses kick up a cloud over me and the wheels crunch by. I stare into the spokes going around and around, my mind as full of nothing as the air between them, and the rest of me aching all over.

'Whoa! Whooaaa there!' I hear the carter calling to his team and the wheels stop a little way past me. 'Hoy, feller, ho there – where you going, nowhere or somewhere?'

A face made mostly of white whiskers looks back at me over an open dray stacked with barrels of beer, and I can only suppose he's talking to me, 'feller' as I've made myself appear, though I hardly know who I might be. I get to my feet, but I can't think what to reply.

'Where you going, I said, feller?' he calls out to me again.

That's the question of the day and I give him one back: 'Blackman's Swamp?'

'Never heard of it,' he says with a frown under his hardworking, sun-bleached brim.

And I could sink away right into the earth and beyond with the certainty now that no such place exists – only I'm just as certainly remembering Mother, so clear I can feel the rise and fall of her breath at my back: *Your grandfather was a boy cutting bark by the river – not this river but way out west – when the white men came and asked him to cut some bark for the roofs of their huts. He learned their language so quick and was so smart in every way, they came back and got him when they needed a guide to show them all the rivers out there. They came back and got him from Blackman's Swamp.* That's what Mother said. Why would it come to me so clear and from her breath if it wasn't true? I tell the carter all else I know of the place: 'It's past Bathurst.' Because that's what Dad always said: *Way out west past Bathurst.*

'Lotta places past Bathurst nowadays,' the old carter says, his whiskers bushing out around a smile as he tells me: 'I'm going up as far as Weatherboard Creek, if you want to save yourself the tramping. It's halfway to Bathurst, near enough.'

Weatherboard Creek. I've heard of that place – everyone would have. It's where the train stops on the Great Western Railway line, for all the well-to-do taking a tourist trip; Prince Alfred, the Duke of Edinburgh, visited there just this summer, had tea with all his *select ladies* on a red carpet under a marquee, looking out at the waterfall where the creek drops off some cliff, before he went back to Sydney, where the Catholics shot him at some other picnic, and he was only lucky to have survived – I read about all that in the *Empire*, read it out for Dad.

Oh, Dad.

My knees start trembling again at the loss of him and I tell the old carter, 'Thanks. I'd be very grateful.' Might not do much for my broken heart, but my feet will be wanting you glorified.

'Hop up, then, young feller,' the carter is urging, smacking the seat beside him.

I can barely lift the swag up onto the dray, nor the tarp after it, I am so over-weary, but I manage a smile for the old man's kindness and the faded pattern of flannel flowers all along the backboard behind him as I climb towards it. And I sigh with relief as I settle there as well: 'Oh dear me.'

So that the carter gives me a wondering glance. Strange feller, this one, I can hear him thinking, and I'm thinking, a bit too late, that I don't know how to sound like a man. I look down at Dad's field boots buckled at my shins, the tops of them folded over at my knees, just as Dad would wear them; but looking like a man and acting like one are two different things, aren't they. I clear my throat, and mumble as deep into these boots as I can: 'Yes, well, it has been a long, long morning. Walk. Warm today ... Isn't it?'

What do I sound like? I might be smart and quick myself at times, I might be all kinds of things, but I am not practised in deceit. I am going to be found out at the first test. I am going to meet the fate of young women who travel the roads alone in this world made for men. No – worse than that – I'm going to meet the fate of a young black woman who has dared to go anywhere at all.

The carter chuckles into his whiskers. 'Yeah, well, walking in the hot sun'll give anyone the *oh-dears*, won't it.' With a shake of the reins, a click of the tongue, the dray is rolling off again, and he winks at me: 'Feller.'

My cheeks go red hot, never dark enough to hide that feeling in my face, which he must surely see.

He gives me another wink: 'Don't worry, whatever you are. You're safe here.' And he's not laughing as he says: 'Tough times for yer, eh?' Because I must be wearing the fact of that on my face, too.

I nod, and look away. I try to drag a raft of peace over my thoughts with the slow and gentle swaying of the dray, the broad backs of the horses shining under the high sun, eight of them, shining like water running over rusted drums, their silky manes all nodding at the way ahead.

Don't cry, Annie. Mother is whispering something else into me: *Don't let them see you cry.*

I won't. Don't give anyone the satisfaction of thinking they might have brought me low – ever.

The rocks and stones by the roadside now hold bunches of green ferns sitting like fat ladies under the shade of the trees, the carter is calling out to his team, 'Gee-up, Jonah! C'mon, Ginger!' with something that sounds like goodness and care, and I am no longer walking. And I am grateful.

Even more when the road steepens further and I see some travellers pushing along on foot, half a dozen of them, and strange-looking, all wearing long blouses and wide straw hats.

The carter shakes his head, muttering, 'Them Chinamen,' as they move off to the side of the road to let us by, and I take a wondering glance at him. I've never known a Chinaman, except in letters to the paper from those complaining of them, that they're unclean, that they cheat on their hawkers' fees in Sydney, tricking the police as they all look the same. *Good luck to 'em,* Dad would say, wanting to get a taste of their broccoli one day, because he'd heard it was like nothing else. Knowing as I do that the rough road of prejudice is never a straight one, I ask the carter, 'You don't mind me but you hate them?'

'Hate them?' The carter blinks at me, seeming offended at the question. 'Not for me to be hating anyone. The Chinese are a whole herd of crazy is all what concerns me. They'll be chasing the gold, these ones here, as they all do, but the time for finding fortunes is over, if it was ever really on. They'll turn around and rush up to Queensland at the next hot tip, then rush all the way back down to Ballarat, and wherever they go they cop a hiding for it, too. Dunno why they put themselves through it – it's a sham, one that keeps 'em all coming. Whole world comes for the gold, and then wants to get home again when they find none – but they can't scrape up enough for the fare.'

I have to nod at that, thinking of Gudge and the other cabbages at Cygnet Farm, for they came off the goldfields themselves, and I'd like to kick them all back across the sea to wherever they came from before then.

'Hoy, you're not going off prospecting yourself, are you?' the carter asks me with deeper warning in his words.

'No!' I just about shriek it to the treetops. The things I've heard and read about the western goldfields, I don't know why anyone would want to go there, either – all full of drunkards and brothels and opium dens and wild men come across from California when the rush ended there. The older brother of one of the boys at Richmond Free Presbyterian, Billy Hirsch, ran off to the big strike at Ophir as soon as he could: fell down a mine when he got there, and that was the end of him. How his mother wailed at the news.

'Not for me to know,' the carter says, 'but you want to be careful out there. Anywhere past Bathurst. No place for ... well, it's no place for anyone getting about on their own.'

I look away again, back over the barrels on the dray, and I see the little crowd of Chinamen coming along now behind. They don't seem to see us, didn't wave as we passed them, as if we passed them from some separate world. What must it be like to be so far from home? I shiver with the notion that I might be about to find out something of that question.

Parramatta, Mother's laugh is a song heard from somewhere beyond some dusty corner in my mind: *It means lots of eels.* Dad laughs with her: *It means lots of pubs.*

'How far is it to Weatherboard Creek?' I ask the carter, to know one small thing of distance, of where I might be going.

He says, 'Aw, only about twenty mile – a bit less. We'll stop at the Buss's Inn and the Blue Mountain Inn on the way for deliveries, then we'll get on to the Weatherboard Inn, get there before the sun sets.'

'That's good,' I say, meaning nothing by it at all, as the hugeness of the earth spins out around me.

'Hungry?' he says, and he pulls an apple out of his coat pocket.

I'm not hungry at all, my stomach is too busy turning itself inside out, but I take the apple from him: 'Thanks.'

*

As I open my eyes, I see the sun is just starting to sink through the trees, and the carter is nudging my arm. 'Here we are, Weatherboard at last,' he says.

I stare at him, forcing my eyes to keep awake. Mack Hathaway is his name and he's in the employ of Bourke's Brewery out of Penrith, new to that district. He knows what it's like to need a hand in tough times and that's all of his past worth knowing, so he told me. I told him my name is Annie, for Annabel, and he laughed, 'Funny name for a lad.' That raised something like a laugh from me, but he's had me working like a lad, rolling barrels into the taprooms of the public houses we've stopped at along the way – 'No such thing as a free ride,' he winked. I've kept my head down and my mouth shut and no-one's paid me the least bit of attention all day.

'G'day, Mack!' A man is coming out of this last inn – a weatherboard inn, and the only building here. Railway tracks a hundred yards or so away run along a platform and over a creek. And that's it, apart from tall forest, everywhere, all around.

'And who you got with you?' the man is asking Mack Hathaway, and I'm shrinking under my hat.

'Offsider – you know how bad me back is these days. Lad's been helping with the load.'

The man takes a closer look at me now, stepping right up to the dray, and he says to Mack, 'You reckon so? I reckon your eyes are getting bad, too, old mate. This young feller is a girl.'

I sit up straight and as I do, I feel my hair fall across my shoulder: it's come loose from its pin, and escaped Dad's hat as I was dozing. One thing I've got plenty of: hair: long, curly, girl's hair.

Something about this man, the way he's looking at me, gives me cause to be alarmed, even before he says: 'And she's a black one.' He turns back to Mack: 'What are you doing bringing one like this here? You know Hettie won't like it —'

'Aw, come on, Jim, have a heart – half a heart.'

'Hettie'll have my heart on a stake when she sees what's here. You know what it's like, Mack – ever since what happened out at Pigetty's Hole when she were a lass – she's never got over it.'

'Aw, c'mon, Jim. You've got an empty stable – she won't know a thing.'

'No, Mack.' This Jim whoever he is shakes his head, and looks straight at me: 'You can't stop here – go on, get off.' He shoos me like I'm a stray dog, flicking a hand at the bush. 'Go on.'

I won't need telling a second time. I've jumped down off the seat and grabbed my swag and tarp off the dray. He's got a nasty missus in there – a Mrs Webb or a Mrs Billington – one who's ready to hit him over the head with a saucepan if she finds a black camping in her yard. I don't know what any Pigetty's Hole might be, but I know all about The Problem With Blacks: they stink, they steal, and they are all shiftless, godless and stupid. I've read it all and I've heard it all, every snipe and sneer behind my back; every assurance from Dad: *It's not true, Annie love. It's only ignorance talking.* And I'm angry again for the lot of it. I give this Weatherboard Jim a look full of curses, for the ignorant stump he is, and I'm off, following the creek to wherever it might go.

'Hoy! Feller! Annie!' Mack Hathaway calls after me.

But I don't look back. I leave him arguing with his *old mate*, and I keep stamping off into the bush till I can't hear them anymore.

The way that man looked at me, like I'm not a person at all. Like I don't even have a name. I say my name to myself as I go, the name my parents gave me at my baptism: I am Annabel Eliza Bird. I am someone, and I'm going to Blackman's Swamp, and maybe there'll be people there who will never, ever look at me that way, like I don't exist – or shouldn't.

JEM

Well, at least it's not damp this evening, at least I'm not condemned to sleep under a tree or on the side of the road, I console myself as I hang the lamp under the awning of the hayshed, back at the Pigeon, my manger for the night. Despite my excellent care of the horseflesh this morning, the Royal could provide no accommodation for me – they're completely full, as is this place, all rooms taken up ahead of the grand opening of the railway terminus.

At least I've been fed well today – Dixon, back at the coach house, couldn't do enough for me by way of steak and eggs and Tennant's pale ale. Not that there was much he could do about the things I most require – such as communication with the outside world. No mail again today: the train couldn't get up past Weatherboard – not the midday service, or, it is expected, the evening service after it – though the word from the railway navvies fixing whatever problem they have with the railway line there is that it will be ready tomorrow. For sure. But if it doesn't come through tomorrow, I've been told, I could always go back east twenty miles to the village of Blue Mountain, where there's another telegraph and Bourke's stout on tap. Could I possibly borrow a horse to get there this afternoon? I had asked. 'Borrow a horse?' Dixon had looked at me as if I were the full barking meshugge. Because I just about am.

I am suddenly overcome by the morbs, that melancholy which hits after ... perhaps a little too much of nothing, combined with the smell of fried bacon coming from Fenderly's kitchen. I sit down on my hay bale, imagining what Pa is doing now. He'll be in our little work room behind the shop on George Street, squinting down the eyepiece at his elaborate repoussé on that ceremonial trowel for the Governor's next sod-turning. Or he's hammering at the mandrel, starting on the setting of that Siamese emerald, which I should have done myself last Friday, but didn't: because I was at the Colonnade, betting on … two flies crawling up a wall. Pa is an artist: he makes exquisite, award-winning epergnes cascading with silver and gold apple blossom and butterflies. He is a businessman as well, a very successful one, and whatever it is he's doing, he never stops working or worrying. He'll be worrying about me, right now. He'll be worrying about his accounts, his investments, the price of his metals, his reputation and his ledger with God: has he been a good enough man today, all things considered? Ruining his sight in the poor light of the table lamp, too cautious over every penny and generally antiquated to get us some decent overhead kerosene lamps for our work room, or God forbid have the gas put on – that sort of luxury, along with arranging lavish Christmas parties, is for the faithful foundry workers who make his spoons and forks. And that's why we're rich.

What did I do today, by contrast? Hung about in a Cobb & Co yard and fell a little bit further in love with that dark bay with the black mane. Zad his name is, Zad for Zadkiel, after the archangel of mercy – and perhaps I'm deserving of none.

The goat in the yard here bleats up at the night, and possibly in agreement.

Wastrel, Inspector-General Fitzworthy adds. *Nuisance to Society* …

Is that all I am? Really?

ANNIE

I dream of falling branches, thousands of branches cracking and falling all around me, and wanting to grab me, chasing me awake, but when I open my eyes, the dawn-lit trees above me are only busy with tiny golden sparrows chirruping over a more practical dread that, if I'm to get anywhere today, I've got to put Dad's boots back on.

Those boots look at me from where they're conspiring together under the tarp, such as I managed to string it up last night: I couldn't get the rope tight enough, so it's sagging right down in the middle, and the pegs for the sides slipped around so much in the sandy ground here, I might as well not have bothered.

There's no way around bothering with these boots, though. I whip out of the swag, take a deep breath as I close my eyes and ram them on, as if not looking and not breathing will make a difference to the feeling. *Oh, oh, oh, oh, oh, oh, oh, oh!* I buckle them up and crawl out from the tarp, where standing brings a higher screaming pitch to each of the individual blisters around my heels and toes: *Oh, please!*

How am I going to walk back to the road like this? I'm beginning to fret about it, when I hear a splash from the creek behind me – a big splash – and curiosity has me forgetting my poor feet to wonder what it is. A fish? That would need to be a big fish to make such a splash.

I step closer to the water, and then I see it – not a fish at all but a slick of black fur, rippling, a blinking glimpse of a tail. A creature as big as a dog, only it can't be a dog – can it? I've never seen a dog swimming with its head underwater like that. Whatever it is, I'm after it, along the rocky bank. Is it a seal? I've never seen a seal but in a picture. I don't think seals live in rivers, though; do they? Or shallow creeks. And there it is again! I see the snout snap at something in a little patch of reeds, and the top of its head, hairy long ears like a spaniel, darting through the water and out of sight once more. I see another ripple, further up, and I keep following the creek, looking for another glimpse, but the creature seems to vanish like it was never there.

I rub my eyes. I hear Mother teasing Dad: *It's true – it's true! He would steal all the fish from our traps.*

What would?

A word I can't hear – *her* language – a reed slipping from my fingers.

You know. Mother nudges Dad with the back of her hand. *They call him bunyip.*

Bunyip? That's not her word. Bunyip is a cartoon in the newspaper – a vicious bogey with blood-dripping fangs that drags its victims into swamps. And bunyips don't exist, not any more than mermaids and faeries do.

Mother laughs; her beautiful laugh. *It's true – it's true!*

But it's only the hazy dream-light of dawn playing tricks with me, playing tricks with my aching heart. Isn't it?

In answer, all I hear is the sound of water – rushing. Not a trickling over rocks but a real fast flow. The falls. I've never seen a waterfall before either, and I can't see the edge of this one from where I stand, but I know they're dangerous, no fantastical story about it. I read only last year that a runaway bushranging convict called Red Mendelson jumped off one, somewhere here in the mountains, rather than get caught by the troopers – that's how brutal the police of New South Wales have got – and he fell two thousand feet into a gorge, never to be found. So I'm treading carefully now, like the earth might give way from underfoot if I step in the wrong spot, or more likely, I might slip on a mossy rock and get carried off. I scramble back up the bank to safer ground.

And the picture before me here is more awesome than anything I've ever seen: the earth is gaping like a great big hole in the world, flat-topped mountains standing all around a valley of cloud – monsters turned to rock. And the creek is rushing and rushing to them, somewhere tumbling away, the sound of water everywhere, that sends a warning roaring through me: *Keep away from here, Annie Bird. Keep Away.*

That voice from the river I heard yesterday, so it seems to me, only it's deep and loud this time, coming up through my boots, and giving me the greatest fright I've ever known – I've never moved so fast. I pack up my camp, spinning like a devil wind, and I bolt for my life back up towards the Weatherboard Inn.

There's no sign of Mack Hathaway or the dray when I get there; only a woman out the front sweeping the verandah like she'd prefer to murder it. I suppose that's black-hating Hettie, and she's the least of my concerns right now.

I look east towards Penrith, towards Sis, and the good sense it would be for me to return to her; I look west towards I don't know. Blackman's Swamp? I don't really know what black anything is, apart from Sis and Mother, rest her soul, and me. Pictures flicker: a dark old face at the door; Dad shaking his head, *No, not here, feller*; I was small, maybe about ten; a barefoot woman at the edge of the market, brown feet on the brown earth under a tree; *Keep away from her, Annie, she's not right in the head*, and then she disappeared.

Keep away from here, the sound of my fear is roaring and roaring over it all.

But which way should I go?

Go west.

Wasn't I so certain of that yesterday? Guidance from the Lord or just the longing inside me, I heard it plain as day. Go find our grandfather, something of our family; find a better place to call home.

Maybe there's nothing out there to find. A dying race, they call the Aborigine, tragical, ancient, doomed to extinction, and maybe that is so. But if this is all I have, then this is mine to know.

I haven't got far past the inn when I hear the sounds of people coming from a railway cutting below the road: a party of men working on the tracks down there, hammering at them with huge and heavy mallets, sweat flying. Working men, too hard at it to be bothered giving anyone a hard time for any reason, and I'm wondering if I might call out to them, to ask how far it is to the next town, to somewhere I might buy a pie, when I hear someone calling out to me – someone real and really calling out.

'Stop! You there! Stop! Whoa!'

A man jumps onto the road in front of me, waving his hands in the air, shouting his lungs out: 'Stop where you are!'

I stop still at his wild eyes – just as a great big bang goes off, louder than any clap of thunder, and there's rocks and dust flying up ahead, flying up from the railway line below, flying up above the trees. The sound shakes my bones, and I stumble back with the shock of it.

'Dynamite!' the man is still shouting at me, but I'm straightaway relieved to know that's all it was – I've seen dynamite go off before, though not this close. Dad took me and Sis to see them blowing up the Lapstone pass for the zigzag rail up from Emu – three years since they finished, and they were at it for ages, too. Bang, boom and it'd be raining rocks out the side of the mountain. I'm so close to this one here, I can smell the dynamite in the air, or what I suppose it is, a coal smell, like dried blood; wounded rock.

'Jeez, mate!' the man keeps on shouting. 'I thought you was gunna walk right into that. Didn't you see the sign back there?' And he is laughing as he shouts.

I shake my head: I didn't see a sign. I must have missed it, busy looking at the ground not thinking about my blisters.

'Well, road's open now!' the man is still keeping on with his shouting, and hopping from foot to foot like he's got dynamite forever going off around him. 'Train'll get through, too – no problem! Took care of that landslip, all right. Oh yeah, we did – yippee!' He's laughing away like the dynamite must have got right into his brain somehow. He smacks his thigh: 'Mate! The look on your face!'

'Must have been side-splitting,' I say, and try to pull my voice down to as low as it can go, since he seems convinced I'm a feller, any ordinary feller; or he's just had his brain shaken up one too many times. 'How far to the next inn this way?' I ask him.

'Pub, you mean?' He squints and I nod; he says: 'Ten mile.' He points up the road: 'Go on past Will's Chimney – that place is closed down. Keep on past Whipcord Pinch, past the police station at Pulpit Hill, and then you'll come to Blackheath, where you'll see Dunn's Inn.'

Maybe I'll just cook up some of my oats by the side of the road somewhere sooner; I'm weary already, too weary, too small, for any ten-mile walk.

But then he says: 'Or you can go on another five mile to One Tree for the best plate of steak and eggs around. Royal Hotel there, right by the Cobb & Co.'

The Cobb & Co. Of course! That's where I need to go. They'll be able to tell me where Blackman's Swamp is: they know every inch of road through all of New South Wales, and from the bottom of Victoria to the top of Queensland. They don't care who you are as long as you're not drunk and you've got the money. I've still got that five pounds, seventeen shillings and bawbees in the swag – less the sixpence spent on yesterday's red-herring pie at Blue Mountain. Depending on how much the coach is, I'll be handing over for the fare. Be done with it – just get there. I smile at this helpful, friendly dynamite man and I shout: 'Thanks!'

Fifteen miles seems like nothing now, and I shake my head at myself as I set off again: if I hadn't been so muddled up leaving Cygnet Farm, charging off like a train, so determined to run away, so little experienced in getting anywhere, I could have asked at the depot in Penrith. And maybe I wouldn't have got this far at all.

'Good on you, digger!' The man waves me off, and I wave back as I go.

Digger? He must take me for a cabbage-headed prospector bound for the goldfields. Good. I hope everyone else on this road supposes the same.

You want to be careful out there. Anywhere past Bathurst … Mack Hathaway's warning rings in my ears.

And I pull Dad's hat right down to my eyebrows. I promise my beloved father and my mother, too: I might have lost my mind this past little while, but it's back in my head again now.

*

Uphill knows no other way. By the time I sight this village of One Tree I reckon my legs have given up and died somewhere along the road so I can't feel my feet anymore. The sun is starting to swing west, towards mid-afternoon. But I'm here; I've made it. These last steps seem the steepest, though. I'll have just enough breath left in me to ask what I need to ask, and fall down for a spell after that. I see a garden outside what I think might be the booking office for the coach, and there's a little patch of lawn there I think would do very well for falling down upon.

I look up at the tall letters on the big stable building behind: *COBB & CO TELEGRAPH LINE OF ROYAL MAIL COACHES*. I send a prayer to them: please don't turn me away. While the mail coach is supposed to take all paying customers, so are inns, and they don't, do they. They can just say, 'You're drunk – go away. We don't like the look of you.' Or they stare through you, like the butcher at Windsor, or the man who sold me a raspberry vinegar and a ham sandwich five miles back, or any number of people passed on any road: they pretend that you're not really there. In sharp understanding, I see how much my father protected me from all this sort of thing; he's not here to give a hard stare to a bigot across my shoulder anymore. Not here to make me feel safe, though now I suppose I never was. I march on a bit quicker with my aloneness and with my prayer: don't you turn me away, don't you dare.

I hear a jingle of bullock bells coming on towards me, around the bend in the road, and I look up again at the sound – always a sweet sound, *plunketty plunk* – and I watch the animals heaving along, a dozen of them, big fellers, curly horns bobbing, hauling a load of bricks. The bullocky is cracking his whip out ahead, more in a manner of telling people to get out of their way than to control the bullocks: they are so steady in their lines. They're not fast at the job, but they're unstoppable, especially coming on downhill as they are – about twelve ton of solid muscle.

For a moment, I'm not sure which side of the road to move to, and as I dither, I look towards the stable yard, the coats of the fine horses there shining a deep golden red, with what now looks like a bushfire racing up behind the Cobb & Co, before I hear the whistle – it's the train. And the whistle is screaming on and on, like they just worked out how to use it.

A whistle that urges the bullocks on to a sudden and mighty pace.

There's the bellowing of the animals and the bullocky hushing them each by name: 'Hey, Fred! Ho, Bonzer! Whoa, Slogger.' And he's cracking the whip furiously, cracking it right above my head. I see he's steering them to the left, so I make my move to the right.

Just a pounding of horses' hooves comes on the other way – what? Two riders walloping up the hill, right towards me.

And I have nowhere to go, unless I can leap the garden fence of the booking office, but I don't think I could make my legs leap to save myself.

I am going to be killed.

'Oh!' I scream, with my hands in the air as far as my burden of swag and tarp will let me.

Because that is all I can do.

JEM

Idon't want to know my fate at all, now it's here with the mail train. I've guessed what it might be: apparently, so Fenderly informed me this morning, there's a second blacksmith needed at Comet's – not at the Petrolia Vale diggings, but a couple of miles further on in Hartley Vale, where the 'kero', as they call it, is barrelled and shipped out. There's your mix-up. And it's just how Pa might think to punish this wayward jeweller: at the anvil, bashing out barrel hoops and horse shoes. How perfectly humbling. In his despair, he's often muttered that I might have best been suited to the baser trades, in darkest mood referring to me in this respect most succinctly as 'Gaulish', both for my somewhat heavier physique and for my many predilections that might be construed as French in flavour and therefore inherited from my mother's line.

Not least among them loitering with lack of intent, as I am doing at present, train steaming and whistling into the station while I ponder how I might remain here with Zad and the other coachers – Harold, Falcon and Poncho. Could I perhaps talk my way into swapping a non-custodial term of blacksmithing for one of stablemanning at One Tree Hill? Tibbins, the actual stableman, is in fact deathly ill – with this so-called river fever, caught, it's supposed, from Simpson, Coach-house Master Dixon's likewise ailing assistant. If I had any money, I'd insist on having the men seen to by a doctor. But then again, if Tibbins expires his last this afternoon, it's difficult to resist calculating that the timing here just might well be excellent – for me.

I watch Dixon bounding across the yard for the train, smoothing down his moustaches in preparation for his most important role: receiving the Royal Mail from the Station Master. I'm surprised there's not a brass band playing. Doubtless there will be tomorrow, for the grand opening.

In the meantime and more immediately, I need to compose a return missive to Pa, an urgent letter begging to be allowed home, promising future diligence and fidelity, foreswearing gambling, whoring, racing … living …

Zad shudders in his withers and shifts beneath me. Quite. He's no happier: the coachman arrived a little while ago, grim fellow as coachmen invariably seem to be these days – I'm sure he gave his name as Grump. Regardless, I'd better get this saddle off this horse and stop indulging in any further fantasy. The whistle has blown.

Just as I'm about to swing down, though, I feel Zad tense again between my boots.

And at the same time I hear a cry of, 'Help! Help me!' coming from the road, with a hell of a to-do going on up there. I hear the cracking of a whip – and what sounds like a stampede of elephants.

'Help! Please, help me!' It's a woman, and in such clear distress I've nudged Zad on before I've thought another thing.

Where is she? I peer at the dusty confusion on the road. A dray careering into the trees a little way down the hill, bricks crashing off it as it teeters; and up the other way, I see a slight-built fellow struggling, it appears, to hang on to the side of a wheeling, rearing horse, while the rider above him is – 'Thief! Thief! You dirty thief!' And I see what is happening: the slight fellow on the road is being relieved of his swag by the rider. What a miserable beggar to steal from a swagman the little he has. This is a new low in highway robbery, surely.

The struggle continues, the horse startling and rearing ever more violently with the ruckus at its side, and I am calling out, 'Oy – you there!' as I urge Zad over the yard fence, at the same time marvelling at what a strong little beggar this swaggie is. 'Oy – let that man alone! Give him back his goods!'

'Help! Me! You! Devil! Cabbage!' the swaggie cries out loud and high as we are upon them, and I now see the swaggie is actually the lady in distress. The hat knocked off her head, chestnut curls flying about as she tries to smack the rider across the face with one hand, while hanging onto what appears to be a billy can attached to the swag with the other. She is tawny-skinned, all tight sinews, and flashing teeth and eyes; even in this dire state she's a lovely bit of jam. Some spark – what!

But just as I get to her, her strength seems to run out, she lets go her hold on the handle of the billy, and the rider is off with the lot. I take in what of his appearance I can: the silver-speckled rump of his dapple-grey mount, stocky thing, possibly a youngish colt and only lately tamed; his black hat, dirt-grey shirt and his face disguised by a black scarf. 'Crack on!' he shouts to another who waits up near the hotel, at the corner of the road leading down into the village, shouting something else, perhaps a name, I don't quite hear. But I know what they are: bushrangers.

This is an outrage. I cannot wholly grasp what I have just witnessed.

Nor can I understand why it is that the swag-girl has grasped hold of my arm, and is screaming at me: 'Nasty! Devil! Thief! You'll pay!' Slapping at my knee; clawing at my wrist; yanking at Zad's reins. She's extremely upset, my word she is.

And she's found a second wind of strength, not going to let go of me now. So, without further consideration of any kind, I've picked the girl up by the back of her trousers, thrown her over Zad's shoulders like a fistful of twigs, and we're after the bastards.

HORSE-BORROWING

ANNIE

If I'm going to die, I'm going to die fighting. If this is how disaster ends for me, let it end with me turning on the back of this horse to strike out at the one who assails me.

'You can take everything from me, but you will not have me!' I screech and scratch at him with everything I can muster. 'You will not have me while ever I'm alive!'

I am kicking and biting and screaming as the horse is walloping along beneath me. I pray to our Heavenly Father that I slip and fall beneath the hooves, and go that way and swift rather than at the dirty hands of this stinking criminal. His elbow is spearing into my side, keeping me held fast to the saddle and hardly able to draw breath.

'Will you stop wriggling about, Miss,' he says with desperate, thumping breath of his own. 'We're gaining ground – I can still see them.'

I can see the little white-clay cottages of the village rushing by, downhill. Petunias are spilling rainbows out of a window box, and I'm thinking aren't they late in the season. A woman is running out into her yard, saucepan in hand, and her apron has a frill all around the hem. I can hear the hissing of the train come in at the station. Sounds of cheering: 'Hooray! Hooray! She's here!'

However it happens, I am going to die.

And now we are as quick into the bush, no more gravel of any road beneath us, but only grass and scrub. And air as we jump a great big fallen log, smashing down onto the ground over the other side of it, to be bolting breakneck downhill once more, this way and that. I might faint from being chucked about across the horse as we go; somehow I don't faint, but I wish I would.

'There they are!' The man keeps racing on through what looks like forest again: a blur of trees and trees and trees. I wish he would stop. I never go on a horse; horses are for ploughing rows and carting goods, and are dealt with by men; I never even go on a pony ride at a fair. I am going to be sick, or I would be if I'd had more than a ham sandwich for my lunch too long ago. I am going to die hungry and chucked about.

And then the man says, 'Damn you,' pulling the horse up, slowing to a trot, chucking my brain around only worse. 'We've lost them.'

I begin to understand at this moment that the man who has got me is not a thief. He's tried to help me, and to no avail.

He brings the horse right to a stop, and his hand is gentle on my back: 'Are you all right there, Miss?'

I can't find the breath or the mind to reply more than a whisper of a groan that means both yes and no.

He says: 'I'm not sure quite what I'd have done if we had caught up with them, though. Hm.'

I look up at him, as far as I can in this predicament, stuck over his horse as I am, and I find his face. He has a scratch right across his cheek, I see as he turns to look behind us: I've drawn blood – from the wrong man. And some kind of a gentleman he is, with his uptowny words. Long side whiskers trimmed close, black on his white face, long black hair flopping across his brow as he takes off his hat to wipe that brow of sweat – with a silk handkerchief. And his hat, resting on his knee right by my nose, is a picture all of its own: a curved uptowny brim, not short in the crown and not tall but something else. He's a flash one – likely plucks his eyebrows, too.

'I am sorry,' he says, still looking out at the bush. 'That was all a bit hopeless, wasn't it.'

I finally find enough breath to say: 'Can you help me down, please?'

'Oh! Yes. Of course. That can't have been the most comfortable ride.' He's quick out of the saddle, hands gentle again around me, sliding me off after him, and I slump to the ground at his feet, my head in my hands, to stop the hurdy-gurdy from all that chucking around. I look at his boots: high-front riding boots, tan-coloured and fancy, with stitches swirling across the pointed toes. One turns around the other on its heel: *crunch*, and a puff of dust.

He says above me: 'Hm. You don't happen to know which way it might be back towards the village, do you? I wasn't taking note as we came down here, I —'

I look up, and around. We are surrounded by bush, scraggedy and grey and mean, in every direction. I don't know at all where we are.

JEM

'Never mind,' I say. 'I'm sure we'll find our way. Somewhere ...'

Her large dark eyes only stare out at the wilderness, bewildered. Who wouldn't be? I am. God, but she's attractive. The line of her jaw gorgeously squared beneath that sweet little daub of a nose – and those unruly chestnut tresses. She'd be stirring the whirlygigs on me if she didn't look so dashed.

I offer her a statement of the obvious: 'Worst luck, hm?'

She hangs her head, and keeps it hung. Oh. Right. I hope she hasn't begun to cry. I never know what to do with one of them – a girl that cries. I say to this one, as one does: 'There, there. We'll work things out.'

'Work things out?' She leaps up off the ground at that, and if she did shed a tear, it's evaporated in the volcanic heat of her temper as she lets me have it: 'Work things *out*? What things? Everything I own is gone. All of my money! My Holy Bible! My certificate of education! My dad's best hat! My billy! My *water* bottle! The rest of my food – my potatoes and beans! My oats, my toothbrush – my *soap*. My *life*! It's all *gone*!' All flashing teeth and eyes again, arms ranging around wild as her curls: 'And now you've got me properly lost? How can you not know where we are? What were you doing going after those thieves? Now I'll never get to – oh! I'm not meant to get anywhere at all – is that it?' She rails at the sky; and then back at me: 'Who are you to tell me *anything* will work out?'

Glaring; sweet little nostrils flaring. And that accent – classic colonial mash of sawn-off vowels, and from her mouth – delightful. Utterly ace. But who am I?

'Er. Jeremy Fox – Jem to those who love me.' I give her an all-weather smile.

She's not in the least bit interested; she has turned away, hands behind her head in exasperation. An exasperation for which I am in some small part responsible.

Yes. Well. I should make some attempt to work things out. I look about at our surrounds once more: bush, bush, bush and a bit more bush. At one mysterious point on the compass, however, as the bush dips away down to a cliff edge, it appears we're above a wide valley of open pasture; other than that, we have approximately three hundred and twenty degrees of eucalyptus-covered hills upon which each tree, each leaf, competes for uniformity. Beggar me. How can we have got lost so quickly? One hears these awful stories of those who get lost in the bush, it is often lamented that whole and outstandingly awful novels of same are written yearly, describing in boundless detail how quickly it does indeed occur, but five minutes? Perhaps ten at the most? Really? We can't be lost. Then again, what would I know? My general sense of the countryside doesn't extend much further than the occasional steeplechase out at Homebush or an impromptu bunny hunt above the dunes of Bondi beach, and then I'm only there for the sport, the opportunity to moke about in tails and get blind on the champagne afterwards.

'Hm,' is about all I can offer, and not for lack wishing things were otherwise: I really must get back to One Tree Hill preferably before both Cobb & Co and Her Majesty's Royal Mail Service set the dogs on me for taking their precious steed out of the yard and making them late for departure. There's some shit on a biscuit.

And swag-girl is now striding off towards the edge of the cliff.

'Oy! Where are you going?' I go after her, with Zad very firmly in hand, and for one horrendous moment I think she's going to throw herself off it, do herself in, for the complete shit biscuit. I see Pa's hands shaking over the police report: *And a young woman was found dead nearby.* 'What are you doing?'

'I'm going to that farmhouse in the valley out there.' She flicks a disparaging hand at the wide expanse beyond and keeps walking. 'Unless you have another bright idea for turning bad into worse.'

I can't see any house; she must have vision even sharper than her tongue. I say: 'How are you going to get there? Fly?'

'No.' She frowns back at me to crush a thousand fools. 'I am intending to walk, as my misfortune demands. I suppose you can't see the track staring at you, either?'

That I can, having had it pointed out to me: a well-worn trail leading to what at first glance appears to be oblivion, but on closer inspection shows what must be a way down – unappealingly steep, but a path nevertheless.

What can I do but follow her as she begins picking her way down this trail? Long black cavalries swashbuckling up over her knees, I'm rather compelled, though every step takes me further from One Tree and deeper into trouble. Horse-borrowing might begin to look rather more like horse-stealing from here on, mightn't it? Add saddle-stealing, as the leather belongs to Her Majesty's Mail. But what choice do I have? When we get to this farmhouse, I'll be asking for directions, and I'll be taking this horse in the most direct way back to his stable with the most abject of apologies ever made.

I still can't quite credit that any of this has occurred – that we are here, so lost, so preposterously alone. Did no-one from the village see what happened back there? It's not as if we weren't making a show of things: two masked bushrangers being pursued at full gallop by a rider on a massive coacher, and in possession of kicking and screaming passenger – right down the middle of the main and pretty much only street. Too distracted by the excitement of the train arrival to notice all that? Merciful God.

Almost as incredible as swag-girl's hips swaying ahead of me right now. Long-legged, lean and sure of her step, she swaggers daintily from rock to rock, and I am hypnotised by her dusty little hind. Perfect little hind.

She flicks another disparaging wave over the shoulder. 'I'm Annie, Annabel Eliza Bird, if it means anything to anyone.'

Annie. Annabel Bird. What a perfect little name.

And she suddenly stops and turns, midway down the slippery slope, hand on one knee, squinting up at me. I think she might be about to give me another blast of her fire, but she sighs, seeming only mildly annoyed, announcing brusquely: 'Thank you for trying anyhow, to get after those thieves. I'm sure you meant well, and I'm sorry I scratched you, Mr Fox.'

'Scratched me? Did you?' I feel my face, and I find the wound, but I am quite beyond distraction as she turns away again.

She says, with yet another flick: 'You lay a molesting hand on me, Mr Fox, I'll bite it off.'

And that almost makes me want to give it a go.

ANNIE

I must have been knocked down dead back there somewhere and I'm having some kind of waking dream while I'm wending my way through purgatory, because this can't be real. Maybe I'll see Mother and Dad soon and everything will be answered. It's all my fighting with Sis, isn't it, that's put me here in limbo to be tested, all my impatience and harping and tearing off and leaving her behind me and – what did she say of me in parting? *Stubborn little streak of snot stain.* Too stubborn to listen to sense when it was trying to tell me to go home to my sister. Well, I'm sorry, Lord. I am very, very sorry for it now – all of it. Even the sins I have committed unawares, and all of the sins I would have committed if I had remained alive.

'God damn!' Mr Fancy Boots loses his footing behind me and goes down with a thump. He's not a small man, and he's real enough. He's rubbing his elbow from the fall. The horse slides around a bit as well, and this queer gentleman scrambles up quick to grab the reins back even as he's brushing the dust off his elbow, saying: 'I'm determined to ruin this tweed in record time.' This Mr Fox. I don't trust him, whoever he is. He's a blasphemer; his eyes are too green; and his fingernails are far too well kept to belong to any honest man.

I tell him, 'It won't be far to that house I saw.' Warning him off again, though it must be a mile yet until we will reach the edge of its paddocks, for whatever good any of that will do me. I keep walking, keep the picture of that little house on the valley flat in my mind, with its chimney puffing and its garden rows dug up from tilling. Get back on the road to where I'm going, for what good that'll do me, too, and keep on ignoring Mr Fox, because if I ignore him, he won't bother me, will he, and I can pretend that I am not three-quarters off my head terrified – of him, the bush and the whole wide horrible roughness of this world I find myself in.

I take another sly look behind me, to see where he is. Never been this near to anyone as flash as him. Not even Mr Webb is outfitted so smart to take the train to the city. Mr Webb wears colonial tweed from the Emu mills – the best of quality but plain in every way. Mr Fox wears something finer-woven, something special-order, and the cut of his coat – fitted at the waist, long lapels, tapering away at the front, twin split at the back for riding – I don't think a finer coat could be imagined. All the while I'm hearing Dad say, *You girls keep away from Richmond today – there's a no-good Jeremy Trickster hanging about*, a 'Jeremy' being the general name for someone flash-looking but untrustworthy. This Jeremy is … together with that coat, he's wearing one of those slim neckties, knotted loose and lazy, nothing lazy about it at all. It's just the way he wants it; unusual colour to the silk, too – not blue, not green, not brown. It's the colour of – Stop looking at him. But not before I get another smile: terrifying.

I warn him off again: 'I'm a good Christian girl. Don't you even think that thought, whatever it might be.'

'I'm sure I'm not thinking anything, Miss Bird.' He only smiles worse, his words smooth as his silk tie.

I bet that silk is softer than anything I've ever owned. And at that thought of mine, grief rushes and floods over me once more, for all that's been stolen from me, for everything I no longer own. How could they have stolen my Bible? Apart from it being my Bible, I had the names of my family written inside it; I wrote those names myself when I was twelve: *Richard Morris Bird, Kathryn Bird, Annabel Eliza Bird, Cecily Jane Bird.* I am lonely now as Dad's felt hat tossed and rolling somewhere on that road to nowhere, and I don't know what I might have done to bring this roughness on me. No-one deserves to lose their Bible or their dad's best hat, however worthless they might be.

'I'm just as sure I will not hurt you. Please, don't worry about anything like that,' says Jeremy Fox with a kindness I can hear, even as I don't believe a single one of those words.

We go on in silence but for the sounds of heels and hooves, and after a while, as the track eases in its steepness, he asks me: 'Would you like to ride the rest of the way, Miss Bird? You must be tired.'

'No,' I tell him quick. 'I'd rather walk.' And that's a lie: my blistered feet are making me want to cry more than anything. With defeat settling into me for this day, I seem to be feeling every bump and bruise in body and spirit both. The trees are a jumble of shadows every time I look up, I'm not even sure I believe we're still following any track; I will walk on and on until I'm not here anymore. Because I'm not getting back on that horse: he's as terrifying as his master: too tall and mightily made.

'Please. Miss Bird. I insist.' Jeremy Fox moves alongside me as the track broadens out through the scrub and the trees. 'Please, I won't touch you except to help you up. I promise.'

'No, thank you.' I glance across at him, not wanting to sound ungrateful, but I'm sure I do. I don't look at his face – I don't want to see the scratch I made there. I look at his arm instead, the right one, furthest away, holding the reins, and I see a thick wrist under that fine tweed, fabric which I follow around to the nearest of him, so close I can see the herringbone pattern in the weave. I can see the breadth of that shoulder, the strength which pulled me up on that horse, walloping along like a Patagonian cowboy – skillful in the saddle. And too strong for me to worry about what harm might come: he could do whatever he likes with me, never mind please or thank you. Terror rising up again and higher, I'm desperate not to have sounded rude or tartish, so I try to make some conversation: 'You must have been together with your horse for some time to ride him so well, Mr Fox?'

'No, actually,' he says, and he rubs his eyes with some weariness of his own. 'We've only just met, back at the Cobb & Co, yesterday. He's rather a champ, is Zad, but I'm afraid I've, ahmmm … borrowed him.'

'Borrowed him?' No-one borrows a horse from Cobb & Co – they don't let horses. I'm not sure I know what terror is anymore as I ask him: 'Did you just take this horse from their yard?'

'Take? There's an interesting idea, isn't it. Not always what it appears.' Jeremy Fox laughs, like a man used to laughing a lot. 'I promise you, honestly. I may be many dreadful things, but a horse thief I am not.'

I don't want to learn what many dreadful things Jeremy Fox might be. I push ahead, into these lengthening shadows, thinking we've got maybe two hours of good light left to find that farmhouse I saw, if we get there at all – and then what? How am I going to get away from this man – tonight? Where am I going to go – with bushrangers probably hiding out somewhere in this forest? Mad ones that would steal whatever I have left – the shirt on my back, and the rest of me. And who will care about whatever might happen after that? I'm just a penniless, scraggedy black girl here. I finally see this bright and clear. I have nothing that says who I am, nothing that says I am anyone. I have only my worst fears all gathering around me.

Jeremy Fox says something, but I don't hear him. I can barely hear my own voice as I say: 'I beg your pardon?'

'I said I hope they're good Christian folk at this farmhouse,' he replies with his easy laugh. 'Because I haven't got a farthing on me, not a copper dot, I'm afraid. Well, I had two – back in my bag at the village – but other than that, I'm absolutely motherless, by order of my father, and the New South Wales Inspector-General of Police – and possibly God, too. And I must admit, that's all as it should be – I have been a very bad boy.'

How bad do you have to be for the *Inspector-General of Police* to be onto you? Please, Lord, spare me, I don't want to know.

'Oh don't worry, Miss Bird, I make that sound a little more exciting than it is. I'm well on the road to reform, believe me. In the meantime, I think I have just enough brass left to talk us into a cup of tea and a buttered bun, before I get this horse back where he should be.'

All I want to do is run, if I had anywhere to run to. I stare and stare, not knowing what to do.

And now, through the shadows, through the trees, I think I see – yes, like a miracle, like my pleas and prayers have been heard – I see what might be a place of safety: not the big farmhouse in the paddock, but a rickety little slab-and-bark hut with hardly a yard around it, only what's being scratched up by chooks – fat, happy chickens, pecking and clucking. It looks just like Mickey Dinnigan's place, not much more than a pile of rubbish, and I've never been so glad to see it.

JEM

'Oh, look! There's a —' She begins to shout as if she would like to attract attention and my hand flies up to cover her mouth, to prevent her from making another sound. She might have a keen eye for spotting farmhouses; I have as keen an eye for horses, and I recognise the grey colt tied up by the trough of this hovel now, its stocky, speckled rump, and with it its less distinctive friend, a dun palomino – those mounts belonging to the bastards who have brought us here. I imagine that it is not out of the realm of possibility that we have stumbled upon their lair.

Annie Bird twists under my grip, exerting one of her own: her little fist pinching up a handful of biceps – arrestingly effective even through shirt and coat sleeve – as she kicks me in the shin, very hard, the toe of her boot nailing right through the leather of my own. It takes a good deal of effort not to cry out, very loud, in return.

I growl very quietly in her ear: 'Stop it.'

She doesn't. Her eyes grow even wilder and rounder. I realise, possibly a little late, that she must presume I'm attacking her.

I growl again: 'I'm not going to hurt you. Look.' I turn her face in the direction of the horses. 'There are your thieves.'

Her eyes grow wilder and rounder still, but she lets go of the pinch, and I let go of her.

We stand suspended, breathless for a moment. Watching. Waiting. For what? My instinct is to throw her over Zad once more and belt off like blazes. I look to Annie Bird for a nod of agreement, but her eyes are fixed on the little house of sticks and the horses outside it. The place has hessian sacks for window screens, which I'm sure they can see out of, even if we can't see in. And those screens are looking right at us, through the flimsiest cover of trees this forest has to offer.

Annie Bird draws in a ragged gasp beside me, glaring, nostrils flaring, and then she says: 'I'm going to get my stuff back.'

'What?' What did she just say?

And she's gone, darting through the trees towards the house, before I can catch her.

ANNIE

It's fury that takes me when I see the tarp-roll still slung to the saddle this side of that light-brown horse. My father's tarp, which he made with his own hands from oat sacks. I am getting my stuff back, or I will die trying, and not only from need of these things that are mine, but the principle of it: I have been thieved from enough.

There is a steady breeze blowing from the west, carrying the voices of men I can't see as I get near them: they must be in the hut, two men, maybe three. I crouch down below the trough to listen above the horses taking their long drink, and the clucking and pecking of the chooks around the yard, a couple of them coming my way, curious.

'Jesus, Dan, but we agreed on four – what is this load o' shit?' one of the men is saying, but not angrily, despite his language: there's a laugh in his words.

'They're revolvers, mate – Colt revolvers,' another replies, with a scratchy voice. 'Police-issue six-shooters. You won't need more than two. Anyway, two is all you're getting, 'cause it's all I got.'

'Aw, it'll do, Jack, I still got mine as well,' says yet another.

'That hunk of scrap?'

'Does the job. It's a good pistol. You gotta know how to use it.'

'The bloody trigger sticks, ya poke.'

'So, still reckon yous are having a go at the Escort, then?' the scratchy-voiced one says.

'Yeah. Friday next, when it comes back through from Eugowra. We'll take 'er at Booralee, just west of Judas Creek, towards Cudal. That's the plan.'

Scratchy voice laughs at that. 'Who yous reckon you are, ay, Jack? Frankie Gardiner and Ben Hall?'

'That ain't fucking funny,' says muck-mouth Jack – worse mouth on him than what comes out of any tannery.

'Yeah, he sleeps wi'a wee little photer of his hero under his pilla.' His offsider is laughing, a wheezy laugh.

'Shut your fucking face, Bill. Ben Hall is dead, long dead – you want to join him? Anyway, it's been five years since they done it at Eugowra – they won't be expecting no-one around there. And it's quiet – there's nothing much going on at any diggings that way. They'll have picked up the load out of Seven Mile from Grenfell, though, by then – and word is that'll be rich.'

'And well-armed,' says scratchy voice. 'There'll be two guards on the Escort, and win, lose or draw, you owe me four pounds for the pair of revolvers, ay.'

'That's fair, I s'pose. We'll settle that today.'

'Too right you will, Jack.'

The offsider is still having a good old wheeze: 'You won't believe what Jack just done, up on the Bathurst Road.'

'Give it a rest,' says Jack.

'He fleeces this poor little swaggie, crossing the road —'

'Fucking shut up, Bill – I thought it was a digger. I seen these pair of smart-looking boots, and the way the bloke was walking in them I thought, here we go, they're new, and that hat – I thought he must've been flush, maybe just come up from Swallow's Nest, and worth the pickings. You know how them new chums'll hide their stash in their swag or under their hat. And we need the fucking money in a hurry, don't we – however it comes.'

'And this bloke it turns out is a little girl,' the wheezy one is going on. 'Jack here goes around robbing off little girls. Robbing their Bibles. Jesus. What would Saint Ben Hall think of that? Little lube she was, too, by the looks. Didn't she put up a fight – we could do with her on our side.'

'She just about pulled me out of the saddle, and I'm not proud of picking her. But here ya're, Dan – here's your four fucking load o' shit pounds. Now shut your fucking faces about it.'

'Yeah, shut up the pair of yous. Let's have a brew, ay. Yous stopping the night?'

'Yeah, don't mind if we do …'

I hear boots creaking on boards and the clank of a bottle or two – men sitting down to have an ale – and I'm taking my chance while they do. For all that I would like to burn down this pile of rubbish house with them in it, for thieving off me, and calling me a lube like I'm just a little black joke, I can't waste time, and I don't have a match anyhow – because *they* have my matches, as well as all else. I sneak around the trough, looking up at the tarp-roll fixed onto the saddlebag on the brown horse, but I can't see the swag anywhere. I suppose it's inside the house with the men – with all my money that they've just used to buy their filthy guns – and that riles me to fuming all over again: *you – you rats. You nasty, stinking rats.*

'Yeah, well you won't get me going into a bank these days – I'd shoot to kill,' I hear that Jack feller say inside the house, the sack over the window flapping in the breeze so that I could almost touch it.

'You bent shilling,' the one with the scratchy voice says. 'Don't take it so personal. Banks rob everyone – you're nothing special. It's only their job. You're not the first to lose a farm – to fire or flood or foreclosing – won't be the last, and you're gettin' yourself a reputation as no good. That little lube ain't the first woman you've stole off, that's what I heard. You done the stage at Blackheath, didn't ya. Black Jack is what they're callin' you now. Watch out, or you'll not have a friend round here soon, ay.'

'Watch out or you can go and get fucked,' says Black Jack. 'I just want enough to get out of here – get to New Zealand, get free of all this shit. Don't need no friends. I'll be gone soon. If the bank had just let me go another season – get the advantage of the rains – we wouldn't fucking be here at all.'

I'm trying to unthread the strap of the tarp-roll from the top of the saddlebag, but my hands are shaking so much with anger I can't unhitch the buckle where it's wedged near the back of the saddle. I've popped the studs fixing the strap of both saddlebags there, though, and the whole thing is slipping towards me. Good. If I can't get my swag back off you, I'll take something of yours instead and to spite you, Black Jack. That makes my hands shake and shudder only more as both saddlebags and tarp fall into them: I've never taken anything that's not mine before. Never.

The horse lets out a big worried neigh and all my terrors return. I don't want to die trying anything more. I've got to get away, but as I go I trip backwards, knocked off kilter by the edge of the trough, and I catch the wing of one of the chooks as I stumble around with my arms full, setting her off squawking – and setting me running through all the chooks now, a dozen of them or so all squawking and flapping around my feet.

I run and I run for the trees. I run towards the outstretched hand of Jeremy Fox, and *smack* goes my hand in his.

'Get up here.' He's pulling me and my full arms onto the front of the saddle, and half by the back of my strides. 'You ace thing,' he says, grabbing me to him as he heels the horse and I'm already closing my eyes.

JEM

Her hair smells of orange-blossom soap, and I breathe in great draughts of it as we belt through the forest in the general direction of escape, avoiding several low-hanging branches along the way and becoming increasingly incredulous that no-one appears to be following us.

I hold Annie Bird against my chest, increasingly incredulous at her mettle. She remains curled over what appears to be mostly bushrangers' saddlebags, and I can see down the back of her red flannel shirt: she smells of lavender there among her underlinens. She is no vagabond, that's for sure, not that I've ever held one of those in my arms before – or not that I recall and certainly not like this. I take another look behind us, and still no-one pursues, and so I pull Zad back to a walk, the better to look at her, and wonder at her. Wonder at the odd stirring she gives me, that's something uncommon, too. Not merely sport, she has me intrigued: I want to know who she is. What on earth she's doing getting about like this.

Leaves scrape across my shoulder to remind me also to look where we're going, and as I do I see lush green pasture spread out beyond the petering edge of the trees. And sheep: hundreds of sheep, bucolically bleating in the golden light of late afternoon. There are several farmhouses dotted about the valley, four or five, and the wheel ruts of a track winding through. All rather pleasant – not to mention a crap-halting relief.

'You can look up now,' I give Annie Bird the good news. 'We have arrived at our destination, so it would seem. Out of the woods, at least.'

'Are we?' She raises her head, those lovely dark eyes gazing out with her question; and she looks dashed again. God, but I could kiss her on the nose.

Instead, I try to assure her. 'Bankable risk there'll be good Christian folk in this village, hm?' The farmhouse nearest even has a white picket fence around their yard. If God doesn't dwell here, he doesn't exist.

But Annie Bird only replies: 'I didn't get my money back.' Forlorn.

'Don't worry about that, really,' I assure her some more. 'At worst, we'll be on our way straight back to One Tree —'

'You reckon?' She crushes me with a dubious eyebrow; she says: 'Maybe there's some coin in here,' opening one of the saddlebags, muttering, 'might as well make my own thieving count,' as she begins to rummage through the contents. 'Matches. Pot of marmalade. Tea. Flour. Soda. Can of boiled beef, sardines, and a packet of barley sugars – I'll survive. You smoke?' She holds up a box of cigarettes.

I'm about to say, no, I don't smoke, until I see they're Grimault's Indian cigarettes, and there's nothing Indian about them – they're Parisian, very pleasant and a bit of a surprise to see here, so I tell her, 'I'm partial to the occasional settler.'

She doesn't care. She pulls out a scarf, a coarsely knitted comforter, and says with some surprise of her own, 'Good wool,' before some dismay: 'Oh – what's this?'

It's a gun. To be more precise, it's a very nice old .436 Deane & Adams five-shot, not that I'm any use with one – pigeon-shoots out at Randwick, or bunnies at Bondi, I am proficient only at missing the target and owing the bookmaker. I do it deliberately, I'm sure – too soft, always have been, couldn't hit a rabbit even if it hit me first. But I do like the look and feel of a gun, that burst of power as it fires – what punter doesn't?

Annie Bird is stunned, holding it with disgust: 'How's this for another *at worst*?'

'Well,' I try for the light side, 'that's the sort of thing that's going to happen when you go about stealing saddlebags from bushrangers, isn't it?'

I get another eyebrow, before she says: 'Maybe. Still not as bad as stealing a horse from Cobb & Co, though, is it. I was only getting my own back.'

'Miss Bird, I did not steal —'

'Good day there! Halloo there!' A woman is waddling towards her white picket fence, some twenty yards or so away, calling out to us. 'Can I help you? You looking for someone?'

Annie Bird shoves the gun back inside the saddlebag and my hand dives in after hers, shaking the weapon from her grip to avoid the possibility of her blowing my leg off with it should it be loaded, and should it, being a possibly temperamental Deane & Adams, want to explode at having its trigger touched at all, as I wave to the woman with my other hand: 'Good day to you! Splendid afternoon, isn't it?'

'Yes, it is,' the woman replies with a smile, but she's holding a rolling pin in one hand, a rolling pin that says she might not be fond of strangers wandering into her pleasant little valley. She looks like a sweet grandmamma, but let's not presume anything here, shall we? She says: 'Are you lost?'

'Yes, we are, as a matter of fact,' I say, moving a little closer, as she does too. 'We're looking for the village of One Tree Hill – or at least an inn between here and there …?'

The woman ceases all pretence at smiling; she stands square at her fence, peering hard at Annie Bird as she replies: 'This ain't One Tree, and there ain't no inn here. This here is The Gap. Seven mile to One Tree – take this road east, through Hartley Vale back to the Bathurst Highway, and up the Mitchell Pass. That'll be One Tree.' She doesn't add, 'now beggar off' but it's implied, and she doesn't take her eyes from Annie Bird.

'Is there an inn nearer-by?' I ask, still hopeful I might get us at least a drink of water – soonish, as I'm rather parched.

But the old woman replies: 'No. I said One Tree seven mile that way. Or you've got Bowenfels nine mile the other to the west. Either way, you get yourselves back on the Bathurst Highway.' She doesn't add, 'right now', but it's implied more firmly still.

'Most helpful, many thanks.' I salute her with a surreptitious extension of the middle finger as I nudge Zad along the track towards the road, snorting under my breath for Annie Bird: 'There you are. Good Christians, told you so, didn't I.'

At which she sighs heavily: 'There's plenty of them that don't like blacks.'

Ah. Is *that* what granny was slitting her eyes at? The brown skin of this girl? I don't know; I throw a smile at it anyway: 'Or perhaps she saw you waving around that gun when she was peeping out of her lace curtains?'

'Nah,' says Annie Bird, staring out at forever. 'Wouldn't matter if I waved a church full of Bibles in her face, she'd still hate me for what she reckons I am – a good-for-nothing Aborigine, out to rob her of something. I'm getting used to it.'

'No,' I must reply, for that is a bit of bunkum, even if I am a little surprised she's a native. I've never met an Aborigine before, other than on the pages of *Bell's Life* informing me that a whole Victorian cricket team full of them are on their way to London to play at The Oval – half their luck. Come to think of it, the closest I've ever been to brown skin of any sort was Ogarita the Indian girl from that dreadful play, whatever it was, at the Lyceum last May, and her make-believe paint came off on my hands in the dressing room afterwards. But I can say the colour of Annie Bird's skin is not the most remarkable thing about her. I must tell her: 'No. No-one ever gets used to being hated.'

'Reckon you know, do you?' she says. And although I do know what it's like to have doors closed and shoulders turned on empty-headed grounds of race, I don't tell her that now. I don't imagine she'd care that the Jockey Club of Pall Mall wouldn't have one like me among them unless my name was Rothschild, and its outpost here only tolerates Hebrews for the numbers – ridiculous not to, since ten percent of all the trade down George and Pitt Streets is Jewish, with a synagogue either side. I don't imagine she'd care that I was always left off the cricket team at Saint Sav's despite my not-insignificant talent at the bat, or that the Latin master not too affectionately called me Fagin's brat, or that a fellow called Orville Peacott used to give me particular hell with his perverted obsession over a certain part of my anatomy, but that I couldn't beat him when I had the chance to do so, not least because his name was Orville. She is stung by unearned hatred, whether it be real or perceived in this instance, and I know enough of this sorry business to know that there is little consolation to be had in it no matter what I might say.

She looks ahead to the road and past it, slung as it is between two thickly wooded hillsides, each topped by lofty, indifferent crags. We're all lost sheep in this Gap to them, I suppose.

'Where do you need to go, Miss Bird?' I ask her as we approach it.

'West.' She says the word with some defiance, her chin pointing the way.

Hm. Of course you'd need to be going in the opposite direction, wouldn't you.

I ask her: 'And where would that be, more precisely? What's west for you?'

'I don't know.' She looks at me with those wondrous, bright-dark eyes. Sad and tired. 'I want to find my grandfather, at a place called Blackman's Swamp, but I don't know where that is, and I don't know if he's there.'

'Right.' I nod. And I want to help her find her grandfather. I shouldn't, but I do. I should make attempts to get this horse back to One Tree Hill right now. But I'm not going to.

ANNIE

'Let me get down now, please,' I tell him, 'and I'll get on my way.'

'On your way *where*?'

Away from here. Away from every horrible thing.

Stubborn.

I tell Jeremy Fox: 'Stop this horse. Please.' Or I'll jump off it.

'No, no, no.' He has me caught between his arms and all his round uptowny o's. 'You will not be wandering off on your own into the sunset, Miss Bird.'

'I'm not going anywhere on a stolen horse,' I tell him. 'Not one inch further.'

'I didn't steal —'

'You might as well have. All very good for one such as you to talk your way clear of any unbelievable thing, but I'll end up in gaol.'

'You won't end up in gaol.' He laughs, and it's the first time I've heard him sound uneasy. 'Technically, I could return this horse to any Cobb & Co depot, couldn't I? It's not as though the mail would still be waiting there at One Tree Hill for me to get back there with Zad. They'll have put on one of the ordinaries, the spares from the back paddock. Inconvenience, that's all this is. Inconvenience. Technically, I should probably do them a favour and drop Zad in somewhere further west for the return trip – perhaps this Bowenfels place, I think that's where they said they rehorse anyway, at an inn called Billing's or Bunning's or something like that. Or what about

Bathurst itself – would that be any good to you? That's where their main depot is, isn't it? Hub of the goldfields and all that? Look, geography is not my best suit, nor the transport routes of New South Wales, but please, I assure you, I didn't steal this horse. What was I supposed to do? Stand there and watch them rob you?'

It begins to settle on me what a brave, Samaritan thing he did do. Those men were armed. He could have been killed up on the road. I could have been too, if he hadn't carried me off again just now. And Bathurst, that is where the Cobb & Co main everything is, their headquarters, everyone knows that. All my longing whispers through me at the name of that town and I tell him: 'Bathurst is where I need to go if I'm going to find out where I'm going.'

'Well, there you are. Good, then. To Bathurst we shall go.'

And that's as far as I will go, to the end of the Bathurst Road. If I was halfway to Bathurst this morning at Weatherboard, we can't be more than a day away here. If I don't find out what I need to know by the time I get there, however I get there, then I will go home, back to my sister, back to whatever that life might bring.

We ride along into the big black shadow being cast by the scarp above us. It'll be too dark to be roaming anywhere soon; too dark to be roaming around with this strange man – with any man. I lean away a little to look around at him, to check once more that he really does exist. He does. The scratch I made on his face is darker for the dried blood, and the bolt of shame I feel at having done that is real enough as well. He smiles: big, sure smile, straight, white teeth, something not right about him, but somehow I'm no longer terrified. Maybe I'm too tired. Except the rush of warmth this smile now brings has me searching my mind for a damp dishcloth to throw over it.

'I'm going straight to the police, the first station we get to,' I tell him, and it's just as much another warning to him. 'I'm going to hand in this gun, tell them what happened and tell them what I heard back there. Those fellers are planning to bail up the Gold Escort, next Friday, at a place called Booralee – Judas Creek, or something like that.' Just the thought of my knowing this makes me feel felonious by some kind of association, makes me feel like having a wash.

'Good idea,' says Jeremy Fox. 'I'll come with you, if you don't mind. It'll count in my favour. Spying on bushrangers, further justification for having absconded on this horse-stealing spree.'

'Absconded?' Terror makes a last effort to overtake me. 'Are you running from some kind of justice yourself?'

'Running? No.' He chuckles like that's a silly idea, and I don't think he's convincing me or himself. 'Not at all,' he says. 'But I am in trouble, as I told you – and mostly with my father. Speaking of which, police station or telegraph office, whichever comes first, I need to get a message to —' He looks out to the sunset slipping through the fold in the hills ahead. 'Ah. What day is it?' he asks with a frown.

And I have to think too, for a moment, before I remember: 'Friday.'

'Friday. Right. Of course it is,' he sighs and I can feel the disappointment in it. 'No rush on the telegram now.'

'Why?' I don't even know why I'm asking the question, why I should wonder anything about him.

'Because Pa – my father – wouldn't open the front door for a fire on Saturday, never mind open a telegram to read it,' he says. 'I won't disturb him until Sunday, if it can be helped.'

'Why?' I reckon I don't want to know that, either.

'Because he's very religious,' he says.

I'm glad to hear that, but I turn to look at him, this Jeremy Fox, not sure if I heard him correctly: 'If your father's religious, why would you want to disturb him on a Sunday?'

'I don't want to disturb him at all, again, any day – God knows I've disturbed him enough.' And even with the blaspheming he does look regretful. 'But Pa is Jewish,' he explains. 'Our Sabbath begins in about five minutes, not that I've been known to observe it for quite some time. My Sabbath usually begins in the back parlour of the Colonnade with a nobbler of brandy in one hand and a – never mind. Suffice to say, I'm a very bad Jew, as all else.'

I wouldn't know a good one from a bad one. I don't know what a Jew is, not truly, apart from the Pharisees being the betrayers of our Lord, Jesus. I know they have a Jewish Orphan Society because their accounts are published in the *Empire*; I know they have different holy days and travel the world – even setting up shop in China. Dad would always say live and let live, but you can't trust a Jew in any business dealings – they're only out for money and their own kind, and they all live in big houses in the city. Hard bargainers – like Mr Lemon, who comes out to Richmond at the crack of dawn Fridays and buys up everything in whole cartloads before anyone else gets a look-in, and who Mr Webb always blames for driving potato prices down, though I've never come to understand how that could be. I do understand the look of regret right here on the face of Jeremy Fox, though, and clear enough to have me wanting for the damp dishcloth again: he loves his father.

I look away into the sunset, too, with the warmth rushing and swirling as I tell him: 'I'm cold and I'm thirsty. We've got to find somewhere to camp.'

And he's quick with the easy, lazy laugh at that: 'Camp?'

JEM

'Yes, camp,' she says, pointing again with that decisive little chin. 'There's a creek up there, we might find a good spot.'

'A creek?' I can only see pasture returning to tall, thin trees once more, and the ever-deepening circles of irony that will see me camping out under the stars tonight. But then, I suppose, this is nothing I haven't earned, and it's not as though I've never slept on the ground before, is it; just not sober.

She looks at me as though she knows, and points more specifically with her hand: '*There.*'

I have no idea what she's pointing at.

'See, near the bottom of the hill, as it comes around from the south?'

'Oh?' No. South? How does anyone *know* where south is?

'Follow it around this way, away from the road,' she says.

I have not a clue what she's talking about, but I move Zad off the road and take us vaguely towards where I think she means, and soon enough I see the creek snaking into the valley and then away into the trees.

'Keep going, keep going,' she says keenly, pointing into those trees. 'Keep well away from the road, so no-one will see us. And that's not an invitation, Mr Fox. It's only that I don't want to get shooed away by any nasty-minded snipe begrudging me the need of rest.'

Does anyone else on earth speak the way this girl does? Her words pluck out some new rhythm on my heart and I don't want to get off this horse, have her orange-blossom loveliness leave this place between my arms.

Only a few yards on, she's giving that the kybosh: 'Here. Here. Stop. Right here.' But a sweet note follows the instruction: 'Oh how beautiful.'

I drag my eyes away from the maze of chestnut curls that is her hair, chestnut spun through with copper, and look up to find a beautiful scene indeed. The stream here pools among mossy rocks enclosed by an alcove of cascading greenery, slender boughs entwined above. The only thing missing is a blast of Beethoven's Pastoral, and perhaps a couple of bluebirds twirling around in the air. And this evening's torture is complete.

'Doesn't this make the long day and all its trials seem worthwhile?' She turns to me and smiles. The first smile she has bestowed: a sudden radiance, infused with wholesome enthusiasm. If I found her attractive before, this wipes out whatever might have remained of my resistance to her.

I say: 'Hm.' And dismount immediately. I take the saddlebags and her roll of whatever it is from her and help her down after them, and as I do desire is eclipsed by concern when she winces.

'Are you hurt?' I ask her, imagining that all my throwing her about has caused some injury. I applied a fairly firm elbow to her ribs trying to stop her from struggling as we belted out of One Tree, and have held her rather tightly since – by necessity. Riding with a girl side-saddling over your pommel is not the easiest way to go.

But she says, 'No, I'm not hurt. I only have sore feet from wearing my dad's boots. They've had enough for one day. Two days ...' She looks up at me from under her hair: she is hurt. 'Having a rest only makes a tenderness sharper, doesn't it?'

It does, that's true, and probably not only as regards sore feet. Several questions jostle but only one seems important for now; I suggest: 'Why don't you go and take those boots off, give those feet a soak?'

'I need to get a fire going,' she says, hobbling off.

'I can do that,' I say, and she gives me the dubious eyebrow over her shoulder. I tell her, hanging my hat on a suitable shrub: 'I'm not entirely useless – just watch me.'

That's precisely what she does. She perches on a rock by the water's edge and watches me even as she takes off boots and socks, plunging her feet into the water with a little, '*Oh*,' of relief, before she resumes the issue of instructions: 'Build the fire here – in front of that tree. No, *that* one. Clear away the leaves.' And: 'Get the branch over there – it'll be dried right out from lying in the sun all day.' And: 'There's some more back along the creek. And that one there with all the twigs hanging off it ...'

I could suggest she rest her voice a while, but I don't. I traipse around and up the creek, picking up sticks. I can't say I've ever made a campfire before, but it seems fitting that I should today. How many times have I grunted resentfully over the workroom forge, barely acknowledging Pa through the smoking ruins of the night before? Quietly uttering my contempt as I lean on the bellows, Pa telling me at my shoulder: *Jemmy, please, you don't have to do this, if it's not what you want to do. Go back to school – it's different here. You can become a lawyer.* Like hell. *I'll double your allowance.* No. I'd rather double my debts and chase women, wouldn't I. Ha! This has gone too far now. I imagine Pa sliding an envelope across the desk of Inspector-General Fitzworthy pleading on my behalf: *You see, it was Friday and not possible for my son to travel after sundown.* How many such pleas have I forced him to make? *He is a good son, really.* Little twists of the truth, little envelopes, all adding up. I should leave chivalry to better men and belt to the nearest Cobb & Co while the light remains. It looks as though it will be a clear night tonight, and once we're back on the Bathurst Road, Zad'll probably knows the way himself. I sh—

I hear a splash, coming from the stream beside me, feel a faint sprinkle of water across my right hand. What? I look back towards Miss Annie Bird, as if she might have flicked this water at me from twenty yards, and see she's presently setting out the edible contents of the saddlebags, Zad victualling happily behind her. Splash again, and a more concerted spray right across my face. What? I look down and peer at the stream, shallow and clear as it is, and see what at first appears to be a rather gruesomely large and slimy eel – but that I see it has fur, a snout, and a black bulbous eye looking somehow malevolently at me, before it slithers away, seemingly into the grassy bank at my feet.

And that's enough firewood. I try not to run back to Miss Bird. Probably only an otter. Are there otters in New South Wales? I wouldn't know. Perhaps it's just a very long and ugly rat. Perhaps this should be enough for me to suggest we might leave for civilisation without further delay, but that the rats are bigger at Circular Quay.

And Annie Bird's feet are ragged – *oh* indeed. I want to hold her toes in my hands until they heal. I'm not going to ask her to put them back in boots to go anywhere.

She doesn't look up from what she's doing, scooping a handful of flour onto a tin plate, as she says: 'Beef from a can is not proper food, no matter how you spice it. I wish there was fishing line in one of those bags.'

You probably don't, unless you want to catch a malevolent otter rat, but I don't mention that – whatever is left of my masculine pride won't allow me. Here is a woman making what I suppose is going to be bread for our meal, barefoot and exhausted by a waterhole on the distant edge of nowhere. While I'm sure I've never tasted beef from a can, never mind caught myself a fish.

I build the fire; I don't know what to say. I'm sure dinner will be lovely? She snips off my glibness with all her capability, her getting on with what needs to be done. I ask instead: 'You've done a fair bit of travelling, have you?'

'No.' She doesn't look up, mixing a little water to her flour, but I wish she would now. She says: 'I only left home yesterday morning. Hardly left the Penrith valley much before that.'

'Really?' I'm surprised, although I'm not sure why I should be – some presumption that indigenes unceasingly wander the continent, I suppose.

'Yes, *really.*' She frowns at her dough. 'The Nepean River – that where I'm from. That's where I was born – so was my mother, and my grandmother, and probably thousands of grandmothers before me.' Long, quick fingers working at soft dough.

I'm not entirely sure where the Nepean River is, although I think I crossed it on the morning of my banishment: back of that coach, crapped out so pathetically it was all I could do to keep down half a quince pie, and just prior to that, Penrith: a vague place of head-pounding potholes that appeared out of an immeasurable tract of gum trees, each of which looked as bored as I was. At this moment, though, I am oddly astonished that Annie Bird and I were in the same place at the same time; paths destined to cross. None of which I am about to offer as further points of conversation. I ask her instead, 'Why did you leave?'

'My dad died on Wednesday evening.' She keeps at that dough. 'A big tree branch fell on him down at the river, the way gum trees do, shedding their branches like bolts of lightning. I – it doesn't seem true. But it is. I saw him take his last breath. He was the manager of Cygnet Farm, at Castlereagh – the only home I've ever known. He was an Englishman, a convict from Liverpool, and he worked for the one landowner, Mr Webb, from the time he got his ticket-of-leave – twenty years. He worked his way up to respectability in every way it counts, but the good Christians of Castlereagh don't want black girls in their village, so we were put out – me and my sister – a knock on the door at dawn yesterday morning. My sister's gone off with her feller, and I've gone off with – well, I don't know, except I'm looking for what I might have in the way of family, looking for my grandfather, looking for another home, if there's one to find.'

'Ah.' There's a reason or two to be dashed. What sort of person turfs young women out into the street like that? Too many: the Female Refuge on Pitt teems with their lack of concern; so does every brothel. 'A wretched blow for you,' I make the understatement of the century. The poor girl has lost her father, her mother as well, I might safely guess – and all while I was complaining about having been left on a mountainside to grow up. If chance meant for our paths to cross, then I would say I am meant to help her. Yes, she's making me yearn in all ways noble and not, but Pa would expect me to help her. He would help her himself, if he were here, just as he makes out a cheque to the refuge every year.

'You'd better get that fire lit,' she says, and throws a box of matches to me. A glance full of sadness, a hint of that smile as I catch them, touching the traces of flour she has touched, I —

Get on with lighting the fire. It takes straightaway, and it's not a helpful metaphor. I do believe I am as instantly in love with her. I've been in love before, of course, most Friday nights. But this is ... Whoa.

I remember that box of Grimault's cigarettes; might be prudent to have one now: calm down. As I step around her to help myself, Annie Bird says: 'Those thieves were kind enough to leave us a jam-tin billy in the other saddlebag, plus this dish and a set of eating utensils – you a spoon man or a fork man?'

Whatever man you want, I'd say, if it was at all appropriate to do so. 'You choose,' I tell her as I put match to cigarette and inhale deeply: nice, very nice.

I watch her arrange the branches in the fire to settle the billy can in the flames to boil, and when it does, she drops portions of the dough into it: dumplings. Extraordinary. And the cigarette isn't helping, either: her every movement is grace itself, even dressed as a man with moleskin trousers rolled and ragged feet – perhaps exactly as she is right at this moment. But if there's one handy distraction these purportedly medicinal cigarettes are good for, it's appetite – tinned squirrel, or sardines in caramel custard, it's all the same: fabulous. But my God, she's making dumplings to go with it, whatever it is.

I'm sure the 'spiced' gravy is tasteless apart from half a pound of salt, but there are dumplings, excellent little morsels of cloud, and this is quite possibly the best meal of my life. We eat tete-a-tete either side of the plate as the sun dims down and down, me the spoon, she the fork. We sip black tea from one tin cup. The breeze lifts one of her curls and brushes it across my forehead, before she points her fork at me and says: 'I'm going to put up the tarp. Don't get any idea you're sleeping under it with me.'

'I wouldn't dream of it,' I say, although I'm sure that's all I'll dream of all night long.

She is busy once more, snatching the plate from me, rinsing it in the stream, before hoisting her 'tarp', her little open-ended tent, between two nearby trees, all in one seemingly fluid action, muttering as she presses iron pins into the ground at each corner: 'Terrible thin soil again.' I could watch her busyness forever.

But I must unsaddle Zad; and tether him securely for the night. 'Sorry, old chum.' I rub his neck in apology for the whole thing, and assure him: 'I'm sharing the indignity, never you mind.' I'll be making my own bed on this terrible thin soil, and given this reality, I'll be indulging in another Grimault's to soothe my way to repose.

The light is almost completely gone now, and as I strike this match, Miss Annie Bird informs me from inside her tent: 'Smoking isn't good for you, no matter what they say. My dad would always say there's a little devil inside every puff making you want another one, and making only the chemist rich. He smoked every day and he didn't think it served him for anything but losing time he didn't have.'

'And I'd agree,' I tell her, 'but this isn't smoking, as such. It's not ordinary tobacco. It's herbal.'

'I don't know what difference that might make, Mr Fox,' she says. 'Smoke is smoke and tobacco is a herb as much as any other.'

Oh no, it's not. These little Indiennes are comprised of Datura stramonium and Cannabis indica leaves, as far as my botanical knowledge stretches and enough to know that if I smoked these with any regularity time would lose all meaning, but I don't think I'd win any points here for saying it. I do have to find something to say, though: I don't want her to leave me yet for her own sleep, I don't want her to stop talking. So I try for what I hope is a happier topic: 'Tell me about your grandfather, Miss Bird – he must be very dear to you.'

'I don't know him.' She sighs inside her canvas fort. 'He's likely as dead as my parents, for all I know.'

'Oh.' Good play – way to woo the girl. I can only say to her what I would say to my own despondency: 'Don't let the morbs get into you. Tomorrow's another day, isn't it?'

And one I hope to see unsavaged by antipodean otter rats, so I step around to the far side of the tent, away from the waterhole, before sitting down as near to her as I can.

'Are you always so cheerful and sure about yourself?' she asks, sounding irritated by the very idea.

'No,' I reply. 'But admittedly, mostly, I am. There's not much point in being otherwise, is there?'

She answers that with silence; the forest around us is silent too, except for something rustling through the undergrowth somewhere.

'What's your grandfather's name?' I ask her, not thinking about that rustling, or the rising dampness of the earth under my arse, or the possibility of my irritating her further with the question as I flick the end of the cigarette into the fire.

'His name is Kulyan.' Her voice is small but fills the sky with wonder and want. 'He's supposed to have been famous, a black tracker from out west, from Blackman's Swamp. A big man in a possum-skin cloak. He was a guide that took the government survey men along the rivers, out to the desert and back, maybe forty years ago. He got a medal for it, or maybe a ribbon, some kind of reward, I don't know. A story I've always been told. Maybe only a story. I don't suppose you ever heard of him, have you?' she asks me and the sky, a sardonic edge to the question.

'No,' I must say, though I wish I had heard of him. 'I'm a relatively recent arrival,' I tell her instead. 'I don't know anyone much worth knowing.' Not really, for all the nobs I've met, and not among the rum chums and over-privileged miscreants that are my usual crowd; men I get drunk with, all good Christians, none of them friends, not reliable ones at least, and I'm certainly not going to tell her that the most famous chap I know, the Governor, is possibly the dullest creature I've ever had the misfortune of being stuck in a room with for half an hour, because I don't want to sound like a donkey's back-end myself, even if I am one.

'Oh?' she asks. 'Did you come out for the gold and strike it lucky?'

'No!' I laugh and share the unedifying facts of the matter: 'My father dragged me out here when I was fifteen – after I was expelled from my school. Valiant attempt to stop me from getting into further trouble, futile as that has been. He also wanted to progress his business, and had gone as far as he could go in London. The rush on metals and minerals here has been merely convenient to him. He's a silversmith, you see, and I'm a jeweller, his jeweller, when I'm not being an idiot. Don't suppose you've heard of S.J. Fox & Son?'

'Oh?' Her voice brightens a little. 'That's interesting. I've seen the advertisement in the *Empire* for S.J. Fox & Son, first Wednesday of every month. *All silver tableware, jewel-setting and bespoke orders.*

Continental craftsmanship. Awarded Intercolonial Exhibition medal Melbourne, 1867. Silversmith and Jeweller to His Excellency the Earl of Belmore,' she recites the script verbatim, dispelling any notion of illiteracy before I could even presume it. Her mind is as impressive as everything else about her, God help me. 'You must have struck it lucky to be all that anyhow,' she says.

'Yes,' I must admit that fact as well, but I don't elaborate on the fortune Pa has wrought, owning four shops, two each on George and Pitt Streets, three of them taking premium rents, as well the foundry at the top of Goulburn, and our not-too-ordinary pile on Potts' Point above Woolloomooloo Bay, situated a pleasant one and a half miles and a sea breeze away from the stench of Sydney Cove. Not bad for a decade in the colonies – he'd be on the same wicket as Belmore, near enough, on the ledger at least, and doesn't have to live next to the sewerage outlet.

I see Pa in the dining room now, among all his splendid things, the silver, the crystal and the cabinetry, alone but for Mrs Kirschbaum, our housekeeper. She has closed the drapes; he, in his silk coat and best hat, has returned from the synagogue, from his dignified and prayerful walk across the city; she has lit the Sabbath candles; and he has sung his blessing over the holiness of the day, over the wine, over the bread, because the Talmud says he must. Sing, even when your heart is breaking; even when your son betrays you. Sing, and always slip the same stale joke into the end of the song in praise of Mrs Kirschbaum's golden loaf of chollah, because the Talmud says he must be joyful every Friday night. How long has it been since I shared that bread with him? Shared a glass of wine: *L'Chayim!* Rolled my eyes at the crumbs carefully retained in his beard to demonstrate how serious he is about this ritual joyfulness. *Yes, yes, Pa, you silly old goat,* I promise him all the time that I'll be home, and I don't get there. I promised him absolutely hand on heart that I'd attend the Israelite Citizens of Sydney representation to Prince Alfred, the Duke of Edinburgh, just a few weeks ago, in solidarity of commiserations for the Duke having taken that bullet in the royal arse from a Papist while picnicking, but thought it the better idea to stay out drinking with the Papists at Randwick Racecourse, instead – anything to avoid the Reverend Rabbi Davis, and Pa's relentless worry and disappointment. His embarrassment. *Shabes shalom* ...

'What are you in so much trouble for?' Annie Bird asks me, perhaps asking why a rich man would go to the trouble of getting into trouble at all.

It's a good question and I give her the simple facts of this, too: 'Gambling, running up a bit of debt, flouting a bit of authority.' I don't tell her about the charge of molesting Cornelia Osborne with an unwanted kiss, because that of course is total bosh. If it were true, I don't know what I should be doing to Annie Bird right at this minute. In comparison, Miss Osborne is not so much a tasty bit of jam as an unset blancmange.

In any case, Miss Bird is scandalised enough as it is; she clicks her tongue in disgust: 'Gambling.'

'Hm.' My shin, where she kicked me earlier this afternoon, throbs deeper still at her reproach.

But when she speaks again, her voice is small once more and searching: 'Have you got any grandfathers, Mr Fox?'

'Had one,' I tell her. 'He died when I was about eight or nine, in London.'

'I'm sorry to hear that,' she says, and I'm sorry she's sorry, but she surprises me with something wry: 'Did he wear flash high-front boots and special-order tweed like you?'

'God, no.' Knock me down, girl. 'He was Polish – very Polish, and very Jewish. He wore a tall black hat and a long black coat. And I don't recall him ever smiling. He was fearsome and frightening. He looked just like an undertaker.'

'Was he? An undertaker?' she asks, and I can hear her amusement.

'No,' I reply, and I tell her to share something that might interest her: 'He was a trader in Baltic amber, in the port of Danzig, and he made a lot of money at it – enough to move to London, so that my father wouldn't have to go into military service. If you're Jewish you have to go into the Prussian Army at twelve years of age – or you did then – to be sure your education is interrupted and preferably ended.'

'Oh? That's not very fair,' she says with the dispassion of one for whom racial inequity is merely the everyday; she'd rather know: 'How do you make a lot of money from trading amber?'

'Fashion. Right place, right time,' I tell her; God, I want to talk to her forever, every night, and it's not just the herbs. 'Meerschaum pipes made the man – they were what every man in Europe wanted – and Baltic amber is used for making the decorative mouthpieces. Grandfather dabbled in jewellery-making as well,' I blather on. 'Traditional Pomeranian designs of silver and amber – but he wasn't successful with any of that. His pieces were austere and old-fashioned, so said my father, which is saying something, coming from him. They influenced my father, though – the silverwork and the gem-setting – and he did have a talent for it, so Grandfather set him up with an apprenticeship and then a shop in the West End, on Piccadilly Circus, changed the family name from Fuchs to Fox, and the rest is history.'

'Piccadilly Circus?' Annie Bird wonders. 'I've heard of that place in London and every time I do it makes me think of dancing bears and marching bands.'

'Not so far from the truth. I had a lot of larks there.' I cannot ever deny. 'I miss the place.'

'I miss my home, too, and I've been gone only two days,' she says, and we sit either side of our canvas wall in silence again; even the forest is hushed.

Then, just when I think she might be drifting, she asks me, 'What's your mother like?'

'My mother?' The facts there are scant, but I give them to Annie Bird anyway: 'I don't really know. I haven't seen her since I was four. My parents are divorced.'

'Divorced?' she gasps. 'How?'

I reel off the story, this odd fragment of life that never quite seems to belong to me: 'My mother didn't like London, and didn't like my father much, either, so I'm told. She's French – and so she went back to Paris, to her family. They're bootmakers and hide-dealers, the Cardozas, little more than peasants, according to the Fuchses, and they'd dabbled with the idea of getting into London as well, but … French Jews are too different, too free in their ways. Gypsies, according to Pa. That's what he calls my mother still – the Gypsy, and not with any affection, if he mentions her at all. But of course that's Pa. I'm sure he made her insane.'

Annie Bird doesn't find that amusing; she asks me: 'Do you miss her?'

And I can only tell her: 'You can't miss what you don't know, I suppose.'

'But I do,' she says. 'All the time.'

Some morbish klezmer violin seeps up from the damp ground, bringing some memory of a woman, my mother: big teeth, big laugh, big breasts, big perfume I've never smelt since. A stranger.

Annie Bird says: 'If it rains or gets too cold, you can come in here under cover, but don't you touch me.'

'I wouldn't.' I wish I could tell her how much I wouldn't dare and how very, very odd that is.

I lean back, rest my head on my hands and look up at our sky: moon on the wax rising through the marcasite sea, fluorescing shadows of rose and mauve and green.

Zad snorts: *You are a bit shredded, aren't you.*

And Annie Bird asks: 'Can you speak French?'

'No, not really. Not more than to read the label on a box of cigarettes.'

'I wish I knew my mother's language,' she says, and her voice is so small I want to hold all her wondering in my arms and never let it go. 'I can't seem to remember a word, and there's no-one I can ask about it, any of it, not now Dad's gone.'

'No-one?' I don't quite understand what she means.

But she doesn't answer me; she asks: 'Do you know any other language?'

I do – a bit of Hebrew, a bit of German, bit of in between the two, bit of Latin and Greek tossed in from St Sav's, but I tell her: 'No.' Because I think I've just understood something unusually profound, for me, a glimpse of it at least. Things change, times change, names change, people come, people go, like tides, Jews flee Tangier once every century, and return to begin again, but there's something about Annie Bird's loss, some lonely-moon marcasite enormity in it, that's overwhelming. The idea of my never having met an Aborigine before suddenly seems the most crushing, dreadful fact – in this, that was once their uninterrupted country. There's all that you read and hear, of course: a cricket team travelling to London; the astounding athletic prowess of native stockmen; the brutality of Stone-Age existence matched only by the brutality of its reportage; actual Christians calling for compassion and some sort of compensation. There's the native camp near Farm Cove on the harbour, where some few dozen or so of some remnant Sydney tribe survive on government rations – I bypass it every time I bother to go home. There's the neighbourhood gossip of a pair of diamond earrings stolen from a house down at Darling Point, a black girl of fourteen charged with it only a month or so ago. But I've never seen an Aborigine personally – not in almost ten years of being here. Not one. Where have they gone? How does one begin to ask that question, never mind live it?

I hear her shift inside her tarpaulin tent; I can sense her back to me, as she says: 'Don't sneak all that barley sugar in the saddlebag.'

As if she's known me since time began. And was born to make me promise: 'Honestly, I wouldn't dare.'

Born to make me promise that I will help this girl find her grandfather, take her right to his door, if I can.

ANNIE

It's still cold when I wake at the first grey haze of this dawn, and I'm scratchy-eyed and panicking from too little sleep and then too much. A magpie is oodling on not far away, telling everyone what a shocking cold night it was – and still is. And how for most of it I couldn't stop wondering when the strange man I've found myself travelling with might come in under the tarp, and if that would be a welcome event for the warmth, or the worst thing that could ever happen. I kept peeking under the side edge at him, but he was out fast; I wondered a couple of times if he'd frozen to death, he was so still, but then I'd hear him snore. I suppose that's special-order tweed for you.

I crank myself off the ground to look out the end of the tarp for him now, but he's not there. The fire's ablaze, though – and then I see him, beyond it. He's at the waterhole, standing on a rock that's just beneath the surface, with his corduroy strides hitched up to his knees. And he's half naked. He's having a wash, splashing up under his arms. The warmth that this picture brings me is not a natural feeling, but then maybe it is: a man who washes, especially in this freezing cold, he can't be all bad, can he. In a different circumstance I'd be approving of his effort.

He stands there for a moment, looking out at the day, and then he pushes his hand through his hair. He has a habit of doing that, pushing his hair back so that it falls across his forehead just the way he wants it. He's more vain than my sister. I could call out to him and tell him that no-one is looking, except that I am.

Something makes him startle and shout out, 'Whoa! Ya!' and he nearly slips off the rock, tiptoeing quick out of there and backwards, and it makes me laugh.

That makes him catch me looking.

'Ah. Good morning, Miss Bird!' A smile on him that just about lights up the gully ahead of the sun, and that's not natural, either: that a man be so cheerful in the morning. I don't get a chance to find a single word in reply before he's telling me: 'I've washed my socks as well.' He points to them where they're drying near the fire, and I'm wondering if he wants some kind of congratulations for it when he adds: 'You could perhaps wear them over your own today. It might help. With your sore feet, I mean.'

He's thinking to forgo socks for me? I look away. It's only a pair of socks, but the simple generosity of it robs me of breath so that I can hardly mumble, 'Thanks,' which makes me even more embarrassed, so that I have to look up again, straight back into that smile, which has me saying, like it's a thing to disdain: 'Do you wake up this cheerful every day?'

'What?' He pushes his hair back again, to make sure he's still as handsome as he reckons he is: 'God, no.'

I do wish he wouldn't blaspheme, even as I'm watching him step closer, picking up his shirt and not putting it on. Oh – my. He has a chest on him like a wrestler I once saw when the New San Francisco Circus Troupe came through town; his name was Boris the Barbarian and he wore leopard-skin britches, and he winked right at me and Sis, but he wasn't near as shameless as Jeremy Fox is now. It's not his nakedness that's in any way shameful – there's nothing wrong with being in the body our Lord in His goodness gave you. It's … the confusing thoughts this chest brings forth. How big a breath must he have to take to fill the lungs inside it? How can this feller with the barbarian chest be a jeweller, someone making tiny, pretty things with that strong body? I've never had any jewellery; I'd never thought to want any. I always thought I might like to have a silver tea tray one day, as my furthest wish away from the bounds of all possibility.

He says: 'I haven't awoken to find myself so battered for quite some time.' He points at his shin: 'Look what you did to me yesterday.' Where I kicked him, a bruise is turning from red to blue as daylight begins to brighten around us. He points to the solid muscle of his arm: 'And here.' Where I pinched him, two little nasty finger marks. And I have to look away yet again, especially so I don't look at the scratch I made on his face as well, but I can't force my eyes to do as I tell them. He says: 'Don't worry about it, Miss Bird. Most mornings I'm only astounded to find that I'm still alive.'

And then he just stands there before me with his shirt in his hand rather than on his body, like this is the usual way he presents himself to ladies. It likely is.

I say: 'Aren't you cold?'

'It's a little fresh.' He hooks up an eyebrow at me. 'But I quite like a bit of fresh sometimes, don't you, Miss Bird?'

'No,' I tell him. I could say as well that I'm still shivering here inside my cami and stays, my cotton blouse and Dad's Crimean buttoned to my chin, with that bushranger's woolen comforter wrapped around my head and shoulders as wide as it will go, but I don't think this is the sort of fresh Mr Fox is talking about. He keeps on standing there before me, not putting his shirt on. He's doing it on purpose. I start pulling my boots on.

He says: 'Aren't you going to wear my socks? They're almost dry.'

I'd forgotten about the stupid socks, he has me spinning so quick one way and then the other. I say: 'No, thank you. I'll be all right.' Regretting the decision straightaway. *Oh. Oh. Oh!* But still, not as bad as yesterday.

And I have to get away – from him, as much as to find myself some privacy for my own necessities. I get up on my feet swift as I can and tell him: 'Stay here – don't you follow me.'

There's a patch of thick scrub a little way back along the creek, where we came in yesterday, and where the sun is beginning to reach into the trees, the slope of gully rising high above the bank on the other side: as good a place as any.

My face is still burning for all that the rest of me is frozen, and I'm still pulling my braces back up on my shoulders from the first and most necessary of my needs, when I hear: 'And what do you reckon you're up to, ay?'

I look up – right into the barrel of a shotgun. One of those double-barrel shotguns. Pointed at me.

I hear the click of the gun as the man makes aim from where he's sitting on his tall, black horse. 'Shy now, ain't ya, this end of a bullet.'

What end of a bullet? That makes no sense to me. I don't know anything about guns, but that Dad would borrow one of Mr Webb's for clearing off rabbits and kangaroos and that I've always hated the sound of the horrible thing firing and firing, with a hundred other guns along the river.

'Get off my land, little black bitch. Get on your way now,' this shotgun tells me.

I nod. I'm trespassing, I reckon. Another click and there's two guns aimed at me, one beyond the trees where the pasture stretches across the gully flat: their pasture, I reckon. I start to back away, towards the waterhole further into the trees, as fast as my trembling knees will take me.

As Jeremy Fox comes up behind me, and he's coming with his shirt on and his hands up, saying to the men: 'Whoa there, chums. We'll be on our way. I wasn't aware that this was private property. We didn't mean any harm. Please excuse us, won't you?'

I'm hoping these tough and mean-looking backwoods sheep farmers can make out his uptowny words, see the harmlessness of us in his good-morning smile.

Maybe they do. The nearer man nods to the other man, who rides off back across that pasture, then he stares hard at Jeremy Fox: 'Your type ain't welcome round here. Tell your mates. I'll give yous two minutes to get off my land.'

'Fair enough. One minute will probably do,' says Jeremy Fox, not letting that smile slip as he takes me by the arm, back to where we made our camp.

I know I am packing up, I can see my hands and my feet moving fast as the farmer stands above us watching, but I don't know what I'm doing: my whole mind is stuck around the words: *Little black bitch*. I've never heard the hatred so plain as that. He likely thinks I dirtied his creek. I start to kick up dust over the fire to put it out, from the habit of always doing so, and I hear the farmer say: 'Leave that and get.'

I can't see from the hatred he's burning into me. I can't feel anything except for a pain come over all my spirit like a rock has been set upon it. What is this hatred for? Why?

Jeremy Fox is back up on his stolen horse with his hands reaching for me: 'Come on, I've got you, up you get.'

Get. Get off my land. I suppose these farmers are free selectors, or 'cockatoos', so Dad would call them, bullies the way they flock together to fix prices and pay their shearers next to nothing, make a mess and move on, not a gentleman among them. Mean, so mean. I don't know if I'm breathing at all.

'It's all right, Miss Bird,' Jeremy Fox is saying something or other, his arms either side of me like a gate, firm and certain, as we return to the road, winding away up a steep hill ahead. 'I have a feeling they might have mistaken us for someone else.'

I don't. My mind takes strange turns away and away from the barrel of the gun and the hatred, through all kinds of pictures, jumbled one after the other: Evangeline Webb spitting on the toe of my shoe in the yard at school, elbows pushing into me one market day with no 'pardon me' from any one of them, my mother making a basket of reeds on the bank of the river singing a song I can't hear, a sadness in her shoulders, a secret. A swan flying out across the water like a great black arrow. Pictures over pictures until hunger pinches in my belly around a ball of anger. Damnation to every horrible, hate-filled soul – may Satan keep your seats nice and warm in Hell.

'If I could do anything to prevent you receiving such an insult again, I would do it,' Jeremy Fox is going on.

And I'm snippety at him: 'I can't be insulted by someone I have no respect for. I'm all right, don't you worry, Mr Fox.'

Little black bitch. How that wounds me and wounds me still.

'Well, good for you, Miss Bird, but I'm not sure I'm too all right. It's not every day one is forced to flee into the hills at gunpoint, is it?'

I can't answer him. I keep looking ahead at the road, listening to the sound of the hooves, the steady speed of the horse pounding at the miles, my bones doing what they can to settle to the jangling thump of the ride, sat as I am astride the saddle now, my mind ridden well past all fearfulness of this. We come around another bend and downwards into yet another wide green valley, and everywhere around are more hills hugged tight all about with trees, almost the same as the valley before. We've been riding maybe an hour when we come to a crossroads and find a proper gravelled highway is being forged here: a steam-roller engine sits idle by a line of big, low box-carts heaped with the blue metal gravel; bullocks are resting in the paddock behind them, several dozen. And as we get closer I see on the sides of the carts is written, 'Cobb & Co'.

'This'd be Bowenfels, then,' says Jeremy Fox, pointing out the puffing chimneys of what must be the horsing inn a quarter of a mile or so distant, huge tin roof the other side of the paddock, telegraph line going along the road like a scalloped edging of the sky. Up the other way, at a similar distance, is a grand-looking homestead, its roof almost as huge, red-and-gold autumn leaves of English trees around it, clipped hedges like bolts of emerald velvet unwound against the forest beyond. I know he should go to the Cobb & Co yards to return this horse, right here, right now. I know he more likely belongs in that grand homestead, ten times grander than the Webb's; I know he doesn't belong anywhere near someone such as me. But I don't want to stop here. I don't want to see another mean face, hear another mean word. And I don't want to get out from under the firm and certain arms of this Jeremy Fox, either. Not yet.

I say to him, 'You should put this horse in here.'

He says: 'Of course I should. But I'm not going to. I promised I'd take you to Bathurst and so that's where we're going.'

'But you'll get into worse trouble for this, won't you,' I say, because I shouldn't let him do it.

And he says, 'Yes, with the law, perhaps. But not with my father, and his is the law that counts. He wouldn't think much of me leaving you on the roadside to fend for yourself. He would expect me to take you to your grandfather, or failing that, ensure your return to your sister or some other suitable place. Don't worry, Miss Bird, everything will work itself out as far as my *trouble* is concerned – Pa will fix it once he has all the facts, and he shall have them tomorrow, for Sunday, which is his usual fixing day, as no-one else is about to bother him, most specifically here being Inspector-General Douglas Fitzworthy, but never mind him. Never mind anything. I will not be abandoning you.'

He might be the kindest man I'll ever know, even if he's terrible in every other way, and I am so very grateful, I can't say anything of it for fear that every feeling in me might tumble from my heart and I'd never be able to gather it all back in again.

We pass right by the inn, right by the yards, and Jeremy Fox tips his hat at a farrier working there by the fence, nailing a shoe – 'Good morning! Beautiful day, isn't it?' – proving that he might have more nerve than any man I'll ever know, either. In a different circumstance, I might want to take a few moments to be amazed at that, but here, my mind and my heart both snag around the signpost at the end of the yard, saying it's *MUDGEE 82 MILES*, to the north, and *BATHURST 43 MILES*, west. I've heard of the name Mudgee before: they suffered in the winter floods there, dozens lost, hundreds of cattle and sheep, two little boys swept away from their mother. But Bathurst: the name here before me now, this famous little city of money and gold and Cobb & Co that's only now forty-three miles away, suddenly seems more foreign to me than anything.

Get off my land.

We follow the telegraph line, starlings sitting up there along it, and out below the road more earthworks are going on, a great cutting in a hillside, a bridge being built, a shed with *GWR* painted on the roof, for the railways. The rock in the cutting is shining in the slant of the forenoon sun, sandy bands of yellow and orange, and I see somewhere, some day, these roads will blast through everywhere, striking a sadness into me like no other that for all these roads I might still have nowhere to go.

'I must say, I'm getting a little peckish, Miss Bird. Aren't you? Time for a sardine and a cup of tea?'

'Yes,' I tell him. 'But I don't want to stop here.' Not in these hills. These dark and lonely hills, with the bush sitting so tight and tall upon them, telling me: *You don't belong here.* 'Keep going,' I tell him, though I don't know what I might be looking for.

The sun is rising higher and higher towards midday, we must have been riding another two hours or more, but Jeremy Fox makes no complaint, though he must be starving for want of something more substantial than barley sugar. The horse must be tiring too, the pace he's been taking these hills. But still I can't see where we can stop: the bush crowds and crowds along the sides of the road and around and around all these endless hills.

Until, on the crest of the next, like a parting of heavy curtains, the forest thins out and the land opens up into great wide rolling waves that look to fold away and away forever. My skin shivers all over at the sight and my spirit flutters out from that rock it's been caught under.

I don't know why, but it feels like I've been here before. I know this place as the first place I've recognised since I left Castlereagh. I don't know how this could be, though. A piece of story locked inside me so that I would always know, when I got here, over the mountains. One day. Now …

'Oh!' I feel the sun on the top of my head and in my heart, lighting me up from the inside, warm and wheaten as the colour of the grasses here. I feel the smile come over my whole face.

'Well, look at that,' says Jeremy Fox behind me, taking a moment of amazement himself; I feel it through my shoulders, through his chest at my back.

There's a little hut down to our left on the side of the slope looking out at the view, one of those knocked-together things made of tin you can buy on special order from America and only have to screw the bolts in, and while it might be humble and start falling to bits within a year, the cockatoo who owns it has bigger ideas: the dam below the hut is a lake, holding its mirror to the bright blue sky, and showing me by the slice of its fresh-cut sink the colour of the earth here: it's a deep, dark red. The colour of rust: alive. And loamy-looking as fresh cake crumbs. I've never seen soil like it. I want to put potatoes in it. I want to put my hands in it. I want a little farm of my own here. One day. I wish Dad was here to see it; maybe he is.

I look back out at forever again and wonder if my grandfather ever stood here with the survey men, looking at their faces all lit up like mine. My blood wants to know – needs to know – if he did. I look down to the right, and on the other side of the road, a spiny anteater curls up into a spiky ball, rolling off into this grass to pretend that he can't be seen. But I can see him: he says the earth here is healthy and full of worms, and he's been here forever, too. I want to clear these slopes of sheep so they don't graze the place out and wreck it for my potatoes. I can't remember ever having felt such a sudden excitement about anything.

A bullockies' camp lies a little way back from where the anteater is hiding in the grass, a circle of bricks around the black scorch, in among some wattles. They're only plain grey wattles you'd see anywhere, along any road, with a little fast-running trickle of a creek coming down off some steep grey rocks behind and a thousand sheep going *baa* at us from above, but it feels somehow safe, somehow welcoming. At last.

It feels like home.

I can breathe here. I can fill my own lungs.

I can tell Jeremy Fox, finally, 'Let's stop here. Right here.'

JEM

'Or perhaps a little further on,' I suggest. 'I need to make a visit to a pub.'

'A pub?' She leans back to look at me, dubious eyebrow preparing to be horrified. 'What do you want to go to a pub for? We haven't got a farthing to spend in one.'

'Something that doesn't cost a farthing,' I assure her, 'but nevertheless something I have no intention of enjoying in the bush.'

She thinks about it for a few seconds before catching the gist. And then she laughs: 'Truly? You have to go to a pub for *that*?'

Her laughter is honey on buttered toast, uncomplicated and delectable, and it seems invariably at my expense, but that's all right with me, early days yet.

I tell her: 'Yes, I do have to go to a pub for that actually, and there will be one of some description very soon, I hope – the next rehorsing yard must be due.' Or it will amount to criminal negligence against both man and beast. But almost as soon as I've said it, we see it: at a junction in the road, nestled into the bottom of the dale ahead, a sagging verandah sits under a long, wide stretch of roof, a small variety of horseflesh watering outside. It's either a pub or a police station and I'm becoming just that bit too desperate to care.

'I want to come back up here, though,' she says, 'back to the bullockies' camp, for that cup of tea, for a rest.'

'Wherever and whatever you wish,' I reply and I'm already urging Zad on, not fifty yards off now, and it is indeed a pub –

Bradley's HIT OR MISS Hotel, says the awning. 'I won't be long at it.'

'All right,' she says, but there is worry in it. For all her chin-to-the-wind defiance, I'm sure she doesn't want to be left alone after that scare this morning, not for a minute, and I don't blame her. Those box-heads: who did they think we were? Grass robbers? Should be a law against the brainless obtaining firearms.

I assure her again, and I'm already dismounting: 'Honestly, I won't be long. In and out – promise. I'll be as quick as I can.'

She says nothing, and a faraway desolation returns to her face as I lead Zad just off the roadside to wait in the shade of a tree there. She looks so young as she gazes out at the hills, so vulnerable, so dainty on the saddle, so astonishingly beautiful, I shouldn't be leaving her alone anywhere, but I can't take her with me – not for this.

I make a dash for the pub, going straight around the back, where I find what I'm looking for: sack-walled and bark-roofed, and conveniently hung with a sign saying *DUNNEKIN* in case it isn't obvious. Inside, it has an open view of these glorious dales, and a handy pile of dual-purpose literature by the box.

Before I pick up one of the newspapers, though, I've already begun reading a notice pinned to the wall at my left shoulder, a local bulletin, entitled *MILDEW FLAT MESSENGER*. Of course. Why would you call your spot on the map 'Glorious Dales', when you can call it 'Mildew Flat'? It's a lively place: there's a dance on next Saturday, May 9th, at St Luke's hall at Honeysuckle Hill, raising funds for the Bathurst & Districts Hospital; in other news, Mrs C. Wiggington has fine bantams to sell, and a Mr George Logue has Cashmere goats; while there's an agricultural show on at Kelso May 2nd – that's today. And I'm done.

When I stand up to reassemble the duds, I can see the stables not far off over the other side of the pub, a couple of the coachers grazing near the fence. This obviously isn't a significant stop on the Cobb & Co route except for the changing of teams, but it's a stop, no doubt about it. I could drop Zad in here; Annie Bird and I could stay here, too, until I'm able to contact Pa. In the interim, I could use the revolver and the information on the turds who robbed Annie as collateral to keep Fitzworthy off my back. With a little patience I could give this present detour from filial duty absolute legitimacy. Or completely hash the lot and perhaps never see Annie again by the unfolding of any number of calamities, such as me being placed in immediate custody or Annie being *shooed* off as an undesirable – or both.

As I'm standing here weighing the impossible against the unthinkable, and wishing I might have just one clarifying ale, I hear voices coming from the back of the pub.

'Yeah, no fear, Sarge Slater, we'll keep an eye out for 'em all right, won't we, Arch.'

I look through a tear in the sack wall behind me at the back of the box and see three fellows standing there.

Presumably it's the one called Arch who responds. 'Yeah, we'll turn 'em right orf, if they come round this way. No fear at all. We'll blow 'em orf the Bathurst Road.'

Arch is a portly, aproned chap with his shirtsleeves rolled, perhaps the innkeeper; his friend, perhaps the stableman, is a stringy thing in dusty cabbage-tree hat, implausibly long stove-pipe legs; and they are speaking with a constabulary chap – a mounted trooper, dark navy uniform, red stripe down the trouser, white cross-belt, compulsorily heavy moustaches, and single-shot rifle strapped to his back. He turns slightly and I see it's a glimmering new Enfield – nice one.

'They are dangerous,' this trooper is saying, whiskers wobbling gravely. 'Do not attempt to apprehend them yourselves without the utmost wherewithal and caution. I have information that, together with the cache of stolen police weapons, they have taken several bundles of dynamite from the rail works at Marangaroo, on their way out of the Lithgow Valley. There are four of them in all counted now. This fellow known as Black Jack —'

'That Black Jack,' Arch shakes his fat head, 'two foot lower than a snake's arsehole, that one. Gone feral.'

'If he weren't born that way,' says Stove-pipes. 'Bastard still owes me for lambs, from two years ago. I don't forget. I don't forget nuthin', by jingoes, I don't.'

'He owes a lot more than that to the Bank of Australasia, let me tell you,' says the trooper. 'All debts and petty rascallery aside,

Black Jack Holly is a violent felon today, and he and Bill Molloy have been joined by two other scoundrels – a man calling himself Fox, who just yesterday snatched a horse from the Cobb & Co at One Tree. Genteel in appearance, tweed coat and corduroys of a city sporting type, and a distinctive brown silk beaver hat, flat-top and not too tall in the crown. Gentry manner of speech, he pretends to be the son of one Solomon Joseph Fox, the Governor's own silversmith, but don't be fooled – he is an impostor and he is sly. He gained the confidence of Ian Dixon up there at One Tree before making off with Black Jack and Molloy.'

'The maggot,' Arch interjects. So could I.

But the trooper has more to say: 'The fourth member of the gang is a female – a half-caste Aboriginal woman by the name of Annabel Bird. She is dressed as a man – tall cavalry boots and red Crimean shirt – and she stole cash from an eminent landowner's residence in Windsor three days ago, the Penrith police have on good authority from the wife there by the name of Webb. And no less dangerous herself, Miss Bird is armed with a pistol. She was witnessed yesterday evening, passing through The Gap – with the aforementioned Fox – and there brandished the weapon threate-ningly at an elderly woman called Irvine.'

As I listen to all this spawn-of-Fitzworthy windbaggery, I have the feeling that a lack of anything but lollies for breakfast is having a lark with my perception of events. This can't actually be happening. I have reached some threshold of absurdity and fallen right in the door.

'Those two sound just like Capt'n Thunderbolt and his lady – she's a black gin, or half of somethin' no good, goes about dressed as a feller,' says Arch, scratching his chin. Of course, there's your mix-up, they do sound just like them – just like *who*?

'Lady Thunderbolt ain't no gin, Arch – she's a opera singer, from Switzyland,' says Stove-pipes. 'Huge bezoombies on her – rock melons.'

See, this is a preposterous dream.

'No, no, no,' the trooper goes on. 'It's not them. Thunderbolt and his lady have moved north. They have had their day in this district, and they were not near so depraved when they were ranging hereabouts. This Fox and his lady are quite a different pair. They are younger – the dandy and the dandizette – and they are not fair players. One witness has said he saw them rob a swagman on the Bathurst Road outside the Royal Hotel while all were distracted at the train coming into the new station. The swagman has not been seen again. We are yet to find the evidence, but they could well be killers. Times are tough, let no man say they are not, but there is no excuse for such violence.'

'No, Sarge Slater, there's not.' Fat Arch cracks his knuckles.

As they say in the Wild West: holy shit.

'Here,' says the trooper, 'a constable from the Hartley District will be coming around with some posters on the matter – be sure to stick one up in the dunny and one behind the bar. A reward for apprehension and conviction is in the offing: two hundred and fifty pounds for Black Jack and one hundred each for the rest – but they are to be taken alive, mind. I repeat: *alive*. No conviction, no reward, and there will be no unnecessary violence or disorder in *my* district – right? Any information you might pick up, send an urgent telegraphic message to the Bathurst Police Court, no matter how trivial a detail it may seem. With that said, however, and speaking of the dunny – you'll have to excuse me, gents.'

'Yeah, Sarge.'

'Sure, Sarge.'

And Sarge is stepping this way.

What to do? What to do? What I usually do when confronted with the law, or with any sort of character I might have displeased: clap on best and most winning smile, and wear it firmly as I emerge from the dunny, in this instance hiding distinctive hat behind my back, which is not, I might add, a beaver, but an equestrian topper – let's not quibble now, shall we.

'Good morning, Sergeant Slater!' I salute him, as if it's the finest one we've ever seen.

'Morning.' The trooper barely nods as I stride past him; too distracted by his own pressing business, he just about pushes me out of his way.

'You reckon shooting 'em in the kneecaps would be unnecessary violence?' Stove-pipes is pondering aloud to Arch as I stride right

away from them as well, and I almost make it to the cover of some
bushes at the roadside when I hear: 'Ay – you there!' Arch steps off
the back verandah, and I salute him, too.

'Morning!'

Keep striding, keep striding. Disappear behind the bushes before
he's located his next thought. And then, as any decent sporting man
would, I run like blazes.

FROM FRYING PAN
TO BLATHERY

ANNIE

Jeremy Fox comes walloping back up the road like the Devil's on his tail, and he's swung up on the horse behind me and telling me, 'Hold on!' before I can ask him what in Heaven's name has happened and what I might hold onto.

'Hold onto that, too.' He's pushing his hat at me and heeling into the horse at the same time, and I don't know how I'm going to hold onto this hat, either, as he bends forward in the saddle, pressing me to the horse's neck.

'Keep looking behind – tell me if anyone is following,' he shouts in my ear and we're flying downhill and over post and rail and through a yard full of Jersey milkers, who are not happy at the disturbance and are slow to get out of the way. I expect I am going to fly headlong right into this paddock and out the other side of the earth.

'And keep your voice down,' he says, because I must have been screaming out my own sudden lack of happiness.

'Is anyone following?'

'I don't know!' I'm trying to look out from under his elbow, trying to hold onto the narrowing edge of his coat lapel with one hand and his stupid hat in my other, and I'm twisted and squashed under him as he half stands in the stirrups, pressing me ever forward. I can't see anything but a special-order tweed window of wide wheaten hills and fluttering treetops, all bouncing up at the sky.

'I said, is anyone following?' he yells now himself, the sound bursting against my head with the power of it.

And I yell back: 'How could I possibly tell!'

He has a look himself. 'Jesus Christ on a cracknel,' he says, and he keeps on at this gallop.

'What!' I'm screaming again. 'What is it!'

He takes another look behind us and tells me over the belting hooves: 'I think we've got away.'

'Got away from what?' I don't want to know. I don't want to know any more about this horrible, rough world that smashes away the smallest glimpse of any good thing.

He's slowing the horse down now and steadying his own breath, his chest still squashing me. 'Perhaps time for that cup of tea, then, hm?'

'What?' I can only look sideways into the knot of his neck-tie and ask him again, despite myself, 'What has happened?'

He's sitting back down, letting me sit up, still catching his breath as he says: 'I'm not entirely sure how or why, but it seems we've been mistaken for bushrangers – those fellows who stole from you. The police think we're with their gang.'

I shake my head at the hills. 'I don't believe you.'

'I'm afraid you'll have to, Miss Bird.' And he tells me all of what he reckons he heard back at that inn. 'A nobbler full of bosh, that all is, except ...' And there he pauses, clears his throat. 'Er.' And then he asks me: 'But you didn't rob cash from anyone in Windsor, did you?'

I don't know how anyone could ask something like that of me, except it has some ring of truth about it, and I ask him, slow so I can understand what I'm saying too: 'Robbed cash in Windsor? Who reckons I did?'

'Some wife called Webster – or Webb, I think the trooper said.'

I believe that, all right. Mrs Webb, the nasty old cow. In some spite at my insulting her on the doorstep in front of Reverend Thorne, and not showing up at Dad's burial to give her the satisfaction of inflicting more grief upon me, she has told a lie to the police about me. It's exactly something she would do, to cover the evil she has done to me – point the finger. She does it just for her own pleasure, destroying people with her slanderous gossip easy as waking up in the mornings. I remember Mrs Bartlett at the Windsor general store once diddled her on oats to spite her for some wicked snipe or other, and to get her back Mrs Webb told the whole of the Richmond and Penrith districts that Mrs Bartlett was having immoral relations with Mr Ennis from Morton's Grain. Mrs Bartlett had to change churches after that, and got a terrible thrashing from her husband before the truth was told. Because that's the nasty old cow that Mrs Webb is. She knows her Mr Webb will be concerned for me when he finds Dad and Sis and me gone, all in separate ways, and she's had to tell lies against me to make it seem right. I should have stayed, to wait for Mr Webb to come back from Sydney tomorrow. I should have stayed with Sis to fight. I would still have the envelope with that witch's handwriting on it, for Dad's last pay, to prove she shoved us out. I wouldn't be here with nothing at all but a madman who thinks I'm a thief, too.

'Miss Bird, I didn't really believe you would have robbed anyone,' says Jeremy Fox.

'Yes, you did,' I say, and I say it meanly for all the bad feeling I have in me for Mrs Webb and for everyone who's ever thought the worst of me or any Aborigine. *Get off my land, black bitch.* I tell him: 'But I never laid a hand on a thing that wasn't mine until I met you.'

'I'm sure you didn't,' he says, and I can feel behind me he's pushing his hair back. He says: 'I apologise if I gave you the impression, ah – I'm sorry for any offence ...' He takes a pause. 'But, er. Miss Bird, um, you're bending the brim of my hat. Could you ...'

I could rip it off altogether in a minute, but I won't do any such awful thing. I look down at it in my hands: it's a nice hat. There's a label sewn on the inside band that says, *Temple & Goldstein, Clothiers and Hatters, Pitt Street, Sydney.* It's an expensive hat, probably worth more than my life. I look at his hand, near my hand, holding the rein, and his skin, where it's got tanned, isn't so different from mine, and it makes me only sad, with that weary, slog of sadness that follows any anger.

'So. How about that cup of tea, hm?' he says.

I look up at the hills again. They are still splendorous as they were ten minutes ago, but there's no sign of a road, or a river, or a trickle of a creek. I don't know where we are, except still heading westerly. I tell Jeremy Fox, I tell the hills: 'I'm being punished for my sins. I know this now.'

'Oh, I doubt that very much,' says Jeremy Fox. 'This is just an extraordinary run of bad luck. Trust me on this – I know about these things.'

No. It's against all reason for me to trust this man on anything.

He says, 'Look on the bright side. There's a hundred pounds on each of our heads. When we turn ourselves in, we'll clear my gambling debts.'

That's not funny. When we turn ourselves in there's only one place I'm going. Mrs Webb will see to it. Oh, but I hope Sis is safe at Yarramundi with Mickey, safe away from all meanness. I want to turn around and go home to her. And now I can't do that at all.

'I don't want to go to gaol,' I tell whoever is listening: *please*. I might deserve a lot of things, but not that.

'You are not going to gaol, Miss Bird.' Jeremy Fox sounds so certain of himself. 'There is no chance in the world that my father would ever believe I'd turned so rogue as to become a bushranger. He knows very well that I lack the industriousness required. He will laugh. This time tomorrow we'll be somewhere in Bathurst laughing about it ourselves – and hopefully with your grandfather or news of him. We just have to make sure we're in the right place at the right time, this time. Present ourselves at the Bathurst Police Court before anyone else gets the opportunity.'

He makes that sound like it's what he does on Sundays.

He says: 'But if I don't get a cup of tea and a sardine shortly, I'm going to expire.'

Me too, probably, for all that I've lost my appetite, and with it my sense of direction. I look and look at the hills, not knowing at all where we might go.

He says behind me: 'Hm. Well.' Because he's got no idea where I might fill a billy, either.

The breeze swishes through the tall, pale grass: *Plenty of water around here …* There'd be water everywhere in such a fertile place as this, but I don't know where it is. I close my eyes, so done in I can't begin to think, but as I do, a memory comes: I see Mother, holding my hand as we walk to Windsor for my new boots, Sis on her hip. It's hot and dry, Rickaby's Creek is down to puddles, and Mother is showing me something there. *Listen, Annie,* she says, but I am looking at the breeze playing in the lilac ribbon of her town bonnet. *Listen and you will hear a little frog.*

I can't hear any frog now, but when I open my eyes I find a streak of green in all the soft gold of the meadows, near the bottom of the rise facing us, a crack slivering down the side of the gully above it, showing where the water goes when it rains.

'There,' I tell Jeremy Fox, 'have a look down there.'

It's only a few yards on and I see it: a creek. I rub my eyes to test the truth of it.

As Jeremy Fox is saying: 'Where?' I'm sure he's got something wrong with his vision, in need of spectacles, but then he sees it too, and he's telling me, 'Now *that* is extraordinary, Miss Bird. I'd be dead without you, you do realise that.'

He wouldn't be here without me, I realise *that*. He's only trying to help, risking his own neck to help, to be kind, and that only makes everything worse.

But, looking ahead, I also see a track winding up from the creek, like a word from our Lord; one word: *Trust*. That track likely leads back to the road and that road likely leads to the resolution of this mistake, this confusion. If I am being trialled here, Heavenly Father, I will accept whatever ordeals you have set for me. I will take this suffering, this small suffering, with a little more humility. With gratitude and dignity. I will not be caught in the snares of my own sinfulness and resentment, nor those of any other.

Further down the gully slope, to the north, a shabby hut of timber appears – no, three of them – one this side of the creek and two the other. It doesn't look as though anyone lives here – boards rotting and falling down, no stock, no gardens, no chimneys going – but I am not so suddenly trusting that I would want to stop here to test anything. Much as I want to get off this horse and stretch out my aching legs, we should keep going around a little way, and I'm about to say that very thing when I see a patch of withering stalks by the hut nearest – potatoes – a fading tangle of pumpkin vine beyond, and someone is shouting: 'Hey! Hey! You there!'

A man coming up from the bank of the creek now, waving a shovel at us.

Oh have pity. *Please.*

JEM

This takes the egg. Some sort of sun-crisped goblin is brandishing a blunt weapon at ten paces, face like a furious prune. What species of being inhabits these parts? Bad-tempered and quite possibly able to communicate with each other through the ether by some occult means.

Annie Bird stiffens her spine on his approach, recoiling; I'm sure I would too, if I wasn't concentrating every ounce of my strength on making some semblance of a friendly face at this unhappy little man.

Who now smiles as he nears: 'Howdy do, travellers!' A Yankee twang, and the smile so broad and transformative, I'm momentarily speechless at it.

'Welcome to Frying Pan.' He plants his shovel in the ground at his feet, and for another fraction of a second I wonder what he's referring to, before he adds with a grin broader still: 'It ain't much but it's home.'

Of course. Frying Pan. That'd be the name of this place. And why wouldn't you call it Frying Pan?

Blue eyes sharp and somehow puckish: 'What brings you along here?' He's clearly excited by the idea, perhaps because Frying Pan is not much accustomed to visitors.

'We only want to stop for a billy, that's all,' Annie Bird tells him, quickly, curtly, before I can lay on any charm. Exhausted and wary, she sighs: 'I don't want any trouble, please. I only want a cup of tea. Then you'll never see me again.'

I want to make her a cup of tea and a better world to go with it.

The man stares at her, and stares at me. He tips his grimy old bowler back on his head as if to see us better, and then he says to Annie, 'It's a free country.' He seems both sympathetic and bemused. 'At least this part of it is. You can have your cup of tea here, no-one to mind if you do.'

'Thank you,' she replies, as she hands me back my hat. I jump from Zad and hold my arms out to her, to help her down after me, with the man asking as I do: 'So, you that Fox and lady bushranger we been hearing about?'

I almost drop her. They bloody well can communicate by some psychic telegraph, can't they. Or perhaps they do it with carrier pigeons.

'Just a cup of tea, please,' Annie mutters as she strides away from us towards the creek. 'Just a cup of tea.'

There is no point in not admitting who we so obviously are; I tell the man, so that he might pass it through the psychic telegraph: 'We are one and the same. But whatever it is you've heard, we're not in with that Black Jack character, whoever he is. There's been an awful mistake made here.'

'Oh, mistakes, yeah, tell me all about 'em.' The man shrugs with an ambivalent nod. 'But I can tell you Jack Holly's all right, whatever you mighta heard about *him*. Man just wants to get free. Either way, it's good to meet you.' He stretches out a hand and adds: 'Somebody's got to stick it to them tarned varmints that oppress us, don't they? Better you than me. I'm Amos Scattergood.'

Amos Scattergood. Of course. What else would he be called? To Americans, ridiculous names are a competitive sport, aren't they?

'We're not thieves,' I attempt to remind him: 'There's been a mistake.'

'That's what they all say.' He laughs over a handshake that's brief but surprisingly firm, before calling out to Annie: 'Hey there, don't go round by the house!'

She's begun gathering firewood, along the bank of the stream, and now mutters something to herself in reply, but she doesn't glance upwards at the warning; she simply changes direction, like a dog responding to a whistle.

I take a sterner attitude with the man: 'I said we're not thieves. Miss Bird is not a thief.' God, the look on her face when I all but accused her, I won't forget that for a while. 'This fact is not negotiable.'

He laughs again, ironically: 'Nothing in there to steal anyway. Unless you want my old pan and sifter, or the quarter of mutton hanging under the tank stand – or my old pal, Gray. And you don't want Gray, no sir, you don't. He's indoors – he don't like folks but me. So don't come too near the house, that's all I mean to tell you.'

'Right.' Each to their own, I suppose. I make an immediate assumption that they are two old prospectors fallen on difficult times, washed up in this backwater after striking it unlucky. I imagine Gray as a pitiful boozer prone to fits of violent melancholy – I've met a few of them washed up in the back lanes of Sydney. 'We'll keep clear of the house.'

As I look over towards it, my gaze travels across the stream, to the other two like dwellings there; long grass grows right up to their doors, one is missing its windowpanes, another its door and half its roof, as if the previous occupants thought they'd take those bits with them when they left, and I ask this man, Amos Scattergood, as if it's not obvious, too: 'You're the only two who live here?'

'Yeah,' he says, 'all moved on but us. Gray didn't eat 'em, I swear.' His laughter thins at this. 'They come and they go, all over these parts, 'cept Gray and me.'

'What brought you here?' I ask him, as one does almost automatically of a fellow curiously displaced, as I am myself.

'Me?' He narrows those sharp blue eyes into mine, a man once handsome, and perhaps not so old as he looks. 'Love,' he says. 'But it was gold in the first instance, o'course. I came over in fifty-three, out of Sacramento, arriving in Port of Melbourne for the goldfields of Ballarat. Same ship as Freeman Cobb, and I gotta say he still owes me twenty from a game of poker on that voyage.'

'Freeman Cobb?' I say the name aloud in part to determine whether or not this is a real conversation I'm having or merely a hallucination extending forth from the dunny at the back of the Hit Or Miss Hotel – Freeman Cobb, of course, being the original founder of Cobb & Co and perhaps, in this cul-de-sac of my imagination, a symbol of all that plagues my conscience.

'Yeah, that Cobb.' Amos Scattergood nods with some reminiscence, perhaps some regret of his own. 'Made his money in three years, sold out, went back to Massachusetts, all pockets a'jangle. Fifteen years later I'm still here and still broke.'

'Goldfields no good to you?' I ask, but I'm looking over at Annie again – I should be helping her with the fire.

'Aw, never too bad, never too good,' he replies. 'We get along all right these days. There's gold in this creek here, but once you've paid your taxes on everything bar your own stinking breath, there's not a lot left. Taxes on candles, taxes on boots, taxes on beer, and that's before they've taxed you for your prospecting right and then more tax for cashing in your gold. Young man, I gotta tell you, I was at Eureka, I fired my pistol across the stockade with the rest o'them, I watched the rebel flag raised above the fray for freedom and democracy. What for? The common man might have his right to vote today, but it ain't much use if he's starvin'. We get along all right, though, yes we do. We ain't starvin'.'

God, but I am. I smile at the man, recalling that he said he had mutton hanging under the tank stand; perhaps he might swap a slice for a sardine. Or for the conversation; I hunt for a line to keep it rolling now. I'm not a voter, never taken my civic duties any more seriously than any other, to Pa's further disappointment – he takes his responsibilities to the common man so seriously, he doesn't allow the fellows at the foundry to work past six pm ever: *Tired men make mistakes, Jemmy. Unhappy ones make them deliberately.* He scrutinises their wages personally, sees to it that they're paid on the dot of Thursday knock-off – because the Talmud says he must. Hm. I ask Amos Scattergood about something I'm less unfamiliar with instead: 'You said you came here for love?'

'Yeah,' he says. 'Frying Pan's been good to us, for sure. We came here after Gray got out of gaol, four, near five years ago now.'

'Oh?' Curiosity slips out ahead of discretion.

But Amos Scattergood doesn't seem bothered at it. 'Yeah. We paid a price for love,' he says, and he explains with breathtaking candour: 'We met in the summer of fifty-nine, Gray was a clerk for the Australasia Bank at the time, and he'd come out to Sofala, where I was whim-driving, working the ponies at Lucky Point mine there, having travelled north myself with the boom of fifty-four. I got two years' hard labour working on the roads, but Gray did his time behind bars at Bathurst hell-hole – a very bad time. The only unnatural thing about it all was the way they beat up Gray in there. He ain't ever recovered. Ain't ever going to.'

'Right.' You poor bastards. I'm in nowise naive to the fact of manly love, nor deaf to the calls of those who want the goldfields 'cleaned up of its abominations' one noose at a time, but I've never met one to admit to it so openly outside the back room of the Cottage of Content lushery up on Pitt Street west – 'going Greek' they call it there. It's a dangerous path to tread, outside of a British public-school gymnasium or dormitory, or occasionally one's own Latin master's room, where my natural lack of obedience for once did me a favour.

'So, you see,' he looks over at Annie, who's crouching to light the fire now, 'we don't want no trouble, either. Right, hey?'

'Of course not.' I suppose he's told me all this to forge some pact of secrecy with me, outlaw to outlaw, but he needn't have. I'm hardly one to throw stones for colonial morality, outlaw or not. I assure him: 'I wouldn't give you up to the police – or anyone like you.'

He says: 'Young man, that's wise of you, and I won't want you sharing what I just told you with your lady friend, but it's not the police that are the ones generally caring about it, I gotta tell you. It's them second-rate, mealy-mouth, middle-class crowd that make every problem known to humanity. The petty boojee-wahzee. They are the enemy of everybody wanting to live free. They hate freedom like nothing else, wanting everyone's life to be miserable as theirs. Taxing everyone for their city footpaths and their paved, blue-metal roads and their prisons. They're the ones chained up in prisons, and they all deserve more'n that, but they don't even know it. For all the years I been here, I've watched them spreading like a pestilence across this land. When I was your age, when I first stepped on this soil, a man could live as he pleased on the road. I thought I got away from them when I left California. But no. They almost killed Gray. Don't you worry about the police, though. They've only got their job to do – they're only doing what the second-raters tell 'em to.'

'Quite.' I think of Inspector-General Fitzworthy, who is both police and staunchly second-rate, and shudder a nod: that man enjoys his job with unnatural alacrity.

Amos Scattergood informs me further: 'Head trooper round here – Slater's his name – he's all right. District Superintendent, he is, but everyone calls him sarge. He's one to leave well alone where no harm's done, and he knows Gray paid bad enough already. A decent man leaves that well alone.'

'Fair enough,' I say, and I look away, with all my own mindless middle-classness and pity for whatever's happened to a man I can't see inside a house not twenty yards from where I stand.

Amos Scattergood leaves me to it, walking off, bow-legged, spry, calling over to Annie: 'There's a fine flame, I gotta say. Not just a pretty face, hey. I'd bet you're the brains behind old spiffy-knickers here, ain't ya?'

She looks up at him from where she is crouching still at the fire. Her curls are tied back from her face with a thread she pulled from her tarp yesterday, made as it is of chaff sacks. Everything about that thought, this girl, her face, stirs me in ways unimaginable before yesterday. Hallucination or not, I am falling more deeply for her moment by moment and at this one making my first realisation that love is not a choice. It's a fact. An outlandish fact.

'Just no-one called Annie Bird?' Amos Scattergood laughs at whatever disconsolate thing she has said of herself, and he tells her: 'You ain't just no-one, little lady. Hey, with that red shirt and them black boots and them pretty dark eyes, you look just like a lady bird. Ha!' He gives himself a clap. 'Lady Bird and The Fox – there's a pair of somebodies, hey. Where you getting along to next? You can tell old Amos. I won't pass it on.'

She glances at me, a look that might slice diamonds for every other outlandish thing that surrounds her, before she asks him: 'You ever heard of a place called Blackman's Swamp?'

The man thinks for a moment, and then: 'Nope. Where's it near?'

She pokes a stick into the fire: 'Nowhere, I don't reckon.' Oh, Annie Bird. Lovely, lost Annie: all that defeats her becomes mine.

And now, as if the stream itself responds, we hear the words: 'Blackman's Swamp is north of the town called Orange.' A well-polished, powerful voice, and it's in fact coming from the hovel behind us: the man called Gray, I presume. 'There was a racetrack there, closed down when the killjoys moved in. That'd be more than a decade ago, I suppose. Always a flurry of banking on those race days, and always a bitter wind.'

Annie Bird leaps to her feet, her eyes wide with hope: 'Blackman's Swamp – it's a real place, is it?'

'Oh yes, it's a place, most definitely,' the voice replies from the darkness beyond an open window. 'Not more than two miles from Orange.'

Annie Bird looks around at the hills, the sky: 'Where's Orange?'

I wouldn't know, apart from it being somewhere generally west of civilisation – we get our copper supply presently from that vicinity, from Mort & Co's Cadia Mine, for our rose-gold. But Amos knows: 'Keep on the Western Road right past Bathurst and you'll get to Orange. Not much more'n forty miles from here.'

'Oh!' The brilliance of her smile tells me I won't be doing any such hasty thing as handing us into the police tomorrow. How could I risk it now? I want to see her face when we find what she is looking for, her grandfather, or whatever answer awaits, for better or worse. I want to be there with her. 'So close! Is it really true?'

'Yeah, true. True as I'm a sad old son of a – a bent-up jigamaree.' Amos Scattergood draws her a map on the dirt with his finger.

'You ever heard of a black man called Kulyan?' she asks him; she asks the map. 'A tracker, he was.'

'Gray?' Amos asks the house.

'Who's that, you say?'

'Kulyan,' Annie says, raising her voice a little. 'My grandfather. He brought the survey men out here, a long time ago, maybe forty years, I don't know exactly when, but he was famous for it, so I've always been told.'

A moment of silence and then: 'No, I'm sorry, I can't say I recall any tracker by that name. There is a famous black buried out that way, though. A man called Yuranigh. There's a gravestone near the village of Molong, twenty miles north-west of Orange, erected in honour of his service to Major Mitchell, the Surveyor General –

interior expedition into what would become Queensland, not so long as forty years ago, but back in the eighteen-forties.'

Amos winks with long affection for his friend: 'Gray knows everything.'

As Annie murmurs into the stream, into me: 'A famous black man ... It's not just a story, is it.'

'Whatever it is and wherever you're going, you might want to stay low anywhere round here,' Amos warns. 'Sarge Slater might be a reasonable man, but he's out for you, and there's the other hundred or so troopers out for you, too, that ain't so reasonable, ain't all decent as him. Less decent'll be the three thousand second-raters of Bathurst wanting to see you swinging from a tree.'

Someone should probably cut the long story short and shoot me now. Instead, I reach into the saddlebag for a settling Grimault's medicinal. Zad flicks me with his tail, but I won't be taking any advice from him, either.

ANNIE

'If I was you, I'd want to get up to the highway at dusk, travel through the night, till you're out the other side of Bathurst,' the old man, Amos, says.

I'm still hearing that California drawl telling me, *Not much more'n forty miles.* Only forty miles, and I'll know where my grandfather is. I'll know where I should be.

'Not going anywhere for a good few hours yet – the horse needs resting,' says Jeremy Fox, offering him one of those herbal cigarettes – those fancy things that smell like perfumed manure, I don't know how anyone could smoke them.

But the old man nods at the label on the box and says, 'Well, don't mind if I do.'

They stand there puffing away as I check the water for the tea, not yet boiling, the old man saying, 'We'll send you along with some vittles for the road, see you through.'

'That's very generous of you,' Jeremy Fox replies, and as he takes the saddle from the horse, checking him over for any soreness from the day, they fall to talking about the creature's hardy build and fine breeding.

I fall to thinking about generosity, about the way righteousness is found in places unexpected, the wisdom of the prophet Amos of Judah coming to me, the lowly farmer trumpeting against the mighty: *They sell the just man for silver, and the poor man for a pair of sandals. They trample the heads of the weak into the dust of the earth, and force the humble out of the way.* Your ways, Lord, are strange. But having me mistaken as a bushranger? Why are you giving me this guise?

'Ten mile on,' Amos in the here and now is saying, 'at the village of Kelso, you'll come to the river – the Macquarie – she's high, you won't miss her, and that'll be Bathurst just on the other side. You'll have to get the ferry across, though – bridge got washed off its piers in the floods, and the new one ain't yet finished.'

'We've got nothing to pay a ferryman with, I'm afraid,' Jeremy Fox replies, and at the whole load of nonsense in these words, fear and doubt strike at me once more. What am I doing here at all? Whatever happens, this is going to be a disaster upon a disaster.

But the old man Amos has it all worked out: 'You won't need no money. You go straight to the Goose & Gander Inn right there at the crossing,' he tells Jeremy Fox. 'Don't worry – it's a safe house, free of varmints. Ask for the ferryman called Bobby McNeil, big guy with a red beard, and when you find him, tell him I sent you. He'll see you across the river, as a favour to me. But careful, the town comes up quick from there at the other side. You'll hear the metal of the road ringing under that pony's shoes – keep to the sides of the road where you can.'

'Where's the Cobb & Co situated?' Jeremy Fox asks. 'It's important we avoid it particularly, for the time being.'

We. I don't want to travel a mile further with this man, madness and misfortune following wherever he goes, but I don't want to travel alone, either, with only my own madness and misfortune for company.

The old man laughs: 'Avoid Cobb & Co in Bathurst? Bathurst *is* Cobb & Co: you got the biggest coaching house in the country right there – the stables and the carriage works, the offices, plus the Prince of Wales Hotel where they put up all their passengers. All the bullock drivers for the overland wool trade come in through there, too, and all the traffic of the mining trade – that town never sleeps. It's the police court you'd be best avoiding altogether.' He draws another mud map on the ground, to show the way through the streets. Then he says: 'Black out that white marking on your horse's forehead, bit of charcoal'll do the trick, and whatever you do, don't wear that hat no more.'

'You don't like my hat?' Jeremy Fox laughs back at him, that lazy laugh: does he take nothing seriously? He takes his hat off and pushes his hair away, making sure he's still handsome.

'It suits you very well, young man,' the voice from the window says; the mysterious Gray. 'But I must agree with Amos. You might attract all sorts of unwanted attention if you wear it any further west.'

And now the three of them are laughing, at what I don't know.

But I burst out begging: 'Mr Fox, please. This isn't fun. I want you to take me only as far as Bathurst, as we'd agreed. You take that horse in to the Cobb & Co. Tonight. If you go on with him, then it *will* be stealing you've done – no question about it. Take him back and take in that gun, tell the police what's really happened, and what's going to happen —' when the real bushranging friends of Mr Amos California bail up the Gold Escort. 'Please, Mr Fox, do your best to clear my name with yours, tell them I'm no thief. But I'm telling you, I'm going on to Blackman's Swamp alone.'

'Alone?' Jeremy Fox stops laughing. 'No. That's simply not going to happen. I'll take you on to your grandfather first, or at least to a place of safety, then I'll put my hands up and clear your name. Besides, I need someone to hold my hat.'

He sounds so very sure of himself, but I can't trust him. I want to but I can't. His beard has grown a little to make those flash-Jeremy side whiskers disappear into it, to make the scratch I put there disappear as well, and make him – oh. He might be my only friend in the world, but he's – oh. He's a man given to self-admiration, too much cheer and getting about without his shirt. I tell him plain as I can make it: 'Hold your own hat. I don't want you to come with me.'

'What you want is beside the point, Miss Bird.' He frowns, showing the spoilt boy he is. He says: 'My faults are many, but a lack of chivalry isn't one of them.'

He stares at me, taking a deep draw on the last of his cigarette. I stare back at him.

He says: 'What are you going to do from Bathurst – walk?'

'Yes. Why not? It must be only thirty miles or so from there.'

That sounds stupid even before he says: 'On those ruined feet? I'm not having that on my conscience to add to everything else.'

'Well, you can lend me your socks, then,' I say, heels too sore to dig in anywhere.

But he says, 'No,' anyhow. 'That offer was rejected, and it's since been withdrawn.'

'Oh?' He is too smooth for his own good. I tell him: 'Have it your way, then. Take me to Blackman's Swamp. But if I end up in prison, it's your fault. If I end up hanged —'

He smiles like he never frowned. 'None of those things are going to happen, either. My father might well make me rot behind bars for a time for this, I might even deserve it, but he won't let any terrible thing happen to you when he hears of your situation. He is a true gentleman, the clean deal, and he's a soft touch. Trust me.'

No. And stop asking me to.

His voice is the softest, most gentlemanly sound I've ever heard, as he says: 'I won't let any harm come to you, Miss Bird. I promise. I'd rather be hanged myself.'

But it's burning me from the inside out and I turn away to pick the billy up out of the fire, the scalding line of heat across my finger where the handle slips down off my stick a welcome place to fix my mind.

'Finished up your lovers' quarrel, hey?' the old man Amos is saying. 'Time to eat, yessiree. I made some raisin buns yesterday – I'll go get 'em.'

Lovers. I nearly spill the whole of the tea canister into the water.

And Jeremy Fox starts laughing again, beside me. He says: 'I was going to make you that cup of tea – honestly, I was. But I'm glad I didn't promise you one of those. I'm sorry, but I think I'm a bit shredded.'

'Shredded?'

'More than the usual quantity of medicine in that lot of herbs, I think.' He throws the end of the cigarette into the fire. 'Very relaxing. Shredded and ready rolled, I am. You should try it sometime.'

'Not likely.'

*

I don't talk to him for the rest of the afternoon, mostly because he fell asleep under a tree and snored until near to dusk. That's how relaxing hemp mixed with devil's snare weed can be, so Amos Scattergood told me: his friend Gray used to smoke those cigarettes all the time before opium became a more effective treatment for his ailments. No, I don't talk to Jeremy Fox the whole ten miles to Kelso and the river, either.

'I am perfectly sober now,' he says, as he's said several times. 'Straight as a circle laid out – honestly.'

Honestly, if I get through Bathurst alive – not drowned or shot or hanged or ended in a fatal fit of nerves – I might reply to him.

At least the highway has been easy enough to follow. The moon is bright, and it's high and shining on the water when I see it: the Macquarie River. I wonder what my grandfather calls it, and as I think this my heart aches for my home, for Castlereagh, for the Nepean, for the river of my mother. A picture slips through the dark like smoke: she is showing me where the swans hide their eggs; she is telling me something about all the different languages that once were here. Once upon a time. *What* languages? *Where?* The memory slips away for another: standing out the back of the house most nights with Dad while he had a pipe, silver all through the water, silver all through Dad's beard and welling in his eyes as he talked and talked of her. I'm homesick. But I have no home, not anymore. *Honestly*, how can this be? The grief catches me again: I want my dad's arms around me. I can't believe he's gone.

'Wait here while I find the McNeil fellow – I'll be as quick as I can,' Jeremy Fox tells me quietly through this shimmering dark, through the soft shadows of posts and chimney pots and a glow of camphene behind dirty glass, leaving me here, wherever here might be, as he goes into the inn.

I can feel the heartbeat of the horse through my hands and my knees, as I listen to the water shooshing through the reeds so near. I close my eyes. I wish I knew what it was saying. I wish the river could truly speak to me.

JEM

'Get the young feller a beer, will ya!' this ferryman McNeil says to the bar on deciding who I am. 'It's the Fox we've got in here tonight! Get a look at him!'

This is not the place to plead innocence as a roar of approval erupts from the tight-squeezed Saturday-night crowd, but I must decline the beer: 'Please, we don't have much time. The police are in pursuit.' Or they will be if you shout my name loudly enough into the night.

'Fuck them.' McNeil lets go of the back of my collar for long enough to lean across me for the beer, shoving it at me, spilling a good deal of it down the front of my waistcoat. 'There's always time for one.'

What can I do? The barmaid leans her plump agreements on the bar at me: 'On the house, Foxy love.'

I drain the glass as the tight-squeezed chat resumes around me, a concertina singing softly somewhere beneath the din, and a chap at my back saying to another, 'It's collusion, I tell you – the banks and the government are in on it together. You know how much the mint made on the gold got from our waste last year? More than ten thousand pounds, and we don't see a penny of it.' His mate says: 'Jesus, strike a light. That's not a tax, that's theft.'

Sounds like it to me. Ten thousand pounds' worth of free gold, and I know for a fact that it's possibly more like fifteen. It's not right; there's an argument that says all that waste gold should at least be spent on improving the state of the roads, one that Pa raised in query once with the under-secretary for finance and trade last year, but it's somehow perfectly legal that it just seems to disappear into the coffers. Like this beer – it's lovely. I have to ask McNeil: 'Is this a local drop?'

'Aye – Maggie O'Meara's, upriver at White Rock,' he says, swaying in his boots as though he might have shares in the company.

'Go on, have another one, love.' The barmaid has a few shares, too, her right hand permanently attached to the tap.

'Not tonight, thanks.' I shake my head, although another would be very good. Annie Bird is concerned enough as it is. I don't need to earn further opprobrium by getting drunk as well, or by staying more than five minutes in here, leaving her alone out there in the dark.

'Stay for a game!' McNeil insists, holding up his fistful of darts. He's at least half boiled or permanently pickled – the colour of his nose just about matches his beard, even in this light – and as much as the idea of a quick game and a second pleasantly wheaty brew is attractive, I have to say: 'I'm really very sorry, Mr McNeil, but time is of the essence.'

'Mr McNeil!' he bellows across the room. 'Did you hear what the lad called me – *Mr* McNeil!'

The room erupts again with shouts of, 'Come off it!' and 'Pull the other one!'

Can't we get on with it? No, not quite yet.

'Come on.' McNeil claps me on the shoulder: 'Stay for another one – and the name's Bobby.' Because this is a workingman's pub, no misters in here – we could be anywhere dockside in Sydney on any Saturday night. The good folk of the Goose & Gander at Kelso are only interested in drinking and gaming and shagging, and possibly a politically ignited brawl among chums at around about midnight. How bitingly apt that this is all so inconvenient to me now.

Look, Pa – I'm telling McNeil the most virtuous lie I've ever told: 'I promise I'll make an all-nighter of it on my way back through, but right at this moment, I really need the ferry across.' And follow that with possibly a dangerous one: 'Black Jack Holly is expecting us.'

'Oh. Black Jack?' He gives me a regretful nod, and the room is momentarily hushed at the mention of their outlaw hero. 'Right y'are, then, young Fox, we'd better be off.' And at last he smacks his glass back down on the bar, reaching next for his cap by the door, and screwing it onto his woolly red head.

In a stride he's out the door, and the crowd is shouting behind me as I follow: 'Go get 'em, Foxy!' and, 'Get what you can from the bastards!' and, most obscurely from the back of the room, 'Bring Jack back with ya next time so I can punch his fucken head in, will ya?'

This is, without a doubt, the most extraordinary thing that has ever occurred to me in a pub, or possibly anywhere. Who am I to these people? Some sort of Dick Turpin, sticking it to the nobs who tax their beer and exploit their efforts at gold-getting? 'Go get one for us, Foxy!' another shouts as I close the door behind me, as if one might do something to reduce the rights fees and duties they pay per ounce by robbing the bankers who rob from them. Would that anyone could, poor beggars.

I ask McNeil, in his verandah-smashing wake: 'Tell me, what is it that I'm supposed to have done that you think is so marvellous?'

'What have you *done*, lad? Giving one to the Cobb & Co, for starters.' The man punches his own chest and belches. 'Bastards come into town and take over – they put the little feller out of business, undercutting on price. It's a misery for anyone in the business of transport what is not with Cobb & Co. I won't take their trade. Flash Yank syndicates – they'll fuck the whole world one day if we let 'em have it. Fuck them.'

'Fair enough,' I say and add: 'But you might want to rein in the language from this point on – I have a lady with me.'

'You do?' he says. 'Would that be your Lady Bird?'

Good God, but these people truly are connected by some supernatural network – unless, of course, a spy was hiding among the shrubbery at Frying Pan to hear Amos Scattergood dub Annie 'Lady Bird' before riding on to Kelso to spread the word, and be a hardly less improbable explanation.

'You've been drinking?' I hear Annie now, at the verandah's edge.

'I had one beer,' I admit into the dark there as my eyes haven't yet adjusted on stepping back outside. I can't see Zad, either, though I hear him shake his head, but as McNeil strikes a match to his lantern, I can see well enough that they're both annoyed, and that McNeil is laughing to himself, mimicking her: '*You've been drinking?*'

Annie sighs, a tremor in her breath, as I promise her: 'I only had one, just to be sociable – I could hardly say no.' But she looks away; I suppose she has returned to not speaking to me at all. Yes, I'm embarrassed about having slept like a bag of bricks all afternoon, won't do it again – not the crime of the century.

McNeil waves us along a pathway down the riverbank towards the jetty, dragging a boy with him as he goes – 'Wake up, box o'rubber nails, y'are' – then he jumps onto the ferry-barge there to light the lamps, calling out something unintelligible by way of instruction to me. Looking downriver, I see there's a surprising amount of traffic on the water – little lights, all hovering back and forth, the remains of the ruined bridge behind them all, gaping at the darkness like a broken jaw.

Just as Zad begins picking his way onto the barge, McNeil trips over his ropes, hitting the deck with a thump, and Annie is sighing again: 'Might be better if I swam across – it's not more than twenty yards.'

I snort: 'Well, then you really would be on your own, Miss Bird – I can't swim to save myself.' Unless you include bobbing around Fig Tree baths that evening last summer, as nude as I was blind, with a girl called —

She clicks her tongue in further disgust, but if she wants to get rid of me she really shouldn't do things like that, for the more contempt she shows me, the more I want to prove her wrong about me. The more I simply want her.

A want that is abruptly suspended as we set out across the river. The barge lurches drunk as its master and I am altogether consumed by a desire to avoid being tipped into the drink; Zad, too – he shifts his weight uncertainly, and we lurch around some more. I'm far too sober for this. McNeil, however, is unconcerned, as he sings at the top of his voice in time with the strokes of his punting pole:

'There was a wild colonial boy, Young Foxy was his name.
A flash but honest lad he was and born in old Tremaine.
He was his father's shining hope, and some'n I can't recall.
He loved his little Lady Bird and hooray cheers to all!
So come along me hearties, we'll range the mountains high,
Together we will plunder, together we will ride!
We'll scar o'er all valleys, and gallop for the plains,
And scorn to live in slavery, bound down by iron chains!
Hooray, hooray! Hooray!'

Belch.

Annie murmurs a prayer under her breath and I hold mine as we veer towards a somewhat larger craft that's suddenly appeared alongside us, its bell ringing urgently, entire carriage and team of four upon it.

McNeil waves to the ferryman there, ringing his own bell, turning around to tell us: 'There's the night coach, Cobb & Co. She runs on the cable way, and can't get away from me. Ha-ha! I like to give her driver a bit of a scare, don't I.' He shouts at the helpless driver now: 'Watch where yer going! Fuck ya!'

Our barge bashes into something else – the footings of the jetty at the other side. Thank Christ. I thank Bobby McNeil, and urge Zad off the barge as fast as he will take it, then up the marshy bank beyond.

'Don't hold me so tight,' Annie hisses.

I have her trapped between my elbows and not merely to enjoy the traces of orange blossom that remain in her hair; I hiss back: 'I'd rather you didn't fall onto the road.'

'We're not on the road,' she says. 'The road's up there.' She points ahead. 'You can't see it, can you.'

No, not yet. I resist telling her I don't possess the keenness of vision she does – that of an untamed grimalkin.

But soon enough, a lamp lights the way: a handsome double-storied place, perhaps a boarding house, followed by a cottage row, and then the town begins to appear, tin roofs reflecting the moonlight, Zad's shoes clashing on gravel. We keep to the right-hand edge of the road here, where it's unpaved, and creep steadily past the tall buildings that emerge at the centre of the town, brick terraces, a shopping arcade, an enormous bank, and up to the left an even more enormous pub. The Prince of Wales Hotel, it can only be: great suspension lamps hang from the ceiling, illuminating a multitude of Amos Scattergood's second-raters inside, all carousing and dancing in their Saturday-night finery. Saloon doors swing, men smoke on the balcony above, and jolly shouts are made all around; none in the least bit interested in us.

'Keep on going,' Annie hisses now, and I hear in it that she is frightened. 'You're supposed to keep on straight past the big hotel.'

'Yes.' I get Zad moving a little more briskly, and I hold Annie a little tighter for the flicker of my own fear as well. I am sneaking through the night, avoiding Bathurst Police Court and its prison just two streets away to our left here up from this hotel; I am, beyond all reasonable doubt, a horse thief from this moment on, at least on the face of things. Zad clips the edge of the road again proclaiming my guilt across the town, but it's only another few minutes before Bathurst begins to vanish behind us, before cottage gardens become bush once more. I can smell it rather than see it: that heady scent of eucalyptus and – Annie in my arms ...

'Truly, please, I mean it – stop squashing me so tight,' she says, and I relent. I let her go, and relax my hands at the reins as well. The road is obvious here anyway, even to me, under this moon: a white trail through the blackness, tossed like a lost ribbon over the hills.

We're to go on another eight miles, past three sets of stately homestead gates, the sheep stations of the district's wealthiest squattocracy, looking for the one called Donnybrook, the name wrought in iron, after which, we were told, we will find another creek and the place to stop until dawn. A creek itself called Donnybrook – the name of which actually does bear direct relation to its location in this instance because, as Amos also mentioned, and as legend has it, two men 'beat the living bawjeepers out of each other there over the claim'. Naturally.

We haven't passed the first of the gates, though, when out of the silence, Annie says: 'I know you're taking a terrible risk for me, and I don't know why you would, but you should know that

I'm grateful for your helping me, Mr Fox. Even if it feels like I've been kidnapped by a madman, I'm grateful for the trouble you're going to.'

I smile with this small but delicious victory: 'Call me Jem. Please.'

She calls me nothing; but then, after another long while, she asks me: 'Do Jews believe in Heaven?'

'That's an odd question,' I must say; I immediately suppose that, like most Christians, she thinks, as legend has it, we're blood-sacrificing heathens who'd sell anything for thirty pieces without a care for divine consequences. But let's give her the benefit of some doubt: 'Why do you ask?'

'Can't I be curious? I just want to know,' she says, defensive but insistent. 'Do you believe in Heaven?'

'It's not such a simple question for a Hebrew to answer,' I tell her. I don't tell her I can't honestly say I believe in Heaven, because, well – it'd put her off me without a further word, I'm sure. Instead, I explain what I think she might want to know: 'If you're a Jew, you don't get rewarded for doing what you or any other ordinary person is expected to do; you don't get a prize for being good. Not that I'm any scholar, but as far as I understand it, unless you were born a perfect angel, just about everyone gets sent to Hell for a time after death – it's called Gehinnom and while you're there you have to rake over all the mistakes you made on earth, every angry or unfair word, every cheat, every lie, and then, when you've atoned for it all, you get to go to Heaven – or, alternatively, you get incinerated and struck from the books.'

'Oh? So everyone goes to purgatory first?' she wonders at the night, and it can only be some power of goodness that stops me from kissing the back of her head as she asks: 'How does God decide if you're good enough to go on to Heaven or not, then? How does He decide to forgive you or not?'

'I don't know,' I must admit. 'Perhaps you have to pass an examination – wouldn't be surprised. It's not God's job to forgive, though. It's our job not to do too many things that need forgiving – and, when we do, to beg forgiveness from the people we have wronged,' I quote my father, and the words churn through the pit of my stomach: I will never cause you pain like this again, Pa.

Never. My wild colonial roaming is finished, with this last ride, this last hurrah. I tell Annie some more of what my father has always told me: 'No-one knows what it's like, Heaven, this place we call Olam Ha-Ba, the world to come, no-one knows what really happens to your soul when you die – and the rabbis like to keep it that way. The thing is, you're supposed to be a good person now, today, on earth, because it's the right and reasonable thing to do – not so you'll get rewarded some time later with some kind of never-ending ecstasy or whatever. I've always thought that idea a bit perverse, personally,' I must also admit. 'I mean, imagine being stuck perpetually on the verge and never able to – never mind.' I just save myself from ruining the moment with mention of things I'm sure Annie Bird has little or no idea of, things that say more about me than they do of her innocence: when was the last time I had a conversation of any length or depth with a woman who is not a whore? I have loved every single one of them; and Pa pays their rent. I am only lucky, damn lucky, that God in his vengeance has not given me a venereal disease.

'Hm.' Annie Bird knows well enough what I am without needing the precise details. I can almost feel the way she thinks, the engine that turns her quick intelligence, and after a few more minutes she asks me: 'What's the most important thing for a Jew to do?'

'That's an easy one,' I sigh at my own failure and the answer both: 'Get married and have children.'

I feel her nod, and her hair brushes my chin. She says: 'That sounds normal enough to me, I suppose.'

'Normal?' I laugh into the dark; and so does she. This is my new most favourite sound, this meeting of our souls inside a laugh; fleeting, but some drug in itself.

Then into the silence now she says: 'I've never thought to get married. I always thought I'd work with my dad, on the farm, doing the accounts for him, doing his reading for him, helping in the fields. I always thought I'd look after him.'

Everything about her shames me and astonishes me at once.

ANNIE

I't's so cold as we go on, colder and colder the more we go on, I can't keep from shivering and shaking, though his arms are still around me with the reins. I can see my breath as mist and the moon as a great ball of ice.

We find the gate we're looking for, or I do, since Jeremy Fox is as blind as he is – whatever he is – and we follow the creek away from it, down past a low rubble bridge and off the road, where the old hut we're looking for sits. Like the ones back at Frying Pan, it's not fit for habitation, but I'm relieved to see it – there'll be basic provisions and blankets inside, stowed there for those who know, for those who are hiding from the law. Save me, but I hope I'll be able to unbend my knees to get off the horse and be asleep in this place very soon. I can't even say how sore my behind is, that's how cold I am: I can't feel it. This might well be my grandfather's country, but I don't know how people live here: it's only the beginning of May; what must it be like in the winter?

'The hut.' My teeth chatter at the words; my whole arm shakes as I point at it.

'Where?' he says.

I'm too cold and too tired to explain more than: 'Stop here.'

He does, and after a moment he says, 'Oh yes, I see.' And then, 'Hm. It's a bit chilly, isn't it,' before taking off his coat and wrapping it around me, telling me as he gets down off the horse: 'I won't be a minute.'

I blink at the night, my weariness fast overrunning me; if he doesn't come back, I might just fall sleep on this horse and never mind if I freeze to death.

'Jesus!' He's bashing around in the hut, something crashes with a thud like a falling timber, but then I hear the striking of a match and he's come back out again, carrying a candle lamp. 'Well, that frightened off the rats.'

He sets the lamp down and when he holds up his arms to help me off the horse I fall right into them. I don't care. He's that strong he's gathered my knees to him before my feet touch the ground, carrying me into the hut, and I don't care even more. 'It ain't much but it's home,' he says as he sets me down on a blanket on the earthen floor in this empty falling-down hut, so that all I can feel is the warmth of his breath against my ear, and I especially don't care about that.

It's when he drapes another blanket over me that warmth becomes a flood of heat and I can't pretend I don't care anymore.

I want his arms back around me. But he's gone outside. I close my eyes and let this warm flood take me all the way to blessed sleep.

Until a noise wakes me again, something moving near me, and I feel a weight at my shoulder: *What?* But it's only the tarp: he's unrolled it and laid that over me as well. He places the woolen comforter under my head.

He says. 'I'm sorry, Miss Bird, but it's even too cold for me tonight. Pretend I'm not here.'

I can't say a word as he gets in beside me. I can't say what it is to feel him so near, right here, for I have never felt any such thing before. A warm river flows within me, wanting him to turn to me, to hold me, and it's not likely I'll get much sleep at all now.

JEM

Patience has never been a particular virtue of mine, but let's make it my best if only one now. If I'm going to further stake my future and my father's reputation on the pursuit of this girl – and let's face it, that's why I'm here – then let's do it properly.

Don't touch her. Don't even try.

This is easier said than done. I was made to love. I was also made with the brake off restraint, which is also why I'm here. And why Annie Bird could well be the most perfect teacher luck could ever have sent me, my greatest personal challenge.

One I will lose if I do not play my cards right.

Yes, patience, so necessary to the long game, isn't it? And this is one game I'm going to win.

ANNIE

He's snoring within minutes, leaving me to count out all the long hours with every other mystifying thing about him. What happened to that warm river? The man can't even swim – what kind of a man is that? And when I've counted around every bit of him a hundred times, I start counting out all my grief, around and around and around. I wonder if Sis has even given me a thought. I wonder where my teacups are, if they're still on the dresser or if they've been thrown away. I worry I'm going to find nothing and no-one at Blackman's Swamp or anywhere for me. I worry that I probably won't be able to go to church tomorrow, that I won't be able to repent for any of my sins before I'm arrested by the police. I worry about everything until I am too tired to sleep.

I worry that Jeremy Fox is taking such a senseless risk on my account: why is he doing this? Just because he can do as he pleases? Too rich, too spoilt, to care, so long as he's being well entertained? He only snores louder and deeper. I want to shove him in the back, the way I would Sis, to make him stop: it can't be good for you to snore like that. But I don't want to touch him, because if I do, I'll starting thinking about wanting him to hold me again.

As the sun comes up it fills the doorless doorway of the hut with grey, but I'm grateful to have something else to think about, watching the colours slowly brighten with the ordinary miracle of every day. The green and gold of the hills here roll and roll away to the west like ripples from stones thrown into water; the sky is huge, deep blue opening with a crack of pink above the land. And the earth all along the bank of the creek I can see is that same rich, dark red. I want a piece of this country. I want this soil under my feet, under my fingernails, like it's already somehow mine.

As if any land could ever be mine.

All those years Dad worked those acres at Castlereagh, land that belonged to my mother's people before it belonged to the Webbs, and there's nothing to show we might ever have been there at all. Dad would always shrug away any unfairness: *Tain't a workhouse in Lancashire, my love. Things could be worse.* Yes, they could. But I can feel my mother rubbing the river mud into my little chest, telling me where I belong: *This is your country. All your grandmothers come from this place ...* Now it's all owned by the Queen, by squatters, selectors – all of them thieves.

And my anger, fierce and mad hot, is more terrible than anything. I get up from under the tarp and the blankets and step out for the creek. I need to wash my face in the cold water before I start to cry from it, for if I let myself do that, I might never stop.

But something stops me in every way, in the grass outside the hut: a tail slithering around a rock making its own trip down to the creek. A lizard, a pattern of stripes and diamonds on its scales, the colour of ashes. And it's huge, maybe six-feet long – powerful legs, ferocious claws – I've never see a lizard like it before. It looks right at me and a different shiver comes: not from fear or cold, but the hugeness of everything I don't know.

The horse stamps a hoof up near the hut, and I look back over my shoulder. I look at Jeremy Fox, but he hasn't moved. He is a beautiful man, and not just in his appearance. He's sleeping in a doorway, for me. I'm still wearing his special-order tweed. Jeremy. Jem. I whisper his name in my thoughts, if a thought can be whispered, and I reckon I know one thing. I've got to get rid of him before I don't want him to go.

I turn away to look for the lizard again, down at the creek, but like the truth, like any wisdom that might guide me, it's gone. It's vanished back into the bush.

*

I can't even get back up on the horse without help, without his touch.

And as soon as I feel it, his hand around mine, bringing me up to the saddle, I tell him: 'I want to go to church. You don't have to come.'

'I don't mind,' he says behind me. 'I haven't been to church in years.'

'You've been to church?' I don't know what I'm saying for his arms are around me again.

'Unavoidable if your father wants to send you to a decent school,' he says. 'Church of England.'

'Oh.' Of course, that's the way things are – you can't be respectable anywhere if you don't go to some kind of church.

'Although technically, I shouldn't,' he says as we head back up to the road. 'Pa would never enter a house of Christian worship. I've endured these things so he doesn't have to, not that it's done either of us any good.'

There's a cold thought: he's a hypocrite, to go with everything else, and doesn't even care to hide it. *Endured?* That's not a way to speak about another's religion. Respectable and respectful are two different things, aren't they. I suppose Jeremy Fox is neither.

And the first church we come to is empty. The whole Western Road is Sunday-empty, it seems, but this church on this stretch of dusty highway, with its broken window and peeling paint, is something too lonely for words. Gold-rush towns spring up and die like weeds, I've read that a hundred times, but there's a sadness here, even in the humming of the flies. A stillness. Not one bird is singing.

'Can we go a bit faster?' I ask Jeremy Fox.

And he says: 'Not really. Not if we're going to make our distance today. Zad is magnificently hardy but perhaps not so used to long treks one day after another, and under saddle, with a burden of two. I don't want to push him to find out.'

There, he turns my head once more: always considering the welfare of the horse. I look down at his hands holding the reins, against my knees, his skin an even deeper tan today from the sun. His shirtsleeves are rolled, tweed stowed in the saddlebags with his collar and tie, as much from the rising heat of that sun as to avoid drawing attention; my dad's red shirt is folded in there with them. Fancy, uptowny hat has been left behind with Amos Scattergood, a payment for kindness, food and a water can, and without its shade the face of Jeremy Fox is darkening too. When we next stop to rest, I make a special effort not to notice that he becomes more handsome to me with every hour.

It's nearing midday by the time we pass the next town, calling itself Lucknow, a handful of shops, two inns and a big mine with great piles of dug-up dirt behind it. But no church that I can see, and likely the reverend is at his rest anyhow, by now, like everyone else in the town.

Except for distant rifle fire coming from somewhere in these long, round hills.

'Hm.' Jeremy Fox brings the horse to a stop, to listen.

Fear shoots through my every nerve. How I hate the sound of guns. I feel his elbows press against me tight, and I don't mind it at all.

'Oh!' But there is thunder with the firing, the sound of hooves, and then I see: it's a herd of wild horses being chased off up the rise of one of the hills ahead, running for their lives towards the sky.

Jeremy Fox has no trouble seeing them, too; he says, disgusted: 'Nothing like a bit of upcountry hospitality. God gave the wrong animal the power to raise a gun. If there's such a place as Hell, I hope it involves branding irons for those who would harm a horse. Hm.'

I can feel his heart pounding into my back, through my blouse, against the lacing of my stays. I can feel every part of him that touches me and I just want to get off this horse. I don't care if I never see another horse.

Please.

But it's three more slow miles yet until the town of Orange finally comes around a bend and over a winding, skinny creek, and once we see it, all I want to do is go straight to the police station here and give ourselves up. I can't take it – any of it. I'll ask the constable if he's heard of my grandfather when I'm safely locked up in a cell. Put my faith in the law of New South Wales to work out what is true and fair; from there I'll write a begging letter to the Honourable Mr Parkes, since he is our Colonial Secretary as well as Dad's hero, make a plea for justice; I'll write a letter to his *Empire* newspaper as well; I'll write to the Premier and the Governor, too; or I'll just write a letter to myself on my own stubborn snot-stained stupidity at ever having run away from home, from the family I do have, from Sis.

I look over this town, down its wide main street, fresh-gravelled and sparkling. It's set in a broad, flat valley like Penrith, except it's got three, no four, banks, all of them with signs saying, *Gold Exchanged Here*, and a great big emporium in the centre of them, with a post and telegraph office right beside that. Money: that's why this town is here. Though it's Sunday and every shop is shut, everything about this place is busy with money. So smartly dressed is this town of Orange it looks like a painting hung between the hills.

And there's a loneliness here, too, a sadness that grabs at my soul. Something bad happened in this place, I can feel it on my skin, and something bad is going to happen to me if I stay here a minute longer than I must. I am probably hysterical with exhaustion and the rest of it, but I don't want the notion tested to see if I'm wrong. *Don't you go off alone, Annie.* Mother grabs me back to her side, in the forest, somewhere. She says something in her language, and something in mine about all the lonely spirits roaming around. *You stay by me, girl.*

I tell Jeremy Fox: 'I don't like it here.'

He says: 'Hm. I'd like to fire a shot right now just to see if anyone comes out for a look. Someone to ask directions to Blackman's Swamp.' He stops us in the middle of the street and asks: 'Which way is north? Left or right?'

I don't know by what miracle he has survived to adulthood; I tell him: 'Right.'

'Right.' There are several options; five that I can see. He takes the first one, saying: 'Unless you've got a better idea, let's just knock on the friendliest-looking door.'

I'm not hopeful there's any such thing as friendly here, but I don't have any other idea.

Of course this road takes us right by the back of the stables marked Cobb & Co, and of course there are a couple of stable boys there raking the mucked hay. One looks up and waves, 'G'day!'

'Not quite the friendly face we're looking for, hm?' Jeremy Fox murmurs in my ear, all fun to him, all a wonderful excitement, before he waves back at the boys, 'G'day there, young fellers.'

The cheek of him, it's almost something to admire, or would be if I wasn't growing so queasy with every kind of fear I own.

Just as we see people at last, on the corner of the next street. A large group of them, maybe twenty, outside a little weatherboard church, a swarm of Sunday-best lace veils and billycocks gathered on a lawn, children skipping and playing, a pony ride, a ginger beer stall: it's a fete. I stare at the cross above it all, on the gable, and drive my prayer into it: *Please, let the way be plain and simple from here. I only want to know if my grandfather is here.* But still, I'm scared, scared like I have never been. Scared to go into a church; and that's not right, either.

I ask Jeremy Fox: 'Can you go over?'

'Of course,' he says and I feel the gentle smile, the sympathy in his voice. 'They don't look like our sort of people anyway, do they.' He takes us up to an apple tree right by the church, where he gets off the horse and pulls me down after him: 'Stretch your legs. Wait here with Zad.'

I'm not going anywhere else. I'm hunched up like an old woman, hiding behind the horse's shoulder, watching as Jeremy Fox goes straight up to the reverend who's standing near the yard fence by a table of cakes and buns. He pushes back his hair: 'Good day there, padre. Lovely weather for it, isn't it? I'm after some directions, if I may. I need to get to a place called Blackman's Swamp, if you'd be so kind.'

All the people at the cake table stop their gossiping to stare like he asked for directions to the other side of the moon.

And I step back out around the horse to hear the reverend answer in a voice as flat as this valley: 'There's no such place as Blackman's Swamp here.'

That makes the fear fly from me and I beg him with every hope and need: 'Yes, there is. There must be. There was a racetrack there – we were told by someone who knew it himself.'

'A racetrack?' A rosy-faced lady says, cake in hand. She has violets pinned to her hat; silk ones.

'Yes.' I beg her and the violets: *please*. While everyone stares and stares at me: the little black ragamuffin blown in from nowhere for no good. Even the little children stop and stare.

'Well,' says the lady, thinking about it still, 'there used to be a track just this side of Narrambla. Follow this very road here, keep on until you come to the sign pointing the way to Ophir, you'll soon see the creek up to your left and —'

'Listen,' the reverend cuts her off. 'There is no such place as Blackman's Swamp here.' He doesn't look at me at all; he's talking to Jeremy, pointing the finger of 'get' at him, and his anger at our asking is as strange as this whole town. Then he looks at me for a second, he gives me a horrible emptied-out stare, and he says to my feet like he can't bear the look of any other part of me: 'Why don't you go off somewhere out past Molong, out past Wellington – perhaps what you're looking for is *there*. But I am afraid it is not *here*. Keep to the Western Road, that is what I would advise.'

I don't believe him. Blackman's Swamp is here somewhere, but he doesn't want me to know. Why? He doesn't want black fellers going there? I don't understand, and I'm not going to get an answer from him. I look away, back towards the main street, over this wide, wide valley and all the hills around, out to a craggy mountain lying like a giant lizard to the south-west, and somewhere deep in my bones, I know like I have never known anything before: my grandfather was born somewhere here. This is where he lived. Where he walked in his possum-skin cloak. This is *my* country.

And I'm going to this Narrambla place to see for myself: see how emptied out of black it is. I start walking, and in a fury. Such fury that I don't know any pain.

JEM

'Miss Bird – Annie – wait, please.' I go after her.

But she won't stop. 'Leave me alone. Go away.'

She wipes her nose with her sleeve as she goes striding up the road, and I can hear in the tremor of her breath that she's crying.

'I said go away!'

How can I? Who could? I don't know what to do with a distressed girl at the best of times, but it's important I do something now. This is horrendous. She is smashing me with her distress.

'I don't ever want to see your face again!' she yells as she keeps striding on up the road.

I wish there was something else I could do apart from follow her dumbly and wince at the thought of her poor ruined feet in those boots with every step, but I don't know that there is, short of turning around to give thanks to that priest with the back of my hand, and what would that achieve? One man's bigotry is another's tragedy, and I've never struck another man in my life. Best to move along and get on elsewhere: my own race makes its way along that very principle, while the worst tragedy I can remember having ever personally known, apart from being ripped away from London and shoved out here, was losing my first horse, Bon-Bon, to gripes just after my bar mitzvah. By comparison, I am beginning to suspect I don't know anything much of tragedy or bigotry to offer a word about it to Annie Bird. No-one has ever told me the place I'm looking for or the place I think I'm from doesn't exist, even if territorial rights have been variously disputed for near two millennia. This is beyond the pale. That priest might as well have beaten her away, and for what? I look at her and I see only an outrage of loveliness; what does he see? Zad rears his head as we walk; yes, I am dragging on his bit, and I can better tell one hide from another than one skin; as I can only follow Annie now, until she chooses to stop.

Which happens when we find Narrambla, about two miles later. No sign that any racetrack was ever here, we see only a flour mill, sitting in a perfectly green paddock by a perfectly trickling stream, with a perfect collection of white-washed buildings and grazing cattle ranged around its white-washed chimney stack. All is still and silent for this Sabbath's long afternoon. Even the forest that surrounds this place appears neat, clipped, held back. I feel her heart crack.

She turns to me. Her face is streaked with dried tears run through the dust of the road. She says, hand on her hip, chin out: 'I want to go to Molong. I want to see the gravestone there, where the famous black man is buried. Then that'll be enough. Then I won't care anymore.'

*

'Black feller's grave?' The publican at this inn at the far edge of the town gives me one of those peculiarly inscrutable Australian squints that could say he's considering your question or considering whether he might want to punch you in the head.

'Yes.' I serve him my best bosh: 'I'm making investigation of it for the Governor, the Earl of Belmore.'

'Right,' he says, very, very slowly, and then: 'It's up at Gamboola.'

'Gamboola?'

'Yarp.'

This conversation could take a year, and almost does. By the end of it I've learned Gamboola is a sheep station twenty miles off, on this side of Molong, a four-thousand-acre run lately purchased by a grazier called Smith who, 'seems a fair sort a' feller'. Meaning he won't shoot on sight? Let's not ask.

I thank him, keen to get back out to Annie, where I've left her with Zad, who's at the trough gathering his fortitude, but the publican wants to know: 'Not having a drink today?'

'On my return,' I promise and his squint follows me out.

'Or we could just turn ourselves in right now,' Annie says when she sees me, so that I promise her: 'Tomorrow.' Because I must have one more night with her. This can't end here, not in such defeat.

I urge Zad on for a burst and we're there well before the sun sets: 'Gamboola' painted in pragmatic fashion on the face of a wooden gate, a homestead of timber and tin set another half a mile from it on the side of one of these interminable hills. Two dogs run out to greet us, barking and leaping about: the happiest beings I've met in a while.

'Afternoon!' Smith, I presume, rises from his verandah, where he's enjoying a beverage with a confrère. They wear moleskin trousers and beaten felt slouches, but there's an air of privilege about them, comfortable in their cane chairs, drinking straight from their bottles. What I wouldn't give.

And I wouldn't dare. Annie has straightened her spine again, her knuckles white on the pommel; she hasn't said half a word for hours, and I'm sure she's bracing for further unpleasantness now.

But the squatter type is smiling, raising his hat: 'All well? What brings you this way?' An English, public-school accent bevelled only a little by its transplantation here – possibly not unlike mine.

'Afternoon!' I reply, just about falling off the horse with the relief one feels upon finally finding something or someone recognisable. I'd rather not lie to him but I must: 'Jeremy,' I give first name for last. 'Making investigation of a grave I believe you have here on your property, for Belmore. The grave of a black tracker.' Whose name I have forgotten, please don't ask me.

'Interesting,' he says, shaking my hand. 'It's not far, back across the other side of the road, at the front paddock there, beyond the first rise. But join us for the moment, won't you? I can't say I know much about the black's grave as yet. Tell us all about your investigation.'

No chance. He glances at Annie, up in the saddle behind me; gives me a curious one: 'But you've brought your own guide, I see.'

'Interpreter,' I say. God, hang me.

He smirks: 'Yes, indeed I see.'

No, indeed you don't.

He says: 'The old sheds are over that way, too – on the southern boundary, you'll see. Make yourself at home. No-one to disturb you.'

'Much appreciated,' I say.

He says: 'Enjoy your gin.'

Some men do need a punch in the head, and I was formerly one of them.

Annie stares straight past the lot of it, still grasping the pommel. I look Zad over as I start leading him back towards the gate: he's not much more impressed, having done fifty miles today, possibly more. It's Annie who needs the apology most, but I don't know how to begin it. We're crossing to the paddock over the road by the time I settle on the utterly inadequate: 'I would never think of you that way, you must know.'

'Good,' she says. 'Because if you ever did, I would curse you to Hell for ten thousand years.'

Fair enough.

The low sun is casting an amber sheen across the bare paddocks, across a dam, making it appear a lake of molten gold, quite a vision, but Annie clicks her tongue: 'Look at this soil – ruined. Next heavy rain and the loam will all be washed away. Sheep are their own disaster.'

I'm only cheered she's speaking again, and now leaning forward on the saddle, pointing at a stand of trees: 'There.'

ANNIE

Among the trees, inside a low and rusted fence, the grass almost as tall as the headstone, here it is. I jump down from the horse without thinking, I'm scrambling so urgently to see.

The headstone tilts backwards, long weary, like me. The stone looks to be crumbling here and there, like it's old, but it's not that old, and the crumbling isn't crumbing: it's bullet holes.

I can read the inscription clear enough, though:

> *To native courage, honesty and fidelity,*
> *Yuranigh, who accompanied the expedition of*
> *discovery into tropical Australia in 1846 lies*
> *buried here according to the rites of his*
> *countrymen and this spot was dedicated and*
> *enclosed by the Governor-General's Authority*
> *in 1852.*

I drop to my knees. This isn't a headstone. It's a monument. I put my hands flat on the ground, the better to feel this earth, to hear it telling me: *Yes, this is your country.*

Hold your head up, Annie.

When I do, I see the carvings made into the trees that circle this place. I've never seen such things before, but I know what they are: something special. Something important. I get up off my knees and look at every one: patterns cut into their trunks where a slice of the bark has been cut away: stripes and waves and diamonds.

I might not know their meaning, but they give me a truth I'd never thought I'd find. This Yuranigh, his countrymen and these government men, they were friends. A truth I never hoped for.

I look around and see Jeremy Fox, standing outside this ring of trees, watching out for me: he really is my friend. And friends don't need to make sense: they just are. Almost twenty years old and I've never had one before.

And that's enough for me. That's worth knowing.

I tell him: 'Thank you. Thank you for bringing me here.'

JEM

'M y pleasure.' It's the girl that's supposed to feel faint, isn't it? What is she doing to me? Every time I think she's left me gasping, she takes astonishing to a new height. I can't know what is so affecting about this place for her, but I know that I never want to be without her – anywhere. How could this have happened? How can I ensure that it *continues* to happen? I'm lost for a line again; all I can think of is: 'Right, then. What would you like to do now?'

'Go home,' she says, 'whatever that might be when I get there. I'll go back to my sister, Cecily. She'll be with her feller, Mickey. He's decent enough, a tanner, and he has a place at Yarramundi, on the river. Or I hope that's where my sister is – it's where I left her. I'll go back and face that Mrs Webb with the truth as my defence, because that's all I can do. I'm ready for it.'

Over my dead proverbial you'll go and live with a tanner in Yarramundi, wherever that is, but I say: 'I meant more immediately.'

'Oh.' She smiles, God but she can smile, as she decides: 'Make a fire and watch the sunset.'

So that's what we do. She selects a spot back over by the dam and we make a fire there; we watch the trees turn black against a pink sky. We eat what's left of our supplies, whatever they might have been. I put my coat around her shoulders as night descends and I leave my arm resting there, holding her beside me as the fire plays along the copper that curls through her hair.

I want to kiss her like I want nothing else on earth. But I can't risk it. These stakes are now dizzying. I could almost laugh at not knowing what to do with this girl, her closeness, her everything.

What I'd like to do is whisk her off to the nearest inn for their best room. I calculate that Molong is only a couple of miles off and that I could perhaps trade the Deane & Adams revolver for a bed somewhere there. It's a fine piece, if a little antique, a little sticky in the cylinder; a little useless for anything much but show or blowing a couple of your own fingers off in the attempt, and only two bullets in it anyway. I want to run away with her – anywhere – but it's far more certain to be on the cards that I'll be handing over that gun to some country constable tomorrow morning and saying, *Before you blow my kneecaps off, let me explain ...* Unless by some extraordinary stroke and continued denial of conscience I can keep travelling with Annie Bird, just until —

'Jeremy,' she says.

And I say: 'Hm?' She called me Jeremy. She is the ace, the pearl, the prize nonpareil.

She says: 'Whatever happens, we'll always be friends, won't we?'

No. Not friends. Not if I can help it. 'Hm.' My voice cracks. 'Always.' Cracks again. 'Friends.'

She says: 'I'm sorry I told you to go away earlier, when I was upset. I'm sorry I've been so rude and ungrateful the whole time. It's been a hard time, a hard shock mixing up all my senses, but I can see things more clearly now.'

She touches my leg mid-thigh and I will die if I can't have her: my heart is going to give way. I stare at her hand on my leg, to try to still the rush. If I am earning points of restitution by resisting temptation, my slate must be gleaming tonight.

Stars dance in drifts across every inch of the obsidian sky; I see its domed immensity above us, as if we ourselves are set inside a stone we cannot comprehend. I could remark that I have never known such clarity of mind myself, never been so sober, except that I have never been so intoxicated as I am at this moment. I glimpse infinity as she falls asleep under my arm, against my chest.

Yes, this is Heaven. And it's as uncomfortable as I ever imagined it would be.

ANNIE

Being such a light sleeper as I am, I feel him keep hold of me all through the night, here on the tarp laid out on the ground. I sleep longer and deeper than I have in years, probably, and each time I wake I take a moment to pretend this is the way things might always be. Such comfort and peace, he doesn't even snore. But it's just pretend, and this new day will bring us back every cold fact, however it comes.

It starts at dawn with the fire gone dead and his waistcoat buttons pressed against my face. I wonder if there are enough coals still going to make a little soda bread with the bit of flour we have left, but I don't want to get out from inside these arms, not just yet. I think I might have fallen back into some dream when I hear the sounds of men talking, strange sounds, of a language I don't know, but I turn my head and see them: black men, two of them, over the other side of the dam, not ten yards away. And I just about jump out of my skin.

They wear canvas strides and flannel shirts like any man would but no shoes. Tall and slim and fit-looking, they're filling water bottles, washing their faces, like any man would, but my heart starts banging with every bad story you hear about a black man, like they must have stolen those shirts and strides and they're going to club me over the head and drag me into the bush next. Like I've got no black in me at all.

One of them looks right at me, says something I can't understand. And I'm smacking Jeremy Fox's arm: 'Wake up.'

'Hm?' He's slow at it.

The black man speaks to me again but in English this time: 'You right? You good?'

I wouldn't know my own name at this moment, but I think he might be asking me if I'm here in this situation of my own free will; shameful as it is, I nod: 'Yes.'

He nods too, and then he smiles, a big white smile out of the misty light; he laughs: 'We thought you was two fellers.' And he asks me again, putting the smile away: 'You good?'

'What?' Jeremy Fox sits up with a start and takes me with him, but within two seconds he is his cheerful self: 'Oh? Good morning.' Unreal.

I'm patting down my hair like it'll make a difference to the state of me, and the black man is saying to Jeremy Fox: 'Sorry to disturb ya, mister.' Then saying something else in that other language to his mate, words I want to grab at and put in my pocket.

They turn away from the dam now; they're going to walk off.

I scramble up: 'No. Don't go.' I've got a thousand questions to ask them, the first one jumping out before I'm properly on my feet: 'Who are you?'

They stop and turn around; and they look alike, as brothers or cousins do, same shapes about their faces, the one that does all the talking, telling me: 'Johnny and Bandy ...' A name starting with Gunda I can't catch, but another question comes tumbling after it too quick to stop: 'Where are you from?'

'We come off Gumble Creek,' he answers. 'Cattle station. Manager tell us to go away last night.'

'Go away?' *Get off my land.*

'Yeah. Go away 'fore the coppers chase us off. He don't want to pay us.'

'Pay you for what?' I ask him, not wanting the sad answer.

'Work. Stock work,' he says. 'We been droving for him, bring his cattle down country. He said big pay coming for us. He give us nothing. Said we was trouble. So we going back home. But we come by here first to pay respects at the grave.'

I nod; I believe them. I ask him: 'Did you know Yuranigh?'

The man shakes his head: 'Nah. Just come to pay respects.' And then he asks me: 'Are you family?'

'Family? No.' I shake my own head, though I don't know what he means any more than I know what family I might or might not have anywhere in the world.

'Cup of tea?' Jeremy Fox is asking behind me, and I could smack him again to be quiet, for the black man's face hardens at the question.

He says something to his mate and then to me: 'Leave yas to it.'

'No.' I almost run after them. 'Where are you going?'

'Family,' the man turns around. 'Out past —' some name he says so fast I don't know what it is, either. 'Up north, long way, past Wellington, past Dubbo ...' and some river I can't catch the name of, either. He points through the bush. 'Going home.'

Home? Family? Please. I beg him: 'Have you heard of a feller called Kulyan? A tracker – an old man, my grandfather. I've been trying to find him.'

The two men talk to each other in their language for a minute and I'm like the little match girl from that fairytale, looking in the window at the family all having Christmas cake while my feet stay stuck outside in the Russian snow. How I wish I could understand these words spinning through the air around me.

'Where's he from, what family has he got?' the man asks me. 'You know, what mob is he?'

'Mob?' Mob of sheep? Mob of kangaroo? 'I don't know. He's from a place called Blackman's Swamp. He's from here.' I can feel that through my feet still, just as I did yesterday, that I am from here, too – *this* land. Please. Please let it be true.

The man says something 'is big country ... lot of families, lot of mobs.' He gives me another shrug, a sorry shrug, somehow grief to grief.

I ask him just to know one thing: 'What did you call this country?'

He says it carefully so that I can hear: 'Wirradjeree. This country – Wirradjeree.'

'Wirradjeree.' The sound is ten times Christmas, in my mouth, my head, my heart.

He smiles that big smile again, his brother or whoever he is does too, before he turns away once more, saying: 'Good luck, ay.'

I wave at their backs: 'And good luck to you.'

I watch them walk away, through the trees off the track, till they're black lines in the grass, and then they are gone. I look at the rocks that are scattered all over this bit of country like little gravestones everywhere, and the loneliness falls over me again.

Jeremy Fox stands behind me with his hands on my shoulders: 'If your grandfather is to be found, we'll find him.'

I want to shrug his hands off me. I'm not going to find my grandfather. He's disappeared into the bush, like Blackman's Swamp.

I tell Jeremy Fox: 'It doesn't matter anymore. I'm finished looking. It's time for us both to get back to where we should be. Face whatever's coming.'

JEM

'Yes, of course,' I say, all the while thinking, bollocks on toast, no. 'I'll see if I can't get a telegram off to my father from Molong before anything need be faced by either of us, though – call off the dogs.'

You can't just change your mind like this, Annie Bird. No grandfather means I have no extenuating excuse for all my pissing about borrowing horses and inadvertently impersonating bush-rangers. What am I to say for myself? Oh, I was just chasing a girl through the wilds for three days. As much as that would not in the least shock or surprise my father – or Inspector-General Fitzworthy, for that matter – it will do naught for my plea of having placed some greater good before obligation and responsibility, and naught for my need to keep her with me.

'I'd rather head east straightaway,' she says, the voice of resignation and reason. 'We should go back to Orange. It has a post and telegraph, I saw the sign for it when we passed through, as well as a police station and the Cobb & Co. We don't know what's at Molong.'

'Except that it's far closer, only a few miles away.' And I am desperate for time: to find both the reason I am here, one which will satisfy Pa first and foremost, and the means by which to avoid losing Annie. I can't lose her. Desperation meets absurdity and they elope with the only solution presenting itself: can I, across the coming hours, make her fall in love with me enough to say she'll marry me? Say she'll return with me to Sydney, where I will diligently get back to stone-classing and claw-setting, and all will be forgiven. *Marry* me? Did I just think that word? Yes, I did. I've gone outback stark raving. As if Pa would find such a marriage fair swap for all the trouble I've caused, never mind the opinion of the law; as if marriage is something I am capable of undertaking – or even contemplating. But what and how else —

She's turned away, begun folding the tarpaulin, saying: 'Well, all right, but let's get going. We might get a better breakfast at a police station anyhow.' Mutters to herself: 'I even sound like a criminal now.'

'No, you don't.' You sound like the woman I should actually marry. I step towards her, to help with the folding, and as I do, what I think is a stick on the ground between us moves. It's a snake – a bloody snake – and I yell, 'Flaming Jesus Jones!' leaping across it to pull Annie out of its way, and even in my panic at never having encountered a snake at such close range before, I'm pleased with the manoeuvre. Perhaps a native stockman might have handled himself a little more confidently, but it's the thought that counts.

Annie's not at all impressed: 'It's only a red-bellied black, and a baby.' She watches it slip sleepily away towards the dam. 'He'd rather eat a frog than you and your fancy boots. You should know they don't bite unless you frighten them – or blaspheme.'

I'll never blaspheme again.

God, but I won't be sending a telegram to Pa from Molong, either. The town, when we arrive at it a short while later, has no telegraph. It has a pub, a general store, a police station twice the size of them both, and a near-toothless fellow standing in the middle of the road informing us: 'Nah. Corp Cruthers ain't here.'

Cruthers being the local trooper, I presume, and ask: 'Is he far off being here?'

'Dunno.'

'Right.' There's Monday morning in Molong, and hard evidence that fortune can favour the foolhardy when it has a mind to. I ask him: 'Where might I find the nearest post and telegraph office, then?'

'Aw.' He scratches his chin. 'Line don't come through here. Yous've gotta go onta Wellington or back ta Orange, line goes along the Burrendong Road through Ironbarks, or out towards Cudal on the Escort Road to Mrs Kite's, if she's there.'

'Wellington?' Annie asks him before I form another thought. 'How much further on is Wellington?'

'Aw.' The man looks up the road. If he's noticed any oddity in these travellers before him, he's not showing any sign of it. He looks as if he might have just now had his soul dragged out through his arse and served up to him on a plate but he's too far gone to be bothered with it. Eventually, he says: 'Few miles north. Not far.'

Annie turns around to me: 'If it's not far, maybe it's worth the trip, to ask one more time. Just one more time …'

Oh yes. Sterling idea. Let's go on to Wellington and ask after your grandfather there. Well played, Foxy.

She asks the man: 'Are there Aborigines living at Wellington?'

'Yeah. I s'pose,' he says, as apathetic about that as anything else. 'Depends where you go.'

She turns to me again: 'What do you reckon?'

'I reckon we'll go to Wellington today,' I tell her.

I can see all birds homing in to roost there, wherever it is: telegram will be sent mid-noble pursuit, and irrespective of the outcome of further grandfatherly enquiries, I'll be proposing to Annie Bird before we hand ourselves in – no fiancée of mine will be charged with anything, one look at me and it will be decided that she has suffered enough even before Pa steps in. She will say yes to my proposal, or at the very least consider it a future possibility; Pa will be shocked but beard-tremblingly joyous, after he's had a little while to adjust to the idea; the police will not only be grateful for our intelligence on the real criminals, but embarrassed; and Fitzworthy can go and stick his head in a bucket. There's the flush of hearts I'm after.

And timing – good timing – will bring it all to me.

*

I might have been a little rash. Several hours later, through what must be thirty miles of countryside whose undulating monotony is marked only by its increasing treelessness, we finally come to another pub, one singular pub, and it's closed – curtains drawn and doors bolted. I don't blame them. This road is clearly not a well-

172

used line of transport, at least not for humans; it is a stock route; it is the road that God forgot.

'We should turn back.' Annie looks at the abandoned pub. 'I'm worried, and I'm hungry. I should never have —'

'It can't be much further,' I assure her again, although I am insanely famished myself – I could eat my bootstraps soon. I've lost a few pounds of flesh for this girl as it is, but I'll lose a few more. Wellington must be just around the next bend. Surely.

But surely it isn't. Obviously, the further outback you go in this country, the longer the miles become and the more you lose your mind. And the hotter it gets; it's probably only a pleasant seventy degrees, but the ceaseless sun is baking my brain. And multiplying the flies. At least there is plenty of water around, a stream every ten thousand years or so to save us from the tragic fate of Burke and Wills, and we stop at the next.

'This doesn't feel good,' says Annie. 'Please. Jeremy. We should go back.'

Jeremy. I'd do this every day to hear her say my name. I say: 'Honestly, it can't be far now – worse to backtrack than to go on.' I dunk my whole head into the cold water of the stream: what in Christ's name am I doing?

Zad looks at me malevolently as he drinks too: *Ten more miles, idiot – and that's it, I'm done.*

And just as well, for that's about what it is to Wellington, at last. Here we are, in the mid-afternoon, arriving at a town of such extraordinary prettiness I must look over my shoulder to check that we did just travel through some back passage of the Netherworld to get here. A small but perfectly formed oasis of hotels and financial institutions arranged surprisingly stylishly above a broad river, a scattering of ladies promenading upon its high bank under their parasols; a school bell ringing, children running out of a gate; a Chinese carrying a pole strung heavily with fish along this main street. I blink at the scene several times to see that it stays where it is.

For the moment, I can't see any obvious evidence of a post and telegraph; it's an advertisement for Tennant's Ale in the window of the nearest inn that catches my eye and my imagination first, and drags them both to the building beside it: the Bank of Australasia. This is the bank that has all Pa's accounts, and there's my decision made: 'I'm going to see if I can get us some money.' To send a telegram and afterwards order a plate-sized sirloin and seven jugs, and then lie down for quite a while.

'Get some money?' Annie gasps, half delirious herself. 'What do you mean by that?'

'Don't worry, I'm not going to rob the bank,' I assure her, and I'd laugh if I could summon the strength. 'I'm only going to employ a little brass, a little khutspe.'

'You're what?'

'I'm going to charm them,' I say.

She is not less horrified. 'Like a confidence trickster?'

Yes, with any luck, but: 'No,' I tell her, dismounting, 'like my father's son.' I'm going to convince the bank teller in there to give me some cash, at the very least a few coins to send off that telegram to Pa.

'Or we could go straight to the police,' Annie makes an attempt at higher logic.

'No. Not yet. Not until I've sent word to my father.' In case, by chance, we are arrested.

She gazes down at me, her eyes hooded with resentful forbearance; let's not make a proposal of marriage until we've at least eaten something today, hm? I leave her and Zad by the river, in the shade of the willows there, and then drag myself back across the road.

Where I have no trouble whatsoever appearing dishevelled and near distress as I lean on the counter at the bank and inform the neatly oiled and starched clerk behind the bars: 'My name is Jeremy Fox. Son of Solomon Fox, the silversmith and jeweller, George Street, Sydney. Silversmith to the Governor, the Earl of Belmore. You may be aware that there is an impostor abroad pretending to be me – a bushranger in league with the one known as Black Jack. But I am the real Jeremy Fox – and I have been robbed, left for dead, and might have died had it not been for the kindness of a native who brought me here. And so I ask for your kindness now in assisting me to get word to my father by telegraph and advancing me a small sum for food and accommodations until my father may reimburse you for your trouble. Please.' *Please.*

The clerk looks at me uncomprehendingly for a very long moment, but when he speaks his words are careful, deliberate: 'Right. Mr Fox, is it? Good afternoon, then. That's a terrible time you've had by the sounds of it. I suggest you go around to the police station, down here on the next corner. Trooper Donovan is who you need to speak to. He's been out at the diggings today, No Hope Ridge, but he'll be back sometime later this afternoon. You should let him know what happened.'

'Certainly will.' Can't hide the smile, either, at the law being otherwise occupied upon our arrival. 'In the meantime, could you be so kind as to arrange for just a little cash, at least for a telegram to be sent? My father will pay, whatever the cost.'

Another very long moment before he says: 'I suppose it would be all right, if it's so urgent.' He slides a pencil and a slip of paper under the bars: 'Write down what you want to say and I'll take it around to the post office myself.'

'Oh, but I could take it to the post —'

'No.' He looks over my face so slowly he must be counting the hairs in my beard. 'I'll take it for you.'

Right. Don't press it. He's an intense sort, isn't he, but I could kiss his savagely nibbled, ink-smudged fingernails. 'Thank you,' I say with all sincerity, and plead again: 'Perhaps a few shillings, too? A loan – just until …?'

'Oh no,' the clerk is quick to squash that. 'No cash. I am sorry, sir. You would have to wait for that to be transferred by your father back down the telegraph. I can't loan a farthing on a handshake, not anymore, not these days.' He leans an elbow on the counter and lowers his voice: 'Tight as a nun.'

I shudder not only at that thought but that this weird man has just articulated it to me. I pretend I am too busy writing my message to respond. *Dear Pa*, I begin with involuntarily trembling hand. *You may have heard by now many awful things about me, but I am innocent – and also miraculously unharmed. Will explain in hideous detail when I see you.* Hopefully not in prison or chained to a blacksmith's forge but over a soothing claret in the library at home.

Please inform I.-G. Fitzworthy that a grave error of justice has been made, and my identity stolen. Please also remit cost of this missive and emergency cash as you see fit to Wellington branch, Bank of Australasia A.S.A.P. Your forever grateful, extremely humble and loving son, Jem. I can't say more than that about the circumstances, can't mention specifics such as misinterpretation of horse-borrowing, without raising unwanted curiosity here. I hope it's enough for Pa to call a halt. Oh – and a: *P.S. I will have happy news to share about future plans for personal improvement.* There, he'll have to rescue me now to find out what it could possibly be.

'They are hoarding gold, too, all the banks,' Clerk Creepy is suddenly chatty, 'and it all goes off to the Bank of England.'

I smile, even as the hairs stand up along the back of my neck; as I shift my weight slightly away from him, the soles of my boots crunch on the earth-encrusted floor, I presume from all the bags of gold-laced dirt that have been through here, on their way home to London. Right. Better make some chat in return to ensure my note gets off. I say: 'Really? What does the Bank of England want with all that gold?'

'No-one knows,' he says conspiratorially, snatching the slip of paper from under the bars. 'You might know better than me. You're a Snide, aren't you? A Jew? Fox the silversmiths, that is a Hebrew business – am I wrong?'

Blood chills a little at what I perceive as the Christ-killer, cheating lowlife accusation in that term 'Snide', but I keep the smile on: 'You are not wrong, sir. My father is a prominent Jew of Sydney.' Not an uncommon fact related in the city's news when his contributions in both vice-regal knick-knack design and charitable donations are reported, or, possibly of more relevance to this chap before me, when Pa's name crops up in the trade of metals in correspondence with this very bank.

'There are Snides at Blathery,' the clerk says blankly. 'Josh Lieberman. You should go to his house while you're waiting for your remittance to come through.' He still doesn't return my smile, and I'm sure he tortures puppies in his spare time, but I think he might be attempting to be helpful. Jews don't turn other Jews away, that's fact rather than mere religion, so the advice is sensible.

And I couldn't be keener to get away from this fellow and his unnerving stare. 'You couldn't give me directions, could you? To – what was the name of the place?' *Blathery*?

'Of course,' the clerk says, pointing at the front window behind me. 'You take this road here towards Molong, and when you come to the second creek crossing – that's Blathery Creek – you'll find an inn all boarded up – that's the Rainbow Inn – turn right up along the track past it and not a quarter mile on is the Liebermans' place. You won't miss it. It's the only house there.'

About ten miles back the way we came. Of course it is. But at least I won't have to attempt to pawn the tweed for food.

As I thank him and turn to leave, he says: 'I'll let Trooper Donovan know what's gone on with you, when I see him. Won't be too long, I shouldn't think. I'll tell him to find you at the Liebermans.'

'Good. Wonderful.' I shudder once more and it's all I can do not to belt out the door.

ANNIE

Two ladies walk past me on their way along the riverbank and one of them gives me a backwards glance, making a point of it. I'm a grubby black stable boy to her by that look, a black mark in her uppity town. If there are Aborigines here, they're not allowed to show their faces. Just like Windsor, or Richmond, or Penrith. Or probably anywhere. My stomach turns around nothing, and it's getting painful.

The lace-edged flounces around the ladies' skirts float above the ground, catching dust. Catching all my envy, too. I wouldn't wear whorish flouncing like that if you paid me, nor a crinoline so wide, but I'm lost in the thought that I might never get to wear a nice dress again. Not that I ever really had any to speak of, apart from Sunday best of decent cotton print, but I did want good fabric, proper dress fabric, fine silk, a heavy brocade, one day. I'll never have such things now.

I look the other way, down towards the water, that's deep and green. It's a picture of the way a river should be: handsome, graceful. I don't even know its name. I want to chuck myself in it, though, just to feel clean, and I wonder whether I'll ever do that again, either.

A swan calls up along the river, a sound like a squeaky door, and I think I'm dreaming it, homesick. But then I see it, a great big black swan, whooshing down upon the water, through the trees, its white wing tips outstretched. A big male – right in front of me, red beak flashing through the reeds. I don't know if he's a cruel reminder that I am nowhere or a sign that maybe I'm only where I should be – waiting to be shooed off somewhere else. Disaster never-ending. Dread quakes out from all the sorrowful nothing in me: I should never have asked to come here, should I – another I-should-never-have to add to all the rest. The horse nudges my shoulder with his nose like he might agree, and I turn around to look at him, looking for some slim blessing in the fact it seems I might have been cured of my fear of riding horses – worthless as that will ever be. What's a girl ever ride a horse for? The circus?

Just as I think that, I see Jeremy Fox, coming for me across the road, green eyes laughing like nothing ever bothers him. Well, why would it? He's a man who can step right in to a bank in any town and ask them for money. A man who, though he is filthy and brown-skinned himself from the road, still looks like he owns it. We are two different kinds of creature.

'Slight detour,' he says, smiling so you wouldn't know where we've been. 'And an interesting surprise – we're off for kosher tea.'

Interesting? Kosher? Whatever that is, I don't reckon it's going to be a good idea.

JEM

As the adage goes, there's a Jew in every town across the globe, if you look hard enough, no matter how small a town might be, even if it's only one house beyond a pub that's closed down, and if you're particularly unlucky, he's looking for a husband for his daughter.

'Jeremy. Fox. Yes, yes, come in, Jeremy Fox.' Josh Lieberman extends his hand after I've given him the very edited version of what I'm doing on his doorstep. 'Of course I know your father,' he says with predictable eagerness. 'I met him only briefly, several years ago now, but his reputation speaks for itself in any case, does it not? Such an accomplished man, a good and honourable man. You must meet my daughter, Shana. Shana! Come out here.' Eureka! 'So, Jeremy, are you in business with your father or are you at the university in Sydney?' Because there is no other possible choice.

I get as far as: 'Ah —'

And, hand still grasping mine, he's moved on to his credentials: 'We have four thousand head of Merino here at Blathery, and ten thousand acres. I am the one and the only Hebrew squatter in this colony. You will not get finer fleeces than Lieberman's!' A modest man, even if I have never heard of him, hawkish face, sculpted goatee, hairy hands, and he is making an immediate and unspoken offer to sell his daughter to me for a reasonable number of sheep. 'Shana!'

I look back apologetically at Annie, who's waiting with Zad in the paddock outside the front-yard fence, beyond the rose garden

on this fringe of the Netherworld, but I don't know if she sees me –
it's almost dark – as Lieberman pulls me inside. When I get a word
in, when I know more clearly where we are, I'll get her inside, too.

It's an old house, brick-floored and wood slips tiling the roof,
but substantial, everything smelling of wood polish, crystal filling
the glass cabinet of the front parlour and an exquisitely enamelled
lamp placed on a table near it to light up every facet, and catch
every glint of gold blocking on the spines of the hefty bookcase next
to it, so that there may be no doubt that Lieberman has done very
well for himself.

'Shana!'

'So it's just the two of you here?' I ask him, wondering if Shana
is somewhere overwhelmed by the endless dusting and polishing
to be overseen in this house, or if she's out in the back parlour
staving languor with chocolates and pulse-enlivening ladies' fictions
with titles like, *The Heiress & Her Many Lovers* and *What Her
Seamstress Saw*.

'Yes, it is only my daughter and myself here at present,' says
Lieberman. 'My son David is away on business in Bourke, buying
rams at the sale yards on the Darling, and my youngest, Simon, is at
school – at the Bathurst Grammar School. I have hopes that Simon
will study medicine.'

Of course you do. I wait for mention of Mrs Lieberman, but none
is forthcoming, and it would be impolite to ask; perhaps the dusting
and polishing finished her entirely, or she's returned to Poland. No,
more likely Berlin: his house is so pristine they must be Germans; and
via Shoreditch says a second look at the walnut cabinetry – nicely
turned but somehow cheap. Whatever they are, there's some strange
agitation about Lieberman himself, eyes dancing about as if I might
run off before I get to lay my own on his prized —

'Shana!' he shouts again down the hall.

And finally she appears at the end of it: 'Papa?'

God, but she is a doll. Raven-haired and rosy, and big blue eyes a
man could lose himself inside, I don't know how it is my jaw made
no sound hitting the bricks. I didn't expect to see that.

'Say good evening to our guest, Mr Fox,' her father commands
her. 'And bring us bread and schnapps.'

'Yes, Papa. Good evening, Mr Fox.' She bobs a little curtsy and goes off to do as she's bid.

'And be quick about dinner,' her father hurls another demand at her back.

I consider Josh Lieberman afresh, and with somewhat reduced esteem. Too cheap for a housekeeper, or can't find one who'll put up with the conditions? Or is he showing off his daughter's obedience? Whatever the case, if he's a man of such blunt expression, so shall I be in return; before he can get on to bludgeoning me with his Ashkenazischer lineage all the way back to Rashi, I tell him: 'I have a friend who must join us, waiting outside.'

'A friend? Why didn't you say so? Of course! Any friend of yours is a friend of mine.' His eyes dance all over the place, and with such excited intensity, I wonder if there's something about the climate here that causes it. 'Where is he?'

'Annie – Annie dear,' I call to her from the verandah, partly for the lark of it, and partly because I'm so light-headed with starvation it just slipped out. 'Don't loiter there.'

'Dear?' Lieberman wonders in puzzlement. 'The native who helped you when you were robbed? Isn't that what you just said to me?'

'Yes.' I grin at him as Annie trudges up the path through the gate, a shadow but for her red shirt, put on against the evening chill; God, but it suits her, my little cavalier. 'We've become close … friends.'

'Good evening – er.' Lieberman's agitation hurtles towards some sort of horror with Annie's every step, as she nears the light now being thrown out down the hall. Oy, the native is a she? I'm sure he doesn't know which is worse. But he doesn't have a choice – here is the son of Solomon Fox in his house – and I'm enjoying this.

'Annie Bird.' She looks up at him with her huge dark eyes, dashed in every sense: 'Annabel. Bird.'

'Joshua Lieberman,' he replies. 'You must join us, Miss Bird.' I'm sure he can't think of anything he'd rather do less.

And no-one could ever outdo Miss Bird for blunt: 'Thank you,' she says. 'I'd like to wash first, please.' While her eyes save a glance for me: I'm not your dear.

I return it: yes, you are. And we are going to sleep in a bed tonight, and I am going to ask you to marry me, after which I am undoubtedly going to kiss you. Yes, I am.

ANNIE

'Wash? Of course. Out through the back, you will find all conveniences in the scullery, and the closet is in the garden.' The man is goggle-eyed as he shows me inside his house, handing me a brass chamber-candlestick off a stand in the hall, maybe surprised that I don't want to roll in the dirt some more like a real Aborigine. But I can't sit at any table in any house the way I am no matter what ignorant thing this Mr Lieberman or whoever he is might reckon.

'Would you like some heated water?' he's asking me, following me down the hall.

I would, but I say, 'No, thank you.' I'm not going to hang about waiting for it.

I don't even look at the house on my way through, I'm so dirty, and I'm goggle-eyed myself when I look in the little mirror above the basin in this nice, clean scullery room: who is this wild thing looking back at me in the half-dark? *Dear.* What game is Jeremy Fox playing now? I don't want to know. I fill the basin at the tap above the laundry trough and wash the worst of the road off me as best I can with one of the flannels folded on the shelf by the mirror, by a shaving cup and razor, a little dish with daisies on it holding the bar of soap. I want to unpeel my cami and stays off me and fill the hip bath hanging on the wall here for a hot soak like nothing else, but I can't do that. I want to go home, to my own warm-brick copper, my own little tin bath. My own soap and flannel. I rinse and wring this one out when I'm finished so that there's no trace of me left on it.

I look out the back window and the sky is that shade of green it sometimes goes at the end of a sunny day before it turns black, the colour I've always imagined the ocean might be, though I've never seen it. Sheep are bleating somewhere at the night against the thump and scratch of the windmill pump bringing the water up from the creek. The land is being washed through white with a million sheep.

I'm going to fall down on this scullery floor if I don't get something to eat.

'Miss Bird?' the grazier, Mr Lieberman, is so quick at my knock on the back door it seems like he's been waiting there, or maybe spying on me from the kitchen, in case I might have made off with his daisy dish or his bath if he wasn't careful. 'Come in, come in.' I think he's trying to smile, but he looks like he's doing himself an injury by it, and I hear him latch the door behind me. 'Welcome, once again.' He gives me a nervous little laugh, taking the candlestick from me so I don't steal that, either. I don't care; I can smell bread, and some kind of stew. Oh, it smells heavenly in here, now I've let myself take a deep breath in. A well-kept house, good food on the stove; I can even smell the lavender in the linen down the hall. Shiny red brick floors, thick carpets and fine furniture, beautiful fire going in the front parlour room. A house to dream about.

And *dear* Jeremy Fox, all cosy on the little sofa with a pretty girl beside him, a young lady, having a drink out of a tiny wineglass. I stop still in the parlour doorway. This picture shows me more of the truth about him than I want to know: that this is the type of picture he belongs in. That he has friends anywhere, in beautiful houses anywhere, with beautiful girls everywhere, and I'm just – stupid and ugly. I've never felt so outside of a picture, and that's saying something.

But he jumps up when he sees me standing here. 'Annie,' he says, and there's no-one ever been so happy to see me. He introduces me to the girl, but I don't hear him until he says: 'You'll never guess what we've been talking about.'

'Shock me,' I say, because I don't reckon he could if he pulled out a pink trombone and blasted it right at me.

He pulls me all the way into the room instead and pushes me down on the sofa next to the girl: 'Perhaps you'd like to be seated before you hear it. Mr Lieberman, tell Miss Bird what you were just telling me – about Blackman's Swamp.'

'Er,' he says, not happy I'm sitting on his sofa, but there's not much he can do about it now, because I'm not moving until I hear what he has to say. 'Ah …' He comes across into the middle of the room, in front of the fire, and he says, 'Well. It's not very remarkable, I don't think. Blackman's Swamp is merely the old name for the town of Orange. I came to the district as a boy, you see, in the early twenties, when the town was only a camp, and —'

'Why did you change the name, then?' I snap out the question at him. I know I sound rude, like he'd done it himself to spite me, like a gentleman should ever be spoken to in such a way, but I don't care about that, either. Because anyhow, I'm not asking him what I want to ask: what did you do with all the black fellers, then? Chase them off with rifles? A bit remarkable for them, don't you think?

He doesn't seem bothered by my bad manners, too busy looking out the window across the room rather than at me, as he answers the question: 'People thought it gave the wrong impression of the town. It was originally named after a settler called Blackman – a white man called Blackman. You see?' He fingers his collar uncomfortably. Good: you be uncomfortable. He makes a strange sound, maybe it's another nervous little laugh, and he says: 'That was twenty years ago now – we, er. A petition of other settlers asked the Governor at the time, Sir Charles Fitzroy, to give the place a new name, and as the wattles were in bloom all around during his visit, Sir Charles named it Orange – evidently not as familiar with the colour of gold as he might have been, or drunk, or both.' I suppose I'm meant to laugh here, but I don't and neither does Jeremy Fox, where he stands beside me. 'Yes. Well,' says this Mr Lieberman. 'Anyway, it was thought better than the original. Some get quite tetchy about it if you call it by the old name, which over the years became rather ill-associated with a racetrack that was on the road to the

Ophir goldfields and its attendant brothel and opium house. The people of Orange are generally averse to that sort of thing – like to think they're gentry, really.'

I could say I hardly noticed, but I don't say anything. I grab a piece of bread and cheese that's sitting on the table right by me and shove it in my mouth before I can say anything else. Oh – that's delicious cheese, and not just because I'm hungry.

'You came here as a boy?' Jeremy asks him. 'So did I. Against your will?'

Mr Lieberman fingers his collar again: 'Long, long story. I won't bore you with it.'

I stop chewing for a second to stare at him. There's likely not that many reasons why you'd have come out here then, to a camp in the middle of nowhere. And even before the time my dad arrived himself. The transport ships might have stopped coming twenty years ago, but they'll always be among us and you'll never know who's who, Dad would say. Mr Lieberman was a convict, I'll bet; or maybe a soldier. No-one special at any rate, though he looks like any well-to-do squatter in his quality strides and his double-breasted vest, jacquard pattern in the fabric I can't quite make out as it stretches around his well-fed stomach.

'Shana!' he barks at the girl beside me. 'Get the dinner.'

And the girl gets up. 'Yes, Papa.' I'd forgotten she was there, she's such a quiet thing. She smiles down at me: 'Excuse me, please, Miss Bird.' Her eyes are so bright, such a pretty blue, they match the flowers embroidered all over the muslin of her dress, but ... there's something tight-screwed about her, too, like she can't blink without being told to. I feel sorry for her somehow, thinking maybe I should offer to help, but I stuff another piece of bread and cheese in my mouth instead: this might be the only day in my whole life that someone else gets my dinner. This time next week, I could well be someone else's scullery maid, scrubbing bedsheets – or worse.

'So there you are,' Jeremy is saying, taking Shana Lieberman's place beside me. 'Blackman's Swamp – isn't that *bizarre*? If I ever wrote a book I'd have to write one about the names of places in this colony, but no-one outside it would ever believe me.'

Whatever you say, Mr Fox. I can hardly look at him. Arms wide across the back of the sofa, knees spread out, taking up as much room as he might. He's so comfortable here, I shrink and shrink.

'Oh, so you are a literary man, are you?' Mr Lieberman asks him, sitting in the chair opposite. 'I've been lately reading the great work of Darwin – *On the Origin of Species*. Very interesting, very exciting indeed. Have you read it?'

'An actual book?' Jeremy laughs. 'Not if I can avoid it. I read *Bell's Life* for the sporting news – not much else.'

'Revolutionary,' Mr Lieberman says as if he never heard him. He looks at the clock on the mantel; he's done that a couple of times now. Maybe counting the seconds until I go. 'The idea that the earth might be thousands of years older than the Egyptians, perhaps hundreds of thousands of years older. And with all this talk of ancient antediluvian beasts being dug out of rocks and mountains that were once in the sea – well, the evidence might be upon us. The earth wasn't created in seven days, it seems. But God is always mysterious ...'

'Hm, interesting.' Jeremy nods, but I don't think he's interested at all, and I don't know what's being talked about anyhow.

Mr Lieberman looks out the front window again now, even though it's gone pitch dark. 'Yes,' he goes on. 'It's Mr Darwin's study of the birds and the tortoises on the Galapagos Islands which is most fascinating. The different species on the different islands, the way only the strong survive to breed and pass on those traits of strength, each according to the precise demands of the environment they live in. It reflects our state of humanity, does it not? Some races are destined to die out.' He looks at me.

I look back at him and I don't say what I want to say: I'm not dead yet ... I push another hunk of bread into my mouth. I'd look at the clock, too, if it would help get me away from here. And where exactly would I go, if I could? Just shut up and be content with the cheese.

'It is no different for us.' Mr Lieberman is going on and on, talking to Jeremy: 'If you tell a man he's only good for business, for banking and trading in gold, he gets good at it, or dies. Is that not so? Jews are very strong, made strong by the many trials of life.

In scientific terms, perhaps this is what it means to be the chosen race, do you not think? Perhaps here is the evidence of this. Darwin himself uses the term *favoured* for this phenomenon of superiority. He would know we were trading with the Egyptians while the Goyim were still living in caves, but he doesn't say that in his book, of course. Shana!' he calls for his daughter to hurry up dinner.

And while Mr Lieberman is distracted, Jeremy leans towards me, touching the back of my hand with a knuckle, whispering: 'This, too, we shall survive.'

I nearly smile, in a nervous sort of way, and for a few different reasons. But Mr Lieberman turns back now and says something to Jeremy in words I don't understand at all. Some different language. And Jeremy replies, 'Yes, of course, who doesn't like potato pie?' What? He told me he didn't speak any other language, but he does, doesn't he. I want to disappear into the sofa. He's a sack full of easy, uptowny lies. Dread prickles all over my skin.

Mr Lieberman is going on and on and on, 'I met him once, you know, Mr Darwin. When he was here in thirty-six on the *Beagle* voyage. He stopped at the inn at Weatherboard, in the mountains, and I was stopped there myself, on my way to Sydney – some business I can't remember. It was a very warm summer. Darwin was sickly and given to sweating. Not inclined to conversation.'

Maybe not with you, whoever Mr Darwin might be. Mr Lieberman is a bragger and some kind of liar, too, I reckon, and he's looking at the clock again, and out the window. Either he's waiting for something, or I should leave. There's something about him I don't trust: I want to leave. This minute.

Especially now he's saying: 'Some races cannot progress, not through education or commerce. They will never be strong in business or in brain – they remain merely slaves and thieves. Weak.'

'Whoa there. Steady on,' I hear Jeremy say beside me, for I have sat bolt upright on the edge of the seat. 'I don't think thievery is a trait particular to any race. Fagin might be a fiction, but there's a grain of truth in him. The London gangs were Jew—'

'Poverty is the true crime there, young fellow. Poverty and disadvantage forced upon us by the Goyim.' Mr Lieberman sits on the edge of his own chair. 'The Aborigine seems to know no other way to be but poor and depraved. He acquires none of the virtues of civilisation but all its vices. The Aborigine does not learn that stealing is wrong. Only a few weeks ago at the Rainbow – the inn on the road, you'd have passed it getting here – a party of marauding blacks attacked the place, stole all of the cash and much of the alcohol on the premises, made off into the bush. Impossible to trace.'

'Come on, fair go, there are bad seeds in every bunch,' says Jeremy, and he's not comfortable at any of this. I'm too frozen with shock to move, as my strange friend has another go at speaking sense: 'Poverty is poverty. When you've been shoved off your land and you've got little hope of getting a job to feed yourself, that's some disadvantage. You can't blame them —'

'Can't blame them for threatening the publican's wife with death? Viciously molesting her as well?' Mr Lieberman says. 'No wonder they are *shoved* off away from our towns. You have not seen the things I have seen, young man. They should live in the bush, way out back, and stay there to live as the savages they are. You cannot employ them – unreliable, coming and going as they please, and if you turn your back on them you've got fifty camping in your top paddock. There are too many aimless white men in need of work anyway these days for black men to take up jobs, with things the way they are on the goldfields, there isn't enough work to go around as it is. But perhaps you are right, young Jeremy Fox. It's not only the blacks who are disposed to such animal violence and treachery. The Goyim are just as bad, I must agree.' He shakes his head at this Goyim, whoever they might be in his mad and dangerous mind. 'You would know, having been robbed yourself by them. I presume you have heard of the bushranger Black Jack?'

Jeremy nods: 'Vaguely.'

Heavenly Father, I don't know how he deceives the way he does, lies and lies rolling off the tongue, so smooth.

And Mr Lieberman goes on again: 'He has caused havoc in this district and inflicted even greater tragedy upon the Rainbow – only yesterday morning, *Sunday* morning, for all that the Goyim here care for their own Sabbath. The good people who owned the place – the Heartfields – are there no more.'

'What happened?' Jeremy asks and we're all on the edge now.

'Well, Black Jack arrived at the inn at dawn, with his accomplices, rapping on the back door demanding cash, and when Mr Heartfield – poor Lyall Heartfield – tried to explain that all their cash was already stolen, Black Jack pushed his way in, wrestling with Lyall, and as they wrestled, the door was forced open, slamming Mrs Heartfield against the wall behind it, cracking her skull. She is perished and Lyall Heartfield is broken in every way.'

'Oh that's terrible!' I can't help crying out.

'It is.' Mr Lieberman's eyes fix on me, terrible as the tale. 'And the night before that, in the dead quiet, Black Jack bailed up the publican at the Post Office Inn – over the river at Wellington. A whole Saturday night's takings gone.' He keeps staring and staring at me with his terrible eyes and his terrible mind, and he says: 'As you should know – *Lady* Bird.'

'What? No!' I stand up; I just about hit the ceiling with fright. 'Whatever you've heard —'

'You are lucky to be alive,' he's saying to Jeremy Fox.

Who's moving towards Mr Lieberman, with his hands up: 'Steady on, old fellow, old friend. This is a misunderstanding. I can explain.'

And you'd better start talking fast, Mr Fancy Boots, because there's someone banging like the devil on the front door this second, too: 'Open up! Open up! Police!'

JEM

Two troopers, two revolvers – two shiny Colonel Colts at full cock – and it's not primarily Annie they're after: it's me.

'You are the man who calls himself Fox? Jeremy Fox?' asks the smaller but perhaps more senior of the two, whom I'm sure is not at all waiting to hear the answer.

Which is, 'Yes.' Because it is me.

And I'm not inclined to say otherwise or any more to the well-buffed barrel accompanying the question.

'You did enter the offices of the Australasia Bank in Wellington this afternoon with the intention of defrauding the cashier?'

I can't answer that. Firstly, I'm just as sure this policeman is not wanting an answer from me. Secondly, as I catch the glint of silver-plate around the trigger guard, I wonder if Pa has forsaken me; received the message and promptly sent one back saying: *Not my son, throw the book at him.* You wouldn't do that, Pa, would you?

'You are under arrest for this attempted fraud, for horse-stealing, for obtaining food and lodgings by deception at One Tree in District of Hartley, for impersonating another, for associating with proscribed persons and for possession of a stolen police firearm.' The Deane & Adams is stuffed under his belt, for all that it must have been a decommissioned museum piece. 'And with this, other offences against the Crown as yet to be determined.'

Shit. Shit. Shit. A thousand times. I could not think of a word other than this one if my life depended on it, and it probably does. You can't have left me in the lurch, Pa. Fair frigging go.

'Turn around. Hands behind your back.'

I can only comply there, too.

Lieberman makes an attempt on my behalf: 'This can't be right. This man is Jeremy Fox – he is a Jew, I can confirm that much.'

He tested me, asking me in Yiddish and in a somewhat challenging way if I liked kugl, which I thought odd ten minutes ago – because why would you ask anyone if they like potato pie? I'll have mine with extra chicken schmaltz – but not so odd now.

And irrelevant anyway. The police are no more interested in hearing this than anything else. My wrists are too broad for the handcuffs the more junior officer is attempting to bolt around them, but that's not stopping these fellows, either. Ouch. You little piece of —

'Stop! You're hurting him!' Annie joins in, to no avail.

'Come along, Miss.' She is taken in the grip of this younger policeman, who has left off the handcuff attempt, but not before taking a fair quantity of skin off my wrists. 'You are arrested as well. Come quietly, so that I can remain gentlemanly with you.'

The senior one, now behind me, is having a go at the handcuffs himself and still can't get them bolted, although he's doing a fine job of taking the rest of my skin off there in his even more determined attempt. I suggest to him, as calmly as I can: 'I'll come quietly, too – trust me. This is rather hurting.'

'Not as hurt as you're gunna be,' he replies, just as calmly, and with quite credible menace, as he finally bolts the handcuffs closed, and starts marching me out, with sweet but slow-witted Shana asking her father as I go: 'Oh? They're not staying for dinner, Papa?'

No, apparently we're not.

*

If he hits me again, Pa, I will go more than quietly. I will marry Shana Lieberman and have twelve children.

'I will ask you one more time. What are they planning to blow up with the dynamite? The dynamite *you* stole from the Wallerawang railway sheds.'

How can I answer that with anything but, 'I told you – I don't know. I didn't steal any dynamite. I stole the horse – accidentally – from the Cobb & Co at One Tree Hill, and that's it.'

Please don't hit me again. He does, of course, another fist belting into my left cheek, and every time he hits me, be it in the face or in the guts, my hands, stuck behind me as they are, feel as if they might be severed by the too-tight cuffs. He's enjoying himself. 'You greedy, thieving Snide – tell the truth!'

He must be enjoying himself, because that's all he'll be getting out of this. Fairly soon, if he keeps this up, I'm not going to be able to say anything whatsoever. His name is Mounted Trooper Donovan, and I think he might believe that if he kills me, slowly and gruesomely, he might earn a promotion. He started by thrashing me around the shoulders with his horse-whip, now punching me, and I'm not sure what he detests more: bushrangers or Jews. Or which is more alarming: his violence generally or his relish at inflicting it upon a man who is purportedly merely *impersonating* a Jew. His lack of intelligence is terrifying. Not that I would hit him back if my arms were free. Reprehensible as I am in so many ways, when it comes down to it, it's against my religion to strike or hate my brother, to want revenge or to bear a grudge, and I've tended to think these are fair enough principles to live by. But there should be a specific law both spiritual and temporal across all faiths against laying into a man who is stuck to a chair wearing handcuffs behind his back. Apart from the agony it's causing, it's a humiliation too far. Or perhaps I merely had it coming, and for quite some time. If I'm to be thrashed for every pound I owe, we've still got a way to go, haven't we. I've never been beaten like this before – too quick with the bosh, too fast to get away from bullies and blackguards, and from the law, to receive anything much but a bit of roughing up. Apart from a few memorable floggings at school, my worst batterings have always come by falling off a horse, or on one occasion, falling through the roof of the Picnic Hotel at Coogee Bay, and I'll never know how that happened. It's all been a lark. Not anymore.

Now Trooper Donovan picks up a baton, smacking it into his hand. He does look a bit as one might expect an agent of Satan to look, in this grey kerosene light.

He says: 'And this one – this is for Mrs Heartfield.'

I feel very badly for Mrs Heartfield, I honestly do, for all that I never met her.

'This is how we settle things out here in the bush.'

I hear Annie somewhere outside the cell: 'What are you doing to him in there? He's not who you think he is. Please! Please listen to me.'

They're not listening to you, Annie, and they're not listening to me. The younger and more 'gentlemanly' copper that has her front of shop asked her on the way here, in the back of the cart they requisitioned from Lieberman, if it was true that she sang opera tunes; I'd sing Florestan's aria from *Fidelio*, if I thought it might help our case. I understand that terrorising people by randomly bailing up stage coaches and robbing pubs, never mind killing publicans' wives, might make the middle-order folks of these parts upset enough to want to see the bastards tortured before hanging – any bastard will do, ten extra points if he's a Jew, or perhaps a Catholic or a black, take your pick. And I do sympathise with their fears – the fear of bastards ruining their nice lives. But I am not a bastard, not that kind at least. I'm not one like this Jack Holly they're after. Now there's a specific, actual bastard I would like to punch in the head for all of this.

If I should live to see him.

The baton comes down across the side of my face. I don't know a thing after that.

ANNIE

'Righto, righto, what's going on here?' This big, tall policeman with a great black moustache comes rushing in.

'Superintendent Slater!' The one that's been sitting here goggling at me and asking me the most stupid questions, jumps up and salutes. 'We weren't expect—'

'No, you wouldn't have been, would you,' says the big, tall policeman, this Superintendent Slater, who must be the boss. 'You wouldn't know what was going on, since you weren't here to receive my message. I've been down at the Ironbarks, as there's been another inn robbery there, yesterday, out towards Burrendong. I'll ask you later why you thought it a good idea to leave this station unmanned all day and all night, Briscomb – what the blazes you two thought you were doing harassing diggers for licence fees out at No Hope at a time like this. But right now I'm asking you: where are the prisoners I've been told you have arrested?'

For a moment all I hear is the sound of the name Briscomb, the name of this rotten cabbage in front of me, a name I won't ever forget, along with that of Trooper Rex Donovan and the sounds of Jeremy being bashed and yelled at in the cell that's down a hallway from this front room we're in here at Wellington police station and gaolhouse. They've been at it for hours; it's past one o'clock in the morning. That Donovan has his wild eye on, a dog to bite your leg off, just because he has a power to. Every time that so-called policeman hits Jeremy, I hear the breath go out of him. He hasn't made a complaint about it or even yelled out in the pain of it. He tries to answer a stupid question and he gets thumped again. Because of me. He wouldn't be here except for me.

'Miss Bird?' The superintendent is looking at me. He's asked me a question I didn't hear, but he's not bothered to wait for an answer anyhow, what a surprise.

'And Fox?' he's asking brainless Briscomb.

Who points at the wall behind me: 'In the lock-up, sir.'

So, the superintendent takes his long, tall legs around there and two steps later he shouts out: 'Jesus Christ!' And I don't think he's shouting that in vain. 'What the – what! What have you done to him?' He shouts even louder and he doesn't wait for an answer to that, either.

As that Donovan starts to explain, 'He was bein' uncooperative, Sarge – I mean, sir,' the superintendent gets right into him: 'I was clear in my instructions. I could not have made it plainer, even to you: there was to be no unnecessary violence in the apprehension of this gang! No conviction, no reward, and that extends to the behaviour of the constabulary. There will be consequences, Donovan, grave consequences, if this man dies. The New South Wales Police Force must be seen to uphold the law in every sense! You are no better than a common felon yourself. This colony will remain in bedlam so long as the likes of you remain in the employ of the Crown.'

I hear a slap; one sharp slap. And the big boss snarls at him with a greater power: 'Get out of my sight.'

Then: 'Briscomb! Get a doctor!'

But before he can get anywhere, another feller comes running in out of the night: 'Stop the arrest! Stop the arrest! You've got the wrong man!' Stiff collar and oiled-down hair like a clerk of some kind, he's run in together with another who's waving a piece of paper and he's jabbering at the superintendent, too: 'We just received confirmation from Mr Fox – Mr Solomon Fox. By every description relayed, the man you've got in here is his son. The man you've got in here really is Jeremy Fox. Jeremy Gideon Fox.'

The superintendent puts his head in his hands. He drops them and looks up at the lamp hung from the ceiling. He takes a deep breath, and then he looks at me. He says, 'Miss Bird ...'

His lips are moving beneath his big, bushy moustache, but I don't know what he's saying to me. All I want to do is go around this wall to Jeremy, to see if he's all right, ask him if it's true that his middle name is Gideon, because I've always liked that name. When the angel appeared to Gideon, he said, 'The Lord is with you, mighty warrior,' and Gideon said, 'How can that be? The Lord has abandoned the Israelites.' But no, Lord, you didn't abandon the Israelites, did you, and you can't abandon him tonight, you can't let him die. This is all *my* fault – not his. And if you should let him die, I'll lose the only friend I've got.

I lose any skerrick of pride I might have had left too: I start to cry, truly cry, in great, big, terrible sobs that I can't hide.

'Tears will not assist you, Miss Bird,' I hear the superintendent say. He's not being unkind; he only wants the truth. It's just him and me in this room now. 'Who are you and how do you know Jack Holly?'

'I don't know any Jack Holly!' I yell with all the frustration of it, and I regret it straightaway, which only makes me cry more.

'Hm.' He scratches his chin and then sits down on the chair opposite, looking and looking at me the whole time, probably thinking I'm just another liar.

'Please,' I beg him, 'I'm just a farm girl from Castlereagh. Jeremy Fox was only trying to help me, when I got attacked on the road, at that place called One Tree Hill. He took the horse to go after the men who attacked me. That's all he did, besides holding onto the horse too long. But he was helping me then, too. I was looking for my grandfather – that's all I was doing. And that's all Jeremy Fox was doing. I'm all alone, apart from him. My father died only on Wednesday, and ...' My heart is so broken in so many ways I don't know who I am.

The superintendent blinks at me and shakes his head to clear it. '*You* were attacked at One Tree Hill?' He looks and looks at me, searching for the truth, and I nod.

'Yes,' I tell him: 'They robbed everything from me – Jack whoever he is and his mate, Bill. But I got my tarp back off them when we came across this place where they were buying guns off a man.'

'Where was that?' the superintendent asks me, elbows on his knees. He looks tired; tired of people lying to him, tired of people doing the wrong thing.

'I don't know,' I tell him; I tell him all I can think of: 'We were lost. It was somewhere in the bush near a place called The Gap. The man they were buying the guns off had a scratchy voice. I didn't hear his name. But I heard clear enough that they're going to rob the Gold Escort at a place called Judas Creek on Friday. And that Black Jack has a very foul way of speaking.'

The superintendent blinks and shakes his head again, at the floorboards, then he asks me: 'The gun that was in your possession, is this one of the guns that was bought down in The Gap?'

'I don't think so. They were inside the hut talking about the money and —'

'How did you get it?' He frowns at me. 'How did you get the gun?' I'm not making sense to him.

But I'm trying as hard as I can; I tell him: 'It was in the saddlebags of the one called Bill – I stole it when I got my tarp back off them.'

'You stole the gun?'

'No – I stole the saddlebags. The gun was in one of the saddlebags, and that's the only thing I've ever stolen in my whole life. I was only getting my own back for them stealing everything off me, buying their guns with the money they stole off me, and calling me a foul name. And I'm very sorry now. I'd give it all back if I could.'

He puts a hand up for me to stop going on and he asks the floorboards: 'What about the money you stole in Penrith? A complaint has been made —'

I stop my babbling and blubbering and find my pride quick enough at that. I tell him: 'I never stole anything from Mrs Webb, not one penny. What money I ever had was my father's – hard-earned.' I grab the front of the shirt I'm wearing: 'This is my father's shirt. Everything I ever had belonged to him – not Mrs Webb.'

'Why would she say you stole money from her, then, if you didn't do that?' He's looking and looking at me; looking for lies.

I give him the plainest facts: 'Because she's horrible and she hates me.'

'Why does she hate you?' He squints like he's got a headache.

'Because I'm black.' I give him the very plainest: 'And I told her off for being the mean and nasty bigot she is.'

He nods and I sniff; he hands me his handkerchief, and he sighs. Then he asks me: 'Who is your grandfather? Can he vouch for you?'

I shrug for want of wailing again; I tell him. 'He's a man called Kulyan, a tracker from Blackman's Swamp, but you likely never heard of him. You likely think I made that up, too.'

'No,' he says, with another big sigh. 'Your story is far too convoluted, Miss Bird, and Kulyan is a name I haven't heard for many years. You couldn't make that up.'

My turn to blink at the policeman, not daring to believe him. 'You've heard of my grandfather?'

'Oh yes,' he says. 'I've heard of Kulyan. If we speak of the same man, my own father knew him well. He was a surveyor, my father, and he employed Kulyan as his chief guide on an exploration of the western rivers, in eighteen twenty-eight. I never met him, this esteemed Kulyan, but I heard about him often enough. Pater admired him very much, spoke of him as a friend, but lost track of him over the years. If he were alive today, he'd be most pleased to find out how Kulyan got on. Where is your grandfather? Did you manage to find him?'

'No.' I hang my head once more, as another pair of boots come stomping in.

It's the doctor. His boots are scuffed and shabby and he smells like rum.

I keep my head hung down and I pray. *Friend.* My grandfather and the surveyor were friends. It's true. Not a story, not a dream: true. And I'll be happy enough at that simple fact forever, Lord, take solace where I find it and be grateful, if you will look over my friend Jeremy now. I will never ask for another blessing. Don't let him die on my account. Take something else from me, instead.

FROM JUDAS CREEK TO TEA-POT AND ON TO BUNYIP'S BEND

JEM

I wonder if there might not be something to the Gentile conception of Heaven when, out of the throbbing fog of agony that is my entire head, I find a vision of Annie looking down on me. Her hair is swept back from her face, and as she turns to pick up something beside me I see that her coppery curls are neatly pinned at the nape of her neck, the tempest contained. I can see the shape of her at last, a bodice fitted to her perfect frame, gay little pansies of crimson and saffron falling along leafy chains through almond air. The neckline of her dress is squared and free of trimmings, the chemisette beneath almost sheer – God, that fashion on a girl is the business. You can *see* her. This girl. Annie. And as she bends over me now, I could almost —

Ouch!

'You're awake?' She smiles at me. She is so very lovely, her smile is so extraordinarily lovely that, if this is death, it's all right with me. I'll get used to the discomfort.

Ouch.

Ouch.

What is she doing to my forehead? With a branding iron.

'Don't worry. Nearly there.' She smiles again.

And I return to the floating unknowingness from whence I came.

*

She's still here when I return but she's even lovelier by candlelight. The moon is in the window at her shoulder, casting its glow about her, too. She's an angel, golden and silvery at once. An angel reading a newspaper.

I try to move to see what she's reading, but moving must be against the rules of Heaven because at the slightest attempt I am sent spinning backwards on a wheel of torture, my head hitting some kind of celestial wall on the way around – no, a series of walls.

'Don't try to get up – it will hurt,' she says, a good minute or so after the event. She touches the side of my face with the back of her hand, and I wish she hadn't because that hurts too.

She smiles: 'Well, you don't have a fever. That's good.'

Is it? I'm beginning to remember that something a lot worse than a bout of influenza has happened to me. I don't think I've come off my horse, either.

She says: 'You look like a colloped old bit of corned beef, but you're all right, thank God. Oh thank God.'

God, the way she talks. Colloped? Is that even a word? It is to Annie Bird. And it could almost distract me from the sneaking understanding that my face is a wreck. And I remember everything now, every blow. This is not the afterlife but the earthly aftermath of all my sins, and a gang of others' as well.

Despite all caution against movement, I try to raise my head again. Where am I? Panic takes me on another turn around the wheel of torture, but the only word that comes out of me is: 'What?'

'Shh. Don't fret,' Annie assures, explaining: 'The doctor said there was a troublesome look about the graze on your brow, but he's a drunkard, wouldn't know what day it is. Still, best to keep an eye on any sign. I've put eucalyptus all around the wound, and the cuts on your wrists, that'll help, and now the bruises are coming out you'll feel better soon. Just like my dad when he was kicked by one of the plough horses a couple of years ago – almost in the exact same spot – looked a horror, but lucky there wasn't more damage done. You only look awful.'

'Oh. Wonderful.'

'I think so,' she says, and she looks down. Even in this faint light, I see a pink flush across her angel face. I'm better already. I'd say

I've just about won her. I had to be pulverised in order to achieve it, but I am achieving it. I remember I'm going to ask her to marry me, and I'd smile at the thought if it didn't hurt too. Let's hold off until I'm capable of kissing her, and everything else that goes with it ...

She's uncorking a bottle on the nightstand as she says: 'You're very lucky. Your father has fixed up everything, with the police and with the bank, he even provided money for all the expenses of looking after you. He must love you very much.'

'He does – he's the best.' Panic takes me on yet another turn around the wheel. 'Is he here?'

'No.' She dabs whatever is in the bottle onto a wad of linen. 'Superintendent Slater put him off with a story about you slipping and hitting your head by an accident – he's not keen to concern your father with too many details of what occurred in the police station.' She gives the linen wad a wry smile. God, I love her again and again. She says, turning that smile onto me: 'You truly are a horror of a sight, I can't tell you. Black and blue. If you were my son I wouldn't want to see you.'

I wish she didn't have to see me; this face is generally the only decent thing I have to recommend me. I change the subject: 'Where are we?'

'In a house, a nice house, here in Wellington,' she says, 'belonging to a woman called Mrs Dutton, the mother of one of the fellers at the bank. They've all been very kind, the people in this town – very ashamed at what happened, I reckon. You'll be happy to know that Trooper Donovan got his marching orders over what he's done – and he deserves it. How any man could look another in the eye and beat him that way – he could have killed you. You've been asleep or delirious for almost two days, be in no doubt about how serious his hurt to you has been. It's Wednesday night, nearly eight o'clock, and except for ten minutes here or there, I've sat by you this whole time to be sure the hurt wasn't worse. I've prayed myself stupid over you. But you'll get well quickly now, I would bet. You can go home soon – and not scare your poor father too much. Your hair will cover the nastiest of it, you'll see.'

I'm not going anywhere without you, Annie; brief but highly informative experience has taught me not to presume anything with her, however. I ask her, carefully: 'What are you going to do? Where will you go?'

'I told you that already,' she says with a shrug and a jut of that perfect little chin. 'I'm going to my sister at Yarramundi.'

No, you're not. Give me a few more days and you'll be coming with me.

'Don't worry, I'll be all right,' says Annie Bird. 'If things go well for the police on Friday and they catch the bushrangers at Judas Creek, I'll be entitled to a reward – that's what Superintendent Slater said. Five hundred pounds for Jack Holly, it is, since they doubled the price on his head, and another hundred for Bill Molloy, if they bring them both in alive.' She pushes the hair back from my forehead, and gentle as she is, I can't help the flinch. 'I'll go halves with you,' she says. 'You can pay off your gambling debts, and I can buy a little farm somewhere – maybe next door to Mrs Webb.'

No. We are not going our separate ways. She bends towards me: her bosom is so close; she cannot leave me. Ever.

She dabs the little wad of linen on my forehead and I just about leave her screaming: 'What is that!'

'Only the eucalyptus oil,' she says, patting me on the chest with her perfect little hand, perfectly firmly. 'I am sorry, sorry for everything you've been put through. But this truly does help the healing. Not that that doctor they have here would know anything about it.' She clicks her tongue in disgust. 'He only wanted to kill you, too. But I tipped his Syrup of Poppies down the kitchen sink and filled the bottle back up with water – fall into a deep enough asleep on that poison, you never wake up again.'

I'm waking up now. Six hundred pounds. A farm of her own. A sister she must surely be missing. I could have some competition for her affections here, if indeed she has any for me other than brotherly, and either way I am doubtless not the most attractive of the contestants, for several reasons, the state of my face not being the worst of them. Must find remedy for that, and as soon as possible. Show her my true character, and with it my intentions. Because I will be bringing this girl home with me. I must. Apologies in advance, Pa, but I've never been more determined about anything in my life.

Or at least I will be, after I've had another little sleep.

ANNIE

'I can't get over your transformation, Miss Bird, every time I see you come out of that door.' Mrs Dutton looks at me over her needlework, her chair set in the parlour room across the hall just so that she can see me come and go at all hours. She doesn't sleep. She doesn't like me in her house, only suffering it because Superintendent Slater asked her especially, since she has the room – six of them, being two parlours, three beds, a dining hall, and sundries out the back. What she's really saying is, *I can't believe you're a thieving native with that pretty dress on.*

I only smile in reply, and pray again that Jeremy does get back on his feet soon, and I can get out from under Mrs Dutton's stuck-up nose. She looks like a storybook lady-of-the-house, with her puffed-up leg-of-mutton shoulders, all green tartan taffeta and plaits wound this way and that on her head, too young for her, and probably dyed. She must be fifty or more, a wealthy widow with nothing better to do than complain about her maid and her cook, and watch me, taking note of every tiny thing. Her home is immaculate. I could live here. And never live here. Not in this immaculate white world. I keep seeing that picture of Jeremy with his arms wide at the back of Mr Lieberman's sofa, sipping at his tiny wineglass, and that's just how he'd be right here tonight if he were able, he'd be entertaining Mrs Dutton. *Such a handsome fellow,* she said to me yesterday: *I saw him from across the road, going into the bank. Strikingly handsome.*

I'm just a strange, untrustworthy surprise; even the maid and the cook look at me sideways – and the cook is a Chinaman.

A trusted friend and nurse, so Superintendent Slater told this house of me, and that's ten times more than a black girl should ever be. I don't think Superintendent Slater approves of any kind of bigot, but he knows how to talk to them: *See to it that Miss Bird has everything she needs for the care of young Mr Fox – bearing in mind that his father has the ear of His Excellency, the Governor.* Everyone jumps at the word of Mr Fox the senior, it seems. Jeremy's father. He's a lot more wealthy and important than I'd reckoned. Too wealthy and important for Jeremy to even be an acquaintance of mine. When he goes home, that'll be that.

Anyhow, every time I look down, I'm reminded I got a very nice dress out of all this, only broadcloth but beautiful quality, printed in France, and a pair of kid button boots I can't believe fit me so well, they might have been made for Cinderella herself, rather than for Miss Shana Lieberman, who is a very nice girl, it turns out, even if I'll likely not forgive her father for the mean things he said to me. I might have ended up with one of her fancy net crinolines, too, five yards around, if I didn't think the only thing they're good for is setting yourself on fire in the home. Whatever is wrong with two-yards' width and a bit of modesty, I will never know. What I'd really like is to properly clean my teeth, but when I asked Mrs Dutton if she might spare the equipment, she looked at me the way she's looking at me right now: suspicious, like I might try to batter her in the night with a six-penny toothbrush. And I might, if I could get my hands on one.

I'll get my toothbrush soon enough. I'll get that charge of stealing against me dropped as well, if Superintendent Slater gets to the bottom of it, as he's promised. And maybe I'll end up with that reward if the crooks get caught on Friday, but I'm not asking for it. I got what I asked for the most – Jeremy will be all right – and that will be that.

'What are you after?' Mrs Dutton asks me as I click the door to him shut behind me.

I look down at the skirt of my dress again, to try to keep my smile on with my good manners. Think of something happy: Sis will be jealous when she sees this dress – it's made by the high-class dressmaker Mrs Mays of George Street, Sydney, who's also a Jewess, so Shana Lieberman told me. *The boutique is just across from the General Post Office*, she said, as if I'll ever go there. Or to any *boutique*. Sis will love this dress and this story so much, she'll have to wait five minutes before getting into me for leaving her the way I did.

I look up at Mrs Dutton with my smile: 'I'm just going out to the bathroom to fill the basin,' I tell her, like it isn't obvious what I'm doing, because I'm holding the washstand basin under my left arm, plain for her to see by the candle in my hand above it.

'And how is young Mr Fox?'

'Much better, I think.'

'You think?'

'Hm.' Oh shut up, you sour old tart full of festering, maggoty gristle.

I keep my smile on as I move down the hall to the 'bathroom' at the back of the house, a room that has me looking twice every time I come in here. It's a room just for bathing alone – I've never seen such a thing before. The great big brass bath is lined with marble and has a drawer beneath it that hot coals go in to keep it warm, and it drains itself right out into the yard and onto the vegetable garden when you're finished. I haven't tried it out yet, of course, but I want one for myself. Who wouldn't? What a mad luxury – you'd never get me out of the bath. There's also a spring-loaded ash-pan lavatory in a privy on the back verandah. It's truly amazing what money can buy, and Mrs Dutton is not even the wealthiest woman in this town. There's a big, sparkling-new two-storey brick mansion up on the corner – what are the baths and lavatories like in there, gold-plated?

I fill the basin from the big brass urn on the hot-water stove in here that constantly burns, always at the ready for Duchess Dutton, and I leave it on the stand then as if I might be waiting for it to cool, to take to him. As if I'm ever going to wash him again. I look out the window at the bright moon, so huge tonight over all my smallness. He can wash himself tomorrow, or whenever he might choose. Yesterday morning, I was praying too hard to think about what I was doing, getting those filthy clothes off him, getting him clean, with that stupid Doctor McTavish swaying behind me and scratching his head like he might have had fleas. I was praying too hard to notice how much it frightened me to see Jeremy Fox in such a bad way, not waking up for hours on end, not snoring either. Tragedy repeating. One disaster too many; one to do me in. I'd wash him every day, of course, if I could. I'd hold his hand all through the night just to be sure he stayed warm. But I can't. And I won't. Because I'm no-one next to him. And that is that.

*

Only that tomorrow is worse, for me. I wake where I fell asleep: on the soft velvet arm of the half-back lounge by the window, but someone's tucked a blanket around me and a good guess says it wasn't Mrs Dutton.

'Good morning,' he says with those eyes too green, too smiling. 'You slept well.'

He's at the wardrobe, nothing on but a sheet around his waist: 'You don't know where my clothes have got to, do you?'

I say: 'You shouldn't be out of bed.' And he shouldn't. Just looking at the marks across his shoulder, blackening, makes me feel wounded myself. Makes me jump out from under the blanket.

'No, no, don't get up,' he says. 'Tell me where I'll find them.'

'I'll get them.' I'm already half out the door. 'You can't wander around the house like that. Mrs Dutton will have a fit at the sight of you.' Never mind me.

His clothes are in the scullery, or the 'laundry room' as it's called here, a whole room set aside for washing clothes – *just* clothes. The maid did them with her usual Tuesday wash and I meant to take them from the table there yesterday. I'll never get a job as a maid. I grab up the bundle now – shirt, trousers, smalls – grab the vest and coat hanging behind the door, all brushed down and pressed, too, and I rush back down the hall.

'Miss Bird?' Mrs Dutton eyes me from her watching post.

I don't look at her as I slip around the bedroom door, telling the boards in the hall: 'Mr Fox is much improved.'

And no easier to look at: turning to me, the light from the window makes a special point of showing every muscle that makes up the front of him above that sheet. He looks fit enough to go another hundred rounds in a wrestling tent.

I couldn't say what his face looks like, because I'm not looking at it as he says: 'You couldn't do me the best favour ever and give my back a bit of a scratch, could you?'

No, please.

'I can't turn my hands to reach,' he says. 'My wrists are still too sore. I'd be so grateful. Annie. Miss Bird.'

Don't you *Miss Bird* me with no shirt on, but he's already turning his back, so sure I'll do as he asks, so sure his body is a reason all its own, and he's right on both counts. I scratch him in a hurried way, like I'm scratching Essie, our old cow, and he says: 'Just a little higher?'

For Heaven's sake. The angry marks around his wrists seem to say: *And so you should.* Every bruise, every graze and scratch that's on him is there because of me. And that only gets all my feelings swelling for him again.

I'm thinking the most sinful thought I've ever had, that I'm wanting him to drop the sheet and hold me everywhere, with nothing between our skins, my hand so close to seeking him in some way that I should never do, when there's a knock at the door – some angel looking out for me.

'Ahem. Is Mr Fox able to receive a visitor?' It's Superintendent Slater.

I make a grab for the nearest worst thing, the chamber-pot beside the bed, with Jeremy Fox's relievings in it, and open the door: 'He's getting dressed.'

'Good, good.' Superintendent Slater smiles at me, tall and kindly. 'I'll wait, then. Thank you, Miss Bird.'

I throw the contents of the pot at the lemon tree off the back verandah, and a tub full of cold water at my face in the scullery, where the maid comes in with Her Majesty's breakfast tray, plates and pots to scrape and rinse; she looks at me like she knows where my mind has been and I'm so confused in my feelings now, I could slap her. Only pride has me telling her down the length of my own nose: 'Mr Fox will want breakfast himself today.'

I'll go and ask him what he wants to eat, because I don't know what else to do. He's already stepping across the hall, though, when I get there, having words with Superintendent Slater; I hear him say: 'Ah. Right. Come to have another go, have you?' Not too happy to talk to any policeman, I would think.

But Superintendent Slater is quick with his apology at the parlour door: 'Mr Fox, let me say first, on behalf of the New South Wales Police Force, how very regrettable these circumstances are. The officer who wrongfully arrested and assaulted you has been stood down and charged with misconduct, a very serious charge, which will most certainly result in a term of imprisonment of at least one year, but of course you may wish to make a separate complaint?'

I'm sure Superintendent Slater doesn't want Jeremy Fox to do that, as he wants to keep it all a secret from Mr Fox the senior – and not just to keep from worrying him further, either. Superintendent Slater probably doesn't want to see the whole sorry thing get into the newspapers – three fat columns' worth in the *Empire* there'd be over a complaint like this one.

Jeremy seems to leave the question hanging there for an age, before he replies: 'No. Let's call that ledger square. The man is wretched enough.'

There's only one man I've ever known who'd forgo an opportunity for vengeance like that, truly turn the other cheek: my dad. My heart doesn't know what to do with this thought; this cruellest of tricks.

'Good. Good,' Superintendent Slater says, still standing there at the parlour door. 'I'd like to ask you some questions, if you don't mind, have all the facts in place before the attempt is made to apprehend Holly and Molloy.'

'All right.' And he follows the policeman into the room.

I should go and make the bed or something, rather than stand here at the end of the hallway.

Mrs Dutton thinks the same, taffeta rustling up behind me: 'What *are* you doing, Miss Bird?'

I don't care to lie to her as I start sneaking up near the parlour door: 'Listening.'

'Is that your place?' she says.

I don't look at her. 'My place is to look after my friend.' And I'm too curious and too drawn to his voice not to listen in.

'Hmph,' she says, and I hear her footsteps quick into the dining hall where she'll be wanting to listen herself.

I hear Jeremy telling the policeman: 'Their horses were a bit scrappy, perhaps recently broken in. Holly's is a grey, with the stout build of Norfolk cob, speckled rump, the other a palomino, pale brown, colour of sawdust. Sturdy but agile – and fast – both of them.'

He gives a few more details of these horses, and I can't help smiling at the thought that I've never met a man that can hardly see two feet in front of him unless there's a horse to be admired, or an inn.

'Good. Excellent.' I can just see the superintendent, sitting in the high-backed easy chair facing the hearth, notebook on the side table at his knee, scratching down the words. 'Most helpful indeed. Right, well, if I can just get you to – ah ...' When he's finished writing he pushes the notebook towards Jeremy, and I step into the doorway, supposing they're finished their business. 'If you wouldn't mind, could you please read over my scribble and give me a signature beneath to say that it's your word? As you might understand, there's been much confusion of late. A formal statement will be prepared if and as required, but for the moment ...'

Jeremy takes the pen from the holder, reading, and, as he puts the nib to the page, I see that not only does it pain him to write his name, because his wrists really are sore, but that he's left-handed. I would never think less of a person being left-handed – you can't help the way God made the workings of you – but somehow Jeremy being left-handed, curving his hand around to stop from smudging the ink, makes me feel even worse about the cruelty of everything. About him. Like we're both as strange as each other. That in a different life, a different time, maybe —

'Before I go,' Superintendent Slater is saying to him now, 'there is one last thing I wish to ask you. Please, do say no if you do not feel able to, and that would be more than understandable, but it would be immensely useful to the Crown if you would agree to accompany the police party tomorrow morning to Judas Creek. With your eye for horses, and more precise knowledge of the offenders' appearance, you might be able to identify them well before they meet the Escort, and with your own superior horsemanship ride on ahead to give us an advantage of time in intercepting them.'

Jeremy's eyebrows rise so high he's forgotten he was ever hurt at all. He says: 'Do go on. What's the deal?'

'Well,' the superintendent explains, 'the Escort is due to leave Eugowra on its run in from Forbes at approximately twelve midday, which means, good weather and good roads willing, it will come through Booralee at approximately three-thirty pm. Judas Creek is just to the east of Booralee and, according to Miss Bird's recollections of their plan, if Holly and Molloy attack the Escort on the west side of the creek towards Cudal, then you might station yourself to the east – the direction from which we have good reason to expect them to come – and when you spot them, ride west like blazes up to us. That's all, Mr Fox. You would not be required to be in any proximity to Holly and Molloy at any time. You would be provided with binocular field-glasses to maximise your distance from them, and you would be kept well away from any action by the police which might ensue – there's an inn at Judas Creek where you might wait for us in safety once your part is played. We do not want any other unfortunate injury occurring to you.'

'No,' he says, and he's giving all this some thought. I can't believe he's considering it. But I can see very well that he is. He asks: 'What's the distance?'

'Fifty-two miles, from Wellington to Judas Creek,' says Superintendent Slater. 'We'll change mounts at Molong, keep the horses fresh. I'd hope to make the journey there in five hours, give or take.'

'Sounds like fun,' says Jeremy Fox. 'Why not.'

My eyebrows just about jump off my face as Superintendent Slater nods with satisfaction: 'That's the spirit, young man.'

What spirit? Spirit of Stupid?

Jeremy Fox is asking him, like he agrees to the most unbelievable things I've ever heard of every day: 'How's Zad? The Cobb & Co coacher – did he pull up all right?'

'He's in fine form,' says the superintendent. 'Don't breed them any tougher than him. Back on the run yesterday.'

'Good.' Jeremy Fox nods, like that horse was only ever his to take.

'Good fellow.' The policeman nods again. 'We'll leave at five-thirty am tomorrow. Any second thoughts about it, that's fine form, too. Let me know in the morning. Until then, Mr Fox.' Superintendent Slater stands up on his long, tall legs and gives a little bow. 'Good day.' He sees me at the door as he turns and I move to let him pass: 'And good day to you, too, Miss Bird.'

He hasn't closed the front door behind him before I've turned back to Jeremy: 'What did you just agree to?'

'An act of redemption,' he says, and he's serious.

'You don't have to redeem yourself.' I just about slice the ceiling in half with the screech of it. 'You don't have anything more to prove.'

'Oh, but yes I do,' he says, inspecting his fingernails. 'I'd better tidy myself up for the occasion, too.' He scratches his chin: 'Have a shave.'

I tell him: 'No, I don't think so.' As if stopping him from having a shave is going to stop him from going.

'Why not?' he asks, and there's that lazy, slow-curling smile, bottom lip with a cut on it, bruises blooming everywhere.

'Because,' I grab for the nearest lie I can find, 'it won't be good for – healing. Your face.' What?

Because I don't want to see the scratch I made to go with all the rest, there under his beard. Because I more than probably like his beard just the way it is.

And he knows it; because he's having fun with me again: 'All right, Miss Bird. Annie. Dear. No shave. But I must demand a toothbrush – my mouth feels disgusting. There wouldn't be a spare on hand here, would there?'

Oh Lord, what do you mean by all of this? Sending me a picture of us both brushing at the basin, passing the tooth-powder between us. Pictures of things that can't ever happen. And with them a terrible feeling this fun of his isn't going to be any fun at all.

JEM

'I want to go home. Today,' she says. 'I want to see if I can get on a coach, to Penrith.'

You will do nothing of the sort. I tell her: 'You won't be traipsing off alone anywhere. I won't have that. I'll take you home myself. Monday. I'll make enquiries this morning for a coachman to take us to the train.' I'm not travelling by Cobb & Co, sharing the journey with chickens and goats and God knows what.

'Make a firm booking, won't you.' She flicks her hand at me, turning away. 'In case you're too dead on Monday to accompany me.'

'There's more chance of that happening crossing George Street at the wrong time of day,' I say, following her back to the bedroom, where she begins attacking the linen. Right. Attempts to inspire admiration are so far failing, but this, I hope, will change when I return to her less scathed than I am at this moment. I catch sight of myself in the wardrobe mirror and find justification number one: this face needs a couple of days yet. Of equal importance is what this police assistance of mine will mean to Pa: a good deal. A reasonable down payment on all I have to atone for, and a handy card to play in compensation to him over my choice of wife. I'd ask her right now – I want to – but I can't. I look at my face again in the vain hope the damage might have lessened across the last twenty seconds. Too bloody vain. So I ask her facetiously instead: 'Aren't you even a little bit impressed?'

'No.' She thumps a fist into a pillow. 'You act like a little boy going after the next exciting thing.'

Never a truer word spoken. By some whim of kindred connection, she knows me: this is why she must be mine. 'I promise you,' I would get down on my knees if I could make it somehow not ridiculous to do so, to promise her the first of every promise I will faithfully fulfil, 'this is *not* a next exciting thing. Trust me.'

'Trust you.' She snorts. 'What do you want for breakfast, apart from another whack to the brain?'

*

She makes an art of not being impressed.

'Since Mr Fox is now recovered, would it be possible for me to be put in another room?' she asks the lady of the house, Mrs Dutton, who, ever obsequious in my presence, sees to it immediately.

And there Annie stays, all morning.

I knock at the door: 'Do you want to go for a walk? It's a beautiful day.'

'No, thank you.'

'Are your feet still sore?'

'No.'

'What are you doing in there?'

'Reading.'

I go without her, walk around the town, go to the bank, fill up, go to the post and telegraph to send off another note to Pa, *Inexpressibly grateful, see you soon*, find a chemist for toothbrushes, find no suitable replacement hat I'd be seen dead wearing, send word around for a coachman, and pass two pubs without going in for a contemplative beer, before I return to her door, which again she refuses to open.

'Yes?'

'Still reading, are you?'

'Yes.'

'What are you reading?'

'A book.'

'Which book?'

'*Great Expectations* – Mr Dickens.'

'Is it any good?'

'I might know that if you let me read it.'

I don't see her all day.

All night.

Before I turn in, I have a quiet chat to Mrs Dutton, who seems to live more or less permanently in her otherwise empty front parlour.

'Please make sure Miss Bird has everything she needs while I'm gone,' I ask her, and add, handing over a couple of pound notes: 'Except money. If she asks, say I haven't left any.'

Mrs Dutton gives me an, 'I see,' that makes me wince at what an appalling act this is, but I can't risk Annie not being here when I get back. I do realise, after having all day to think about it, that she is possibly resentful at being forced to stay here in this mausoleum far longer than she should have to when she only wants to return to her sister after what has been rather an arduous time. I mutter more ludicrous dreck at Mrs Dutton's steadfastly second-rate fish-face moue: 'Ah, no. Miss Bird has, um, she has suffered a series of dreadful shocks in recent days, and I don't want her to do anything foolish.' There, that's fixed it. 'Without me here. Ah. I mean to say it would be best that she doesn't leave this house. Without – er. Me.' God, shut up and go to bed.

Where I don't stay awake all night tossing and turning it over because I really am looking forward to the morning's ride. Why shouldn't I? For once I get to do the thing I love beyond the usual objective of pleasure-mongering. I get to be useful at it. Do it for the greater good. For a change. Besides, that slick of shit custard, Donovan, nearly killed me; I deserve this ride. When I succeed at its purpose this time, she'll see. She'll see what I'm really worth.

She appears in the hall before dawn as I'm leaving to wait on the verandah for the police to arrive. I suppose she's relented, come to say good luck and goodbye; but she says: 'So, all ready to go and get shot by bushrangers.'

I say: 'Not unless they catch me, and that's not going to happen. I'll see you tomorrow. When I get back.'

The nightgown she's wearing is too big for her, bunching on the boards at her feet, sleeve voluminous at her elbow as she shields her candle from the draught. There's a wariness in her gaze, dark eyes asking me not to go, I'm sure of it. I could step back up the hall and kiss her now, take her with a passion, make her gasp, but I'm just as sure she'd slap me if I did. And wouldn't it be marvellous – except I don't do things like that anymore.

Instead, I ask her: 'Did you finish your book?'

'No,' she says. 'It's a big book.'

'Are you enjoying it?'

'Yes. I've never read anything by Mr Dickens before. I've never read a novel before. It's a good story.'

So good I don't want to go. I don't want to leave her. I want to stay here and read novels with her – that's how changed I am by her gaze.

But I hear the sounds of ready hooves coming up the street, and I'm as quickly champing to be off again.

I turn back to her, to say hooroo, see you soon, but she's gone.

*

Naturally, the police ambush doesn't go quite as expected, either.

I am stationed alone on what I'm told is the eastern side of this creek named for the ultimate betrayer of Christ, just obscured by a stand of trees but with a clear, long view of the road as it emerges from between two steep, heavily wooded hills. Bit of a headache, but otherwise terrific, after a day's brisk ride out in the sunshine, even if the terrain has mostly been a little dull in its endlessly hilly Netherworldish way, and a little more so after this past hour hanging about on my own just watching and waiting, shifting the binoculars from hand to hand because they weigh half a ton in these wrists that remain somewhat weak from their ordeal. It'd be insufferably boring if it wasn't for this mare I'm on: she's called Rosie, a pretty red bay who looks so much like my old Bon-Bon it could be her, bless her black socks, and she's bored too. Shifting her weight around every few minutes with the threat: *Get off my back or get going, will you.* She will start playing up any moment; I can feel her shoulders twitching for it through my knees.

But at last I see the grey cob in the distance, the palomino coming on behind, and at a steady canter, coming on quickly so that I suppose they're heading straight for the Escort to take her on at speed.

And speed is something I have: Rosie is off before I've got a heel in, first down across the narrow creek to avoid being seen on the bridge, and then cross country through open fields for a mile or so – bloody marvellous! – and now we're back to the road where Slater and his party of three other troopers should be waiting to take my signal. Yes, and there they are. I wave, and at it, off they go.

While I head on for the pub. This is splendid, I'm so very glad I came. I'm also a little bit impressed myself that I didn't get lost or jigger things up in some other way.

I can see the pub. Oddly grand place of thatch and clay, flung out here as it is amid nothing but sheep paddocks broken only by dense and rugged woodland, but apparently, all the inns along the Escort Road are fairly grand affairs, from all the endless cash bestowed by wool and gold. I'm looking forward to a beer, just the one, or maybe two, and a game of billiards, having been told there'll be a table here, a licensed one, and I'm setting my limit now at two pounds, maybe five – or maybe just a beer. The pub is situated very pleasantly at the foot of steep, round hills, nestled above the looping meander of Judas Creek, and beneath the shade of expansive eucalypts, all bathed in that warm light of the lowering sun that's rather an excellent feature of these parts. But Rosie is thirstier than I am, ladies first. I'll take her for a drink before watering myself.

'Well, there was an outing.' I rub her shoulder and she nods: she enjoyed that last burst herself.

But what's this? Just as we're about to cross the little stone bridge over the stream, a fellow comes bellowing out of the bushes below it, as if he's the troll that lives there. Good God. Waving his arms and shouting: 'Go back! Go back!'

The mare rears up beneath me.

There's one almighty, thunderous explosion of fire and earth.

And I don't know which way is arseward.

ANNIE

I reckon I understand now why so many warn against the reading of novels – I haven't been able to put that *Great Expectations* from my mind since I finished it, hours ago. It's the most amazing story I've ever read, such a warning against what money can do, and such people in it I seem to know so well I can't believe it's all been made up from Mr Dickens' imagination. Since reading that final page, I can't believe Pip would even consider being friends with Estella – the thought of it has made me cross. She doesn't deserve him, not as a friend or anything else. But then, in a way, they're both as bad as each other, aren't they? Around and around it goes until I remember they're not real! And I don't know if reading such novels regularly would be a good thing for taking my mind away from my own troubles, or if I should never open another one.

There's a bookcase full of them in the back parlour, one called *David Copperfield* in particular that keeps looking back at me every time I think about it, but it's twice as long. Anyhow, I don't want to go out there again. When I left this bedroom to return *Great Expectations*, Mrs Dutton followed me up the hall, stood there and watched me put the book back on the shelf. Mr Dickens should put her in a story and push her down a well. I'll just sit here looking out the window at the roses in the garden down the side of the house, losing their leaves in the fading light, not thinking about everything that's unbelievable in real life.

Like the horse and rider I can now see tearing up the road, kicking up a cloud of dust as they go. It's not Jeremy. Unless he shrank, and changed his clothes.

It's almost five o'clock, not that that means anything. He won't come back until tomorrow.

But what if he doesn't come back? How am I going to get home? How am I going to get on anywhere knowing my last words to him were, 'It's a good story'? Like I don't care. This is a terrible story. I stand up. I sit down. I listen to the clock ticking away: telling me something bad has happened. Because too quick I've come to expect the worst? Or because I'm sure it must be true in this new life of mine.

A hurrying crunch of boots on the front verandah has me snapping up on my feet yet again.

Bang! Bang! An urgent knocking at the door: 'Mrs Dutton! Mrs Dutton! News is in! Come to the courthouse! News is in!'

She rustles like a pudding in a paper bag, rushing up the hall, the maid and the cook after her. And me as well. I'm the fastest into the street, though, having the full misfortune of knowing where the courthouse is, too – right near the gaol.

'And where do you think you're going, Miss Bird?' Mrs Dutton is as quick to try to stop me, with her claws grabbing around my arm: 'You are not to leave this house.'

I have no words to tell her where I reckon she can shove her claws, her house and every nasty spike of iron lace on it – and no time to give it another thought. I smack her hand off me, and I run, with the rest of the town, to hear:

'Word has arrived from Cudal! The bridge is blown at Bushies Inn!' So shouts that Constable Briscomb out the front of the courthouse, standing on the top step, chest puffed out like you wouldn't know he was asking me only days ago if the rumour was true I'd been raised in a convent in Switzerland and if I was sure I couldn't sing him a song while his mate was busy bashing an innocent man. Or practically innocent. I look around at the crowd: a hundred people or more gathering now, and half as many prams – I've never seen so many babies in one lot. Nor so many Chinamen with their strings of fish and baskets of greens, doing a good trade for dinner, since everyone's here.

'Three men down in the battle!' Briscomb reads out another bit of the news from the message he's holding. 'Gunshot wounds!'

'Ooooh,' says the crowd, all excitement at that.

'Holly and Molloy are captured! They are captured alive!'

And everyone shouts: 'Hooray!'

'The Escort detours by the back road through Nashdale!' But no-one's listening to that bit. Billycocks and babies are being thrown in the air; the town of Wellington is having a shindy tonight, celebrating that the thieves are off the road.

I could be excited myself at the thought of the reward that's maybe coming to me now, only I'm sure more than ever that Jeremy has been shot.

'There is no more news,' says Mrs Dutton coming up beside me. 'You must return to the house at once.'

'Get my black face off your street, you mean?' I look at her with all the hatefulness and fearfulness in me: 'There's nothing I want more than to get out of your town and never come here again. If you'd give me the money for a ticket, I'd leave today.'

She sucks in her fat duchess cheeks and clutches at her heart: 'No, no, no! Miss Bird, no!'

'Yes, yes, yes!' I yell and then I hoof off away from her, away from the whole town, my belly full of lit rockets of terror, each one a tumbling madness all its own. I think I'm going to be sick from it. But I start running instead. I start running like I might run myself towards a different ending to my story, and I don't stop running until the fact of the river decides it for me.

The water shooshes at my feet, fast flowing, and I walk along beside it, matching its pace, away, away, but in too short a time it only comes to a fork with another river, wider, faster, darker in the dusk, trapping me here, telling me I don't know where I am. Somewhere north of the town, I am, great high hills rising up ahead, and I stand and stare into them across the water, until I take in the sight of something here I could almost laugh at: the red-and-yellow signage of a Cobb & Co coaching yard, just on the other side of the river. Because I don't think it's real.

'You right there, miss? You lost?'

I turn towards the voice of a man, as gentle as it is rough. An old man, stepping up the bank towards me, from where it seems he was tying up a little boat. He has hair like a mess of fencing wire, face scooped out and grey with a life of worry and hard work: he looks just like Magwitch, the convict and Pip's benefactor from *Great Expectations*, so I don't think he's real, either.

I ask him, testing this dream: 'Why is the Cobb & Co over there and not in the town?'

'Horsing yard's always been over there,' he says, real enough. 'Long before it got took over by Cobb & Co. You need to get across? I can take you.'

'I've got no money for that.'

'Don't matter to me, I won't be taking money from a young lady to see she gets to where she needs to be. Georgie up there at the punt'll take you for nothing, too, if you're quick, as he'll be going across for the coach in a minute.' A punt and a ferry wharf which I can see behind his face now that he's said it.

'That's so kind, thank you.' But I tell him I mean: 'I've got no money at all.'

'Oh.' He shrugs. 'Where would you go if you could, then, ay?'

'Home.'

He nods: 'Wouldn't we all.'

I ask him: 'How long have you been here?' Like I'm asking him how long he's been condemned to ford the rivers of purgatory.

'Since eighteen hundred and thirty-three,' he says. 'Since the village was over there, with the horsing yard, and it wasn't a town called Wellington then.'

Thirty-three was the year my dad arrived; I want to keep talking with this man like he's an old mate of his I've never met before. I ask him: 'What was it called, the village?'

'Montefiores, it was, not much to it then, and a bit less these days – the floods winter last took the boathouse and half the Chinamen's huts that was there. A pig farm, too.'

'That's a strange name, Montefiores.' It sounds like Monty-fee-ories and I don't know why but that I must have read something in the *Empire* to make me think it: 'Is it Mexican?'

'Mexican? No.' The man laughs, his voice even gentler with the sound: 'Mr Montefiore was a merchant of iron, from London, ran his sheep out here, and started up the Bank of Australasia to put his piles of money in, a'fore he went back to London to enjoy it all.'

'Oh,' I say.

'A Jew,' he says. 'They're a clever lot, them Jews.'

Except for the one I know, and just as my heart was steadying, it's walloping again. Please, for all I've used up every prayer, don't let him be one of them who was shot.

'Miss Bird! Miss Bird!' That Constable Briscomb has chased me down, charging up on his big white horse. 'Miss Bird, you can't be walking alone at night.' He gets off his horse. 'Are you all right?'

No. But I say: 'Yes.'

He says: 'I must escort you back to Mrs Dutton's, where you'll be safe.'

Safe? I don't think anywhere is safe for me.

But the kind old man says: 'That sounds like the thing to do, Miss. It's getting cold now.'

And I don't have anywhere else to go, so I go along with Constable Briscomb, who's saying some cabbage-headed thing to me about it being a good opportunity for him to apologise for his behaviour the other night.

I don't look at him. I watch the river blackening with this night. A dog barks, and a campfire is glowing in the trees some distance across the water.

'They're blacks over there, Miss Bird, you see,' Constable Briscomb is saying. 'No-one wanders around here alone at night. They're real blacks.'

Real blacks. Like I'm not a real anything at all. I'd like someone to apologise to me for that. That's never going to happen, so I ask him what else I most need to hear: 'Has there been any more news? About Judas Creek?'

'No, I'm sorry, Miss Bird,' he says, 'there's not.'

JEM

'Bajeez and Jiminy Jake, we thought you were gone, boy, we did,' the Welsh publican of Bushies Inn smacks me on the back again and hands me another free ale. Free because one of the local squatters, a fellow called Trenton of Mandagery, has put his purse behind the bar; while a Mrs Kite, who is the other most notable resident of the area and possessor of the present end of the telegraph line, has brought a fatted pig, which is roasting on a spit out in the yard.

I'm quite drunk already, after – hm. I'm not sure how many I've had. But I knock this one down, too. It would be rude to refuse. And quite silly. It's world-famous Aitken's pale ale, they have here, and, being a brew imported from Scotland, it tastes like the world is small and excellent. Oh, it's a good drop. Just what the doctor ordered too, as I suppose I might not enjoy being smacked upon the back quite so much if I were sober, my back having taken the landing when I got thrown in the blast. Not to worry. If there's one thing I can do with a bit of style, it's fall off a horse; I've had practice. Everything is all right. Rosie's all right – very unimpressed, but all right. I'm all right. The tweed is fairly much destroyed, but I'm —

'Lucky to be alive!'

I'll drink to that. There was one essential piece of intelligence the police ambush lacked, and that was knowledge of the existence of a third member of the gang, some poor beggar called Riley, who was tasked with destroying that bridge over the creek. Ingenious scheme if Holly had pulled it off. The idea was to both stop the Gold Escort from getting through, and to bring into uproar the inhabitants of this pub, and thereby round up and rob the lot in one go. Exhausting to imagine that; the planning and concentration required to be an actual criminal. That'd be a full-time profession, wouldn't it. But it's not funny. It was Holly and Molloy who were rounded up in this deal, and who are both on their way to Bathurst Gaol presently, with Riley, and Molloy with a gunshot to the leg.

'Two seconds ahead of yourself and you'da been dust!'

Yes. And two of the troopers were shot in reply, not causing any dangerous wounds, but Holly and Molloy will hang for the effort nonetheless: there can be no clemency for them now. Miserable thought, that a man might hang for any crime. No chance of reform once you're dead. This is my last Friday night ever getting crapped: cheers, Pa. I wonder if they have a bottle of the porter – I do like an Aitken's porter.

'You must be made to bounce.' The publican smacks me on the back again.

I say: 'No. I am made for love.'

'You are drunk, young Mr Fox.'

'I am.' And I'm all right. Of course I am. The best thing to do when you fall off a horse, or anything, really, is to get yourself drunk immediately afterwards, or better still, beforehand. 'You haven't got a porter, have you?'

'I have.' He smacks me yet again. 'Good lad.' And he goes off back behind the bar to get it.

I'll drink this next one slowly – I don't want to be too boiled for billiards. I mean to have a game with the distinguished Superintendent Slater, or Sarge as he is to his chums, and Bert for Cuthbert to his mother. Cuthbert Ulysses Slater, in fact – I'd like to meet his mother. But in the meantime, I think I might have a crack at dragging myself around to her son right now, where he's sitting with a handful of other squattery types. He's a terribly nice chap, this policeman. I love him. I'd like to sit on his knee, but I won't. He's a dour man, wears his responsibilities as heavily as he wears that moustache. And, as I learned on our long, long way here this morning, he's a man of letters: written a monograph in his spare time on the mineralogy of New South Wales and Southern Queensland. How fascinating is that?

'Should be drawn and quartered,' one of the squattery types is advising Slater sternly.

Another adds: 'Castrate the bastards. Hanging's too good for them.'

I lean against the wall to stop it moving with the long, flat aaaa's in *caaastrate the baaastards*. That grazier is at least half sheep. And I'm suddenly a little too drunk. Perhaps nearly being disintegrated by dynamite has been a bit unsettling. I wonder what Annie's doing. I wish she was here. I'm quite glad she's not.

'Now, now,' Slater is saying in his settling, super-policeman way. 'Jack Holly was a dog gone mad, there is no doubt, a man of the most desperate kind. He deserves the full weight of the law as it is, but no more. It was his anger and despair that brought him undone, a weakness to which any might succumb.' This man should have a pulpit. I could listen to him all night, or for a little while, anyway. 'Holly had lost all,' he goes on grimly, and a lone harmonica joins him from some dim corner of the room. 'He had lost almost the entirety of his flock to the drought the summer before last, then the floods made off with the rest of them, and his fences. So, when he had no clip to sell this summer just past, he defaulted on a loan from his stock agent and his mortgage to the bank, who then took everything that remained on his selection – the house, the furniture, the pots and pans, the lot. Even his wife, who took up with a butcher from Bowenfels. It appears that all he wanted was a fresh start, an escape to New Zealand – as do we all at times – a letter to that effect having been found among his few possessions that were stowed in the Wellington caves. He won't go anywhere now. He is losing his very life. And if I were able to make the laws of this land, I would bring some punishment against the banks for their part in his demise.'

Reverent nodding around the table at inarguably sage words. I'll drink to that, too. Bankers: they're allowed to gamble with *your* money and lose whole countries, but don't you think for a second it might work the other way around. Hearty squattorial condemnation of the banks turns to hearty condemnation of 'half-cocked cockatoo selectors with no bloody idea', which then turns to complaining about their leasehold costs and how no-one appreciates how tough it is out here for them making a fortune off land they didn't have to buy. Boohoo. Someone says something about 'idiot diggers making a track through my place' and someone else says: 'Sodomites!' Cheers to the Great Australian Whine, to be enjoyed at any pub across the country. If this was Woolloomooloo dockside, it'd be the wharf labourers moaning about the seamen, all united in moaning about Customs House; if we were half a mile up the hill from there at the Rushcutter's View, they'd all be shaking their careworn heads over the delay in municipal kerbing and guttering playing a merry hell with real estate prices along the New South Head Road, and shouting bribery and corruption. Yawn.

But someone has asked me a question. Have they? 'Hm?' I'm still holding up the wall with my back, which, on second thoughts, might not be as all right as I'd prefer it to be. I think I should lie down. The smell of spit-roasting pig is not helping. Gah. Is there a bowl of nuts somewhere? I really should have something to eat.

'I said, that's a good-looking gin you got for yourself.' One of the squatters is talking to me. I look at the bottle in my hand: it's a porter, Aitken's stamped upon the glass. I'm not drinking gin. 'That pretty little Lady Bird,' he says, 'where'd you find her? I might want one of them myself. Has she got a sister?'

'What?' I don't like the little man in front of me. I don't know who he is or how he could know anything about me or Annie, but I might want to punch him in the head, since I never got my go at Jack Holly. I'd like to punch him a few times: once for every time Annie and any girl like her has suffered that name – *gin*, as if she were fair game, anyone's at the price of a drink – and once more because I haven't *got* her at all. Yet. I'll punch him again for the box-head who set me back there by wrecking my own pretty face and one more time each for every dickless ball-sack who's called me a Snide, a Shiny, a Wedge, a Shylock, a Fagan, a dirty fucking Jew, or ever had an unfair go at anyone in the history of human existence. I'd like to punch him until I break my fist. But instead, I find a good deal more satisfaction in telling him: 'She's not half as pretty as your sheep. I've heard they all look like you, too.'

'Now, now,' Bertie Slater rescues me, 'Miss Annabel Bird is a respectable young lady, Cam. I won't tolerate a bad word said about her. She is responsible for the apprehension of the gang – without her information we would not have been able to ambush them as we did. And, you might be interested to know, she is the granddaughter of Kulyan.'

This gob on a flyblown turd called Cam tips his hat back on his head: 'Get out with you, no – is she? Gawd strike me, I haven't heard that name in a while.'

'Oh,' says Slater, disappointed, 'I was rather hoping you had. She's looking for him, her grandfather. I'd hoped to bring her back some news.'

Then some other, older squatter says, above another round of bottles in his arms: 'You looking for Kulyan?'

I make an attempt to straighten up at that.

'You've seen him?' Slater says.

'I haven't seen him for a couple of years, no. But I'm not surprised you haven't heard that name for a while ...' the older grazier pauses to place the bottles on the table and I almost fall off the wall with anticipation. After a couple of thousand years, he says: 'No-one calls him Kulyan these days. He goes by the name of Kel Creekstone. Last I came across him he was head stockman for Arrowsmiths out at Tea-Pot.'

I hear that as 'head tea-pot out at Arrowstock', thank Christ for Bertie Slater, who has found a pencil and a scrap of paper, to make a note.

And I slide the rest of the way down the wall.

'Mr Fox! Jeremy! Are you all right?'

Possibly not really much all right at all.

ANNIE

'Would you like a cup of tea, Miss Bird?' the maid asks me, knocking at the bedroom door. Her name is Hilda, and she's being so nice to me I think she must know something, even though she couldn't. She just feels sorry for me. I would too. When Constable Briscomb brought me back here last night, Mrs Dutton shook a finger at me: 'You will not leave this house again. Mr Fox was firm in his instruction.' I'm a prisoner in a frilly-edged cage, sitting here by the window all day, *David Copperfield* in my lap, not being read because I can't make sense of the words.

I find enough of my own to tell Hilda, 'No, thank you. But I'd like to have some string, please.' I've made a decision, the last of a hundred I've made today: when Superintendent Slater, or some other policeman, finally arrives to tell me that Jeremy Fox is dead, I'm going to ask for help in getting home, and I need to be ready: I need to tie up Dad's clothes and boots into a parcel so I can carry them with me, and take them home as well. If they don't help me, I'm going to start walking. If Jeremy Fox is not dead, I'll be walking right past him out the door. *You will not leave this house.* Who does he think he is?

'String?' Hilda's voice is soft and small, but I can hear that she's concerned I'm not well.

I'm not well. It's almost half-past three in the afternoon; I don't know how much longer I can sit here without running into the street screaming in want of everything I don't know. Frightened no-one will care about me if he's dead. Frightened they'll throw me across the river to fend for myself with the real blacks over there, throw me out with the rubbish like they would have done Dad's old tarp. Frightened I'll never see Jeremy Fox again. I say, 'Yes. Just string for making a parcel.'

And it's right this second I see them: Jeremy and Superintendent Slater, riding slowly up towards the house like there's no urgent need for them to get here. I scream out something, I wouldn't know what, as I fling open the door, running past Hilda and out into the street, where I scream at them: 'What took you so long!' Like they haven't ridden some fifty miles to explain it.

His back is to me, getting off the horse, and I see now: something is wrong. He's moving very slowly, holding onto the saddle, one foot on the ground, the other still in the stirrup. 'Jeremy!' I rush to him out the gate. 'What's happened?' He turns his head to me, but he doesn't say anything. He looks as if he might as well be dead: his face is pale, bruises even blacker for it. I think: oh dear Lord, he has been shot. 'Jeremy!' I yell at him again.

'Give me a minute,' he says, still holding onto the saddle, and I smell the alcohol on his breath. He smells a lot worse than he looks – like a brewery that's been rolled in muck.

I ask him: 'Are you drunk?' All the upset makes that come out of my mouth like Dad never once came home so well revived he was rolling pie-eyed – like I'm not grateful at the thought that drunk might be all he is.

'Yes,' he says, getting his other foot on the ground. 'And I do apologise. I drank far too much last night, and haven't drunk nearly enough today to get through it. Christ alive. But don't worry. I've done this before.'

'Got drunk? I don't doubt you have.'

'Ha.' He laughs like he'd rather cry: 'I meant to say, I've come off a horse before, kinked my back.'

'Oh.' Oh dear. He leans forward, hands on his knees. 'I see.'

'Quite a journey that was.' Superintendent Slater is saying behind me, sounding exhausted from it – the ride and the state of Jeremy both, not a lot of doubt there, either. 'Best get the lad straight to bed. Sleep it off.'

'I'm sorry, Annie,' Jeremy tells his boots. 'I really am.'

'Don't stand there like dolly.' Here's Mrs Dutton. 'Help the man inside.'

I tell her: 'Why don't you go and turn down the bedclothes.' And I don't need to look at her stupid face as she hisses, 'The insolence!' I hear Hilda skittering back across the verandah to do it herself, as Jeremy manages another laugh: 'Ha.' And he does smile with it. 'You don't need to help me, Annie. Only a little patience required and not much of that, either – it'll right itself in a day or two. Always does. Honestly.'

I help him anyhow, holding him by the arm for all the good that might do apart from allowing me to feel the strain of his every bent-over step up the path and into the house.

He says: 'You're so lovely.'

I don't say: you're so drunk. Inside the bedroom, I close the door and help him get out of his dirty clothes, thinking I've dreamt too much of seeing this man naked in every way I shouldn't, but not like this – again. I don't want to be his nurse. I don't want to be his friend. Getting his shirt over his head is another and worse agony for him, raising his arms so he groans, 'Oh shit on me,' but it's here I see the cause of it: an angry red mark all down the right side of his back, and it's hot under my hand. 'Horses,' I hiss at it.

'It wasn't her fault,' he says. 'She was scared. Whoa – when the bridge blew up. Scared me too. I deserve everything I get.'

Maybe you do. 'You're not having any trouble breathing, are you?' I ask him, not sure of the injury I'm looking at but that a knock to the back can pierce a lung with a rib and kill you.

'No. Honestly. The vet gave it all a good poke. Awful.'

'Lie down,' I say. 'I'll see if I can find some liniment.' I leave him, and not just to find some liniment. I can't be near him now without my heart being twisted and torn in seventeen different and painful ways.

I go out to the kitchen, where I stare at the bottles Hilda gets for me from the pantry, a choice of two: Dr Jayne's American Counter Irritant or Farmer's Friend. Dad used Farmer's Friend on his sore knees and shoulders; it's liniment for horses – strong and smelling of rosemary and peppermint.

'I'd go with the Farmer's Friend,' Superintendent Slater says from the doorway. 'Swear by it myself. Sprinkle the stuff on my porridge.'

Maybe he does. I pick up the bottle and hold it to my breast like a shield against why ever he's followed me into the kitchen.

'Mr Fox did a very courageous thing yesterday,' he says. 'I daresay he'll be handsomely rewarded for it.' His voice so deep and serious, the first thing I reckon is that I am going to be told I'll be getting nothing, instead. I press the bottle harder into my flesh and try to tell myself it doesn't matter. Remind myself that I just want to go home: that's all I need. Rich white men get all the money, that's the way things work. Handsome ones get to do anything they want. Only Superintendent Slater adds: 'Although he's requested that any and all reward is to go to you.'

'That's nice,' I say, and I can hardly see as I rush past him. 'Pardon me, please.'

'Miss Bird, there's something else I wanted to discuss with you. I —'

I'm not going to cry again in front of Superintendent Slater for everything else that's not mine to have. The bulk of which is lying flat out, stinking and stewed, where I left him.

He says into the pillow he's cuddling with: 'Annie, I thought you were never coming back.'

'Well, I'm back.' I pull the bedclothes over him as necessary, then I sit behind him, soaking a flannel with the liniment and the smell sends me only more grief as I do, the smell of home, of all I want returned that can never be returned, but I let the tears go quietly here as I rub it as gently as I can into his back; he can't see.

He groans, but I think it's with contentment at the warmth of the rub; he says to his pillow: 'I'm going to marry you.'

Because this day just has to get more and more horrible. I want to tell him he'd be better off finding himself a good mare to settle down with, but I can't speak for the torment.

He says: 'I'm going to have to ask your grandfather, though, I hope.'

That makes me snap, annoyed: 'Ask what?'

'If I can marry you.'

'What are you talking about?' Apart from inebriated rubbish.

'When we find him,' he says. 'We found out at the pub that he's a stockman, Kel Creekstone, he is, and he's at a place called Tea-Pot Swamp. Why wouldn't you call a place Tea-Pot Swamp? We can get on the road tomorrow, if I can convince a coachman to take us.'

'If you think you're being funny, Jeremy, you're very mistaken.'

'I'm not trying to be funny,' he says. 'I wouldn't try to be funny about something like this. Isn't it wonderful?'

I don't believe him. I can't believe him. 'You're too drunk to know what you're saying.'

'I'm never that drunk,' he says. 'I would never be false to you about anything, Annie. But I should probably ask you first, shouldn't I. To marry me. And I will. When I'm sober. This isn't quite the way I planned to propose. Let's pretend I didn't mention it. Hm?'

JEM

'I'm sure you won't remember anyhow,' she says.

'Oh, I'll remember,' I promise her. I'll remember the touch of her hand on my skin most of all, with some gratitude at being so incapacitated at present that I can't attempt to do any of the things I would otherwise like to do to her. I wish she'd take her clothes off and get into bed.

'I'd prefer it if you didn't,' she says. 'Marriage isn't picking a puppy up off the street and taking it home.'

'I'm aware of that,' I tell her: 'You're not a puppy.'

'But you are a child,' she says. 'You need to go to sleep.' And now she leaves.

'Don't go.' But she's already closed the door.

I'm not winning this hand, am I. That's all right. I'll turn it around. When she sees what a herculean effort I'm about to make to deliver her to her grandfather, she won't be able to say no.

*

Beginning with getting out of bed before the house is awake. At first I'm not sure it's achievable, but eventually I get one leg over the other and crawl out backwards, and once I'm standing up it is all right – much better than yesterday. Face is looking somewhat less like raw meat, too – there's a bonus. But Jesus am I crapped out. Brass band playing something lively in my head. Someone has thoughtfully filled a jug on the nightstand, though, thank you, Annie. I drink all of it. My clothes have been brushed down as well, a fresh shirt found, no collar but never mind, it'll do the business. God, but my poor coat: one of the buttons at the back is chipped, the split below it a little ripped, but I don't suppose anyone will notice. On second thoughts: let's not bother with the difficulty of getting it on. It looks as though it will be another fine day out there and, pretty little city of the Netherworld though it may be, I'm not likely ever to come back here. Besides, trousers and boots are far more essential. And far more difficult: I have to lie back down to get it done.

But done it is and the walk will fix me up. I know where I'm going. I asked Bert Slater yesterday where I'd best find a coachman willing to take us into the indeterminate, and he recommended a fellow called Arthur Trundle, 'good man in need of the work', husband of the local publicaness who was robbed last Saturday evening, and who is having a bit of hard luck generally from the downturn in the coaching trade for those who've missed out on Cobb & Co runs. I watch the sun rise over the river, turning it to honey as I wait at the jetty for a ferryman to see me, a gristly old fellow with a tiny dinghy that all but destroys me to get down into, but gets me there: the stables of the Post Office Inn, over at the part of the township called Montefiores – do another Jew a small favour, won't you?

'You that Fox bloke, aintcha?' I find the coachman, Trundle, unsmiling over the sack of oats he's carrying. 'Yeah, I'll take you where yous are wanting to go. Done a good thing by us here, ay. Nine-pence a mile plus expenses.' He nods.

'Come around to the house when you're ready,' I say before I've done the arithmetic. Nine-pence a mile over something like a hundred of them to get to Tea-Pot Swamp – that's not five pounds, is it? Not even four? Whatever, I think we'll be giving him a tip.

He says, 'Righto,' and something that sounds like 'see you then' or perhaps 'won't be long'. Whichever suits him is all right with me.

Back in the town proper, I almost have a spring in my step. I could have a hair of the dog somewhere, too, but I don't. I'm not going to drink anything today. Today, Annie will see the man I am. *But you are a child*, she said to me yesterday, with all her disappointment and worry. I am going to prove her wrong.

'Your coach will arrive shortly,' I tell her when I find her waiting on the front verandah, as I'd hoped I might: she sleeps like a squirrel that's had one cup of coffee too many before bed; she'll have heard me drumbling about and getting out the door.

'Coach?' she says.

'Yes, coach,' I say. 'I meant everything I said, even if I didn't say any of it as I would have liked to. But for the moment, if you will excuse me, I'm going to have a bath.'

I don't wait for a reply. The verandah steps have sent a set of blades into my spine: it's the lower portion of it that goes out of kilter, every bloody time, no matter how or where I land. A hot bath will be just the thing. And a little bit of cool from me for Miss Bird will not hurt, either.

*

Not that any of it works terribly well. Annie is less inclined to conversation than our coachman. Her nose raised indifferently past Mrs Dutton in farewell remains raised all the way out the gate and into the coach. Perhaps she's nervous, and understandably, not wanting to give in to hope only to have it dashed once more if we don't find her grandfather. Perhaps she's weary of my company, too. I wouldn't blame her; I'm rather tired of me myself.

Our coach is an open, two-horse britzka, attractive in all appearance but sprung like a cement trampoline, so that almost immediately we're inside it, whatever benefit a hot bath might have given me vanishes inside such a ferocity of pain I think I'm going to faint again. This vehicle is made for the suburbs of London. It is furnished with a hundred compartments that convert into all manner of storage and seating configurations for long-distance travel to one's baronial estate, but never intended to be actually used beyond Harrow. Perhaps that explains Mr Trundle's discounted price. The mere thought that I'm going to spend the next few days in it makes me want to faint.

'Your father is very good to allow you to do this for me,' Annie completes her first full sentence of the day as we leave the bounds of Wellington.

I don't tell her he doesn't know, not that he'd mind if he did know, in principle. He'd approve of both the gesture of assisting a lady in need and my torture by britzka. I tell Annie what I've told her in various ways already: 'My father is a very good man.' Just as the britzka makes a sharp left across a shallow pothole in the track. *Fuck.* I grip the edge of the seat as a poor substitute for letting go of a few similar expletives. That vet who examined me at Judas Creek said I might have cracked a rib, but that is nothing compared to what is going on just above my arse, where surely my back has now been ripped open and is being fed upon by hungry crows.

I can't stand it anymore. 'You'll have to forgive me, Annie.' I'm too desperate to care what sort of a child I'll look like. 'I have to lie down.' On the floor of the carriage, with my feet up against the door.

She moves her feet out of the way, and stares out at the country-side: 'You're not fit enough to be travelling.'

Perhaps not, but optimism is determined to hang on to its own opinion: 'It'll settle down. It already is.' Optimism or bloody-mindedness – because I have to keep going, keep at the table, for one more hand, one more throw, even though I am losing.

She clicks her tongue and shakes her head, but the relief for me is almost instant, no opinion about it. She peers down at me over her skirts, the lowermost hoop of her slim crinoline brushing against my cheek not unpleasantly at all, and she frowns: 'It's all too much for me, Jeremy. All this. You do whatever you do, whenever and however you please. I've never even travelled in a carriage before, of any sort, only the little cart at Cygnet Farm. I'm just a farm girl. You don't want me.'

I can't help smiling at that: she's thinking about it, isn't she. Ha! Of course I'm still in with a chance – and a better one, now my body has given me back my brain. I say: 'Annie, I do want you, like I have wanted no-one else ever. I'm really not what you think I am. Pa is wealthy, yes, but we're just tradesmen, when it comes down to it, and I'm at least half peasant myself, from some grubby little backstreet of Paris. I'm no pedigree. Don't you worry about that.' Unless you're a rabbi or a matchmaker.

'Don't worry?' She clasps her hands on her knees. 'I'm not *worried* about that. I'm happy to be a peasant. I'm happy being just who I am, thank you.'

Right. Well. Good for you. Condescending little bint.

ANNIE

'Far be it from me to stop you being who you are,' he says. 'I've never been known to perform miracles in any case.' He closes his eyes.

I earned that chide. 'I don't want to seem ungrateful, Jeremy, but I —'

'You're owed a grandfather,' he says, keeping his eyes closed. 'The last thing I'd like you to be is grateful.'

I look back out at the bush: it's lonely country here along this Burrendong Road, and everything looks thin and mean: the sandy soil, the trees, and me. But I'm not going to pretend that I'm anything more to this man than entertainment. How many girls does he lead along this way? What does he really want? Something I'm not giving any man who might turn around and throw it away when he sees something else. What kind of a man proposes marriage – drunk – after knowing a woman hardly more than a week? That answers itself, doesn't it. Much as I might want him to get back up on the seat here, rest his head on my lap so I can stroke his hair, I'm not going to. There's no point.

Twenty miles and a sad and slow eternity later, when we stop to eat at a place called the Diggers' Inn at Ironbarks, the want of a point could not be made plainer. He's stretching and yawning awake, and blaspheming, 'Oh God, Jesus, no, really?' getting himself up to his feet as a woman comes out of the inn – a shabby, bark-roofed, rough-slab thing – and she's saying, 'Are you who

I think you are? You our hero, Mr Fox? The Fox and his black missy? You *are*, aren't you. Well, what do you know. Come in and give us a yarn.'

She's not a horrible person. She's happy and welcoming. You don't have to be a horrible person to insult someone with skin darker than yours; by some unwritten law you're just allowed to. I'm just a black missy, a toy for a man, a tart, a whore, no matter that I've never even kissed a man before, and together with all else, I've been fretting that I've missed church now two Sundays in a row, to repent for all the other ways I've strayed since leaving home. I'm tired of keeping my chin up as it is. Being his black missy every day until he gets bored – the exhaustion of it would finish me before the heartbreak got the opportunity.

Jeremy Fox is having a laugh with this woman, making sure his hair is just how he wants it, covering the graze on his brow, like he hasn't been unconscious on a coach floor half the day: 'I see you haven't got the latest telegraph. Miss Bird won't have me, I'm sorry to say.'

'Won't have you?' The woman is holding out a fat, happy hand to me to step down after him: 'What's wrong with you? Oh, but you're a dainty little piece to look at, aren't you,' she says as I get down. 'I heard you were a bigger lass – can't believe half what you hear these days, though, can you.' It's good she likes a chat, because I can't manage it at all today. She's at the coachman next: 'And if it isn't Arthur Trundle – Artie, my love, haven't seen you for donkey's. How's your Jilly going?' before she's back at Jeremy: 'What'll you drink, darlin'?'

'A pot of tea, thanks,' he says.

'*Tea*? What's wrong with *you*?' But she's in a hurry to get it for him anyhow.

And inside the musty, dusty empty Sunday bar-room, he's pulling out a chair for me: 'I take you to all the best places. I can't believe you're refusing to consider me as matrimonial material. *Are* you? Refusing?'

But I can't find the courage to say yes, or no.

I say, 'Ham, please,' for my sandwich; he asks for cheese.

He says: 'Annie?'

I say: 'Shh. How do you feel now?'

'Dreadful.'

That makes two of us.

I say: 'You don't have to continue this journey.' I'll find my own way, ask to borrow some money from him. 'You should be resting.'

He says: 'I've spent most of my adult life at rest. I'll take you to your grandfather, or I'll take you home. Whichever comes first. That's not open for discussion.'

Neither are the overnighting arrangements another twenty miles further on. We stop again at a more substantial-seeming place called the Starlight Inn, a few miles yet from the town of Orange, and after a plate of corned beef and tomato salad we're both too tired to taste he insists I take the one available bedroom here, while he sleeps with the coachman on miserable little camp beds out the back. 'I've settled it with the publican.'

'You can't do that,' I hiss at him. He might have spent the rest of the way here sitting up like a normal person, but he was so quiet all the while, shifting around every five minutes, I'm sure he's still suffering.

He says: 'I'm not going to allow you to sleep with the coachman, good chap that he is.'

I want to say, well, sleep with me. Hold me in the night, make up my mind for me. But I can't. I'm just as sure he's paid the publican more than the room is worth so that I can have it.

He scratches his beard to make it worse, for all that I want my hand touching that face, kissing that beard. 'Good night, Annie.'

And I can only stand here and watch him leave, as the maid watches me from the linen press in the hall with a look on her face that could be disgust at what's blown in to her nice, clean house or could be asking me: are you out of your little black missy mind?

JEM

I will wear her down. Mile by mile. Minute by minute. I will have her with unceasing courtesy and consideration. I will give her an understanding of the life she should expect with me.

'Tough customer, that one,' says Trundle, rolling a cigarette in the gloom of bunking-class at Ploughman's Shitheap or wherever it is we are.

'Hm.' She can't refuse me. She won't.

'Best kind,' he says. 'For marrying.'

'Hm.' I lower myself to the floor and crawl onto the bed. Coachmen: they might tend towards the taciturn, but they have eyes in the backs of their heads.

'Need a hand getting them boots off, lad?'

'Hm.'

ANNIE

I listen to the frogs all singing along the creek outside, and I can't
picture saying goodbye to him. I picture a beautiful house with as
much Staffordshire china as I could ever want – probably Wedg-
wood. I see the silver tea tray I've always craved. A wardrobe full of
silk and the finest French brocades. A hot-water stove. The softest
linens never washed nor wrung nor hung by me.

But when I fall asleep I dream that the craggy mountain in
the distance really is a lizard and with a swish of his tale my
house is smashed. I'm running through the forest, not knowing
if I'm coming or going, if I'm running towards something or
running away.

I wake up with a sore throat. Not the sort that's got from ailing
with a cold, but the sort that comes from too much silence brought
down upon too much to say.

'Did you sleep well, Annie?'

'Yes, thank you. Did you?'

'Yes, thank you. Could you pass the pepper, please?'

'How is your back today?'

'Excellent. Much better.'

'That's good.'

'Nice egg?'

'Mmm, very nice, thank you.'

On and on it goes into the day. But by lunchtime, I know what I
must do.

'By gee.' Mr Trundle turns to Jeremy as we see the village where he'd planned to stop. 'Pigetty's ain't what it used to be. Was only the inn and the store last time I come this way.'

Pigetty's. I've heard this name before, but I can't think where or why. Piggety's Hole. Whatever it might have been, it's hundreds of tents and bark huts now, set all around a street that's a river made of mud.

'Heard there'd been a strike,' says Mr Trundle, tipping back his hat for a better look. 'Didn't know it was coming on like this.'

Squalor like I've never seen the further we drive into it. Rubbish in the street, the smells of every kind of waste, children running around with matted hair and filthy clothes and mud all up their little legs when it's Monday and they should be at school. But it's the colour of this mud that sends me a shiver: it's that rich, healthy red of the earth I saw near Bathurst, only churned up and spat out as it is with the gold diggings and the pumps thumping all around, it looks like the land is so wounded it's running with blood. My heart starts walloping at the sight, though I don't really know why.

'We can push on, but there ain't much between here and Carcoar – ten mile. What do you reckon?' Mr Trundle is asking Jeremy, who says to me: 'Why don't I go in to the store and get some things to eat on the road – picnic? Somewhere a little bit elsewhere?'

'All right.' But my hand has grabbed his before I can think to stop it. 'Don't leave me here on my own.'

'Of course not.' He smiles and gives my hand a squeeze. 'Best to put you in charge of lunch anyway, I think. I'd come out with a tin of preserved peaches and a cricket ball.'

His joke doesn't do anything to ease my fear in this place, and I know he can feel it through my hand.

His voice is gentle and deep by my ear: 'There are worse slums not far from where I live, but there's never anything to be worried about – people are people and circumstance is rarely a good indicator of quality.'

I'm not worried about the people, but I still can't say what it is that's got me in a panic. It's the same feeling I had in the mountains near the waterfall at Weatherboard Creek, that feeling

I'm being told: *Keep away from here.* I can't tell him that – I really would sound mad.

I keep hold of his hand down the step and tighter when I feel it hurts him to lift me across the mud to the hardly less muddy verandah of the store, and tighter again inside: it's crowded. No-one is looking my way, but the crowd seems to press in against me. The walls of the store are all stacked with shelves – boots and pots and pans and swag blankets; belts and bridles, shovels and drapery – bright checked shirts hanging everywhere from the ceiling, and that all presses in on me, too.

'Right. What shall we get?' he asks me, looking around.

I spot the grocery counter at the back of the shop, all the usual tins and bins, and there's a shelf of baked goods above some barrels of fruit as well, so I say: 'Bread? Some pears? Some ham if they've got any?'

'Perhaps not ham. I don't eat pork,' he says, pulling me through the people and over towards the counter.

'Don't you?' I'd think ham was a strange thing to be fussy about not eating but that my heart is still banging too loud for me to make much sense of anything. 'Get whatever you like, I don't mind.'

We have to wait in line to be served and as we do he picks up a newspaper from a table in the centre of the room. 'Ha,' he says. 'Look at that.'

I look at the paper in his hand and I don't recognise any of the words on the page at all. It doesn't look like English – the type down the columns doesn't even look like letters I recognise. It looks like something King Arthur and his knights might read. I think it's a trick of my mind, and I look up at Jeremy, confused.

'The German news,' he explains and says a name that sounds like ostrich pudding. 'Pa subscribes. Only place he can go to check that Poland is still being ripped apart three ways. It's from Adelaide, the paper – funny to see it here.'

He's reading it. I can see his eyes following the words; I can see it in his half-blind squint. He says, 'I can't read a word these days,' putting the paper back on the table where he found it, but he did read it, just like he understood Mr Lieberman, speaking in that other language about potato pie, caught out at a lie that's got lost in all that's happened since. Jeremy is lying again right now, and it's this lie – this one tiny lie – that makes up my mind. I push my hand out of his again and I stand alone in the middle of this terrible place.

I asked him the very first night of our talking together, there by that waterhole at The Gap: *Do you speak any other language?* He told me no. Jealousy slips through my panicking and strangles it: he and his father speak some other language, don't they. Why would you lie about a thing like that if you weren't a liar in everything?

That's a big conclusion to jump to, isn't it, and I'm just about to pull myself back from it when a feller in front of us turns around and starts talking to him in German, too – or I suppose that's what language it is. It could be Abyssinian for all I know. Jeremy's very happy to chat to him, in that cheerful way he has, and here he is laughing, suddenly laughing, and shaking hands in this language I don't know.

I don't know him, and I never will.

JEM

How is my father? Gerhardt Hegel has asked me, and I'm still a little stunned at seeing him here. He's a carpenter, from Wiesbaden. If it's true that there's a Jew somewhere in every town across the world, there's also a German tradesman of some description, and in Sydney many of them at some stage make their way to Pa's door for advice – because he is able to give it to them in German and help them decipher employment contracts. The usual run of events for such immigrants is: young tradesman is accosted by sea captain in a pub in Hamburg and told that Australia is the Working-man's Paradise, with eight-hour days and five pounds a week, where a carpenter can buy his own house and wallpaper it in cash; sea captain collects payment of fares from the various colonial govern-ments for every young tradesman convinced; young tradesman discovers, once here, that the contract he couldn't read says he has to work twelve-hour days for two pounds, nine shillings; Pa gives the poor chap a sympathetic ear and advises he's stuck with what he's signed until the expiry of the terms but promises to put his name forward for better-paying government tenders when they come up. And that's precisely what happened to Gerhardt.

I tell him Pa is, '*Sehr gut*,' or he will be once I eventually get home to prove the worry was worth it, and I ask Gerhardt what he's doing here: '*Was machst du hier?*'

He gives me a two-ton Teutonic shrug and says the government tender Pa helped him get was for the New South Wales Police Force, at present building a lock-up between here and Cadia copper mine, and that it won't be finished quickly enough: he thought Germans had a problem with drinking too much until he came out here. Now that I'm looking at him, I recall the last time I saw Gerhardt Hegel was at the Marrickville Hotel, but I can't remember what I was doing out there. A wedding? Yes – a German wedding. Gerhardt's? No idea. Too budgerigarred.

I'm still laughing at that as he says: '*Und du?*' asking what I'm doing here, saying I look a bit rough, he almost didn't recognise me, and I look around for Annie, to introduce her, but she's gone.

'Excuse me.' I leave Gerhardt and the queue.

I find her looking intently at a kettle near the door. 'What's wrong, Annie? Was someone unpleasant to you?' I can't think why she seems so troubled at being here.

She shakes her head: 'I'd just like to go. Can you hurry up. Please.'

Can you be a little less unpleasant yourself, I don't say. I'm not here for the lark of it, I don't say. I'm here on your account, I don't say. You want to see unpleasant, I could show you the tenements of Darling Harbour or the Rocks, with their rats, their flea-infested hessian walls, their overflowing outhouses, and the Pitt Street pipes emptying directly into Circular Quay – but I don't say that, either.

I hurry up.

Gerhardt Hegel says to me at the counter: 'Every time I see you, you are with a different woman. I don't know how you manage when one is hard enough.'

I tell him: 'I only want one, now.'

'*Dieses Fräulein?*' he says, looking over at her, where she's moved on to inspecting a stand of turpentine drums, and where it's also true that one or two glances inspect her, too. It's not only her colour that draws a stare, though I'm not sure she's aware of her beauty. I don't think she understands it at all: that I would do anything to hold that hand every day and on any street.

'Yes,' I tell him, 'that one.'

He looks at me for a long moment, no doubt taking in the remnant damage to my face, as if she might have done it. She might as well have.

'*Viel Glück,*' is all he says, though: good luck.

Yes, I need some of that, don't I. I need a grandfather, and in the meantime, a night in the best hotel this district can offer. One last roll of this dice.

ANNIE

There are little children playing in a garden, running around a well, beside this big, grand brick hotel. The early-evening colours are washed-soft and misty, the air is fresh between high, steep hills, and every tree and every building in this slim gully is set either side of a trickling river like God put them there especially to please Himself. Only ten miles on and it couldn't be a more different world: it looks like a scene on one of my Staffordshire teacups. It looks like a home. That word comes back to me strong as it did when I first saw those wide rolling waves of the land at Bathurst. That feeling I should be here – in *this* place. Or maybe I'm just missing my teacups.

Jeremy says: 'I'll go in and see what rooms they've got.'

I don't care. They can give me a tent and I'll go and sleep on the riverbank.

'Good little town, Carcoar,' Mr Trundle says, turning to me in his seat. 'She's small but she's rich. Real rich.'

'Why's she so rich?' I ask him.

'Gold. All around her, same as everywhere else. But this one don't change for any of it.'

I wonder if this town really could be mine, even though I've just about let go of that dream of belonging anywhere. I ask him: 'How far to Tea-Pot Swamp from here?'

'Not more'n twelve mile,' he says. 'Be there tomorra morning. I hope yous find what yer lookin' for. Yer grandfather, ay?'

'Yes,' I say, but I've just about let go of that dream, too. I'll be on my way to Yarramundi sometime tomorrow afternoon, knocking at the door of Mickey Dinnigan's asking for Sis, asking for her forgiveness, before I send off a letter to Superintendent Slater to let him know where I am, to see if I'll get any of that reward. If I do, maybe I could see if I can get some land out here. I don't really want to share a town with Mrs Webb if I don't have to, not now I'm getting so close to the fact of it. She won't be happy when she knows I haven't been charged for her lies, but she'll find another stick to hit me with. I ask Mr Trundle, just to know something of this here: 'What's the name of that river?'

'River? That's the Belubula,' he says. 'Flows into the Lachlan, Cowra way.'

Doesn't mean anything to me, but maybe it will one day. If nothing works out, maybe I could learn how to serve and be a maid in this nice hotel.

'You never know what you're gunna get, love,' Mr Trundle says, like he's overheard my thoughts, and he nods towards the river. 'Manager at the Commercial Bank over there, he's on his way back from getting his lunch one day and gets shot dead by the Hall gang on their way out from trying to rob the place. They never got no money out of it before they run off and Ben Hall got hunted down and shot dead himself when it all caught up – they all come to grief one way or another. By gee, if yer gunna take a risk make it a good one, ay? I'll tell you what, though, good thing them shoot-on-sight laws weren't around for you and our Mr Fox – then ye'd have nothing to worry about, would ya.' He laughs at my blink of surprise. 'All I mean by it is, yer a long time dead. Don't chuck away your chances. And don't listen to me. The wife doesn't.'

I don't know what Mr Trundle is talking about, strange old man not given to chat suddenly giving it a go, so I just smile, probably relieved Jeremy and I weren't shot on sight. That's a wild enough ride we've had, and I'm glad it's just about over.

He's been a long while in the hotel. I stare at the doors of the saloon – for another ten minutes. He must be having a beer. Maybe run into another Abyssinian friend.

I ask Mr Trundle: 'Is there a church here in this town?'

'Too right there is, Miss.'

'What denomination is it?'

'Church of Scotland, up the hill. St James, I think it is.'

My spirit flutters all around this gully and up among its gold-kissed clouds: *The church is Presbyterian? Could it be true?*

Another five minutes of telling myself it's not likely a girl such as me would find acceptance anywhere so nice and a woman comes out of the door along from the saloon – the door to the house, I suppose.

'Miss Bird,' she's saying, gliding over, a lady in every way; she's got fine, fair hair like the children playing in the garden and I guess she's their mother. 'Welcome to the Hotel Victoria, I'm so pleased to meet you. I'm Mrs Galbraith.'

Are you? I don't believe this town. I pinch my leg through my skirts as she steps up to the carriage. I've already decided I'll work for her, if it comes to it.

She reaches for my hand to help me down: 'Such a pleasure to have unexpected guests. I shouldn't complain of it, but it's been too quiet here of late and my husband is away – so *often* away. The navy is a shameless thief.'

'Is it?' I hardly hear her; the touch of her hand reminds me of Miss Madden, my old school teacher: sunshine on a cool autumn day.

'Mr Fox is upstairs,' she tells me, 'in the private parlour there. Your apartments are each either side of it. I'll show you up. How was the journey?'

I've forgotten it already, but I say, 'Long.'

'Isn't it always far too long?' she says. 'You must make yourself at home, Miss Bird. Should you need anything at all, pull the bell in any of the rooms and the maid will be with you.'

'Thank you.' For every unreal thing that's happened since I left the farm, this one goes straight to the top. *This* is the one that Sis will say I made up. I nearly start laughing at the thought, that way laughter comes when something is just too mad to believe.

But there's nothing to laugh at when I see Jeremy, in this very nice little parlour, looking over this very nice little town, turning to me, saying: 'Annie, please don't sit down.'

My heart has never known such a force, such a quake, as he gets down on his knees in front of me, taking both my hands in his.

He says: 'I know you think I'm a rake. I am. I was. I'm not anymore. Annie, I love you. I want this to be your everyday. Our everyday. I want you to be my wife. I don't expect you to say yes, here, not now. But please, please tell me that you'll consider it. I can't imagine any kind of tomorrow without you.'

'Jeremy ...' I don't know how to tell him. I don't want this sort of everyday. I want a potato farm, if the Lord will let me have one. I want something of my old life back, even with its hardships. I might not know much about men, or much about life itself, but the things that warn me off Jeremy Fox are things that don't just go away because you tell them to: he's vain, he's a liar and good at it, he's not the right religion, he's a gambler and skilled at losing, a heavy drinker, and he doesn't really have a job – not one that he needs to go to in any hurry. He smokes herbal cigarettes and sleeps all afternoon, sleeps on carriage floors. He snores. His parents are divorced. He's too handsome and he's too rich. He's paid a nice white hotel-keeperess who knows how much money to pretend that I'm a lady. He knows too many tricks for making me look at him, for filling up my mind with him. Once he gets what he wants, he won't want me anymore. Then, I really will have nothing. I have to tell him the simple truth: 'Jeremy, I'm sorry. I can't.'

'You're saying no.' I've hurt his feelings, I can see the wound there in his eyes, those eyes too green, and that is awful, but there are more awful hurts than this.

I tell him: 'That's right. I'm saying no.'

'Absolutely no.' I think I've hurt his feelings very much, but it won't last long. He'll find another girl. He'll find a hundred.

It's for the best: 'That's right. Absolutely no.'

JEM

I am smashed. There is nothing else to say, for the moment. Apart from, *What do you mean by absolutely no?* And that can wait until I'm prepared to humiliate myself further.

Whatever might have remained of my dignity deserts me at this moment, too, as I can't get up off my knees without gripping the settee beside me and not quite suppressing a grunt of both pain and despair.

'Are you all right?' she asks.

Obviously not. But I tell her: 'Nothing a good lie-down won't fix. I'm sure you could do without me this evening. Thank you for being so clear in your answer. Now, if you'll excuse me, please, I'll leave you in peace.' It's mercifully few strides across the room to the door.

'Jeremy. It's not that I'm not fond of you,' she says. 'It's just that —'

'You don't need to explain, Annie. I understand.'

And I don't want to hear it. Leave me with that one shred of *fond*. I have one last tomorrow left to change her mind. I know I've lost, I do realise it's over, pointless, finished, done, but I can't let it go. I can't let her go. I'm down to a grandfather still yet to find, and that could well change the game. Maybe.

*

'Never heard of any feller called Kulyan,' says the station manager of Arrowsmiths. Of course he hasn't. But then he says:

'I can tell you Kel Creekstone isn't here, though. He moved on from us last winter, when we moved the bulk of the stock off, up north.' He looks across the property that comprises half of Tea-Pot Swamp and is about to be no more: a sign affixed to the front gate declaring ten thousand acres will be auctioned off for smaller holdings next Thursday at a hotel in Blayney – by a Mr Benjamin Meyer, of course, such is the power of my father's prayer. Or it's a conspiracy.

I look over at Annie in the britzka beyond the gate. She won't be surprised her grandfather has not been located here. She's already asked me this morning if she can borrow the money for a fare to Penrith on the Cobb & Co. I didn't say no, despite having wanted to shout the word at her, not least because my back is now making me insane and, today, seems to have begun an argument with an increasingly alarming ache in my side. I don't know if it's the sustained sobriety or the smashing from Annie, but whatever is going on in my body, I have to stop travelling and sort it out – soon. Still, it was a good excuse to give Mrs Galbraith at breakfast for why the wooing hadn't gone quite to plan – and she smirked over her sympathy, getting quite the wrong idea about what I meant by 'got ahead of myself' and 'come off a horse', wouldn't charge me for the dinner I couldn't eat.

But let's see this pointlessness through to the end, shall we. I ask the station manager: 'Do you know where Mr Creekstone has gone?' Please let it not be 'up north somewhere'.

'Handy stockman, is old Kel.' The manager shrugs and I think he's going to say something helpful like 'dunno where he is', but he says: 'He's up at Bunyip's Bend, just this side of Spring Grove, back towards Blayney and up the Guyong Road.'

It can't be that easy. I ask him: 'When did you last see him?'

'Few days ago,' says the manager, eyeing me as though I might be the bailiff, squaring at me defensively. 'I seen him Friday. Usually see him in Blayney on a Friday, picks up his rations at the store. A tidy man. Ask anyone, ask Neville McKenzie – the horse dealer he's been working for since he left here. Old Kel's rounding up bush horses these days, up in the hills, breaking them in and that. Best wrangler there is. None can rope and ride like him, not men half his age. None fairer to a horse, either.'

Sounds like a sterling chap to me. Well, chums, this is it. If I could, I'd run to her with the news.

ALL'S WELL THAT ENDS

ANNIE

'Found him,' says Jeremy, and he's talking to Mr Trundle about it being only a few miles on to a place called Bunyip's Bend.

'*Bunyip's* Bend?' Is that what he said? Some strange creature flips about in my belly. 'You've really found him?' I ask him and he says, as he's getting back into the carriage beside me:

'So it would seem.'

I don't reckon I've ever felt such excitement as this. What will my grandfather look like? What will he think of me? Will he be happy to see me? Will I have a whole family to meet? Will he not want to know who I am at all? I've been in this world nearly twenty years and he's never come to find me. Maybe he doesn't know I'm alive. I can't stop checking my hair for curls come loose in the breeze as we go, brushing at my dress to keep off any dust, like it will matter.

This last hill is the longest I've ever known, and it's not only from this excitement I'm feeling. This hill is huge – huge and so, so round that as we get near the top, I stand up and lean out of the carriage to look back at the world from here. And the world is an amazing place of thick green grasses and bright blue sky and earth I want to get my hands in.

A little grey kangaroo bounds across the track behind us and all I can think is that I'll be wanting good fences for my potatoes here – like this place is already mine.

'Annie, please sit down – you'll fall out,' says Jeremy behind me.

And I laugh at him: 'You're just the one I'd listen to for advice on reckless.' But I sit back down beside him anyhow, and I tell him: 'Thank you. Whatever happens today, I want you to know I'll always be grateful for everything you've done to help me.'

'Make that the last time you thank me, hm?'

I see that little cloud of sadness in his eyes; I know the last thing he wants is my gratitude. But it's all I can give.

Mr Trundle turns this way and that with the bends in the road and I nearly jump out of the seat again with each one just for the joy of knowing I'm closer and closer. We pass a sudden farm: a hawthorn hedgerow, a happy crop beyond, bean poles already picked clean, great big pumpkins sprawling ready for harvest, too; happy pigs in their pen; a little cottage made out of stone. All gone to bush once more in another blink and then we come to a wide, sweeping fork to the left that meets another fork from the right, and only a little way further, I see broad blankets of pasture, the high post and rail of a horse yard, and I know this is it. I've jumped out of the carriage before Mr Trundle's got the brake on.

I can see a man in the yard. Just an ordinary working man in moleskins and riding boots, an indigo shirt faded to the colour of chicory blossom by the sun. He's not a big man, he's no huge, tall legend of a man as Dad said he was; he's not got a possum-skin cloak on, either. But I know he's my grandfather. He has to be. His arms are dark below the roll of his sleeve; his hair is grey, almost white against his black face. He's busy with a rope around a horse; he looks over at me.

Me.

All feelings flood at once and I'm letting myself in the gate and I'm taking these last steps towards him until I've walked right up to him, and I'm asking him: 'Are you Kulyan? Are you Kel Creekstone?'

He looks at me for a second with a frown. Lines all over his old face, like a map. Bringing me here, now. He starts to smile, and when he does I see my mother in that smile. But he's got one tooth missing, an eye tooth.

He says: 'I'm Old Kel, that's right, girl, and who are you?'

I start to cry. His voice: it's the river in me, all the rivers, swirling and racing all around. Calling me here, to this place, all this time.

He says, 'It's all right, girl. You gunna tell me your name?'

I tell him: 'Annie. I'm your granddaughter.' And that's all I can get out of me for the minute.

He says: 'Annie?' And then he holds me to him, tight against his canvas shirt.

Home.

JEM

There we have it: Annie in the arms of her grandfather, and me standing awkwardly in every sense by the roadside.

'Good-looking country,' Trundle says, taking a stretch himself.

'Yes, it is.' I can only agree. It is good-looking country. We're at some altitude here with a panoramic view across the hills that's as crisp as the air, while behind the yards is a forest of sturdy timber, a wall of rustling leaves, all very picturesque. Good-looking horses, too: half a dozen, one in this yard and five in the one behind, fine of fetlock, thick at the shoulders, the look of Arabs about them, the type to fetch a price as stock horses when they are broken in, I would suppose.

Wish I smoked tobacco, give me something to look busy with. I should do the manly thing, go over to the old chap and shake his hand, as the hand of the much-preferred man, and make my farewell.

I can't do it. I don't want to say goodbye. Neither do I want to leave her at a bark hut, which appears to be the only dwelling on the property. It has no chimney. She can't stay here.

'Might as well give it another crack,' says Trundle.

I didn't really need the encouragement.

The grandfather is holding on to her by the shoulder, as if he might not ever let her go for the marvel of it, and why would he. A dog of indeterminate breed is wagging its tail in celebratory circles as it dashes around them, trots over to me for a sniff, then back to them.

'Oh, Jeremy.' The face of the happiest girl that ever lived turns to me. 'This is my grandfather.' And to him: 'This is the man who brought me here. I'd never have found you if it wasn't for Jeremy.'

'Fox,' I hold out my hand and with all my superfluity add: 'Jeremy.'

'G'day,' he says and he looks at me for a disconcertingly long time as he shakes my hand: 'Kel Creekstone.' A trace in his tone and in his grip that suggests he's got no time for fools. 'That's good of you to bring my granddaughter here,' he says as he lets the shake go, but he doesn't take his eyes off me. 'I'll make us a brew, ay?'

I can't think of anything worse than sitting through a cup tea for any reason right now, but I say, 'Thanks.'

As the old man walks away towards the hut, to the fireplace in the dirt in front of it, Annie turns back to me, and I say to her: 'I'm not leaving you here.'

She says: 'Yes, you are. Please, Jeremy, don't make this harder than it already is.' *Please go away* is what she is saying to me.

'I can stay somewhere nearby, in case —'

'No.' She is not having one bit of me. 'What you want isn't possible. It's just pretend. I can't pretend that I could ever live as you do. You go and find some girl who fits in your picture.' *Please go away*. 'I'm sure you won't be short on choice.'

'I've made my choice.'

'So have I.' She throws that at me through gritted teeth. 'Now stop this. Please. You're only making a pest of yourself.'

Ouch.

ANNIE

I should shut my mouth. No – I should apologise. I have hurt him enough.

But he says, 'Annie.' Pleading with me like I've kicked him to the ground.

That turns me around again and again, twisting my heart every which way.

And so I give him the very worst of what I've got to say, the nastiest of all my fears: 'Jeremy. Nothing about you is real except for trouble. You can't even tell the truth about what language you can speak. My place is here, not with you.' I smack my heart with my own pleading. 'I need to be here. My history is here, and I need to know it. It's thousands of years old.'

'So is mine,' he says, and I've only confused him. 'What lie did I tell you?'

'You told me you didn't speak any other language, and you do.'

'What?' But then it dawns for him. 'I didn't mean to lie about that. I just didn't want to sound like a pompous idiot when you asked. You sounded sad about not knowing your mother's language. I didn't want you to feel —'

Now that we're bickering about it, I can see very well he was only saving my feelings, but I have nastier words to come. 'And you forgot all about it because you were too *shredded* from smoking those fancy cigarettes.'

'Well, yes,' he says, but I don't let him get another word in.

'How can you love a woman, Jeremy?' I hiss at him like the worst snake ever made. 'How can you be true? You don't even love your own mother – she's out there somewhere in the world, in some *grubby* place and you don't even care about her. You don't even know who she is. You're the type to get bored of a girl and then forget she even exists – it'd be in your blood, and I'm not falling for it. I'm not going to be your fun little bit of black missy for five minutes. So just go – please, *go*.'

'Right,' he says. 'Point taken. I won't bother you again.'

'Good,' I say, and I don't watch him walk away, for the shame of what I have just done.

JEM

What did she say to me? I don't love my mother? That's the most callous thing I have ever heard. I can't understand why it has just been said to me. I've never been an angry sort of fellow; I'm rather angry now.

'Didn't go too well?' Trundle says and I don't answer him.

I see the bundle of her father's clothes stowed under the seat, with the calico bag that has her night things in it, the bloody toothbrush I bought her, too, and I throw the lot over the fence. And that's only another self-inflicted punishment: 'Fuck this.' I hold my side as if that will help.

'Should probably get you to a doctor, lad.'

I tell him: 'I just want to get back to Sydney.'

Forget she exists? Let's see what we can do.

ANNIE

The clop of the carriage going away goes on and on across my heart.

My grandfather is asking me, pouring the tea: 'That feller change his mind?'

'Yes,' I say. I hope. Charles Dickens should write a book about me and give me the ending I deserve.

My grandfather passes me the hot tin mug: 'He your feller?'

I look at him and his old map face. I don't even know who my grandfather is yet, he doesn't know the first thing about my story, but I am that plain.

And I lie anyhow: 'No, not my feller. No, nothing like that.'

JUST DESSERTS

JEM

Seventeen hours later I'm back at One Tree, just as the sun is rising. After parting company with Trundle at Bathurst yesterday evening for another private coach to take me the last fifty miles overnight, I'm too wretched to be angry, too bereft to be embarrassed about anything beyond how much cash I've burnt over these last few days. All I want to do is retrieve my bag from the Pigeon, before going back to the Royal near the railway station, where I will have a shave and then lie flat on the floor until it's time to board the train – another eight hours from now.

'Are you sure you wouldn't like me to wait for you, sir?' says the present coachman, probably the most polite coachman in the world. I'm not polite. When he offered to take me the whole distance to Sydney I told him I'd rather be eaten alive by rabid dogs – even with the wait for the train, even with a fresh team guaranteed at every twenty miles, the coach is far slower over eighty, and the next pothole will undoubtedly reduce me to rubble.

I tell the coachman: 'No.' And take myself the few yards from road to inn. If there is any pleasure left to me, it might be knocking on Fenderly's door at six o'clock in the morning, just to give another a little inconvenience, but I've never been much good at schadenfreude and Fenderly is too happy to see me.

'Well, look who it is!' he greets me, blinking and scratching at his undershirt, 'A sight for sore eyes, you are, young Mr Fox, me lad. Didn't we get you in a mix-up, ay, my word we did.' He's not in the slightest bit embarrassed about whatever his part might have been in wrongfully accusing me of being an impostor of myself; somewhere, deep down, we all know he was at least halfway right. But he is keen to ensure there are no adverse consequences for him: 'What can I do for you? Anything you like. We hear you turned out quite the hero.' He's stepping aside to welcome me in. 'You'll be wanting to have some breakfast with us, won't you?'

'No.' I'm not interested much in food, less so in anything that comes with extra bacon. For a moment I can't remember why I am here, though, as Annie's rebuff smashes through me again, and again, like the relentless swell of a savage sea: I don't love my mother? My mother is the one who didn't love me, not enough to stay in London. I was only four years old. Never a pleasant thought, and this is why I don't think it. I don't think about her; why should I?

'You all right there, Mr Fox?' Fenderly peers more closely at me. 'You don't look quite yourself.'

What would you know. But I now remember why I'm here, for the one small thing that could possibly raise my spirits one grain's width above shit level: 'I'd like to pick up the bag I left here.' And the shaving case that's in it. And a fresh pair of socks.

'Bag?'

'Yes. A carpetbag. I left in around the back.' In your manger.

'Oh, I don't know anything about any bag,' he says, and his eyes dart in every direction in the attempt to avoid mine. Because of course my bag is not here. Some good Christian would have stolen it, wouldn't they.

I walk back towards the village. It doesn't matter. I'd have too hard a time carrying it anyway. I don't need a shave. Pa's been at me the last few years to let it go, start looking like a man.

*

The views out over the mountain gorges are something to see from the train, and I might appreciate them another day. I will bring Pa up here one Sunday for lunch, drag him away from work, start behaving like a son.

Four hours and twenty minutes later, coming in to Sydney in the dark, I can barely raise an arm to hail a cab, but I have to; it's three miles yet from Redfern to Woolloomooloo and I'm not capable of walking that far now. It's a Wednesday night and the streets beyond the hub of the city are shut-up quiet under the dull glow of the lamps. The stench of the place is exceptionally disgusting after this fortnight's worth of too much clarity, but it's pushed aside by the sea breeze on the rise of Potts' Point above the bay, as it always is.

And Mrs Kirschbaum is opening the front door before I've set foot: 'Jeremy!' Running down the steps, into the street, apron billowing under full sail.

'Where have you been!' she yells. She can't talk without yelling. 'Get inside. You look thin. We've been so worried.' She pulls me by the sleeve in through the gate, and I look up at the house, all lamps blazing across the wall of otherwise restrained Italianate sandstone that is home, to be sure I can't accidentally walk past it.

'Is Pa home yet?' I ask her on the steps.

'Is he home?' she yells. 'Is he *home*? He hasn't left the house.'

There's a fact to send me sub-shit level, and here's Pa.

'Jemmy! Jemmy, it's you!' He runs out of the library into the hall, beard trembling, kissing my cheeks. 'Oy oy oy! *Boruch Hashem*!' Crying in three languages.

As Mrs Kirschbaum continues to yell at me: 'Look at your face! What happened to your *face*?'

The faces of Pa's man, Lozinski, and the maid, Clarinda, appear at the end of the hall, as Mrs Kirschbaum pushes back my hair to find the worst of mine: 'Go up to your room and get into bed.'

Is it any wonder I've had some difficulty growing up?

'Jemmy, say something.' Pa is wiping his eyes. 'Are you all right? What's wrong? Are you upset with me? I was only going to make you stay at the Comet forge for a month. Only to give you time to think about things. I wasn't going to make you stay there forever. I feel so bad about it now. Can you forgive me?'

'Pa.' I kiss him on the head, because I have shrunk him, and because I can't begin to answer that ridiculous question.

'Fitzworthy says you helped the police. He says you will be honoured. I'm so proud. What did you do?'

'He also said you hit your head,' Mrs Kirschbaum's voice is getting higher and higher. 'What happened to you? Can't you talk?' She turns to Pa: 'Mr Fox, why isn't he talking?' She doesn't let anyone talk before she's decided: 'I'm going to get Doctor Feinberg.' And because she is never as insane as she sounds, she narrows her eyes at me and shakes a finger: 'You are hiding something. You've hurt yourself, haven't you. Don't you lie to me. Don't you lie to your father. You've hurt your back, haven't you. I know when you've hurt your back. You go upstairs now.'

'I will in a minute,' I say. I want to see Raj first, and not cry myself in front of my father or Mrs Kirschbaum.

'Jemmy, you're not going out, are you? Please.' Pa is following me down the hall.

'No. I'm not going anywhere,' I promise him: quite possibly ever again. That he's asked me the question is a scalding regret, but why wouldn't he ask it? I can't remember the last time I cried, it's not been a feature of my personality, but I'll remember this time.

I keep walking out the back door, across the lawn to the stables, and I hear Raj snort before I get there, *Where have you been?* When he sees me, he kicks the back of the stall: *I've been locked up in this yard for Christ knows how long.*

'I'm sorry.' I give his nose a rub and he pushes away my hand: *Going to have to do a bit more than say sorry to earn my forgiveness, old chum.*

*

'You might kill your father before you kill yourself,' Doctor Feinberg tells me, making his inventory. 'How did you get these cuts on your wrists?' he asks. 'And these bruises across your shoulder – you look like you've been whipped.' He's unsure if he should be amazed or repulsed by the possibilities.

It's a humiliation I don't want to revisit, and I gave my word to Bert Slater I wouldn't be making any deal of it, so I give Doctor Feinberg my most plausible evasion: 'I don't remember.'

He issues a threat I don't need to hear, either: 'If you take another fall, you will break your back and you won't be riding anything. Is that what you would like to achieve with your life?'

No answer required there; we've had this part of the conversation before. He starts poking around everywhere for the flinch and when he finds the one that makes me yell – that place in the middle of the side of my back, right beneath my left shoulder – he mutters: 'Oy.' I've managed to shock him now. 'What possessed you to travel anywhere in this state?'

'I didn't think it was anything much to worry about, at first.' I was otherwise occupied trying to get a girl who hates me to agree to marry me: even I don't believe I did that. 'I thought I'd only kinked my back again.'

'How drunk were you this time? Did you see a doctor at all?' he asks me.

'No.' The vet, who was quite possibly as drunk as everyone else, doesn't count.

He says: 'You have three dangerously fractured ribs, that I can ascertain. You will not be leaving this bed until I instruct it is safe to do so.'

That's all right. I don't want to.

My father is at the door: 'Do you want some soup, Jem?'

No. But I say: 'Yes, please. Thanks, Pa.'

'Mrs Kirschbaum wants to know if you want kneydlekh in it, or only the broth.'

'Whatever she thinks is best.'

She and Doctor Feinberg have a long argument about everything that's best, from the placement of a pillow to the temperature of a linseed poultice and how often it should be applied. 'No, he is not to have a brandy to sleep. He'll be after the bottle,' Feinberg is firm about that, and I don't dispute it with any finer point of fact that I suffer from generalised idiocy rather than alcoholism. He takes something from his bag and smacks it on the nightstand: 'He can have these if the pain is bad.' It's a box of Grimault's medicinals. There might have been a time when the prospect of spending a few weeks shredded in bed would have been appealing, but it's not anymore.

'Is the pain very bad?' Pa asks me with all the anxiety I have given him.

'No,' I tell him, and it's not. 'Not now.' Not pain that is of any treatable kind.

He kisses me once more, pressing my cheek to his: 'I'm so happy that you're home.'

God love him – I do.

It's not till after midnight that they all leave me alone, and I cry again: I will be a good son from this day on, I have no doubt, but I don't think I'm going to have an easy time of it forgetting Annie Bird.

ANNIE

'Get up, girl,' my grandfather says at the crack of dawn Friday, but I don't want to put one bit of me outside the blankets. It's so cold up here in these hills. I don't have enough of his blood in me to bear it. This one-room hut is no shelter against it, the gaps in the slabs almost as wide as the slabs themselves – not that this grandfather of mine cares. He sleeps outside with his dog under the verandah, if it can be called such. Inside is where the saddles and blankets for the horses live. And he has no sympathy at all for me: 'Get up, we're going to Carcoar.'

'Carcoar?' I ask him. I asked him yesterday if I'd be able to somehow get to Carcoar on the Sunday coming, to go to church, and he said he wouldn't be going to Carcoar on Sunday, like going to Carcoar was the most stupid thing he'd ever heard, never mind going to church. I don't know how we're going to get along. I know this is only my third day here but he says more to the horses than me. I've tried to talk to him – about Dad, Mother, the farm, but he doesn't seem to want to know, doesn't want to hear about his own daughter, he just grunts and walks away, too busy – and I don't know how I'm going to leave him to it. Yet. I don't have any money, and every time I remember that, I think of Jeremy, and the fool I am for not borrowing the fare to Penrith from him before I thought to be such a vicious little snake to him. The fool I am for making him go at all.

'Get up and do as you're told,' says my grandfather. I don't need to ask him why it seems he lives alone. There's something about his impatience I recognise as maybe in the blood – that makes me think I am getting exactly what I deserve. I don't know if he's been intent on taking a measure of me, or just doesn't like what he sees.

'Can't I know why we're going to Carcoar today?' I get up out of bed, if it can be called such: a camp bed, barely six inches off the cold, bare ground, and I deserve that, too.

He gives me a question for my question: 'You planning on stopping here for a while?'

How do I say no to my grandfather, my only one in the world? I say, 'Yes, well, I hadn't thought —'

'No, well, you wouldn't have thought, would you. Got to take you down to see the boss, Neville McKenzie, get rations for you, if you're staying,' he says, and he goes back out the door, such that that is, where he tosses the frying pan on the fire with a clunk. 'Get your name in the book at the Blayney store.'

'Rations?' I say, like I don't know what they are, like labourers of all kinds don't get stuck on getting paid in provisions and getting nowhere for it, but I'm more intent on almost tossing myself at the fire right now just trying to get unfrozen.

'Yeah, rations.' He shakes his old white head at the cabbage that is me before him: 'Tell Neville McKenzie you're working here with me.'

'Working here?' There's nothing much here for me to do, except get water from the creek, which isn't far, and cook if he lets me. Apart from that and fretting over the awful thing I've done to Jeremy, I've been fretting about what I'm going to do when my monthly bother comes, which will be soon, and will have to involve cutting the hem off my nightgown, this cast-off nightgown I was given by that Mrs Dutton, and am now wearing under Dad's Crimean like I don't know how to dress myself. I'm so ashamed.

'Yeah. Say you're looking after me.' My grandfather cracks an egg into the pan, but then his face cracks into a smile as he looks back up at me. 'You don't have to if you don't want to, girl. I don't need no housemaid. But if you're staying, you gotta eat and I've only got rations for one.' He keeps cracking eggs into the pan, tossing the eggshells onto the pile over the other side of the fire. A whole pile of rubbish over there: egg shells and yabby shells, from the sweet crayfish in the dam, and old tin cans, the dog sniffing through it all. I can't live here, like this. But when he asks me: 'So what do you reckon? You staying for a bit?'

I say: 'Yes.' He's my grandfather. Smiling at me with my mother's smile. It doesn't matter how he lives. I have to know who he is and take everything that's coming to me along the way. This is what the Lord has provided for me. And in Carcoar, I can send off some letters, one to Sis, not saying very much, and one to Superintendent Slater, care of the police court in Bathurst, asking him straight out if and when I'm going to see any of that reward. Maybe I can ask that Mrs Galbraith at the hotel for a little notepaper, and some envelopes, a few pennies for the post. She was so nice to me; I don't see why she'd say no.

'Good,' my grandfather says. 'Another name in the book is another name they can't say ain't here.'

'What do you mean?' Now he seems to have started talking to me, finally, I don't want him to stop, ever.

He says: 'White fellers don't like writing things down when it comes to black fellers, and if they do, they say you live somewhere you don't, give you a name that's not your own.'

'Is that what happened to you?'

'Nah. I got in first,' he says. 'Long time ago, when they were doing one of their black feller musterings, the missionaries, they come out and asked me who I was, and I said Kulyan, told them I'm from Wirradjeree country, from the Wambool way, that's the Macquarie River, and they tried to call me Jack Dalton after the station I was working on at the time – Daltons – giving me a blanket and a Bible in exchange. I took the blanket but not the Bible or that name. They said, you gotta have two names in our book and so I gave them two names I chose myself.'

'Kel Creekstone,' I say, smiling back at him with all my wonder and gratitude renewed at being here with him, the small miracle of it. We are blood all right. 'How did you come up with that name?'

'I dunno.' He laughs at the fire. 'Just made it up when them fellers come along. I wasn't gunna have them call me Jack Dalton. I wasn't gunna have them write that down in their book.' He stops laughing, and looks hard at me for a few moments, like he's thinking about whether or not he might say something more.

Please say something more, I try to ask him with my eyes. And then he does: 'You've gotta understand something if you're gunna stay, Annie. This is my land you're standing on here. This is my mother's country. The government might have the law that says the Queen of England owns these yards, these paddocks, this bush, but I have another law that says it's still mine. From Ophir, on the Wambool where I was born, to this place here at Bunyip, out to Bathurst, to Blayney and all along the Belubula River. We never surrendered.'

I don't want to ask him who the 'we' is; I don't know if I want to know that they're not here anymore, maybe like Mother's people on the Nepean. But I don't want to put him off telling me anything – everything.

He changes the subject anyhow: 'Neville McKenzie, he's all right. He knows who I am. We do each other a favour. It'll be all good with him.'

'A favour?'

'You don't need to know anything about that.' He hands me a tin plate and slops an egg onto the tough old bread there: 'Be quiet and eat your breakfast.'

I do, and afterwards, as I'm washing off the plates in a bucket, he says: 'So, what horse you want to take?' He nods over at the yard nearest the hut and horses in there. 'Pick any one you like, apart from that one on his own.'

'Horse?' I have to tell him: 'I can't ride any of those horses.' I might not be as fearful of them as I once was, but —

'If you don't get on a horse, you don't come with me.' He's frowning, not understanding what I'm worried about.

'Grandfather, I can't —' Those horses are all too tall and wild, however they might be tamed by him – and they're horses.

He says, frowning deeper: 'Didn't you tell me you rode from One Tree to Wellington with that feller? What did he do, tie you in a bag first?'

My face goes red hot at that, because it's just about true. I say: 'No. But he held me the whole time so I didn't fall off.'

'He doubled you? All that way?' He laughs, the biggest laugh I've heard come out of him. He says: 'There's a feller that doesn't mind trouble.'

'Hm.' There's a feller who got thrown off a horse. I tell my grandfather: 'You can laugh as much as you want to, but I can't ride a horse on my own.' I grab up another excuse: 'And I'm not doing it in skirts.' Not wearing strides, either. Because why? I'm a *lady*?

'You'll be right.' He pats me on the shoulder as he walks past, going into the hut; comes back out with a saddle: 'You missing that feller yet?'

'No,' I say, shaking the drips off the plates, busy hiding my face altogether. I miss Jeremy Fox like I'm missing half my heart. But I'll get over it, when I do. I'm sure he's got over me.

*

I've got sixteen miles of learning how to ride a horse to Carcoar, my hands trembling most of the way, scared of the reins, Grandfather saying every five minutes: 'Look out at the country. Don't look at the ground.' Him and the dog both barking at me: 'You gotta learn, girl, if you're gunna stay here. Sometimes I gotta go off with McKenzie, bringing horses in. You gotta know how to look after yourself.' Maybe I've got to look after myself all the way back to Yarramundi, not on a horse. He's telling me: 'Take it easy and the horse will too. She's a good girl. She just wants you to tell her what to do.' Yeah, well, there's the problem, isn't it: I don't know what I'm doing.

'Can we just slow down a bit?'

'Not if we want to get there this week, girl.'

But we get there all right and, with my knees still weak from the whole, long morning of it, I'm standing on my own two legs again being introduced to this Neville McKenzie, at his yard full of horses on a steep paddock above the town, a tall, fat man in a cheap checked shirt with a wide-brimmed hat and a gold tooth; he looks just like a horse dealer: fast. And that's also the way he talks.

'Good you're gunna take care of the old man – Annie, is it? Pleased to meet you,' he says, not interested one way or the other, before he's thick in chat with my grandfather. I'd like to say, no, as a matter of fact it's Miss Bird to you, but what he's saying has got my attention: 'The next sale of land looks like it'll be gazetted in July sometime, a parcel at Spring Grove, small lots – one, two, three hundred acres – good soil and at two pounds per acre expected at auction it'll all go quick. And Bunyip'll be next after that is my bet. We're going to have to move on then. I'd reckon by the end of the year.'

Grandfather gives the man one of those long stares of his, but he doesn't say anything.

Neville McKenzie shrugs with his palms up: 'Not much I can do about it, Kel. I'll find somewhere else.'

As a bell goes off in my head: there might be something I can do about it. I feel that little flutter of excitement rise up through me, that maybe, truly, I can have a piece of this place – that *I* could own a piece of my grandfather's country. If I get even half the reward, I could do it – a *third*. It would change everything. It would be the most wonderful thing ever to happen, except I'd build a proper house on it, and for the moment, I'll be keeping it to myself.

I don't know what horse thing they're talking about now as I interrupt them: 'I've got to go into the town and send off some letters.' Thinking I'll sneak off on my own, down to the hotel, to see Mrs Galbraith.

'Letters?' Grandfather blinks at me, and then he gives me a strange little frowning smile, before he's telling Neville McKenzie, 'Gotta get going. Things to do. See ya.'

We start walking the horses down the hill and my grandfather is quick to ask me: 'You going to write them letters yourself, are ya?'

'Yes. One to my sister, Cecily, and one to …' I don't want to tell him anything about it so I say: 'A friend.'

'You can write.' He says that with such pride, it takes the breath from me for a second.

Before I tell him with pride of my own: 'Yes, I can write. And I can read whole books, too.'

'Good on you, girl.' For the first time since that first moment he saw me, I feel like he's pleased, really pleased I'm here.

But when I tell him, 'I'm going to ask at the Hotel Victoria, see if I can have some paper, borrow a few pennies —'

He cuts that down: 'What do you want to go doing that for?'

'Well, I haven't got any money or things to write with, and —'

'Go to the post office, get what you need there, put it on McKenzie's account. That'll be all right.'

'But I know the lady at the hotel,' I tell him. 'We stayed here last Monday night.'

He doesn't say anything. I don't know what he's so disapproving of, but I jump at it: 'We stayed in separate rooms.'

He only grunts at that, 'Here,' holds out his hand for me to give him the reins of the horse: but I soon find out what he means.

I knock at the door of the house and a maid goes to get her mistress, who comes down the hall and looks down from her step at me now: 'I'm sorry, you are?' She's very nice about it, such a fine and fair lady, but she's not going to give me anything. 'I don't recall …?'

'Miss Bird,' I say. I might be a bit *grubby* from the road, but I don't look that much different than I did four days ago. I'm not wearing any crinoline cage under my skirt, for obvious reasons, but I've tucked up the waist neatly, so that you'd have to be looking for faults to tell. I look smart enough, I don't need a mirror to know it. I don't need to know anyone who'd mark another down over a petticoat, either. But it's not that, is it, not really. I'm no-one to this woman without a rich white man paying the bill, I suppose. For all that I'd like to slap her to set the memory, I smile back with an equal sweetness. 'You might recall who I am another time.' And as I turn away from her I close my eyes and I pray my hardest for something I shouldn't: the land. Only souls should ever be prayed for, not money or material things, but it's my soul that's wanting this piece of land.

Grandfather says: 'She ain't all she seems.'

Whoever is. I say: 'She'll keep.'

He says: 'She keeps a squatters' brothel up there.'

The river takes my laughter and tosses it in the air, up to the post office, where my grandfather is not unwelcome on business from Neville McKenzie, where the postmaster there says, 'How's it going, Kel?' And he replies, 'My granddaughter's got to write some letters.'

He watches me writing them at the counter, looping out the words, blotting up the ink. He says: 'Your mother and your father did a good job on you.'

I am blessed and blessed, wrapped up in the warmth and the rightness of family, as I tell him: 'They did.' And I call him for the first time: 'Granddad.'

I tell Sis only that I've found him and I'll write again soon, and I'm halfway through choosing my words for Superintendent Slater, when this granddad of mine says: 'You writing to that feller?'

I frown at him now: 'No.' And I'm not going to. I say: 'That's a feller who's not going to want to hear from me.'

'Why not?' says Granddad. 'What did you do?'

And I grunt at him: 'You can just leave that be.'

JEM

'Ah, Jem! I have something for you.' Eli Abrahams, my tailor, is thrilled to see me, pulling out a couple of bolts of tweed before the shop bell's stopped ringing. 'These came in only last week.'

I need a new winter coat. That's why I'm here. But I'm inclined to say, you choose, I don't care – because my entire personality has been stolen by the morbs, thrown on Death's boat and pushed out to sea.

'Your father says you've been indisposed – all right now?' Eli asks, and he's asking at least fifty percent on Pa's account, as much for his own curiosity.

'Never better,' I tell him, genuine as gimcrack. I heal quickly, always have, barely more than a month and not an ache left in me: nothing. Although Feinberg insists on exacerbating the nothing by continuing to forbid me to ride. Feinberg can go and get —

'I like the beard,' says Eli. 'Looks good.' Schmoozing as a tailor should.

I choose the blue whatever it is, he tapes me up, I wander out. I need a new hat, too, but I can't imagine dragging myself around the block to Pitt Street, so I start walking back to our shop, to Pa. Only a matter of weeks ago, the idea of wandering about town hatless was unthinkable. Undoable. Now I'm finding it difficult to remember that man – that child. I remember promising Pa I would reform by Yom Kippur, and I'm well ahead of schedule, but

I'm not sure what I've done to myself this time. Back in bed, the sheer weight of boredom drove me to a Grimault's and, inside a nightmare that had me convinced I couldn't breathe, it only made me hurl up – which in turn gave Mrs Kirschbaum cause to fear I had pneumonia. That was fun.

I take the lane to the back of the shop, a dank and sunless passage, the rotting bowel that runs the length of Sydney's most glittering strip. What am I doing here?

I'm back at work, my second day. Pretending to be a jeweller. I *am* a jeweller. I open the safe and take out the jacinths Pa needs me to set into a pair of earrings. This isn't work. The stones are beautiful in colour and cut, such depths of red, they are fire and blood; and silver is soft and predictable. Gold is too. And it's all excruciatingly boring. That's not the morbs talking: it's always been excruciatingly boring. I've never wanted to be a jeweller. Just because you can do something doesn't mean you should. Pa's the artist. This is his life. He can spend days on end designing and refining a candelabrum. He's front of house, in his showroom at this very moment, with one of Belmore's men, discussing plans for the Sydney Intercolonial Exhibition. A man in the midst of all his beautiful things, serving God and the Governor both with his gifts. While I'm ...

Wishing I could see these jacinths glinting against Annie Bird's skin, along her slender neck.

Then wanting a claret with lunch – at all fifty-seven public houses in the metropolitan area. And not wanting that at all. I am horrified by the quantities of alcohol I've consumed, so horrified I can't even share a glass with Pa. I might have just lost a few weeks to bed, but that is nothing compared to the weeks on end, the months, the years, I have lost to drinking. And what for? Because I can't think of anything else to do. And I can't do nothing – because I am my father's son.

If I said to Pa today, sorry, I can't finish this, I've decided I want to go to university, or I'd like to be a dentist, or even a tailor, he'd slaughter a calf in the street, he'd move a mountain to see I achieve it. But I can't see myself doing any of those things. Although, I must admit, this period of contemplation has also caused me to realise there are occasions on which I simply don't see very well at all. She was right: I do need spectacles, if I'm going to read anything longer than the track news. I look up from the eyepiece now and the tools hanging on the back wall are a blur – I can't tell the difference between drill, chisel and mould-cutter, except that I know what is where. That's nothing to do with the lighting in here, and nothing to do with any post-spree blear. My vanity has not diminished quite enough for me to face it yet, though, even if it goes some way to explaining my abiding aversion to study, as well as sustained tweezering of stones into microscopically tiny claws.

'Jemmy, I didn't hear you come back in.' Here's Pa at the workroom door. 'How is Eli?'

'Good.' I get on with it, blinding myself in lieu of alternatives.

'Belmore and the Countess are going to establish a house in the countryside,' he tells me the gossip and its significance to him. 'They will require full sets of silver – everything, top to bottom, front to back.'

'And you've been asked to oblige?'

'Yes.' He's so happy. God, I love him. Then he says: 'Reverend Davis called in earlier and I've invited him to dinner tonight.' Probably the last person I want to see. I haven't been to synagogue yet; another bridge left to cross, and Pa hasn't asked me to for any reason. But if Feinberg was quick to tell me the fate of my father is in my hands, I'm going to get it tenfold from the Reverend Rabbi Davis in a glance. I look up and see clearly enough that Pa's going to give it to me himself, right here, with a smile that can barely contain itself: 'We've found the perfect wife for you.'

Jesus Christ. I don't want to yell that at him, so I say, 'Hm?'

'She's from Danzig.' Pa is so delighted, his eyes almost leap out of his head; Danzig is where he was born. 'Her name is Danya Blankowicz – she is the second cousin of Reverend Woolf's wife – you know, the new rabbi in Geelong? She is very smart and very beautiful.' No, she's not; she will be cross-eyed and look like the back end of a dray. 'She speaks a little bit of English already, too.' She will speak none. 'She is a distant relative of Joe Montefiore on her mother's side …' He goes on about her family for a few more centuries, and then he says: 'Isn't the timing incredible? We can't ignore it.'

I can. She could look like Bathsheba naked in the woods and I wouldn't want to know about it. I have to tell him: 'Pa, I'm not up to it – please, not tonight.'

He'd be crestfallen if he didn't find something else to panic about: 'Are you too tired? You're not feeling ill, are you? Did you come too soon back to work?'

'No,' I can only tell him because I don't know how to describe to him this illness that I do have. I can't tell him I'm too smashed yet to imagine that I will ever be able to love a woman again. I don't want to disappoint him, either, though, so I do what I do best: put him off. 'After Yom Kippur, I'll be ready to think about it. I promise.'

'Ah! Good. I see.' He claps his hands together, thinking I'm going to wait until after I've atoned, and part of me hopes I do feel differently then, though the rest of me doubts it very much. He says, 'I'll tell Reverend Davis not to write to her father just yet. Something better might come along in the meantime anywise.'

Something better. My father's only real fault. A woman is not a 'something'. I've always known that, always been a respectful if prolific lothario. Pa has a different view, and it's one that's robbed me of my mother. I've had a lot of time lately to think about that, too, and every shade of grief and guilt about it forces me to lay down that hand at him here: 'I need to write to someone myself, before I make any decision about marriage. I need to write to my mother.'

'What are you saying?' Pa is more than disappointed at that: 'You want to delay marriage forever, is that what you mean by asking me this?'

'Not at all.' Perhaps. 'I only want to write to my mother and remind her that I'm alive. Why is that wrong?' We had a similar conversation like this once, before my bar mitzvah in London, but I didn't press the point, and then my first horse died the week after and all thought of my mother was lost; within a year after that I was lost in Deb Jacobs' dugs and jugs of ale. This time I will press and I will know if and what my mother thinks of me – *why* she left me.

He says: 'She wouldn't care to know about your marriage plans or anything else.' But he doesn't say this into my eyes; he turns away from me, waving at the air.

I don't believe him anymore; or at least it's a one-sided truth I have to shake. I have to tell him: 'I'm a big boy now, Pa. I have to know this one for myself. Can I have my mother's address, please?'

'I don't have it.' He walks off. And my father just lied to me outright: you don't lose the address of another Jew. It just doesn't happen. She could be living in a tree-house in Timbuktu and someone would have the street number.

I walk out, too, back into the lane. I need a drink. No, I don't. Yes, I do. I'm going to drink a bottle of claret and finish myself off properly with a pipe at Hong Sing's at the Rocks.

'Jem!'

No, I won't. A familiar form has grasped me by the arm on emerging from the lane at Hunter Street.

'Jem! It is you, jolly old cock.' It's a face I know, a chap from the Jockey Club, stockbroker, but the name eludes me for a moment – Peterson? Paterson? P-something. Long night at a bagatelle table not so long ago. And the goats at the Colonnade? He'd be ten years older, blotched and bloated – there's my future down that road. I shake his hand anyway. He says: 'Join us for lunch?'

'Ah. Hm. Bit busy today, sorry.' I'm compelled to get away from him as quickly as possible, but old habit keeps me on the spot, hedging bets.

'Busy? Heard you have been,' says P whoever he is – Pisspot. 'Go on, come down to Tatts for lunch. We heard you got shot. You have to tell us all about it.'

'Shot?' This entire country has a problem with fact-distortion as well as grog. A problem with the truth. I tell him: 'Had to happen eventually, didn't it. Who doesn't want to shoot me? But really, must dash. Enjoy your lunch.'

I take the corner of George Street at a brisk clip, every intention of going straight back around to the shop – like a man, like the son of a man who's recently wiped his slate at City Tatts and everywhere else in this town, explain to Pa that he's got nothing to worry about. Whatever happened between him and my mother, it's not for me to judge. I only want to know her, and if she's as dreadful as all that, so be it. Then I'll know, won't I.

But I don't get there before: 'Mr Fox! Oh, Mr Fox!'

It's Miss Osborne. Cornelia Osborne. Inspector-General Fitz-worthy's niece. Waving a handkerchief to get my attention outside the toy shop two doors down. Because I need to wade through a higher tide of my own shit today. I look at the Bondi omnibus across the road at Wynyard Square, as though I might make it before it sets off. It's three-quarters empty. I watch the name on the side of it – *THE LOTTERY* – disappear behind a baker's cart, behind Cornelia Osborne's head.

'Mr Fox, what a coincidence.' Somehow, I don't think so; Cornelia Osborne is never a coincidence. She giggles behind her hand, like the scandal-waiting-to-unfold that she is, and then she says: 'I was with Uncle Douglas only yesterday and we were all saying that we shall have to organise a celebration, a toast to your courage out there on the goldfields, now that you are recovered, and ...' She giggles again, blinking rapidly: 'We shall have to clear up our little misunderstanding, too, won't we?'

'Misunderstanding?' I have nothing left to prevent myself from letting her have it: 'You mean when you told your uncle I molested you in a public park?'

'I never said *that*!' She bats it off as a silly thing, and she's gone as violently pink as the rosebuds around her bonnet.

'What did you tell him, then?' I'm going to find that out at least. It's an irrelevance I have not thought about at all of late, but I'm suddenly angry at every frigging lie that's ever been told, including and especially my own. I'm also slightly terrified that Cornelia Osborne is going to resume her pursuit of me. She's not unattractive, if you like fluffy things that giggle, but I want nothing to do with her, or her uncle. I've said all I need to say to the police, made my statement, refused the reward, spent many hours in contemplation of men who will hang because second-rate people like you make their lives impossible. You want to resume harassing me? No cheese.

'Oh?' She opens and closes her mouth, a shrug protesting innocence.

But I'm pursuing her now: 'Why did you tell that lie about me?' I have never molested a woman, never gone anywhere there without an invitation. What's your problem, sweet pea, miffed I didn't accept yours? As if your family would ever allow you to make off with a Jew, for any money. 'Tell me.' And I don't care if that sounds like a threat.

She takes a step back, but she tells me: 'It was only a little game. It was Gertie's idea.' Her duplicate, her silly, giggling friend. 'She'd thought if I got you into trouble then you might see.'

'Might see what?'

'Me.'

On another day I might find that admission quite sweet, but this is not that day.

She says: 'I didn't think it would go that far. I didn't think you would come to any harm. Quite the opposite.'

Yes, another day, I will find that very sweet indeed, but this day, I tell her: 'Don't come near me again. Let there be no misunderstanding about that.'

Or the new low I've just achieved: abusing a lady in the street.

'Mr Fox, I'm so sorry.' And I've made her cry. 'You've every right to be cross with me. But Uncle Douglas, he really does need to see you. He wants to talk to you —'

I've already walked away. I don't care for anything Fitzworthy might have to say. There's probably some newly discovered creditor that needs to be quietly placated and paid off – he can talk to Pa about it. I can't talk to anyone right now, including and especially Pa, so I walk right past the shop. I walk the mile and a half home, away from this city that's not my home.

'Where are you going!' Mrs Kirschbaum chases me up the stairs.

'I'm getting changed.' Into corduroys. Leave me alone. 'Close the door.'

She doesn't: 'What are you doing?'

Apart from changing my trousers? 'Going out for a few hours.'

She chases me down the stairs: '*Where are you going?*'

'I'm going for a ride.'

She gasps: 'No! Doctor Feinberg said you're not to.' She chases me through the kitchen and out the back, across the yard, so that the city can hear her scream at me: 'Jeremy! Don't be such a fool. You're not better yet. You will fall from the horse and you will be crippled forever!'

I take the saddle from its rest and give Mrs Kirschbaum a piece of her own hysteria: 'If I don't go for a ride right now, I will kill myself.'

*

We belt along the beach at Bondi, Raj and I, but we don't last long at it, too out of condition, both of us. The sea is empty, grey and cold, the waves high and crashing a wide, white wash upon the sand. A weight lifts and settles again: this is the one thing I have any true enthusiasm for and I can't do anything with it.

I look back over the dunes, as if I might see her there across the hundred and fifty miles between us, but there's only a line of thick, dark scrub against cold, grey sky, soon to be carved up for waterfront views. And the pub: probably the only pub I've never owed anything at apart from a pane of glass for a cricket ball through a window. I want to fly to her: take off, into the hills. Today. Immediately. I want to ask her if it's true: that she could never consider me. Ask her every day until she says yes. I want to tell her: do you know, I spend more energy in any given day trying not to wonder what you're doing than I do at anything else? She'd probably say, with her marvellous contempt, that I'm only shocked a girl said no. And she would be right, but far from entirely. The rest of what I feel for her is a weight I have no idea how I can begin to shift, either.

Perhaps I should consider marriage. I'll be twenty-five in a few weeks' time; that's no longer embarrassingly young – as though I didn't make a ludicrous proposal for it myself thirty-seven days ago. Perhaps I could let Pa take care of it. Close my eyes, swallow that pill, take up the responsibility and the cure will come. Raj tosses his head with his own contempt for that idea. And he's right, too. I rather marry my horse than some girl I don't love, especially now that I know what love can do when it's misplaced.

We go slowly back across the dunes and through the falling night, nothing else to do but return home and smooth things out with Pa, and afterwards write Cornelia Osborne a note of apology. Possibly send flowers – no, not flowers. Just the apology. It's only been a month, I must remind myself, and hearts are made from more brittle stuff; I won't always feel this way – I hope.

'Did you even eat lunch today?' Mrs Kirschbaum gets me coming back through the kitchen, a smile of unknowing but genuine sympathy from Clarinda at the stove as I go, holding my tongue: no, I didn't eat lunch today. I can't eat as I used to; but that will change as well, when I get fitter.

'You're too thin.' She follows me back through the house. I am not thin by any interpretation.

I ask her: 'Is Pa back?'

'Is he back?' she shrieks. 'Yes, he came back. But he's gone out again.'

'Where did he go?'

'Oh, you care, do you?'

'Yes, I care. Where did he go?'

'He went to Doctor Feinberg's.' Oh, excellent, more and more shit to come for me. But she says: 'No, not to talk about you. Not everyone wants to talk about you.'

I need to get married so I don't live here anymore.

She says: 'You want lokshn with your stew or will I throw it out?'

'I'll come back down and eat it in a moment. Thank you.' I'll eat the lokshn – I would have to be dead not to eat those noodles. And dessert. Please, don't follow me.

She doesn't.

Upstairs, in my room, I light the lamp on the dressing table and see my face in the mirror as I do. I wonder what Annie would think of the beard; it's the first thing I think every morning when I see myself. I don't know if I'm growing it for Pa or because I think she might like it. I should put a cloth across the mirror, shouldn't I.

I should write that note to Cornelia Osborne before it falls out of my mind – *Dear Miss Osborne or Dear Cornelia?* – but as I look down to open the drawer I see a note left here for me: the meticulous flourishes of Pa's copperplate script spelling out:

CARDOZA, 24 Rue de Grenelle, Saint-Germain-des-Prés, Paris.

My mother's address. It must be, as her family name is Cardoza, even if he's omitted her own name – Eva. Thanks, Pa, you mad old pretzel. Now that I'm looking at it, though, now that it's here,

I can't think what I might say to her. What does one say after an absence, a silence, of twenty-one years? I'm not sure I want to say anything in a note. I look out the window, the lamps of the ships in Woolloomooloo Bay swaying. Perhaps I should go to Paris myself and say it to her face. My face. That would solve quite a lot of things, wouldn't it?

ANNIE

I've never seen so many bricks in one place as in this town of Bathurst, now that I'm seeing it in broad daylight, the only truly big town I've ever seen. All roads from the west lead into here, traffic of every description coming and going up and down every great wide blue-gravelled street, to the Cobb & Co Booking Office, the Crown Lands Office, flour mills – I've counted three – and foundries smoking all around every type of business you could think of. Twice as many prams as Wellington, too – they must have a baby factory here as well.

And they have my money. Our money. I've hardly noticed the twenty-five miles on the back of this horse to get here. We're on our way to see Superintendent Slater. For six hundred pounds. Dad would have had to work near ten years to see that amount of money, and it'd just about always be gone, month to month, with expenses so you could never get ahead. Six *hundred* pounds in one lot. I never dared to expect it, and not the full amount, either, but my prayer for the land has been heard, it has to have been, and I don't care that I'm so cold on the back of this horse the first thing I'm going to buy myself is a coat, and maybe a little cart, so I never have to travel on the back of a horse again – wearing a blanket and trying not to think what I must look like in the middle of this rich and busy town. We look like a couple of penniless blacks come down from the hills, is what me and Granddad look like, because that's what we are.

'Courthouse is up this way.' Granddad knows where he's going: all this is his country, and Bathurst was where he first got work through the missionaries, going all over the place fencing for them, getting tucker and Bible lessons in exchange, 'about a hundred years ago', or more like in the early forties, he couldn't tell you exactly when, because it took him a few years to get used to the idea of what a date is and how they roll around a calendar, so he'll never know how old he is. And he'll never see the inside of a church with me. I'll have to go on my own, when I get the courage up to get myself there, maybe next Sunday, to give proper thanks and praise.

Neither of us has ever had a cause to go inside this Bathurst Police Court before, though. Neither of us is a criminal, but we get a rough look from the young policeman standing guard outside as we tether the horses at the rail here, like we'd be that stupid we'd steal horses and tether them outside a courthouse under a policeman's nose. I do my best to make myself look somewhere near to decent, unwrapping the blanket and taking off Dad's Crimean underneath so that for however long we'll be here I can freeze in my nice French cotton dress, my only dress.

'What do you want?' The policeman at the counter says, as we approach, like we are manure under his boots.

'We're here to see the superintendent,' Granddad says, pulling himself up to his full height. He might not be a giant, he might not be more than three or four inches taller than me, but he is not going to be denied. He hasn't let on to me what he thinks of all this talk of reward, I'd reckon from so many long years' being denied. But now that we're here, we're getting what is our due.

'Oh, are you?' this young feller says. He's got a thin-lipped way about him like that Trooper Donovan: if he was a dog you might be inclined to shoot him so he doesn't breed. And that thought shakes me, as it does sometimes from dreams: I can still hear that animal hitting him; I can still feel how frightened I was that he wouldn't live that night. Don't think about Jeremy *here*; don't think about him giving all this money to me without a word. Don't think about the loss of his kindness and his bravery from my everyday life being probably the greatest regret I'll ever know.

Too late. My voice is shaking, my whole body is shaking like a leaf in a storm as I tell Constable Thin Lips here: 'My name is Annabel Bird. Superintendent Slater is expecting me today. I'm here to collect a reward for what I did in turning in Jack Holly and his gang.'

The policeman looks at me with such a blank I wonder if I dreamed getting the letter back from Superintendent Slater to tell me to be here. Today. Wednesday. The eighth of July. I stand here waiting to be told that the court proceedings against the bushrangers failed, that there was no conviction after all, even though I read in the Bathurst paper at the Blayney store only last Friday that the convictions have gone down and appeals for clemency dismissed with them because of *the plethora of police evidence and eye-witness accounts of the innumerable crimes of the gang*; even though they are all Irishmen and so guilty before the trial began. They're donating my reward to the Prince Alfred Hospital, instead. After all these weeks' waiting and freezing, I'm ready to beg in the streets for that warm winter coat. It's not as though Granddad can put something like that on the store account. Even though he makes cartloads of cash for Neville McKenzie – who is a criminal. A fraud. All those wild horses Granddad catches for him are supposed to be held and sold on for the government, as Bunyip's Bend is Crown land and Neville McKenzie is not paying a penny in leasing it, but he takes the best-looking, unbranded horses for himself, selling them on at a premium to new cockatoo farmers every time the next bit of Crown land gets auctioned off. I could tell this young policeman all about it, but I won't. Because Neville McKenzie lets Granddad live on his own land as he pleases in return. It didn't take me long to work all that out. Because I'm not stupid. And I'm not getting any money today, either, am I.

'Miss Bird!' I nearly jump through the ceiling as the superintendent himself steps out from a door at the side of the counter, with his long legs and his long moustache, smiling and beckoning us over. 'Yes, yes, been expecting you. Good to see you. And Mr Creekstone,' he says, making a big show of shaking Granddad's hand, while all I can do is put one foot in front of the other to get in this door. '*Mr* Creekstone, I'm very pleased to meet you at last.'

Granddad, being who he is, gives the superintendent one of his hard, measuring stares.

But Superintendent Slater isn't bothered by it: 'Wonderful,' he's saying, showing us down a hall and into a room off it. 'Sit down, please, sit down.'

We do, on chairs set in front of his desk, and Granddad continues taking him in, quiet and steady.

'My father searched high and low for you, Mr Creekstone,' the superintendent is going on as he sits down too. 'A great regret of his not to see you again before he passed away. Where were you all that time? You must tell me.'

But Granddad only shrugs: 'All round.' And that's all Superintendent Slater will be getting out of him on the subject. Granddad will just not talk about the past unless it's at a time of his choosing and on his own terms. But he adds: 'Your father and me, we had some good times together.' Must have been special for him to say a thing like that.

'My father lamented not having written down much of what you taught him.' The superintendent leans his elbows on his desk and his smile is a sad one. 'Observing the behaviour of water, observing the seasons, the colours, in ways that had never occurred to him before. He moved around, too, for many years, to a posting down in Adelaide. And, well, life takes over, things get lost, don't they?'

That's an invitation for Granddad to talk about it to the son now, but he only says: 'Yeah. You lose your looks, too. We were handsome fellers in them days.' Granddad laughs then, and he's laughing him off, saying that's enough of that.

I hope the superintendent doesn't take it personally; I've asked Granddad about the survey of the rivers myself, only asking him if it was a medal or a ribbon he got, just trying to work out the story I'd always been told, and he shook his head, *Be quiet, all your questions, you'll make a man deaf*, then telling me hours later, by the fire, *It was a medal on a ribbon*, before walking away. I know Granddad's got his reasons there somewhere, for keeping things close, and maybe Superintendent Slater knows it as well; he says: 'Handsome? I have no doubt about it.' Dismissing it with a wave of his long superintendent fingers to make it gone, and then he frowns, down to business, with me. 'I have some bad news, I'm afraid, which I thought best to tell you face to face.'

Oh my dear Lord, here we have it. We're not getting the money, are we. I take a deep breath. It's all right. I'm not going to fall off the chair. I'll only be as poor as I was this morning. It doesn't matter. I have my grandfather. I have family, the tiny amount that there is. Even if Sis hasn't replied to my letter yet, and I'm not worried about that, either, because she's so lazy it could take her another month yet to get around to it. Days at a time I'm contented there at Bunyip, since Granddad and I have worked out something of a routine, since he's getting used to my cooking, since I've started tacking old oat sacks to the walls of the hut to keep the draught out. Days at a time I can go without anyone looking down on me up there. Everything will be all right. Except that the land is soon going to be sold out from under us. Oh, please.

'I'm sorry to tell you, Miss Bird.' The superintendent finally brings the hammer down, but it's not the bad news I'm prepared for. 'We weren't able to retrieve much in the way of what was stolen from you.' He opens the drawer at his desk and I might fall off the chair anyhow with relief as he pushes my Holy Bible towards me. He says: 'This was all that could be found.'

'Oh.' I'm overcome at the sight of it, taking it in my hands. I open it and see our names in the only book that matters to me: *Richard Morris Bird, Kathryn Bird, Annabel Eliza Bird, Cecily Jane Bird.* I'm going to put Kel Creekstone, Kulyan of the Wirradjeree in there, too, whether he likes it or not. And that's not all: my *Certificate of Completion of Primary Education* slips from the back cover and floats across the floor, stopping under the toe of Granddad's boot.

He picks it up and hands it to me, saying: 'What's that? Instructions on how to save your soul?'

'Maybe,' I tell him, and I hand it back to him, even though he can't read it. 'That's the piece of paper that says I finished school.'

'Is it now.' He looks at it, then he folds it back up and puts it in his coat pocket: 'That's not getting lost again.' He says to Superintendent Slater: 'This granddaughter here, she's a clever one.' There's no money that can give a person what he gives me by that look of pride.

'Clever and very patient,' Superintendent Slater says, but I can see he's not yet finished with the bad news. He says: 'Right. Well. As to the monies of the reward, there is a small administrative problem we must overcome before you might take any benefit from it.'

'Small?' I squeak out the word because it doesn't look like it's going to be a small problem.

Superintendent Slater shifts around in his seat, uncomfortable; he says: 'Before I explain, you must know that I do not approve of the situation, but unfortunately I can't do anything about it. I can't release the monies directly to you, and there are two reasons for this. The government treasury will not allow me to hand such a large sum in cash to you, stipulating that it must be deposited into a bank, but I have been unsuccessful in having a bank agree to open an account for you.'

'Why?' For all that I don't want this answer.

He tells me: 'As I said, I disapprove of the reasonings, but there is no malicious intention here. It is felt that it would not be in your interests to have such a sum at your disposal.'

'They're worried I might spend it all on lollies and grog?' I'm too weary of the insult to be angry about it at this minute.

'Something like that,' he agrees. 'And there are four reasons given for this: you are under twenty-one years of age, you are female, you are unmarried and you are an Aborigine.'

'Well, put it in Granddad's name, then,' I say and I know I shouldn't have bothered there, either. Granddad's looking out the window at the sky: he's left the room for this bit.

Superintendent Slater shakes his head: 'It's the last of those reasons that is the crucial one. To be blunt, I can't hand over that amount of cash to any Aborigine.'

Give me half, then, for the half of me that isn't an Aborigine, I could say, if I had any humour for it, but I can only get blunt too: 'So I'm not getting any money.'

'No, I didn't say that. But if you're to have any of it, you must have a trustee to administer the funds on your behalf.'

I can hardly hear what he's saying. Only a few months ago, I was in charge of Dad's books at the farm, I had money in my pocket, taking Sis to a drapery sale. Now I'm not allowed to have any?

Ever? It's not the money I want, I could scream. I'm honest and I'm hardworking. I just want to be able to buy a coat when I need one.

'Miss Bird, I can see you're upset, and you have my sympathy. In fact, you can have more than my sympathy. If you would agree to it, I would be most happy, and most honoured, to act as your trustee. Unless, of course, there's someone else? A husband would have an immediate right of claim.'

Would he? Good for him. There might have been a him, a big white him, once upon a time for about five minutes, but there isn't anymore. I say: 'There's no-one else.' What's the difference between one and another? Except maybe Jeremy Fox would have spent it on a hat and a day at the races. I'd thank Superintendent Slater for his decency and generosity, but I'm too caught up in looking at this picture of my future where I have to ask a policeman for money to buy things that I need, no matter what a good-hearted gentleman he is. I know what a trust account is; because I'm not stupid. A trust account is for children and people of feeble mind and things that aren't people at all, like the business dealings of the Railways and the Roads.

'We can make these arrangements today, and in any way you choose,' the superintendent is saying. 'Is there a particular bank which would be convenient to you?'

'The Commercial Bank at Carcoar.' I stab the words into the air. 'They have four percent on deposits advertised in the window.'

'I shall see to it.' He nods. 'Do you have any thoughts on what you might like to do with the money?'

'Yes,' I tell him: 'Land. Granddad and me, we want to buy some land.'

'Now there's a good idea.'

*

No land comes up for sale anywhere in the hills for the whole month of July, though.

'Strange,' says Neville McKenzie. 'That Spring Grove parcel looked a certainty. Dunno what the hold-up is.'

Maybe they're onto you and they're laying a careful trap, I could say, but I don't. So long as the land at Bunyip isn't auctioned,

Granddad doesn't have to move off elsewhere. Even when it does come up, if it comes up, it won't ever be ours anyhow: it'll be held in trust, too, because an Aborigine isn't allowed to own anything at all, especially not their own land. It's not against any law for me to own a piece of this country, not against the law for Granddad to roll up at a general election of government and cast his vote as a man, either, only a thousand ways to prevent these things from happening, a thousand faceless, nameless government men saying no. I don't understand why: all I want to do is build a house and put potatoes in the ground. You'd think that would make me a model colonist.

I make curtains for the hut instead, and make Granddad and Neville McKenzie bolt some tin on this roof and build another hut for the saddles to live in. I have a home, and I'm not going anywhere soon. I have everything I need: coat and gloves and a warm suit of wincey for working. I have a cart and a comfortable bed got for a good price from a farm sale at Spring Grove. The bank at Carcoar wasn't the smartest choice, as the telegraph doesn't go across from Bathurst yet, so getting whatever I might need is as slow as a donkey ride, but that's all right. I've learned my lessons in patience. And I enjoy leaving the cart outside Mrs Galbraith's hotel when I'm down there, for the purposes of helping that memory of hers – one day. As well, I'm waiting for a load of bricks to come up for a chimney, so I don't have to cook outside, and next, the building of another room so I don't have to sleep where I cook.

'Don't have time for all that,' says Granddad. 'Only going to be more to move when we gotta,' he complains, but he'll do it, and continue to sleep on the verandah in front of the fire if that's what he wants.

At this rate, Sis'll have a proper house and a crop in before I do. I've heard from her and her sloppy spelling telling me Mickey Dinnigan has made fools of us all, buying her three acres of prime near Kendall's Londonderry on the high ground between Richmond and Penrith. There's what living in a rubbish heap for a time and saving your pennies can do – if you're a big white man. Dad would be so happy for her. Maybe not so pleased that she's also pregnant and not yet married, and to a Catholic, but you can't have everything go your way. She went and got my Staffordshire teacups for me and a whole load of things – my hairbrush, my good boots, my favourite skirt, my Sunday best – she went back to the farm that terrible day we were shoved off, and she piled what she could onto a cart the tanners sent around when she told them what happened. I love my only sister, even if it'll take her another two months to get around to sending it all to me. I've sent her a letter back asking her to come herself, to meet Granddad, but I don't know if she will. She didn't know Mother as I did, and she doesn't have to be black if she doesn't want to be, near fair as Dad as she is. And it's a long and winding way to come.

Like the truth sometimes, but we get there, however we do, in the end: Sis also told me that Mrs Webb and Mr Murgett got caught at adultery and, as well as there being another new manager at Cygnet Farm these days, Mrs Webb hasn't shown her face in any town in the district almost since my leaving. It's wrong to take comfort in the misfortune of others, but let's make an exception for that one. She tried to say Sis was a thief of our own things, too.

I look out at the patch I'm longing to till here at Bunyip by the dam, wondering if I ever will, wondering if the heavy frosts up here are going to defeat a winter crop of anything except beets and spinach, and garlic … maybe. I'm dreaming of where I want my apple orchard to be, sheltered from the bitter west wind by the edge of the forest on this land that can never be mine except for maybe, when I hear the dog bark.

He's barking at the sky. Just standing there, barking at the clouds, wagging his tail. 'Ha. Pepper,' my grandfather says his name as he walks by on his way to the yard, to his new lot of horses. I don't call Pepper by his name, though he's a good old dog, curling up with me on the couple of rainy days that Granddad was away gathering that new wild bunch. I don't call Pepper by his name because the word 'pepper' makes me think of Jeremy every time, for the picture I have of him in my mind grinding pepper on his eggs that morning at the inn at Ploughman's Creek.

When do you stop missing someone you hardly even knew?

Two weeks, that's all it was, for all that there was a load gone on in it. Just two weeks and since two months have now gone by. He wouldn't ever have wanted to live here as I do, and I don't want to be anywhere else, so why, Lord, why can't I shake him from me? What am I meant to learn from this?

Pepper's still barking at whatever he can see, up there in the winter clouds, their bellies full of what looks like some more rain. Maybe he's telling me to hurry up to the creek for the water I need before it starts bucketing down. The tops of the tall trees behind the hut all of a sudden shoosh together in a gust, and then stop still. And so do I, as I see it's not rain that's falling from the sky.

It's snow.

I've never seen anything so beautiful in my life, watching it falling onto the palm of my hand.

'Ha,' says Granddad, walking back for a saddle. 'You thinking about that feller again?'

'No.' Not again. Only always. Beautiful and gone: a snowflake melting on my skin.

JEM

'Don't worry about it,' Pa says with blithe irony, on our way to the synagogue, and this is his attempt to gird my loins for the challenge. 'No-one expects you at shul these days. No-one expects you to be observant and I've let go of any hope that you might start now. Everyone is too pleased you're not bringing us kharpe un shande anymore.'

I am only too pleased to know that I'm no longer considered a source of shame, but it's too heavily morbish that I longer seem to go anywhere. I go to work, I go home, I go for a ride, I go home, I lie awake and stare out at black water. I have more meaningful conversations with the lad who mucks out Raj's digs – Davey Simmons, son of a dockside fishmonger, wants to be a jockey, let's see what we can do. Other than that, I have avoided social engagements of every kind; but I am not going to avoid this one.

'I know it's difficult for the young to consider religion,' he goes on across Wynyard Square. 'I've only ever wanted you to know where you come from and where you are going. To be a good man, a good Jew, that's worth more than this.' He gestures down York Street towards the synagogue, its edifice of pale sandstone and diamond panes, elegant, Egyptian simplicity telling me it has a five-thousand-six-hundred-and-twenty-nine-year-old memory and can recall in every detail what happened last time I was here. Pa had quite reasonably demanded I straighten up and face myself in the assembly of my fellows, to begin the Hebrew new year a better man: I turned up late to Ne'ilah, the final evening service, wreaking at the weary end of the Homebush Spring Carnival, and fell asleep on the floor against the back wall. Given my record, that doesn't seem a spectacular transgression, but it was: I didn't disgrace myself so much as I disgraced him. There would have been at least three hundred people here for Yom Kippur, from all over New South Wales and anyone visiting from elsewhere.

There'll only be about thirty people here tonight and in the hall, not the sanctuary. But they will all be looking at me, sidewise, and every other wise. The windows of Sydney Central Police Station, so conveniently located next door, look down upon me, too, for it seems the greatest revelation of my reform to date is a newfound capacity for cowardice. I can't even mention the word Paris to Pa. How could I even think of leaving him before I've made some very concerted amends? How could I imagine asking him for the money, never mind his permission to go? I can't even write to my mother. What if it's true that she doesn't want to know me? What if she says: where have *you* been? What if it's true that I'm not capable of real love at all?

Pa says as we turn into the gate: 'You know I only want you to create the family for your children that I wasn't able to create for you myself.'

Only? My stomach clenches with what feels like knowledge that every step I'm taking this midwinter Wednesday evening is only going to lead to further disappointment for him, and for me. In a contest of excuses for making the mistakes of life, Pa wins. He was forced to leave home at the age of eleven, to escape conscription, his father was cold and often as violent as the Prussian Guard itself, he didn't know his mother because she had died when he was born, but by thirteen Pa had completed school in a foreign language, by twenty-three had his own business and has not stopped working since except for Shabes to give thanks for it all. I am twenty-five and I've done nothing.

I owe him this.

'Jeremiah.' Reverend Davis pointedly calls me by the name that's on the register of births in the Great Synagogue of London to remind me that the whole of Israel is looking at me, too. 'You look well.' He can't say whatever else he might want to – such as, *Where have you been?* – because Something Better and her parents are here. Somewhere. I can't look at anything but the back of Pa's head, the stitching of the silk yarmulke pinned there.

'Jem.' Eli Abrahams is at my shoulder, the friendly face of my tailor: 'I'll get you a drink. What do you want?'

'Nothing, thanks.'

'Nothing?'

'A glass of water.' Something to do with my hands. This is, on the surface, only an informal gathering, a drink to welcome the family to Sydney. The Ashers are from Dublin; Irish Jews: rare and universally loved, father is a lawyer, emigrating for mother's health, top philanthropic pedigree, rescuer of Syrian orphans, wholly Ashkenazic lineage, and an Irish Republican sympathiser, which might provide a moment of amusing awkwardness with the inevitable toast to the Queen later in the proceedings. But it's the daughter they've brought with them, their youngest, Esther, who is the real reason we're here: to attempt to solve the problem of me for good. Pa's already agreed that if I say no, it's no and no badgering, but I am as nervous as an adolescent. No: I was *never* this nervous as an adolescent. What has happened to me?

'Jeremy.' Mrs Davis has me by the wrist in a pincer grip – she could get a job next door as a handcuffer. She's an attractive, cultured woman and highly efficient at her role as hostess, but she has one of those pained smiles that begs one not to break anything, especially pronounced for me. 'I must introduce you to Miss Asher.'

Must you? Yes.

Oh my God. She turns around and she is gorgeous. Esther Asher is the fizz, the complete package. Creamily spilling from her dress, I would be diving in there at the earliest opportunity if I hadn't lost all vigour. A little mischief in that curious eyebrow, holding out her hand for me to kiss, nothing coy about her: 'So, Mr Fox, the famous sportsman.'

She even says that with exactly the right amount of contempt, and she more than speaks English: her accent is as lovely as she is. But as I bend to her hand, I can't kiss it; I brush it with my breath and give it a squeeze of vague apology.

'Sportsman, yes, that might be one description.' I give her an apology in that, too. 'Pleased to meet you.' You'll find someone more entertaining to talk to in a moment. Like Doctor Feinberg, who's boring her father with the plans for the new synagogue, which will bring the two Hebrew congregations of Sydney together, when they stop arguing long enough to settle on a site.

I stand in this room full of people who love me and forgive me, and who might love me in times to come, but there's only one girl I want to marry – the one whose only endorsement comes from a coachman on a backwoods road from nowhere to nowhere. Sometimes I can almost believe it never happened at all, until the fact bludgeons me in the guts, as it does right now.

I excuse myself to find another glass of water, but Doctor Feinberg follows me, taking me aside: 'What's wrong, Jeremy? Why are you so quiet? What's happened? What have you done?'

'Nothing. I'm getting a glass of water.'

'You look uncomfortable. Have you injured yourself?'

I could laugh at that if I had one in me: 'No.' Not in any way you could imagine.

He says: 'You should forget about riding altogether. Think of your father. You're making him ill with worry, every time you get on that horse. Grow up and grow out of it.'

'You're making him ill with worry, putting that thought in his head,' I tell him, and I don't look at his affronted face. If I can't ride my horse, I would rather be dead – nothing hysterical about it, just a fact. It's the only recognisable part of me I have left.

'Pa.' I catch him by the arm, interrupting him with Mrs Asher: 'I'm sorry. I've got to go home. I think I've eaten something bad.'

He touches my face, his thumb rubs against my cheek above the beard: 'All right.' He nods. He knows I'm sad, but he can't imagine why and I can't tell him. How can I even start to explain it? I don't understand it myself.

How much it still hurts that she sent me away. How she lingers, strands of her hair curling through every thought. Looking at *Bell's* last week, just waiting for the barber, I read the latest on the Aboriginal Cricket Team's tour of England – beaten by Surrey, drawn with Mote Park, picking up their stride – and there was the rest of my day gone. Lost to this odd, unreasonable bereavement that sits like a magnet in my chest, pulling me, telling me: *Go west. Beg her to look again.*

I walk home in the dark that's spotting rain, and sheeting with it by the time I get there.

'Jeremy, what are you doing home?' Mrs Kirschbaum follows me up the stairs. 'You're soaking wet.'

'Can't get anything past you, can I?'

'No. Why are you early? Didn't you like her?'

'She's beautiful, lovely.'

'What's wrong, Jeremy?'

I can only tell her: 'I don't know.'

'I do,' says Mrs Kirschbaum: 'You're dershlogn.'

That's exactly what I am: depressed.

She says: 'I'll make some kneydlekh.'

Kneydlekh. Dumplings. Matzo dumplings in chicken soup. The cure for all ills. But all I can see or feel is Annie making dumplings out of nothing by an open fire, flour on the tips of her quick and perfect fingers.

ANNIE

It's still snowing. The ground is white around the fire. So cold, I've turned the collar of my coat up around my ears, but I can't think of going inside, excited like I'm small again, seeing a rainbow or a bubble for the first time, except this is going on and on. It's been snowing for hours.

Granddad keeps laughing at me from under the verandah: 'Thought you didn't like this weather.'

I'm so full of this unexpected joy, the words float out of me without my thinking: 'I don't know how you can't believe in God, Granddad, looking at this.'

'Never said I don't believe in God.' Granddad grunts. 'You reckon a man with a long white beard put snow in the sky just for you to squeal at, girl?'

'No.' I turn around and look at him there with his cup of tea under the kerosene lamp that's hanging from the awning above, and I dare to ask him, maybe because it's so cold I don't reckon he's going to get up and walk away: 'What's the word in your language for snow?'

'You don't want to know anything like that.'

'Yes, I do.'

'Anyone hear you talking language, they'll pick you up and take you away.'

'Take you where?'

'Wherever they want to.'

I shiver at that and all it might mean, but I say: 'Tell me anyhow. No-one but me and the dog will know.'

He says something too soft for me to hear.

'What did you say?'

He says a word that sounds like *daa laa raa*, rolling that r around his tongue; I wish he could tell me how to spell it.

'*Daa laa raa*,' I say.

He says: 'That's enough of that.'

I say: 'I want to know everything you know. I want to know all your stories.' And I dare: 'My mother told me all kinds of things, but I can hardly remember any of them. I was only a little girl.' All my longing and all my not knowing pinch in my throat. 'I don't mean to upset you, Granddad, I just need to know.' Who are you? Where is everybody else? What happened? I tell him: 'I need to know who I am.'

He's quiet for a long time, before he says: 'I've got stories, girl.'

I think that's all he's going to say; but then he asks me: 'You seen a big lizard out here sometime? Real big feller?'

'Yes.' Just once. 'A big grey lizard, with white stripes and diamonds all over it.' Down by that creek on the west side of Bathurst, that first morning I knew I was falling in love, with that man and this country.

'That's the one.' Granddad nods. 'That's me, that lizard. He's a good hunter, a good fighter – strong, fast, smart – but he ain't good at losing. All his hunting grounds have been taken from around here. All the grasslands have been grabbed up and bush cleared where it shouldn't be, dams and waterholes where they shouldn't be. And I'm one of them that opened the door and let the thieves walk right in. I thought I was something special in them days.'

'What days?' I ask him.

He tells the fire behind me: 'After the war.'

'War?'

'Yeah. War.' He points his mug at the darkness of the bush. 'I was only just made a man of my family, here, a hunter, a warrior for my mob – right here over the other side of Spring Grove. So when they came for us, the white fellers, I was younger than you, about fourteen or fifteen years old, I reckon. There was trouble here and there, round Bathurst, and at a place near where Blayney is now. One of the farmers there shot a feller for pulling down a fence that was going through a burial ground, then the farmer got a spear in him, then another couple of fellers got a bullet in them. At first, one of my uncles thought it was just a story the mob from the mountains was spreading to keep us all off the kangaroo there. We weren't ready for what come at us, no-one could have been. It was bad and it was fast. I saw my father, and nearly all my uncles and my older cousins get killed at a place the other side of Carcoar, a place called Pigetty's Hole nowadays. They weren't just farmers – they were soldiers sent to get us. Over all the days and the places of the war, there was maybe a thousand of us mob round here, I don't know. No-one writ it down. Today, there's you and me on the book at the Blayney store.'

I don't know what's more shocking – that name, Pigetty's Hole, that horrible place, or the thought that there could be a war I've never heard about.

'You want more story, girl?'

'Yes.'

'I ran with the women, north,' he tells me, into the flames. 'We went up to around Ophir, on the river. That's where we'd go in the summertime, we'd meet up with lots of other families there. But this was the end of summer, the weather was turning, and everything went wrong. Some women got sick, babies died. The uncles I had left went away with a war party, and I was left looking after women and babies – they said to me, you're too small. My uncles never came back. The shame was hard to carry, but my family wasn't the only one this happened to – it happened to all our mob across the whole of Wirradjeree country, as big as England.

'The leader, our chief warrior, he was called Windradyne. He took a party over the mountains to Parramatta to make peace, to put a stop to all the killing. He was tall and real good-looking, and he knew what he was doing, or thought he did. We was going to get an agreement with the Governor – Governor Brisbane it was then – we'd keep the peace if we could keep them off some of our land. I stayed on the Wambool, waiting. But no agreement was made, no treaty for peace was got. They just laughed at him, called him Saturday, said go away don't bother us again. We've got guns and you don't.

'Next thing I knew, white fellers were cutting a road up from the place they called Blackman's Swamp, heading towards us. But I had an idea: if we were going to survive I had to get smart. Make peace myself. Make friends with the enemy. I started cutting bark for the farmers that came, all around what's Orange now, so did some others. We'd cut all this bark for their roofs and get a sheep or two off them to share. And it was there I found out I was smarter than the rest – I was good at picking up the language. I got picked to go on the survey of the rivers. I thought I was pretty good. I thought I would get to keep that bit of land on the Wambool for my mother and my aunties if I did a good job. I thought I'd get a girl from one of the families further up north when I came back, as my mother wanted me to, as the law said I should, and everything would work out all right. It didn't.

'That surveyor feller, Graeme Slater, that superintendent's father, we became good mates, we had respect going both ways, there was a few good fellers back then. When we finished, he said, "Come to Sydney with me. You want your land, you've gotta have money, you want money, you gotta have a job, want a job, come to Sydney – I'll get you a job as a tracker." He did get me a job, with the police at Emu, near Penrith. They wanted me to go and find all the Mulgoa people left along the river there – the Yandai, as your mother would have known it. Sheep would go missing, fences would get ripped up, but they could never find who did it. When I found what was left of the Mulgoa on that part of the river, I knew it wasn't them. We didn't speak that much of the same language to begin with, but it was easy to see – there was only women left there, too, all from different families, about twenty, and no babies at all. No hunters – not one. They were living at Warragamba. And that's where I met your grandmother.'

He stands up and comes over to me. He wipes my tears with the palm of his hand. He says: 'You look a lot like her. I was having a drink at the river when I first saw her. I was looking at all the eels in the water. You don't get eels out here, I'd never seen 'em before. When I saw your grandmother, it was like I'd never seen a girl before, either. I didn't stay long at Warragamba, though. The police didn't pay me for my work. All I got was a medal for the survey, go away little black feller. And I had to go home, to my family. I promised my mother and my aunties I'd come back and get a girl from the north, from the Burrendong mob, as they said I should.'

'Did you?'

'No,' he tells me. 'When I got back, my mother was gone, she'd passed on, and the Burrendong mob moved north up past Wellington, causing a whole lot of trouble up there, though I didn't know that then, because I moved on, too, looking for work because I had to eat. I never went back to Mulgoa country. I never saw your mother born. I knew she was coming, but I never saw her. Your grandmother's mother didn't want me there anyway, and a man can't talk back to her. That's no joke – it's the law. I had no business doing what I did at Warragamba. I was too sweet on myself and my own chances. Your grandmother knew what I was – she was already thinking about going to see if she could get work at the church in Richmond, worried about how they'd eat when they were moved off from the riverbank. You do what you have to do to survive. Eat your shame before it eats you.

'Too much gets broken in a war and this war isn't finished all its breaking. Only ten years ago there were still corroborees around Mudgee way, but they stopped when the gold rush came there. What do you do?' he asks the fire. 'You've got to do whatever you've got to do, go where you gotta go, to survive, when everything is broken. And white fellers gotta make up stories to pretend none of it ever happened at all. Or they have to say we're a bad lot, we killed their women and children. Pretending that they didn't kill ours. They killed hundreds of us; maybe thousands. There's one thing we all know, and that's right from wrong – it doesn't have a colour. Neither does shame, and shame catches up one day. That's my story. That's all I'm gunna say.'

I say: 'Thank you.'

He says: 'Now make an old man another cup of tea.'

I put the billy back on the flames and as I do, he says: 'You and all your questions. You wanting me to find you a black feller, are ya?'

'What?' No. 'I'm not wanting any feller. You just said there aren't any to have.'

He laughs at me again then: 'Just because your name ain't in a book doesn't mean you ain't there. I can rope you in a nice black feller from Cowra way, if you want one. Nice God-bothering shearer near Woodstock looking for a girl right now – yous can go to church together every day.' He rocks back on his heels at that, crunching the snow and laughing like it's the funniest thing he's ever said.

I narrow my eyes at him: 'I'm not looking to get married to anyone.'

'Ha! Ha!' He smacks his knee. 'Reckon you're special, too, ay?'

'I do not.' I try to change the subject. 'We're running low on sugar – you have too much in your tea.'

'You're gunna drive a man mad, you are,' he says, 'if you ain't already. That white feller you sent away. Best slapped face I've ever seen.' When he stops laughing he says: 'You still missing him?'

'I am not.' Stop teasing me about it.

'You gunna write a letter to him?'

'No, I am not.' Snow swirls around, wild white streaks against the black, making my head spin. 'It's not funny.'

But Granddad is serious as he says: 'You listen to me. I wish I had gone back to your grandmother. Break one law, you might as well break 'em all. I wish I'd had the guts. Why don't you write to him, girl?'

'He won't want to hear from me,' I tell him, pass the shame.

'Wouldn't be too sure about that,' says Granddad.

And I tell him: 'I'm pretty sure.'

But Granddad only needles me more: 'What did you say to him to send him off like that?'

'None of your business.'

'Ha!'

NEVER TOO LATE FOR MORE DESSERT

JEM

September 25th, 1868

Dear Mother,

I finally get to it, in the last few hours before the fast for Atonement begins and writing is not allowed. After all this time wrestling with the words, I decide to keep it brief and plain:

I don't know what has kept us from each other for all this time, and I don't much care about the details of whatever might have occurred between you and my father, but I am desirous now that I might come to know you.

As you would probably be aware, I have recently turned twenty-five. The time has arrived for me to consider marriage, and with all the considerations involved, I would like you to be a part of my future family life, however that might be achieved.

I hope this note finds you well and happy – and inclined to write back. I would like nothing more than to hear from you, and, most hopefully, to meet with you in Paris if you would like that, too.

Your son,
Jeremy

No, it doesn't matter that I smudged the 'y'; I always smudge the 'y': it's authentically me. Blot it, fold it, envelope it, and it's done.

A small but gold-weight burden lifted, as well as a politically acceptable reason to delay things with Esther. A twenty-thousand-mile round trip, for both the correspondence and me, should give us at least a year until we can announce an engagement. She's already told me she doesn't want to marry me until I'm thirty. She's dug the dirt and so has her mother: they're waiting for me to backslide. That's not going to happen. But what is going to happen is that Pa will be content with this compromise when I tell him, tomorrow night, when we break the fast together: my gift to him, as well as attending the entire day of prayer tomorrow, just for him. Just this year, this one Yom Kippur, to show him that the only thing I might collapse from is a lack of food and water.

I lock up the shop and I do feel an odd lightness as I start walking towards the post office. Or perhaps a normalness returning. Spring helps: the warmth in the air, a certain brightness re-enlivening the sky. And Esther herself has helped. We might not love each other madly, but that's not the point of marriage, is it. We are a match. We're chums. She routinely beats me at battledore and shuttlecock. Her laughter might be a little too sharp, her gaze a little too cool at times, but she's intelligent and gorgeous and good company. What more do you want? Well, a little bit of lust would be useful, but perhaps that'll come later, when the reality of unlimited shagging settles in. Perhaps that's not her fault but mine. I'll feel differently after five years of no shagging, won't I. Five years. There's a commitment. Hm.

Though it's only half-past two, the post office is Friday-afternoon bedlam and the harried clerk behind the counter tells me: 'You've missed today's dispatch to Europe, sir. Your letter won't go off until next Thursday.'

'That's all right,' I tell him. What's a couple of days on a journey of somewhere around twelve weeks. It doesn't matter when it gets there; I hope she loves me when it does. Either way, there's nothing more I can do about it.

I walk home with a sense of some power in my step, a feeling that things are, at last, coming together and in the scheme of things I've probably made good time in this regard. I smile at the thought of what I'm most looking forward to discussing with Pa tomorrow night: what I plan to do with myself in terms of an occupation. I'm going to ask him if I can take over the business side of things – something that would have been unthinkable five months ago. Laughable. You wouldn't have put me in charge of the takings for a charity fete for the certainty I'd go and chance the lot punting on the winner of a cat-herding competition around the corner. But now I see that, while arithmetic is probably never going to be my strongest suit, deal-making is a highly transferable skill. It's all gambling and bluff. I could sell an Arab his own camel back to him at twice what he paid for it – and sober I won't lose it five minutes later. I know Pa will be as cautious as Esther, but Lozinski can mind me – as Lozinski minds the money as it is, more secretary than valet – and, more importantly, Pa can take on a fellow artisan who cares. I will be the gentleman he's always wanted me to be. It'll take some time to convince him, but I have plenty of that. As well as a fantasy that business will take me out to Bathurst, to Cadia, to the goldfields generally, inspecting Pa's investments in ore getting, but let's not dwell there.

I have one last act of repentance to perform before the sun sets. Inside, the house is steeped in the aroma of Mrs Kirschbaum's chicken soup, the soup she cooks every Friday for Shabes, and, today, all the other dishes she's cooking for the breaking of the fast tomorrow night – the pickled herring, the kugl, the honey cake. She's too busy to notice I've come in – the only day of the year on which this could ever conceivably occur. She's on her own as Clarinda has gone home to her own family for the holiday, and she's only got a couple of hours left before she must hang up the tools, too.

'Mrs Kirschbaum!' I shout into the kitchen and her wooden spoon flies up into the air.

'Ah!' she screams. 'Jeremy! You terrible —' She doesn't stop moving at the stove. 'Go into the dining room and behave yourself.'

I will in a minute. We will eat together there when Pa gets in himself, from his final spot of business, inspecting the first batch of a new tableware design up at the foundry – gum leaves and wattle sprigs set into the handles. My father is a genius. We will eat on the dot of half-past three, and enjoy the best and most beautiful of all we have, in thankfulness for all we share.

But now I step over behind Mrs Kirschbaum and put my arms around her waist.

'Jeremy, what are you doing?'

I kiss her on the cheek: 'I'm saying thank you.'

'What for?' She bats me away to look under the lid of another pot.

'For looking after me. For every kneidl.' Seventeen different kinds of dumplings in her repertoire.

'You don't have to say thank you,' she says. 'Please, go away. I have too much to do.'

I leave her for the dining room, to wait for Pa, in this sparkling heart of home. I hear him at the door now: 'Mmm. That chicken soup smells so good,' he says, coming down the hall, as though it's not the same smell every Friday night.

I laugh with something that seems remarkably like happiness, but that also seems strangely like goodbye.

*

In the morning, as I'm knotting my tie and squinting out at what might be a distant ship glistening silver in the sunrise or something in my eye, I'm making my first contemplation of the day a study in why I have failed as yet to see an optician – when I hear a knock at the door downstairs.

It won't be someone that anyone in this house can do business with today, unless there's a fire or a risk of someone's dying, so the knock goes unanswered. I continue dressing, making my second contemplation of the day the fact that I am already thirsty and there are thirteen hours of fasting left to endure.

The door-knocker has another go. I decide to go down and tell them politely to go away. It's probably only someone knocking at the wrong house, or a chimney sweep after a job. Who else knocks on a door randomly at seven o'clock on a Saturday morning? Or maybe it's bad news. The rap at the door is firmer again. I think of the boy Davey Simmons, having got him a spot as a groom at

Randwick only last week, and I suddenly worry he's taken a kick or a fall and his father has come to condemn me – he's such a slight fellow, that boy. And I'm taking on my father's tendency for fast accelerating dread with each step.

But it's not the fishmonger Simmons; it's the Inspector-General of Police, Douglas Fitzworthy.

All thought is suspended around the words: *Shit. No. Not. Today.*

'Good morning, young Mr Fox,' those over-waxed moustaches say. 'Just the man I was hoping to see.'

My mind races through what this could be, a litany of all my outstanding guilt: that lurking creditor waiting out there somewhere; a notice to sue for some destruction of property I can't remember; a child I might have fathered to a woman of consequence; a child I might have fathered to a woman of no consequence I'll never know about and certainly not from the Inspector-General of Police; the piece of my heart that will always long to redress any kind of hurt I might have caused by my debauchery; the other piece of my heart that beats in permanent disbelief that I am not the syphilitic mess I probably should be; and, as well, a creeping fear that this is, after two months' silence, an invitation to have afternoon tea with Cornelia Osborne.

He's tapping the outside leg with a riding whip. He's not a horseman. He's a blinkered, bourgeois bag of gas who spends his working life in an office next to a synagogue and hasn't bothered to learn a thing about his neighbours. Whatever he wants, he's not disturbing my father with it today.

'Inspector-General.' I step out towards him onto the porch, closing the door behind me: 'It's not a good time – it's the Day of Atonement.' Which means, among other things, that I've solidly forgiven your fluff-brained niece, as well as the despicable little sock full of turds who almost killed me in your Wellington police station. How about next Good Friday I turn up on your doorstep with a bottle of whiskey under one arm and a banjo under the other?

'I won't take up your time.' He couldn't care less. He's come to tell me and he's going to: 'I merely wanted to be the bearer of glad tidings, deliver the splendid news to you personally, on behalf of the Governor himself, as to the reward that has been decided upon for your part in the apprehension of the gang of Jack Holly and his evil conspiracy.'

How this man drags himself through every day with those sorts of sentences unfurling like sheet lead through his mind is a divine mystery itself – and that was a brief one. One that brings little relief to me.

I tell him: 'I've made it clear in every dealing with the police that I'm not interested in a reward.' My guts turn: it was all supposed to go to Annie. If it hasn't I might accelerate quickly towards anger.

But Fitzworthy explains: 'This is not the reward that was posted seeking information which might lead to the arrest and conviction of the criminals. This is for your assistance to police on the day, for the personal risk taken by you to render that assistance, and in compensation for the injury received by you on that occasion.'

'Whatever it is, donate it to the Children's Asylum. I don't want it.' Let it pay for a few excursions, packets of Faney's chocolate pastilles to go around; which reminds me: I must make that train booking to take Pa to lunch at the Blue Mountain Inn, next Sunday. In the meantime: 'If there's a piece of paper I have to sign, I'll come in during the week.'

I'm about to turn away to go back inside.

'Oh no, Mr Fox,' Fitzworthy says with what I suppose is a smile of some satisfaction. 'No piece of paper need be signed. The Earl of Belmore put his signature to the necessary documents yesterday evening and the transfer of title has been made.'

'Transfer of title?' I shouldn't be asking that question. I'm thinking, there goes my resolution to be observant, just for one day. Fitzworthy is pulling an envelope from his inside pocket and handing it to me, and I take it, just to make it even worse: 'What is this?'

He says: 'A bestowal of Crown land.'

It looks to me like a bribe. I tell him: 'If this is to ensure my discretion on a certain matter of false imprisonment and battery, it's not in any way necessary.' Pa will never find out about what happened; I have been scrupulously vague about the entire affair because I don't need to revisit a moment of it – never will. But this is too extraordinary. Why should Belmore want to give me such a gift if there's not some desperation behind it? An avoidance of scandal – yes, that's what this must be, and Belmore is keen to steer clear of one with the Hebrew community, as he already has his hands full with a few hundred rolling eruptions of sectarian uproar as a result of Prince Alfred's shooting earlier in the year, culminating most recently in the nervous collapse and resignation of popularly beloved Colonial Secretary Parkes. That would do it. I attempt to hand the envelope back: 'I don't need any such incentive to stay schtum.'

Fitzworthy clears his throat indignantly: 'Now, now, young man, you have an imagination. It's nothing so far-fetched as that.' He explains: 'It was submitted by Superintendent Slater that you would in all likelihood not accept a monetary compensation and he made the suggestion himself as to what parcel of land might be attractive to you. He holds you in a very high regard.'

That's really very touching. Bert Slater, you good old stick. But Fitzworthy is not finished surprising me.

'The land in question is three hundred and twenty acres of quality pasture in the District of Carcoar.'

There's something far-fetched. I tear open the envelope for a further transgression, but I can't help it: my heart has stopped.

And then it just about explodes when I see the words: *Horseyards Lane, Bunyip's Bend, and all dwellings, improvements and effects upon it.* It can't be any other pasture: there is none there.

'Superintendent Slater expected that you might be so pleased.'

'Pleased?' I don't know what might describe this blaze of confusion. A gentleman might shake another gentleman's hand at this pass, if it didn't constitute doing a deal on my father's doorstep on the most inappropriate day for it. Any man might say thank you, say something, but shock prevents me from anything other than a charmless: 'I have to go. Sorry.'

Back in the hall, I stuff the envelope and its contents into the depths of the umbrella stand. This might well be the word of God on where I'm supposed to be. The word on my future. My forever: Annie. But I don't know how I'm going to break it to Pa. Break his heart. I don't know if I can.

*

I have twelve hours to think about it, with Pa occupied all day, in prayer, in song, in greeting friends he hasn't seen since yesterday and some for many years. And I have fairly much only one contemplation the whole time: Annie. I shake a lot of hands, I give a lot of well wishes with them, genuine every one. But all I can think of is getting myself on that road – tomorrow – and asking her again: Please, can you love me? How could I not try again? What if she tells me to go away again? What if she's not there? Every question, every doubt, is meaningless. I have to go.

Every few minutes I look up at the gallery, where the women are, looking for Esther, but I don't see her until the break between the special morning service and the afternoon Torah reading, when I go outside to stretch my back, aching from sitting hunched over the storm of my thoughts. My one thought.

She says: 'You look like you're suffering.' That careful, curious eyebrow of hers making the suggestion I might have done something to warrant it. And I have: a thousand things.

I tell her, 'I'm starving,' because that's what one says, but then I warn her, because I'm not going to embarrass her with what I'm going to do over the days to come: 'I'm also worried.'

'About?'

'Our plans, such that they are.'

'Oh.' She looks away, grips an iron fence-post: 'Are you saying what I think you're saying?'

'Probably.'

And I think I've played this badly, but when she looks up again, she's smiling: 'I've been worried too.'

'I have no doubt about it.' She doesn't want to marry me at all.

She asks me: 'Is it someone else?'

I nod. 'That's the hope.'

She says: 'Same here.' She wants someone who smokes a pipe and quotes Schiller and Shakespeare, a crisp and witty Verdelho by the fire.

As we hold each other up with a quiet laugh, half delirious, Mrs Davis frowns fondly over at us, and I look up at the sky above this city I'll be leaving very soon: God, if you really do exist, thank you. Now, please, be as kind to Pa.

I watch him, only him, throughout the final service: head in his hands, making his last entreaties before God decides if he will live another year or die, praying that his name, by all his good deeds, his service and generosity, is written into the Book of Life. If God exists, it should be. I more than love him: I am proud to be his son.

The prayer goes on: Hear, Israel, the Lord is God, the Lord is One. The shofar sounds, the ancient ram's horn trumpeting in the New Year as it's done for thousands. And I'm about to break this tradition. How can I be contemplating doing this to him?

Pa grips me by the elbow: '*L'shone toyve.*' To a good year. Tears in his eyes – tears of happiness that I am here with him. I have tears in my eyes, too.

I can't do this to him.

*

Yes, I can. I wait until everyone but Mrs Kirschbaum has gone from the house. 'Good luck,' Esther whispers at the door as she leaves with her parents. Pa is sitting in his library, on his reading chair by the window, sated and tired. A man who's had an excellent day, finishing a well-earned glass of muscat. The time is now. It's either confess or skulk off in the middle of the night, run away from home, and I'm not doing that to him.

He opens his eyes as I sit in the chair opposite him, and he says: 'I forgot to mention to you – Nathan will be giving an open lecture on Tuesday on Judaism in Ireland. It should be interesting.'

'I bet it will be.' My not-to-be-father-in-law is an interesting man. Between the tribe of Catholic grandmothers, Anglican clergy, Reverend Davis, and Nathan Asher's radically progressive ideas on republicanism and socialistic democracy, they'd better make sure no-one at the lecture is armed.

Pa says: 'You look like you've got something on your mind.'

I nod.

He looks at the envelope I'm holding; he says: 'Did you hear from your mother?'

'No,' I must admit, 'I only managed to write to her yesterday. In the post.' And it's impossible that I might have received a reply by now even if I'd written to her back in June.

He nods, perhaps a little sauced, and he gives me a sleepy smile, taking that news on the chin – good.

I have to tell him: 'That's not what's on my mind right now, though.'

'What's on your mind, my boy?' he asks me.

And I begin the smashing of his wishes: 'I'm not going to marry Esther.'

'What are you talking about?' He shakes his head as if to clear it of some bizarre flicker of a dream.

'We've agreed, we don't want to do that,' I tell him. 'We're not suited.'

He sighs: 'Well, that's a disappointment, Jemmy, but if you've agreed, I suppose that's just what it is, then. Perhaps spend some time apart. You might feel differently in a while.'

'No.' I say it quickly and cleanly: 'I love someone else. She's not Jewish.'

Pa stares at me, uncomprehending.

Mrs Kirschbaum is not so uncomprehending, appearing at the door: '*What* did you tell your father?'

But Pa keeps his composure, prepared to reserve judgement, not going to undo his pact with God today. 'What does her father do?' he asks me what's important to him. 'Is he an educated man?'

'He's no longer with us.' And I make the facts as plain as I can again: 'He was a farm manager, at Castlereagh, near Penrith. He grew vegetables.'

'What?' Mrs Kirschbaum looks ready to hit me with the empty platter she's holding. Farming is not high on the list of respectable professions for a Jew, unless it's a hobby or it's made you rich.

But Pa continues to keep his composure: 'She's, what – English?'

'Partly,' I say; no point holding back the truth here, either. 'The other, more distinctive part of her is Aboriginal.' All said and done, Pa probably wouldn't care if she was a headhunter's daughter from Borneo so long as she was a Jew, and not a French Sephardic Jew like my mother, with her bronzed Arabian skin. As a Gentile, Annie would have to be an Englishwoman of some note or nobility to be considered worth smashing five and a half thousand years of unbroken tradition for.

'What religion is she?' He looks terrified by the answer before I give it.

'Presbyterian, I think.'

He doesn't have a quarrel of any kind with Presbyterians, but he clenches his fists on his knees and leans forward, at me: 'You can't marry her.'

'I know it sounds impossible,' I admit to him, and the more salient rest of it: 'She probably doesn't want me anyway. But I have to try to ask her – again.'

'Again?' He raises his voice just a little. 'You are saying that she doesn't want *you*? So she is mad also, apart from being in every way unsuitable?'

'No. She's suitable in every way. It's her rejection of me that caused me to wake up,' I tell him. 'She is the reason I'm a better man today.'

'Where did you meet her?' Pa is trying and failing to understand, and who can blame him.

'It's a long story.' I tell him what's important in it: 'She helped me, when I got lost, out west. She told me the truth about my arrogance. She's a good person. She's perfect for me. I could give you every adjective to describe her: strong and capable and funny and lovely and fascinating and absolutely herself. But none of that can describe what I feel for her.'

Pa only repeats: 'You can't marry her.'

'I know,' I repeat that too. 'But if she'll have me, that's what I'm going to do. And if she won't have me, I'm leaving Sydney anyway. I'm going to breed horses near Bathurst.'

'I preferred you better when you were a drunk.' My father is losing his composure. I've just told him I want to be a peasant myself. 'At least I knew what to expect from you. Don't think I'm going to give you any money.'

'I'm not asking for any, Pa. I'm going to make my own way.'

'How?' he says. 'Pht.' Dismissing the idea.

And here lies the real problem, Pa: I've never had the opportunity to make my way except by making hell for all concerned in kicking against the comfortable box you'd rather put me in. But I'm not going to hit him with that; I say: 'I've been gifted some land out there.' I show him the title: 'For helping the police.' I've robbed him of taking any pleasure from that or Belmore's personal commendation, but what else can I do? I have to do this. 'I'm going. In the morning.'

'You are *not*!' Mrs Kirschbaum is distressed to the point of shattering the glass in the cabinetry. 'Why are you saying these things to your father?'

My father loses his head completely: 'Go then. Get out. You haven't changed. You've only swapped one selfish mask for another one. You are just like your mother.'

*

I pack straightaway and it doesn't take long: my saddlebags aren't the roomiest, never having been required to carry much apart from a change of essentials and a shaving case I no longer possess or require. I trim my beard with a pair of nail scissors if it's untidy between haircuts. I have a feeling I'm not going to have my hair cut for a while, however things go. I have a feeling of such intense sadness and intense hope I'm not entirely sure I'm moving through the world at all, the world that exists between my bedroom and Raj.

'Jemmy.' I hear him behind me now at the stable door. 'I'm sorry.'

'I'm sorry too.'

'What's her name?' my father asks me.

'Annie,' I tell him. 'Annabel Bird.'

'Annabel Bird?' I can feel him frowning through the dark: 'Do I know that name from somewhere?'

Perhaps. There must be at least one highly inaccurate story of the momentarily infamous Lady Bird and The Fox that made its way into one of the more entertaining pieces of privy literature. I hope one day I'll tell him all that and he'll laugh as we should. He's had enough to shock him for the time being, though, so I only say: 'It's a name that's been on my mind so constantly perhaps you've seen it written in my eyes.'

'Perhaps,' he says, and he has a shock for me: 'I was in love once. I wasn't sensible or realistic then, either. She was too vivacious, too beautiful for someone so old-fashioned as me. She left me for someone else.'

He pauses; I guess: 'And then you made a bad choice by marrying my mother on consignment from a rabbi who knew a rabbi in Paris?'

'No. That *was* your mother. Eva,' he tells me, and for a moment everything is still, the breeze, the sea, the sounds of the neighbourhood, everything except the splash of stars behind his face. He says: 'She left me – and you – to return to her family, and to divorce me, because all along she loved another man. She married him, a musician called Max van der Felden, a violinist. The van der Feldens are Dutch Sephardi, liberal, intellectual, every way in vogue. I couldn't compete with that. I was just a jeweller with a little shop in London then, commonplace, no-one, and with a father who criticised her from the moment they were introduced. In Paris, she could do as she pleased – dance in the street, wear her hair around her shoulders, fall in love with musicians. And so I wouldn't let her take you there. I couldn't forgive her. I still can't. Perhaps one day I will, and I want to, but the wound is very deep. Love is a dangerous thing, my boy, whether it is done properly or not. I don't want you to be hurt.'

So you kept me from my mother out of spite, instead: perfect sense. But I pull him towards me and kiss him; I tell him: 'I will probably get hurt.'

He nods, and there's his blessing: 'Yes, you probably will.'

ANNIE

It is simply ludicrous to act as we do. Not only do we allow Maoris who are uneducated and ignorant of the English language to sit in the Parliament of New Zealand, but we allow them to vote in matters which are not of any concern to them, and to reduce parliamentary debate to the level of their gibberish....

No wonder the government here in Australia prefers black fellers to be illiterate. Why do Maoris in New Zealand get to vote and Aborigines don't? They have a treaty in New Zealand, so says Granddad – that's what's supposed to happen after a war. He's still waiting for his. I tear up these newspaper pages into squares for the pit of necessity, wondering where Granddad is – somewhere north of Orange near Ophir, bringing some more horses in. I wonder if he's happy or grieving when he goes up that way on the Wambool, remembering his family; I suppose he'd be both. Like me, today: it's my birthday and I don't have anyone to mark it with, except Pepper, and he doesn't care.

I look back at the hut, looking more like a little house these days and that gives me cause for some joy. We might not ever have any land that's ours, and I don't have a potato crop in as I'd wanted, but this house is a good house. I've got that chimney and that second room on the back; I've got the verandah bricked to keep the mud from the door. I want to get the slabs clayed up and white-washed, too, some nice paper on the walls inside so it's almost like the home I lost, only smaller, but I won't do that. We're moving the lot next week. This land has been taken up by someone, don't know who, and we're shifting down to Blayney as soon as Granddad and Neville McKenzie get back, onto another Crown-land run – we've got until October the seventh to get everything off this place or it'll belong to whoever this land belongs to now.

I don't want to move anything. But that's life, isn't it. You can't get everything you want the way you want it, and I definitely never will. I'm never going to have a hot-water stove; I'm never going to have an ash-pan lavatory on a back verandah with views over a rose garden; I'm never going to have those pretty dresses – and what would be the point if I did have them? I don't even wear my Sunday best Sis sent with all my other things, because I don't even go to church. Granddad really doesn't want me to. He doesn't say it so plain, but he finds reasons to keep me here – something needs mending at dawn of a Sunday, there's bad weather coming that doesn't come. I think he's worried I won't come back, that I'll get grabbed by some missionary as soon as stepping in the door. It's been five months and nothing is better or worse for me not going. It's the intention inside that's important, isn't it. The thought that counts. Even if I can't yet move myself on from the Book of Jeremiah: *This is what the Lord says: 'Stand at the crossroads and look; ask for the ancient paths, ask where the good way is, and walk in it, and you will find rest for your souls ...'*

A piece of land on Granddad's country will come up for sale eventually, and that is where we will rest. In the meantime, the interest on that trust account has risen to five percent, so there's only a gain to be had in waiting; no loss, if you don't think about it too much. *It will all happen in its own good time*, is what Superintendent Slater said when he passed through last week, stopping for a cup – then giving Granddad the tip that a big mob of good horses was up Ophir way. If everyone was as good as Superintendent Slater, the world would be a better place. It'd likely be Heaven.

Oh, but my one biggest and most useless wish for this birthday is that we could somehow stay. Here. I've put some spinach in and it's jumped out of the ground, for all Granddad complains that he doesn't like it. He doesn't eat enough vegetables. And I want *this* soil. I just hate thinking it's all going to be put under sheep and destroyed by some cockatoo with no care for the earth at his feet. But more than this, I don't want Granddad to have to move. Sometimes I hear him singing to himself in a moment now and again when he forgets I'm here; I don't ask him about it, they seem like private songs, and he's not going to tell me anyhow, but they seem like sounds that belong here, some ancient path of his own. I've seen where he goes when he walks off: over the other side of the forest, about half a mile: he sits on the ground there and looks at that big craggy mountain. He won't be able to see it from the valley in Blayney.

Sometimes, when it's misty, I think I can see the warriors in their possum-skin cloaks in the forest and it's the strangest thing: it doesn't frighten me to think they're there. I want them to be. I want more family. I must have more family out there somewhere. When Granddad left the Wambool all those years ago, when he left all those aunties and cousins there to go off and find work further afield, they wouldn't have all just disappeared into the ground. They would have done whatever they had to do to survive. They will have had families themselves; my Mulgoa family would have as well.

I'm lonely here. Maybe I'll go down into Carcoar today and get a loan of a novel for a sixpence from the circulating library that goes there of a Wednesday, get myself that copy of *David Copperfield*, save talking to myself for the next day or two that Granddad will be away; hook a few eyebrows, too. Maybe I'll have a read of it in the saloon of Mrs Galbraith's hotel; have a ham sandwich and a raspberry vinegar while I'm there.

'What do you reckon, Pepper?' I ask him, but he's looking up at the track with his ears forward.

I see the slow dust of a walking horse through the green twist of hawthorn at the bend on the edge of the farthest yard; someone's coming. Someone mistakenly taken the sweeping fork from the north here off the Guyong Road, I would bet that sixpence. Someone should put a sign there for the weary few who have to turn back a mile and a half. But Pepper is running flat out with a hello bark like it's someone he knows: Granddad? Can't be, unless he didn't rope anything at the river and that doesn't seem likely. Granddad can walk up to any horse and they're friends in five seconds; and Superintendent Slater said there must have been fifty of them that he saw, they're getting to be such a pest to farmers as diggers abandon more and more of them with their dreams of striking it lucky. It's only the gold-prospecting companies that are making any money – employing half those diggers on work-for-rations terms until they hit pay-dirt themselves. It's a disgrace. I used to think those poor men were a load of cabbages, and they might well be, only I've come to understand a bit more what hard luck it is to want for what you can't have. Maybe it's one of them now, about to ask me for directions.

I stand here like a lonely person with too little to do, watching the rider come around, supposing I should start walking up to the gate, be a kind face on another's long road.

And when I get there I'm grabbing hold of the latch with a startle at what I do see, thinking that loneliness is playing its cruellest on me: he looks just like Jeremy. Of course he does: what else would I be wanting for my birthday?

His beard is thicker; he's wearing ordinary moleskins and black top-boots dusty from the road, his forearms dark from rolled shirtsleeves. If I could paint a picture of what a man should look like, this'd be it. So he's not real. I'll blink in a second and he'll be a cabbage off the goldfields with half his teeth missing.

No, he's got all his teeth.

He says: 'Annie. Good morning. I hope. Hm.' Pushing his hand through his hair.

But it's not until I'm watching him get down out of that saddle that I see it really *is* him.

'Jeremy.'

JEM

I'm quite certain she's not overly pleased to see me; quite certain the last thing she wants to do is open that gate. I've planned my exit in advance – I'll go back up to the inn on the highway and get appropriately drunk while I work out what to do next. But for the moment, I need to work out something to say. How does one say: 'You'll never guess what. The chap you despise is now your landlord.' Perhaps she's already aware.

I don't get a chance to say anything at all, though, before she's through the gate and her arms are around my neck.

There. That was worth the trip. Three and half days of trying not to be too hopeful, and she's saying: 'I'm so happy to see you. It's my birthday today. Would you like a cup of tea?'

ANNIE

'Many happy returns.' He laughs into my hair; he says: 'I've come to ask you again if you'll marry me.'

I say: 'Yes.' And I still haven't let him go because I don't want this dream to end.

'Is that an acknowledgement of the question or an answer to it?'

'An answer,' I say, and I'll never be able to say much about what happens after that, except that he makes the inside of my little house look like a tiny corner of a cupboard and my hands are shaking so much getting my teacups off the shelf, the rattle can surely be heard in Bathurst.

'I don't really want a cup of tea,' he says. 'But I would like to kiss you. May I?'

I suppose I must tell him yes, because he does, and what happens after that is nobody's business, except that I never want to be without his skin touching mine ever again.

*

It's sometime in the middle of the afternoon that I wake inside his arms, this new home I find here; he's still asleep, snoring and making me love that, too, but I'm so excited – so full of happiness and fear – I have to wake him up: 'Jeremy.'

'Hm?' He opens his eyes and I have to kiss him.

And I have to stop myself; I have to say: 'We've got a lot to talk about, a lot of differences to overcome.'

'None that matter to me,' he says.

'What will your father say?' I begin with the fundamental of fundamentals. His father might be the most generous man in the world, but this isn't a matter of generosity.

'He's already said it.' Jeremy doesn't pretty the truth: 'He's not happy. But he'll understand, in time. He'll see the sense of it when he meets you.'

'Meets me?' All my trepidation skips a hundred steps and says: 'I don't want to go to Sydney. I couldn't live in such a place.' Not that I've been there, but the thought is bad enough: I'd be lost and frightened every day.

He says: 'I'm not going to ask you to.'

'Where will we live?'

'Here.'

'*Here* here.' I can't let myself believe that might be true.

But it is. I can see it in his smile before he tells me: 'Yes. I now own this land, and all improvements and effects upon it. So you'll do as I say.'

Oh – *what*? 'Did you buy it?'

'No,' he says. 'Reward for falling off a horse at Judas Creek. You must know, I don't have any money, Annie. But I don't have any debts anymore, either. What you see is what you get.'

I see he's walked away from riches for me: he is everything that I could ever want from a man. I tell him: 'I've got money.' And then I remember what Superintendent Slater said: 'As soon as we marry it becomes yours to claim.'

He says: 'What do you mean mine to claim?'

I explain: 'I'm not allowed to have the money myself, because a girl who's an Aborigine, under twenty-one and unmarried can't be trusted to manage her own affairs. Superintendent Slater holds it in trust for me.'

'Superintendent Slater?' Jeremy frowns: 'He's behind my acquisition of this property, too – he made a submission to the Governor on my behalf to see that I got this place in particular.'

We blink at each other for the revelation: Superintendent Slater is probably God. He's at least the kindest and wisest man alive, to take such care to see both our needs so well met.

But while that might all be so, I have to say to the Jeremy Fox I know, even inside his arms and especially inside his arms: 'You spend a penny of that money on gambling or any other wastefulness and I'll walk away from you.'

He says, 'I know. If that weren't the case, I wouldn't be here. You'll have to look after the money yourself anyway – I can't add up. Don't ever trust me to keep a pound in my pocket unchaperoned.'

Oh my. I don't know what happiness means anymore, for all that is being restored to me now.

He says: 'I want a stud here. I want to breed Arabian-thorough-bred crosses, for the track, and for the pleasure of it, and to make a reasonably good living for us. I hope your grandfather will want to work with me.'

I start to cry.

He kisses a tear: 'I don't have anything else to offer, except perhaps a trip to Paris.'

'Paris?' For a moment I don't know what he means.

Until he says: 'I've written to my mother. Depending on her answer and my financial ability, I might want to go at some time. I might want to meet her, and for you to meet her, too.'

I see the aching in his eyes, I see that little boy kept from his mother, and it brings my shame down on me, all my vicious, fearful words; I tell him: 'I'm so sorry for those horrible things I said.'

'Don't be.' He holds me tighter: 'It was just the kicking I needed.'

No. No-one needs a kicking like that. Not from me, not from anyone.

I close my eyes and listen to his heart, my own so rich in gratitude, and I promise him: I will never cause you one moment of harm again.

*

Two days we stay there in my little house, all alone, with me learning things about the way a body works I could never have dreamed inside the wildest one. He makes my bed too small and wide as the sky at once. He shows me everything that's beautiful in a man. All the songs of Solomon: *Behold, you are beautiful, my love – behold you are beautiful.* He might not be able to add up, but he has the sum of every last part of me – and the measure of every last worry.

I ask him: 'What will our children be?'

He says: 'Wonderful, because you'll be their mother.' He says: 'I hope we're making the first of them now.'

There's a terror. I say: 'We'd better get married quickly, then.'

He says: 'As soon as I can arrange it.'

Oh dear Lord, but: '*Where* are we going to get married? *Who* will marry us?'

He says: 'The Wesleyan Methodists of Tremearne will marry us, at the Cornish Settlement across the highway. They'll marry anyone, especially a woman who saved her man from the drink, and especially the son of one of their most reliable Sydney donors. I've already made the enquiry.'

I say: 'That sounds like you were a bit sure of yourself.'

'No, not at all,' he says. 'I was more than half sure you would turn me away, but if you didn't I wanted to be able to answer your four hundred and fifty-seven questions without any delay which might give you time to think about it too much.'

And it's this second I hear the crack of the whip, up on the track, coming down from the fork, the thundering of hooves, and I tell him: 'Granddad's home.'

We're quick out of bed then. I might make comment that he seems a little too practised at this, only it's him that's looking worried now, checking his hair, his teeth, putting his waistcoat on, taking it off again. He's a wonder to watch. I could tell him not to worry; I could tell him that Granddad has been needling me and teasing me all this time to write to that white feller I sent away; I could tell him I'm sure Granddad will approve. But I can't tell him that, because I'm not sure myself. I couldn't ever say for certain just what Granddad might do. And anyhow, I've got to run out and open the gate.

JEM

He brings seven horses, and the one under him, into the yard, sitting back in the saddle, loose and light in all his limbs as though he's out for an early-evening stroll. He's in unquestionable control of their every move, while the boss, the McKenzie fellow, I presume, waves some kind of hooroo from outside the gate. Let's make that a permanent hooroo. Slavery might have been loudly abolished in America of late, but it continues quietly here; and not here on this piece of land as of today.

I'm quietly dissolving my internal organs in the juices that are made when doubt begins to crush desire. If Annie's grandfather puts the kybosh on me, I have no idea what I'm going to do. Give him the title to the land? That would be meaningful – in every impractical and pointless sense. He has a rifle slung at the saddle: he could just shoot me.

He cleaves one of the horses off from the others with such a careless toss of rope I hope he doesn't shoot me before I can ask him to teach me how to do that. A mare, I think, he takes her off to the yard adjacent.

I look at Annie, walking back from the gate. Her blue work dress is the same colour as the distant hills; her apron as white as the thin clouds above us. She does all her washing outside with water she brings up in buckets from the stream a quarter of a mile away. As much as the home she's made is delightful, the sweetest thing that's ever been made, I want to build her a house with a tank and a laundry and someone else doing it. I want her front parlour to look out at that view over the yards, over the hills; our bedroom, too. I'm not at all confident that Mr Creekstone will be impressed with any idea I have of the future.

I start walking towards him as he starts riding back this way; I will take this on the front foot.

He sees me and beckons me over to the yard rail between us.

'Good afternoon, Mr Creekstone. I'm not sure if you'd remember, I'm —'

'Yeah,' he says, 'I know who y'are. Come back for that cup of tea, have ya?' He's looking at me as though he knows what I've been doing with his granddaughter for the past two days, how irretrievably distracted I am by the shape of her ankles, the shape of her – shut up. I don't know if he knows what's happened with the transfer of the land, but this is his territory. He's not getting down out of the saddle; the muzzle of the rifle is hovering somewhere over my left knee.

Be direct, be brief: 'I've come to ask if I might marry Annie.'

'What did she say?' He continues to stare down at me, inscrutably, in a way that challenges what I think I know.

'She said yes.' Didn't she? Yes, she did: in every way possible.

He nods. Another disconcertingly long and silent stare before he says: 'You ride bareback, feller?'

Not sober and not recently, but I can. Raj enjoys the odd jaunt without the rigging, even if my arse doesn't the next day. Foggy memory of extremely sore arse after pulling up too sharply to avoid a Bondi 'bus and coming off, perhaps four, five years ago, possibly causing original injury to my back, but I nod: 'Why do you ask?'

'You see that filly I put up there on her own?'

'Yes.'

'She wants some more weight on her than me, to get her going. She's a nice girl, but she's slow, a bit scared. You want to have a go?'

At breaking in a wild horse bareback? Not really, no. Not today, when I'm not feeling so brassy myself. I don't know what a heavier weight on a horse might do except make her slower, but this is clearly a test of my character. I have to say: 'All right.' Don't I.

He says: 'Right. Come up.'

I walk around to the inside gate of that yard, preparing to make a fool of myself. She's not a big girl, but I'm sure I'll jigger it up getting my weight on her at all. I will end up on the turf, and then we can all have a laugh. I can recover my dignity later; never had difficulty with that.

He slips a bridle on her and she looks quite docile as he walks her over. She's a pretty thing: chestnut with a white stripe down her fine nose, shy, and looking at me warily: *I know what you're up to – don't you get on my back.*

I give her a rub on the cheek, a scratch down the crest of her neck, and she shakes her head. I can feel her nerves; and I whisper to her: 'Don't worry. Me too.'

Grasping a handful of mane at her withers, I swing up and, as fortune occasionally favours fools, I stay up. She tenses all over, and I rub her shoulder to reassure her, but she only stands there, petrified. Nothing at the gentle nudge to move off. So I lean forward and scratch her on the poll, between her ears: 'A hundred yards, that's all. Then I'll jump off. We'll both be champs.' Nothing.

I should jump off her now, but I don't. I lean forward a little more instead, and give her another nudge, but with my knees just behind her shoulders. She stamps right fore, she seems to know what I mean; I release the pressure and then, without further question, she moves off. Mostly sidewise, but she's off, and within a few strides she's in a trot. I think I've done it.

Annie's grandfather laughs from the fence he's leaning on, watching: 'Yeah. That's the way, feller.'

I think I am an unexpectedly gifted horse-breaking genius – something possibly quite handy to future plans. I turn her back to him and say: 'Well, she seems to like the extra weight, doesn't she?'

'Ha!' The old man keeps laughing: 'Dunno about that. I just wanted to see if you'd give her a smack.'

That's a test I appreciate. I've never hurt a horse, except to avert some worse consequence, such as flying off a clifftop or into the side of a 'bus. A horse can feel a mosquito land on its hide; there's no need to converse via thrashings and spurs. Kel Creekstone and I are going to be excellent partners.

I put a little pressure on the bit to pull her up and now, as though she might only have been slow to show her resentment, she tenses again; she kicks up her hind and throws me – over her head, and with such speed I have no time to brace or turn. The only fortune here, as I meet the ground, is that she doesn't trample me to emphasise the point.

ANNIE

I don't make sense of the picture at first. I don't understand what's happened. The horse bucked out with its back legs; Jeremy was on the horse and now he's not; and Granddad is pulling it away. Pepper is barking and jumping around.

And Jeremy is lying on the ground.

He's not getting up.

JEM

'Jeremy!'

I've recently enjoyed a few lonely-moment fantasies involving Annie running across a field towards me: this wasn't one of them.

Her grandfather is more interested in the horse. I can't of course be certain, given the majority of my mind is occupied with other concerns, but I'm sure he tells her: 'Didn't want ya to chuck him that hard.'

'Jeremy! Are you all right?'

No. I think I'm still mostly winded, though, so I tell her: 'I'll be all right in a minute.'

But I can't get up. I don't know what I've done, apart from having planted my left shoulder in this paddock.

ANNIE

He has the unseeing stare of shock in his eyes. I can't think anything but that disaster hasn't finished with me yet and it has a will to punish the men I love. I remember the promise and the prayer I made as my father lay dying: seeing my whole life laid out caring for a crippled man and being happy at it should he be allowed to stay alive. I make that same prayer and promise now for Jeremy. If this is the destiny the Lord has chosen for me, I accept it. If my sinfulness has caused this to happen, I repent. I repent every breath.

As I yell at my grandfather: 'What have you done?'

'Had to make sure you couldn't scare him off this time,' is what my grandfather says to me with no shame.

'This is no time to be making a joke!' I yell at him again, but he ignores me.

He kneels over the other side of Jeremy: 'Sorry, young feller.' He says to me: 'Push him back this way. Make it quick.'

'God! No!' And some other words. There's nothing wrong with Jeremy's lungs as we roll him over, but he is all right, in a manner of speaking: he sits up, holding his arm – that looks somehow askew to me.

'I'll fix you up,' Granddad is telling him.

'Well, there's something new,' Jeremy is telling him. 'I've never come off over the top like that before.'

And he laughs; Granddad laughs too: 'Yeah, it was a good one.'

I'm not sharing their amusement.

'I'm getting a doctor,' I tell them both. One that's not drunk, or a vet – or wrong in the head.

JEM

S he flies off out of the gate on a horse at a canter and I'm not sure if I'm actually seeing that or if I've lost consciousness. I say to Mr Creekstone, who's unbuttoning my shirt: 'Annie's ridden out of the gate. On a horse.'

'She can do what she likes,' he says.

'She is extraordinary,' I say, and then I ask him, 'Where's the doctor?' because, given that this is really occurring, I don't like the idea of her riding off alone anywhere.

'Carcoar,' he says.

'How far is Carcoar?' I can't remember the distances around here.

'Sixteen miles,' he says, and I very much don't like the idea of her going. It must be near three o'clock in the afternoon as it is. Her grandfather says: 'You won't need a doctor after I fix it. Don't worry. I done it ten times myself.' He pulls my shirt off downwards and says, 'Hold your breath in,' then twists my shoulder back into place. Excruciating and extraordinary at the same time. Not what I would call fixed but not anywhere near as bad as it was.

Now that I'm capable of thought, however, I am annoyed. An hour ago I was the happiest man on earth, and here I have achieved two bollocking spills inside half a year. This is not fair. Fuck off. In some way or another, I usually thoroughly deserve whatever kicking I get; this one is unnecessary. Except perhaps as a message from Feinberg asking me when I'm going to grow out of this, as well as the answer: quite possibly never. Horses being who they are, these things will happen; hopefully not ten times to me. All things considered, I would do this again tomorrow. Or possibly not tomorrow. And not with Annie going off alone through the bush on a horse I don't know as one of the results. I think I'm going to hurl.

'Don't do that, it'll give you grief.' Mr Creekstone sits down beside me on the ground. 'Stay here a minute till you settle that.'

So we do; we look out at the hills until I'm not going to throw up.

I don't know how long it is we sit here like this before he says: 'You gotta understand something, young feller. This is my land, and Annie is my granddaughter. I'll get you worse than what you're feeling now if you do the wrong thing by either one of them.' As though he has a power to; perhaps he does.

Whether he's aware of the formalities at the Crown Lands Office or not, I tell him now: 'I understand that whatever claims I have are subject to your approval.'

'Good,' he says; and then he adds: 'Don't make me regret it.'

'Regret what?'

'My approval,' he says; and then he nods at the hills: 'I've waited too many a day for this.'

As though he might have plotted out a long game himself; I'm sure he has. But when I ask him, 'What is it you've been waiting for?'

He only says: 'Waiting for you to get up. It'll be cold soon. That girl will give us trouble if you're still out here when she gets back.'

I wish she hadn't gone; it's too far, it's too late, and this is hardly an emergency, just uncomfortable; very uncomfortable getting up, but it'll be all right as soon as I sit down again. Don't throw up. Choose instead to appreciate how very extraordinary Annie is. I tell her grandfather: 'You know, she was frightened of horses when we first met.'

'Yeah.' He tells me: 'She still is.'

I hurl.

He says: 'Bet that hurt.'

It did.

*

She's back in only a few hours and I suppose she's turned around after having seen sense. As soon as she's in the door I say: 'Annie, please don't ever do that again.'

'Don't do what?' she says, hanging up her coat. 'Not fall off a horse trying to impress someone?'

'Fair enough,' I say. 'Well, I'm glad you changed your mind.'

'What do you mean, changed my mind?'

'I'm glad you didn't go all the way to Carcoar.'

'Of course I didn't go all the way to Carcoar. I had word sent out from the Blayney store. Because I'm not a reckless lunatic,' she says. 'There are two doctors at Carcoar and one will come when he can get away. Unless you'd like me to take you in the cart tomorrow? Nice rough road down there – you might remember it.'

'No, thank you.'

I don't think there has ever been a moment of unmarriedness between us, not since I picked her up by the back of her trousers and she cracked me one in return.

Although others may be slow to understand what we're about. The doctor who comes the following afternoon to swathe and sling all else that's obvious is a pleasant chap called Brierley, and he doesn't acknowledge that Annie is here at all, except to say to me: 'Have your maid warm the bedclothes of an evening.' I don't remark that she's an expert at it already. I tell him: 'I don't have a maid. I have a Mrs Fox.' And an instant apology: 'Oh, I do say, I'm sorry, I didn't see you there.' Instant lie.

When he's gone, she says: 'It's always going to be like this. Are you sure we're doing the right thing?'

'Yes. There is no life I want to have without you.' I am in unmedicated pain and incapacitated and I don't care, because of Annie, and only Annie. Is there a more accurate gauge of affection? But we must get down to a lie of our own in that regard: 'I need you to write to Pa and tell him you've said yes but not tell him what I've done to my arm. He'll be waiting by the letterbox now to hear from me.'

'I can't do that,' she says. 'I'm not beginning this life with such a deceit. Why can't he know?'

'Because you don't know anything about worry until you've met my father. He'll be upset and he won't be inclined to lend me the money to purchase breeding stock.'

So she sits at her little kitchen table and writes the letter to him:

Dear Mr Fox,

I read it over her shoulder, kissing the line of little orange-blossom ringlets at the nape of her neck.

'Stop that.'

My name is Annabel Bird and I am delighted to inform you that I have accepted your son Jeremy's proposal of marriage. He would have written to tell you himself but he left the property immediately to inspect stock and asked me to write instead, fearing that his inclination for forgetfulness in this respect might cause you undue concern ...

And – bonus – he will immediately relax at the elegance of her handwriting. He will be surprised, as I was, at her literacy, and then embarrassed, as I was, at the question; he will worry, always, at every unkindness we will face. But what is the alternative? Allow the middling rump of unhappiness that is the bigoted among us a win at a game they aren't even aware they're playing? *That* is unreasonable. To give in to it would be absurd.

To illustrate just how absurd, we meet a pair of Carcoar's top-shelf second-raters the following week, when we go in to begin the business of tidying our affairs with the bank. 'Mr Fox, isn't it?' It's Mrs Galbraith – who I've learned since our first meeting not only runs an occasional toffs' tail-house upstairs at the hotel, but that she's slighted Annie on its doorstep. She's with her husband, the Captain, a man who appears to be both affable and distinguished, and in this kerbside exchange says to Annie, 'Yes, my word, the district is abuzz with the news that Mr Fox is to settle here and marry. You're from the West Indies, we hear? I'm only recently returned from the Caribbean myself – dreadful rioting in Havana. Which of the islands do you call home?'

There's a whopper. I'm still failing to fathom from what possible dreck-filled swamp that one has crept when Annie replies with an unreadable smile: 'Whichever island might make you sleep easier at night, Captain Galbraith.'

How could I *not* marry her?

'Mr Fox, you must tell us what happened to your arm.' Mrs Galbraith graciously paints over Annie's words as if they hadn't been spoken. 'Doctor Brierley said you had a bad fall last Friday.'

Yawn. 'All lies,' I tell her. 'Annie smashed me with her frying pan.'

She and the Captain laugh: 'Ha, ha, ha. What cards you are.' We laugh too: 'Must make tracks.'

There are very few people with whom we'll share this road.

But that's all right. You can't invite everyone to your wedding, can you.

ANNIE

The day wouldn't be right if it didn't begin with Sis and me fighting like we never drew breath since last time.

'How can you not want flowers in your hair, Annie?'

'Because I'm getting married, not tarting myself up for a shindy.'

'You've never tarted up for a shindy, ever. No flowers, no bonnet, no veil. You look like you're going to school.'

'I do not. This is Italian silk I'm wearing.' It's so soft and smooth I never want to take it off, though I'm looking forward to that, too. It's the colour of the creek at dawn, palest silver with threads of blue and gold whispering through it; a plain scalloped collar and fifty-three fine pin-tucks all down the skirt, it's everything I'd never dreamed I'd ever have. 'And it's enough as it is.'

She sighs: 'Just one flower, then. Please?'

'Oh all right.'

I let my sister pin one of her silk flowers into the plaited roll she's made of my hair, and it does look good. So do our faces here together in the mirror. We often seem cut from such different cloth, but we share our mother's nose; her smile.

I tell her: 'I'm so happy you're here, Sis.' She stayed with me last night; stayed up talking all through it, cuddling as we haven't done for years.

'I wouldn't have missed this.' She gives my shoulders a squeeze, my cheek a kiss. And then her baby cries. My sister has the prettiest baby that ever was born: all fat little arms and legs and big blue eyes, I could spend the day kissing her, instead – a little girl, and they've called her Kathy. I go to pick her up from her basket at our feet and Sis says: 'Don't do that – she'll make a wreck of your Italian silk and then we'll be late.'

Like my bother. I'm not sure, but I think maybe my own baby has just begun in me, and I'm looking forward to that more than anything.

'Don't sit there smiling at yourself. Our granddad is waiting out there.'

I laugh at my lazy little sister giving me a hurry along away from a mirror, but she's been changed too, in all the best of ways, doesn't mind claiming an old black feller for family now she has one of her own, and she's right. Granddad is waiting and he's been a sack full of nervous wonder all morning: he doesn't want to go to church; isn't happy in his suitcoat, even if he looks smart in it. He's polished his boots twice.

He's sitting in the cart that's been decorated all around with ribbons and button daisies, bells on the bridle of the horse, and he looks like he'd rather be anywhere else. But when he turns and sees his granddaughters, he straightens his back in that proud way of his. He says: 'Don't you look good.' Too proud to say any more.

He should be proud. He's on his own land and no-one can ever shove him off. There's a paddock full of new breeding mares behind his hat that wouldn't be there without him helping Jeremy select them, from Kelso, from Oberon and Hartley. There's another paddock beyond full of wild bush horses that wouldn't be there, either, getting sold to farmers at fair prices and making us a living in the meantime, hard luck if Neville McKenzie doesn't like the competition and is still looking for another wrangler. If we get any kind of success from this place, it will be because of Granddad – his knowledge and his skill. I can't say I enjoyed him and Jeremy going off together up to the Wambool for the first time, just two weeks ago, but they came back, with a deeper friendship, and all parts intact.

'Hooray! Hooray for Annie! Hooray for she's getting married today!' Mickey Dinnigan meets us near the gate where he's been camping with a cartload of mates – the band he and Sis have brought as our surprise wedding present. How they will be received by the Cornish choir that's supposed to be singing today is something I'm not going to worry about – or the alcohol they will have brought with them. Not my business. Sis's wedding will be an event, though, that's for sure, when they get around to it.

We'll bring the potatoes. I look over my shoulder at my crop, already thick with leaves, only half an acre to start, to see how they go: they are going like they're meant to be here, too. With our house, our big house, that's halfway through to being finished, looking east over all this country, over all my longing fulfilled – and more. It's going to have a bathroom, a laundry, and a sun room just for me, all designed by Jeremy's German friend, Gerhardt Hegel. Granddad might always sleep under the awning of the hut; Jeremy might never really know which way is east; and whatever might happen otherwise I will try not to worry about the eye-popping amounts of money we have borrowed from his father for this house and those mares. By all accounts, it's a more economical arrangement for Mr Fox than the previous one he had with his son.

My belly flips with my own nervous wonder at that thought: I haven't met Mr Fox yet but by our correspondence. He and Jeremy, and the others that are coming from Sydney, stayed in Bathurst last night. Will they like me? Doesn't matter. Will they like the wedding? Doesn't matter; we've made sure there won't be ham sandwiches at this shindy. Will they like my dress? Yes: Jeremy's tailor, Eli Abrahams, made it to my measurements and suggestions and sent it in the post.

The bridle bells jingle as we set out along the ten small miles north to the chapel, and my joy, only joy, sweeps over all. This day is blazing bright and hot with the summer sun; the breeze weaves through broad, satin carpets of green grasses tall as me. I've only been this way once before, to meet the pastor, Reverend Pascoe, but it is my new favourite way through anything.

We come to the crossroads and behind us the drummer in the band begins to play, then with him a fiddle and then a banjo, reeling. They'll hear us coming, won't they – and let them. Why not?

For it's only us. Hidden in the bush, the tiny church of blue rubblestone stands alone except for a hall of weatherboard beside it: a tiny world made ours alone, between a highway, a Methodist village and a copper mine.

How I wish my parents were here to see me married, to see Sis and me arriving with our grandfather, side by side, a baby in a basket at our feet. But they are here. The flesh of us that came from them says so. The stories that brought me here along this path say so: a giant of a man in a possum-skin cloak our father kept a light upon in my heart for no other reason than to speak of his devotion to our mother.

How blessed I am in every way.

It's Wednesday, the eleventh of December, chosen because it falls best for everyone between Sunday and Friday, and before the start of Hanukah that then rolls on into Christmas. The Lord has lit all candles for this day – the most beautiful day of my life.

JEM

'It's almost two o'clock.' Pa snaps his watch shut beside me as we wait within the chapel, more pleased at this day than I could ever have expected him to be. I'm still amazed that he's here at all. For him, entering any house of worship other than a Hebrew one couldn't be a bigger deal: it's forbidden. I can't imagine how he has struggled with his conscience over this. That he has crossed this threshold for me – there's no word in any language to describe such a gift. And this look of glad anticipation on my father's face right now, well, it's the ace I never knew he held. Marvellous.

Until he grips me by the shoulder: 'Are you ready?'

'Ready?' I wince: Pa's grip is always surprisingly strong, enthusiastic, and he's precisely struck the sinew there that's not quite as glad yet as it could be.

'Ah.' He nods, and releases the clamp. 'A little tender still, is it?'

'Is what?'

'Your shoulder.'

'How did you know about my shoulder?' Jesus. I immediately see Feinberg scanning the accident reports out of Carcoar Hospital, watching, waiting for me to fail in some way. I'd like to tell him my back is remarkably cured since that fall, as though something was finally jolted into place; I'd like to tell him to keep away from my father.

But Pa smiles with his secret: 'Annabel. She told me, in her letters. I know I shouldn't betray her confidence, but perhaps you should know at this moment just what a good woman you have chosen, that dishonesty would weigh so heavily on her.'

There I was thinking they'd been discussing interest rates.

He says: 'Jemmy, you know I can't wait to meet her.'

I can't wait to see her, as though I didn't see her yesterday morning before I left; as though each day with her doesn't bring me a new revelation of what it means to be outrageously lucky.

He says: 'She already seems so much my daughter.'

Oh God. Don't cry. Think of why: she sent him an itemised chart of costs for the house, and asked his opinion on such decisions as to whether he thought the verandah should be paved in stone or tiles, the windows casement or sash, the roof tin or slate, on the balance of durability, price and style. If she'd set out to enchant him on the page, she couldn't have done better, only she didn't set out to do anything except seek his advice, because she was born responsible. She'll be getting more than the tea tray she suggested as a present; I can't wait to watch her face when she opens those boxes sometime later this afternoon.

I think I hear the cart outside now and turn, but it's not her. It's Bert Slater – good he could make it. I look at my watch: still almost two.

I look up again and Esther catches my eye: she mocks me, pretending to bite her fingernails. She invited herself to the wedding, and her chum Susannah McLeod, whom I suspect might just be her crisp and witty Someone Else, getting away for a week together, under the pretext of looking after Pa. Whatever the reason, it's good that she's here: a Sydney friend for Annie, for when we go, as we will eventually, possibly next summer, when Raj's part in the business brings us foals – I won't be handling cash trackside without her, and Sydney is too far away, too long a time away from her.

Too far, too long. I wonder if my mother is opening my letter today, somewhere in the centre of Paris. Twelve weeks and one day since I sent it off. Has she written back? Sobriety plays havoc with the emotions, doesn't it? What's the time? Two minutes past. Hm.

The pastor smiles at me. Nice chap: he's a metallurgist at the mine when he's not doing this. He and Pa and Bert Slater will have a spree on discussion of valuable rocks over tea and bride-cake when we're done with the business at hand.

Where is she?

Mrs Kirschbaum's fan behind me keeps time in the close air; she doesn't know what to do with herself since she has been prevented for the last fifteen minutes from brushing imaginary lint off the back of my frock-coat, which I am very much looking forward to removing. It's a forge in here. Only twenty-seven people in this church, including the choir and a few locals nosing in, but it's a cosy fit.

I think I hear a violin – and think it's a quirk of the heat, of the wait. There'll be no music but the choir today, some hymns from the Wesley Collection, seven hundred and sixty-nine to choose from, and did we want to make the selection ourselves, the pastor asked us. No, we trust the choir; if there's one thing the Cornish can do without instruction, apart from mining copper, it's singing songs. But I can still hear that violin.

It is a violin – a melancholy klezmer note strung somehow around the world.

No, it's not. It's Mendelssohn's Wedding March. And a banjo. What else would it be?

Annie. Here she is, on her grandfather's arm, holding a bouquet of golden button daisies from our dam.

'Oy,' my father whispers, gripping my arm again; Mrs Kirschbaum gasps and the crowd sighs: 'Ahhh.'

Because Annie is astonishingly lovely.

She smiles at me.

I cry.

She takes my hand, and the pastor begins:

'Brothers and sisters, be welcome into this humble house of the Lord. We are gathered here today to solemnise the union of Annabel Eliza Bird to Jeremiah Gideon Fox in Holy Matrimony. We are gathered here today, in this great land of Australia, a people of many faiths and colours, believers and unbelievers, those of us who have found our faith and those of us who are searching still. And yet among us we share that which is most universal and the highest of truths, that God is the creator of each miracle that brings us into being. The one truth, the only truth, is here in every face, proclaiming that God is each of you, that God is almighty, that God is love.'

Amen to that, to us, and mazel tov.

AUTHOR NOTE

How does this story really end? Annie and Jem live happily ever after. They raise a large healthy brood of gorgeous tawny babes, seven of them. They and their children after them raise horses – stock horses and race horses, a few of them big winners – and make quite a lot of money at it. Jem takes Annie to Paris several times and she loves it there, for her Aboriginal heritage is of interest to just about everyone she meets, especially her mother-in-law, Eva, and Jem's half-brothers, Louis and Gabriel van der Felden. They consider living in France often, but home, there in the hills of central New South Wales, calls them back each time. Home: where they employ Aboriginal wranglers, gardeners and household staff, and pay them wages; where Annie is never happier than when she is among her crops of potatoes and peas, except perhaps when she's reading a book in her coal-heated bath or corresponding at length upon Jewish theology with Pa; and where Jem doesn't have too many more equestrian mishaps despite never growing up in this regard. Although they become people of note in both Sydney and Bathurst circles, and despite their many contributions to their world, in terms equine, vegetable and charitable, they'll never receive much of a mention in the annals of the day. The detail of their lives is white-washed away.

It's a trick of history Australians are champion at, a crime of theft against the identity of others, those who sit outside what the mainstream decides an Australian should look like, and we do it all the time, every day, today.

The year after this novel ends, 1869, those men who went over to England to play in the Aboriginal Cricket Team, returned to a country in which the laws had been changed, at least in Victoria, to ensure an Aboriginal person couldn't leave these shores again without government permission; those men could now also have their applications to marry arbitrarily refused.

The year this novel was begun, 2014, a beautiful, vibrant Aboriginal woman, Miss Dhu, died of complications of septicaemia and pneumonia in a police cell in Western Australia, there for unpaid traffic fines. The same year, in the case of another young Aboriginal woman, Lynette Daley, who was raped so savagely that she died of her injuries, the New South Wales Department of Public Prosecutions decided that the white men who attacked her could not be charged despite coronial recommendation and the glaring evidence against them; an injustice that has only been overturned, by the determined efforts of her family, as I write this note more than three years later.

Throughout the writing of this novel, I came up against immeasurable holes in the historical records of what happened to the Mulgoa and the Bathurst-Wambool Wiradjuri (or Wirradjeree, as used in the novel to reflect the spellings of the time) after colonisation. Half-sketched or absent acts of war that remain unresolved by truce or treaty today. Open wounds that can only be closed by the telling and acknowledgement of the truth.

What really happened and is continuing to happen is that Australia has a devastating problem with racism.

As an Australian of European descent, I wrestled for a long time with the ethical dilemma of taking on the voice of a First Nations, Aboriginal character, but Annie's is a voice that's been with me a long time. This woman is my friend. I grew up at La Perouse, on the northern, axe-edged tip of Botany Bay, where half my friends were Koori and the other half came from all over the world. Few of us fitted neatly into the white-bread square of what an Australian should be. The Aboriginal people in my life today are not only people I'm proud to call friends, but are among my oldest friends. Maybe it was inevitable that I would one day try to write a bold, determined and triumphant black woman to match the examples in my own reality.

It was a chance encounter that really got Annie Bird whispering, and sometimes shouting, into my ear, though. I was roaming through some research, wanting to discover the history of the wild west of the New South Wales goldfields, where I live today (and indulging my long-held love affair with that period, the 1970s TV series *Rush* and my abiding crush on the actor John Waters), when I came across a fleeting footnote to the white male history of the times: the real-life bushranger wife of Captain Thunderbolt, Mary Ann Bugg. Bugg was the daughter of an ex-convict English farmer and an Aboriginal woman of unknown nationality (possibly Worrimi or Biripi) from the Hunter Valley area; she was boarding-school educated in Sydney and variously said to be exceptionally beautiful and articulate, a cracking good opera singer and a resourceful, britches-wearing bushwoman; some time after her husband was shot dead by police in 1870, in one account, she stated that her heritage was Maori rather than Aboriginal, possibly in order to obtain work and perhaps to retain her independence, to avoid being corralled on a mission station and having her life controlled by church and state. Her story, or the wisps of it that remain, intrigued me for what it says about the nineteenth-century myth of the First Nations peoples' inability to make their way in the white world or between cultures; and what it says about survival.

My story is not an Aboriginal history, though, and doesn't pretend to be. The intricacies of that history are not mine to tell. Like all my stories, *Lady Bird & The Fox* is an expression and invention of the love, curiosity and despair I have for the country I call home. There are many First Nations writers exploring stories of dispossession and survival and triumph through their fiction today, the complexity and diversity of that experience infused with living, contemporary culture: Anita Heiss, Alexis Wright, Kim Scott, Tony Birch, so many more – discover them and be richer for it. It's my hope only that I inspire readers of all kinds to go and find out more – more and more of the truth.

As for my credentials as an 1860s larrikin Ashkenazi Jew, well, perhaps there's a fair amount of that in my DNA, both Prussian and Irish, an intense need to know what Sydney was like when they stepped off the ship, and to understand how and why that element of my family identity has remained so strong so far down the line. To have an Irish Catholic great-great-grandmother, as I do, is one thing; to have an Irish Jewish great-great-grandmother as well feels, to me, like I've inherited some kind of cultural jackpot.

But Jews have often been painted out of the picture of Australia, too. It's a consistently overlooked fact that they have been a significant part of the fabric of Australian life since British colonisation, and have contributed to this country enormously – far beyond their weight of numbers, and despite religious and racial prejudice. Among the approximately one hundred and fifty thousand convicts transported to Australia, it's thought that around one thousand of them were Jews; by 1868, when the colonies had swelled to a population of about one and a half million, about six thousand Jews had come to call Australia home. From the beginning, they've comprised only about half a percent of the population and yet gave us our first Australian-born governor-general, Sir Isaac Isaacs, and our first and most famous military general, Sir John Monash – both of them born here during the gold rushes.

As always, I could not have written this story without the wonderful newspaper and pictorial databases of the National Library of Australia's Trove. I also owe a massive debt of gratitude to Jacquie Seemann Charak for helping me not only understand necessary religious and historical details of the Jewish experience, but for her generosity of spirit and enthusiasm for what I was trying to achieve – and for the very kind assistance of her mother-in-law, Danielle Charak, in researching the Yiddish terms and spellings used throughout. I hope I have honoured that generosity here. Profound thanks, too, to Wiradjuri Elder, Neil Ingram, for reading this novel with an eye out for any cultural carelessness on my part; while any errors remain my own, I hope that my story in some small way makes a contribution to understanding and healing. To those friends and comrades who put up with my endless need to discuss this story – Narelle Woodberry-Daniels, Liz Hovey, Sarah Ferguson-Long, Greg Johnston, and Chlöe and Jason Roweth especially – thank you for understanding what heart country lies in these pages for me. To those publishing colleagues who also braved early drafts – Selwa Anthony, Lou Johnson and Jo Butler –

thank you for the wisdom and faith you shared along the way. To my editor, Alexandra Nahlous, thank you for the care you have lavished on my words; to Joel Naoum, thank you for making this publication possible. And most of all, thank you to my boys, Tom and Cal, who gave me vital encouragement to crack on with this manuscript exactly when I needed it.

None of it gets done at all without Deano, though, my muse de bloke, Dean Brownlee, my best bits of life. A man who knows what it is to be a prodigal son and to welcome them home, too. A man who knows the best risks ever taken are those we take for love.

KIM KELLY

Kim Kelly is the author of seven novels exploring Australia and its history. Her stories shine a bright light on some forgotten corners of the past and tell the tales of ordinary people living through extraordinary times.

An editor and literary consultant by trade, stories fill her everyday – most nights, too – and it's love that fuels her intellectual engine. In fact, she takes love so seriously she once donated a kidney to her husband to prove it, and also to save his life.

Originally from Sydney, today Kim lives on a small rural property in central New South Wales just outside the tiny gold-rush village of Millthorpe, where the ghosts are mostly friendly and her grown sons regularly come home to graze.